The Owl's Mirror

The
OWL'S
MIRROR

A Novel

Wilfried Wlochal

iUniverse, Inc.
Bloomington

The Owl's Mirror
A Novel

This is a work of fiction. All of the characters, names, incidents, organizations, and dialogue in this novel are either the products of the author's imagination or are used fictitiously.

iUniverse books may be ordered through booksellers or by contacting:

iUniverse
1663 Liberty Drive
Bloomington, IN 47403
www.iuniverse.com
1-800-Authors (1-800-288-4677)

Because of the dynamic nature of the Internet, any web addresses or links contained in this book may have changed since publication and may no longer be valid. The views expressed in this work are solely those of the author and do not necessarily reflect the views of the publisher, and the publisher hereby disclaims any responsibility for them.

Any people depicted in stock imagery provided by Thinkstock are models, and such images are being used for illustrative purposes only.

Certain stock imagery © Thinkstock.

Front cover by: Kit Foster Design

ISBN: 978-1-4759-6509-4 (sc)
ISBN: 978-1-4759-6508-7 (hc)
ISBN: 978-1-4759-6507-0 (e)

Library of Congress Control Number: 2012922735

Printed in the United States of America

iUniverse rev. date: 12/4/2012

Other books by Wilfried Wlochal:

87 Cents
A Whale Ate the Moon
Through Hell and the Thousand-Year Reich

PROLOGUE

My romp through the other side of life started with a scheduled flight from the Interior of British Columbia home to Calgary, Canada. We crashed…

CHAPTER ONE

The belt - the damn belt...

Trying to focus my mind, I rivet my eyes on the burning wheel slowly rotating in its bearings. Choking acrid stench of burning rubber is drifting my way but I am unable to escape the putrid fumes of aviation fuel gradually blanketing the crash site. The fog-bleached sickle of the waxing moon casts a cold, pale light on the sparse shrubs surrounding me. Vainly I struggle to free my right foot trapped in tough branches of a tree. From my hanging head-down position I strain my ears to catch anything above the faint crackle of fire; even an anguished human grunt would comfort me by knowing that I am not alone. I feel blood trickling from my chest, slowly creeping its sweet stickiness down my neck, my cheeks and eyelids. I am unable to reach the seat buckle with either hand.

An icy moist breeze rolls in. Except for an occasional gentle rustle of leaves it is deadly still. I struggle to turn my head but I'm firmly wedged in the branches.

"Help!" My voice is raspy. Is anybody there? "Help," I try once more, but then I become aware that no one can hear me. Again I attempt to reach the buckle, turn my shoulders, push hard against the thorny, vicious brushwood.

There! A swish. A crackle of faintly approaching steps, the breaking of small twigs underfoot; then quiet again. "Somebody there?" But my voice comes out a low moan. I can sense it, feel it subconsciously: a person is standing very close to me. "Help," I groan once more.

"Who are you?" A woman's voice.

The words lash me like an electric jolt. "My belt. Open my belt!" I speak my words slowly, carefully, hoping that she would understand me.

"What's your name?" What does it matter who I am? The voice insists: "Who are you?"

"...that button on my..." The voice... The voice... I had heard it before.

"Who are you?" the interrogation continues. The tone of her voice is cold, cutting, hurtful. Vaguely I recognise her as the woman next to me in seat 4A.

"Help me. Tony Parker." Can she understand any of it?

"Tony who?"

"Anthony Parker. Hurry!" I am not certain if she can make out my croaked words.

Her footsteps crackle through the underbrush again, moving, receding, then returning and approaching me from the front. I beg once more, straining my voice. "Please, don't leave me like this. Help me."

Now I am able to see her feet coming closer. The moon casts only a faint light through the mist, yet I can make out from my hanging position that she looks unruffled as if she had walked away from the crash intact.

"Parker? Your name is Parker?" Her query is angry, laced with derision. "Who is Parker?"

"I beg you, help me. I'm nobody." Could she understand me?

"Why were you on that flight?"

I don't answer; instead I swing my body back and forth. A few inches at first, then almost a foot; back and forth, back and forth. The blood keeps running. Unexpectedly her voice is suddenly very close behind me, almost whispering into my ears. "Save your strength. Rescue will be here the moment the fog lifts. You'll make it out alive. You are not seriously hurt." She sounds somewhat more comforting.

What kind of a person is she? Will she leave me here to bleed to death? Damn bitch! I continue to swing my body to and fro, a few inches at a time. Suddenly I feel her hand at the nape of my neck, pushing me up, up. "Catch the edge of the seat," she commands. "Hang on, pull yourself up. More!" With an audible snap the seat belt opens. I slide down, roll off her back and fall flat onto the ground where I lie for some time.

"Get up," she urges. "There's nothing wrong with you. A few scratches, so don't expect any favours from me. And don't whine. I can't stand whiners. Get up and clean yourself. You are disgusting."

Slowly, painfully I claw myself up to face her. She looks clean and acts calmly - too calmly for me to comprehend. I try a few steps, and then my knees buckle and the world around me fades to black.

✳   ✳   ✳

When I came around I dimly perceived that someone was watching me. I tried to gather my thoughts but could not make out if I had been dreaming or if perhaps I had been driven in a car, swaying with the motion. A man's voice: "Good morning, Mister Parker. You are safe now. No, don't move yet. Lie quite still for awhile. Let energy flow back into you slowly."

"Who... who..." My throat was dry and the words didn't come out.

"I am Max. I'm the butler. I carried you up to the attic here and you are lying on a cot now. You are okay, but rest a little while longer."

"How long..."

Max the butler completed the question. "How long have you slept? All day, but now you are coming around again. Can you see me now? I'm standing near the window."

I craned my neck and then saw him, a muscular man with strong biceps and a broad, friendly face. The man came closer and wiped my forehead with a towel. "You will be in good shape very soon. It's still early now, but I'll go and bring you a cup of soup. A growing boy needs some food. And then we'll try and have you get up for a couple of steps. Just so that you get used to it again. In a day or two you'll be as good as new." He silently left the room.

Where was I? I tried to raise my head but the room spun and left me disoriented. Max the butler - did I perceive a German accent? I closed my eyes again and promptly drifted into a nap.

"Just a few scratches, Mister Parker. Nothing broken." Max was back again. "There, I brought you some consommé, but first let me put this stuff on here. Can you lift your left arm a bit? Just a little higher, please. Does it hurt?" Yes, it was definitely a German accent.

The potion burned like fire but I shook my head. "Are you a nurse?"

The butler laughed. "No, but I've had plenty of bruises myself once. - Another patch here - don't touch. You'll be fine again very soon. It's your head I'm worried about. I mean, the shock. When you found out that you had expired. - Oh my, she didn't tell you yet, did she?" He gently helped me into an upright position, feet on the floor. "Dizzy? In a little while it will all look normal again. Had it myself often enough. Now, can you hold the spoon? Don't worry if you spill some."

"What do you mean..." my voice slowly came back. "You said 'expired'." Surely I had misheard or that man was making a mistake. I tried to focus my thoughts on something familiar, anything, any event to which I could relate. I would tell my wife... my wife. What was her name? I would tell her...

The soup was tasteless, and then Max was gone again and left me alone once more. Was I losing my mind? How could I have forgotten my wife's name? Laura, Laura...

CHAPTER TWO

L ater I remembered vaguely that I had been up once or twice with the butler's help; now slowly I worked my mind through the haze. Max was already in the room, holding a steaming big mug of soup. Was it still the same day, or perhaps the next even? I had lost track.

"What happened?"

"You're doing fine, Mister Parker. Slept for hours again. A little bit more of this? I took your vital signs while you were out; you'll live. Or whatever. Once you cried, like a child almost. More like a whimper - being knocked out like that... It's evening now. I'll let you get up, but slowly. Come, I'll help you get into the shower. Take very small steps first."

My legs were unstable and I held onto the butler until I could sit down on that narrow seat in the shower. It felt like emerging from a meat grinder, but gradually I gathered my energies and let the water wash away pain and anxiety.

Coming out of the shower I stepped in front of the mirror, wiped off the condensation and looked straight into the eyes of a teenager. Who is that person? I was middle-aged with greying temples and pouches under my eyes, but instead I now stared into the face of a mere child. Oh, it was Tony Parker all right, but I saw myself as I looked some forty years earlier. I was still wrapped up in my own image when the butler came back with an arm full of clothes.

"I dumped your old stuff," Max explained, then noticing me staring at my own image. "Yes, they all look at themselves.

Nobody is aware of his cosmic age until they come here. You are lucky, you even look like yourself. Some find themselves as old women, old men... Yes, yes, some arrive here and find out they had even changed gender. Others turn out to be children again. Or they want to hide, but there's no place to run. I guess that's why so many change their names."

"Max, how old do I look to you?"

The butler studied me carefully. "You must have been in fairly good physical condition. It would show if you had neglected yourself. Your age? Eighteen, perhaps. Nineteen at most."

"I am fifty-eight. This is all a dream, isn't it?"

"Is it a dream? Isn't everything a dream? Is any of it real? Does it matter? You're asking the wrong guy."

"I know who I am. I'm a mature man nearing my retirement age. I've started making plans. Max, what the hell is going on?"

"Just goes to show you how screwed-up things are when you're here." He sat down on the bench. "Come here, Mr. Parker. Please, sit here next to me. Please. Nobody here is dead - not really. At least, we are not motionless. But we are on a different frequency. Some call this the Level Two, but they may just be guessing like everybody else. You are the same you, but you have resettled in this other reality and in your own cosmic age. Anyway, that's what they say. I don't know myself where we are - nobody does. What is real, what is illusion? Is a dream real? Certainly – but it's not factual. Perhaps some philosopher can come up with the right answer, but I don't know."

"Then who am I? Just a dream?"

"You might as well be. Here you may be nothing more than a squatter. An alien, a trespasser. I really don't know where you belong, if anywhere at all. Perhaps in one of the other dimensions. There are so many of them - some say seven. But now that you are here you must fit into this one."

"Is there no way of going back? After all, this may just be an illusion."

Max shrugged his shoulders. "There's no way back. You must integrate; become part of us. Miss Lynch has already arranged matters for your transition. There will be an inquest." He stalled, searching for words.

"What kind?" I asked. "The way I see it, I'm dead or dreaming, and this is just some kind of a movie. A mind trick or something."

"There are many ways of being dead," Max slowly continued. "Like there are many ways of being alive on another level. I know it's terribly confusing, and that's what the inquest is all about. To see if they can fit you in."

"And if they cannot?"

Max did not respond to my question head-on. "You may hear rumours about... you know... about the end of everything. Ignore them. Don't pay any heed."

"What kind of rumours, Max?"

"About the..." He fidgeted nervously before continuing. "We are not supposed to ever mention it. Especially if you are a squatter. Beside, it's only hearsay anyway."

I hesitated to continue this line of probing, seeing that the questions made my newly found friend uncomfortable. "I'm not worried about any rumours, Max. I'm more concerned with me. How about you? Are you one too? Are you also a squatter, as you call them?"

Max looked at his shoes as if to collect his thoughts. "That's just it. I don't really know. I woke up here one day and I didn't have the nerve to ask. Miss Lynch took me in."

"Then what the hell are you talking about?"

"There is no need to get excited, Sir. I have a personal viewpoint on where we are. It may not hold water, but it sort of puts a face onto our position. At least it comforts me. Some say this place here is built from memory, brick by brick, and all the regulars here are incomplete. Some say they are underachievers, that they have not delivered the goods when they had the chance. They still have a debt to pay. That's what some say."

"And you? What was your potential?"

"That's just it. I may not even be in that group. Besides, all this is just hearsay anyway."

"Before you - what did you call it? - before you woke up here yourself, who were you? How old were you? And, dammit, stop calling me Mister Parker. I'm Tony. Look at us, I'm half your age."

"Goes to show you, Mister ..."

"Tony."

"That's just it, Tony; there is no certainty anywhere, not even in numbers or names. Nothing is as it appears; all is illusion. It's like shadow-boxing. Who was I? I bottled Coca Cola, that's all that comes to mind." Max put his arms around me. "Just let it go, Tony. Let it all go on its own speed. Drift with the stream wherever it may carry you. Perhaps we are all just drifters. I cannot give you much advice, but be prepared to panic now and then. Who knows, perhaps there is a way out of it all." He cradled my head as he carefully applied some patches to cover the lesions, then cleaned my face. "Just let it flow past you, Tony. Let it go. There may be daylight at the end somewhere."

I don't remember how long I sat there, cradled by Max. It didn't matter. What did time matter anyhow? "This woman, she's a real bitch, isn't she?"

Max shook his head. "Miss Lynch? She would lay down her life for you. She did for others, perhaps even for me."

"How long have you been here then?"

"Must be over thirty years now."

"Ouch!"

"You must hold still now, Mister… ah, Tony."

"But you're only what? Forty? You can't have been here all that long."

"See what I mean? Time here is all messed up. It comes in big chunks, it comes in very little attoseconds. It can even stand perfectly still. Years can turn into minutes, minutes blow up into years. Some grow older, some don't." He put the towel down. "There! You look as good as new now. And a lot younger." He smiled. "And we better get you on your feet fast. Day after tomorrow is your first meeting with that council and we have to get you into shape."

CHAPTER THREE

Max had patched me up with professional care, bent my knees, twisted my arms, arched my back and pummelled and kneaded me until it hurt, but the next morning I was in pretty good shape again. Max hinted with increasing urgency that I was now expected to pick my own lodging as far away from my rescuers as possible. "To put Miss Lynch at ease," as Max explained. Nothing personal. "And here are sixty bucks," he added. "To start you off. It's from her." I knew he was lying because I had seen him earlier go through his own wallet fingering his folding money.

"Of course, I'll pay her back," I hastily added, playing along with his pretence.

I felt surprisingly mobile, and, after the first tense moments, gained enough strength and confidence to investigate my neighbourhood. I managed to slowly walk for blocks, then studied the houses: three-storey, old-fashioned working-class residences which promised stability and advertised vacancies. *Furnished Room for Rent* signs in some windows, *Chambre a louer*, if you came from Montreal or Moncton. One card read in small scribbles under the head banner: *Refund for non-drinker, no visitors, no radio, no TV. No squatters.* A greasy-looking woman, her face framed by unkempt strands of reddish hair opened the door and mustered me suspiciously. What does that refund thing mean, I wanted to know.

"They pay us thirty loonies per week, we kick back five." Is that legal, I wanted to know.

"Are you not one of them squatters? You look like one."

"So?"

She snorted and slammed the door in my face. Kawuumph.

Another window sign added: *Beautiful view, moderate up-charge*. A hefty hulk of a man of African ancestry, a man with a big, friendly face and thick round black-rimmed glasses opened the door. A forty-year old Harley biker no doubt. What's the up-charge, I asked. The biker studied me for awhile, then said "five bucks". We went up past the vacant second floor, then through a door and up the bare wooden stairs to the attic. One large room sparsely furnished, an attached kitchen with a big window leading out onto a diminutive landing on a flat roof. The advertised 'beautiful view' was an outlook onto a neglected, weed-covered garden. "You can climb through there," the biker said. "Take a sleeping bag out, stay there under the stars on hot nights. Are you by chance new here?"

I nodded. "How can you tell?"

"You smell of camphor and iodine. Big bruise on your forehead. Accident?"

"Squatter."

"I had a hunch but that's okay with me. Any money?"

I nodded and showed him my sixty loonies. "My name is Ted." He handed me the door key.

The roof area looked barely big enough for escape manoeuvres, but still the idea of a possible retreat into quasi isolation appeared attractive at this moment. There was altogether too much going on and I yearned for some seclusion. Besides, I was suddenly quite tired from all this walking.

�֎ ✷ ✷

After a short rest on the well-worn sofa I was ready to see more of my new world. First I ambled through the neighbourhood, then, daring to stray further afield, I took a bus to the end of the line. "Hertha Pavilion, last stop," the conductor announced. It was a decrepit former dancing palace the size of a Zeppelin hangar precariously balanced on its rusty I-beams rammed into the bedrock under the mud of the bay and slowly wasting away. Here the bus made a P-turn and stopped and the last four passengers disembarked. The driver and conductor unscrewed the tops of their thermos flasks and unrolled their coffee break snacks. The sign above the former ball room had long ago disintegrated with only *ertha* and *avili* still in place, albeit without their bent neon-filled glass tubes.

I walked all the way back to Henry Street by foot, a trip that took nearly an hour and blistered my already swollen feet. Everything was cheap. Hot-dogs twenty-five cents. Coffee ten, with buttered toast and jam twenty-five. By and large, the city looked bedraggled. A happy place has dogs and kids who laugh and play in the streets but there were very few of them to be seen. A side trip also showed me the seedy side of the city, the abandoned factories along the shoreline, the car wreckers and the old slaughterhouses with the cattle pens framed in paint-peeling white wooden fencing. Such valuable real estate, I thought. Why does nobody do anything about it? Depression and decay everywhere. Was the city dying?

Four blocks further I changed my opinion. Craig Street West, hustle and bustle, construction cranes, heavy-duty trucks carting enormous scoops of dirt from deep excavations, DANGER - DO NOT ENTER signs, a woman in red-and-yellow safety vest redirecting the traffic. What are they building here, I wanted to know. That? Oh, that's the new shopping centre. The Craig Market Arcadia.

Two blocks over I found myself in a section of town which could only have been a movie set. Baker Street of Sherlock Holmes fame, complete with gas street lamps, cobble stones, a cigar shop with an open door, the eternal flame dropped from the ceiling inviting to light up. I heard the clickety-clack of a horse pulling a hansom with drawn curtains, then waited for the megaphone amplified 'cut - save the light - take ten' command, but it never came.

The city was a hodgepodge of incongruous junk and superficiality, abandoned dreams, fabricated instant nostalgia with some assembly required. What's going on? How could I find out, who would tell me? I waited until the gas lights came on one by one, throwing patches of yellow disks onto the cobblestones. Tired I went to my new home and to bed where I dreamed that I was running uphill on a treadmill.

Before six in the morning I was wide-awake, washed up and went out again. The expansive park two streets further down had a calming effect on me. Lush trees, shrubs, their leaves still moist from the night's dew; a guy passing on a mountain bike; someone walking his dog, the first I saw. The city was waking up. The Imperial Garden Shop opened and I bought a whole pushcart full of necessities such as a razor, soap, two T-shirts, jeans, sneakers, a stack of dish rags, food, food and more food - and a jug of milk. A growing boy needs lots of milk.

When I returned home my landlord Ted saw me coming with my paper bags and opened the door. He said there had been a call for me to remind me of tomorrow's meeting at two. The biker helped carry my stuff up, then we walked down again and he invited me to a mug of very good coffee. The biker was Russian and his full name was Taddeus Ramelov. He had been a miner first, and then, when the seams ran out, an oil rigger. Now he held a temp job at the Carlisle Book Depository, working together 'with half-wits and retards'.

"I steal books. Actually, they are free to the poor anyway, a free library for the illiterate - isn't that ironic? But stealing them is a sport." Sure, he could get his Book Draw Pass, two items per month, but stealing has the aura of danger, adventure and plain asphalt jungle piracy. "Come," he said, and we went into the adjacent living room with wall-to-wall bookshelves. Books on the table, books in boxes, books on the windowsill, books everywhere. "There! These are all my friends."

He pointed to an overloaded rack with editions printed in Cyrillic. "Pushkin - do you know him? He was such a romantic fool - died still in his thirties. Got killed in a duel no less. What could this man have written if he had lived his full life? Listen to his Ode to Liberty."

There was reverence in the big man's voice as he recited the complete poem by heart. "Russian is such a beautiful language," he said. "Just pay attention to the richness and resonance, the colour, the sheer musicality of it. So full of sad melody. Like bel canto you need not understand the words. Can you not hear its big Slavic soul hiding behind every syllable? Hm? I know much of what he wrote by heart."

Ted recited some more and he was right; the words had a hypnotic effect with their harmonious interplay of tone and timbre, the cadence, the embroidery of their intonation, their rhythm.

I studied the bookshelves: Sociology; mathematics; Roman Architecture; a heavy tome on Light Polarisation; Advanced Abstract Geometry; Salinity of Selected Bodies of Water; Porosity of Stressed Membranes; Geothermal Turbine Design; Myths and Legends of Penal Rehabilitation; Das Röhren Vademekum; on and on and on.

"Isn't it ironic," Ted said with a sweeping gesture. "All this knowledge here in my hands. And now I'm turning blind."

Next day I continued my adventure through town. People seemed lethargic, so I decided to conduct a small test. At the *Consolidated Hardware and Camping* store I noticed a pile of oddly shaped combination hatchet-and-claw tools on sale, which for some reason had been put on display in the paint department. They might be useful for taking pallets and skids apart, so I wandered over to the opposite side of the store where they sold hammers, saws and crowbars. I finally found a couple of salesmen in deep discussion with each other. "Do you have any of those hatches with a claw at the other end? For taking crates apart?" I had to ask twice before the shorter one noticed me and asked: "Yes, can I help you?"

I repeated my question once more upon which the man replied: "Ah those. Yes, I know what you mean. I think I have seen them once. If you don't find them here we must have run out. I doubt we'll order them in again. They didn't sell very well." Then, without waiting for my response, he nodded, turned back to his colleague and continued their conversation.

As I left the store the uniformed lady at the exit door asked sweetly: "Did you find what you came here for?"

"No, I was just looking."

"Looking for what?"

"Nothing special. Just looking around."

"Why?" She wiped her forehead and looked deeply puzzled.

CHAPTER FOUR

The meeting took place around an oval table in an otherwise barren conference room. Two men and two women sat along one side and around the ends; I sat alone. The officiating man directly opposite me introduced the group but I paid scant attention and promptly forgot their names.

"Before Miss Hanna sets up your education funds…"

I must have looked puzzled, so he added: "Oh yes, we expect you to be frugal, study and amount to something. Before she sets up your account, there are a few questions I must ask. Anthony William Parker…" He stroked his thick black handle-bar moustache and paused to let the significance of his position sink in. "This is an integration council expressly assembled to deal with problem migrants such as you. According to this memorandum from the courier, the name of you, young man, is not as per manifest, to writ: Timothy L. Vanderberg." Turning to the woman on his left: "What's the L standing for, Miss Hanna?"

"Lionel."

"You're not Lionel, are you?"

I didn't know if to nod or shake my head. "No."

The man continued. "You were escorted by our courier, Miss Lynch. Either there had been yet another error in her data bank…" pouncing the desk with his middle finger and turning to Miss Hanna again. "That's the third one from her this year already. Will this now finally trigger an official inquest?"

Miss Hanna already expected his question. "Of course, Paragraph sixteen, chapter four. We must be very strict about this."

"At any rate, this meeting will be very informal and brief. We have been assembled to ease you into our society. First we must get this - this ugly incident out of the way. Tell us in your own words how you ended up in seat Four B. And don't try and fool us. Both Miss Hanna and I are familiar with the airline business."

He glanced sideways at Miss Hanna, then added barely audible: "And some of us still are, aren't they?"

This remark was obviously directed at his secretary, but Miss Hanna ignored the barb. She looked at me, raising her eyebrows, expecting an answer.

I had trouble remembering all events in detail. "The baby. It cried it's head off and I upgraded into business class. Yes, a baby. It howled while we all waited in the boarding pen, and when finally I took my seat in the plane, there it was again; right on the seat behind me. 'It's those diapers,' the mother said."

"And then?"

"I asked the stewardess... the flight attendant... I asked her if I could upgrade..."

The doctor raised his eyebrows. "There was a free seat then?"

"Yes, Sir. A cancellation or something. Normally they are all taken but this one was still free. The upgrade costs thirty dollars but you usually have to do this as you check in. It's a bargain. This one was a no-show probably."

"After you had resettled, did you talk to the person next to you?"

I tried to remember. "Yes, I believe we talked."

The Significant Man smiled forgivingly. "Yes, yes, I know. It is difficult to remember every detail from before - well, from before the event. It comes, it goes. However, try hard: did you have a conversation with the occupant of the seat beside you?"

I shrugged. "Probably, but not much."

"Describe what you saw when you sat down on seat Four B."

I cautiously studied the people in front of me. The man who addressed me wore a well-tailored dark-blue jacket, a gold-coloured vest and a bright yellow tie. I couldn't see his shoes but judging by the man's closely cropped hair I imagined them to be black laced wingtips, Argyle socks, pants probably held up by both suspenders and a belt. He looked as if there was a faint odour of moth balls around him. Age? Forty-five to fifty, I would guess.

The man's secretary on his left was the professional type: turtleneck sweater under smart grey jacket, sensible low-heel shoes, hair cut short, straight, combed; no earrings; no bracelet; instead she wore a big round no-nonsense man's wristwatch such as aviators do. The only other jewellery I saw on her was a black oval pendant with a sprinkle of small diamonds behind what I thought was a rocket of sorts. A rocket in flight set against a starry night sky. I guessed her age at thirty-five or so.

Clockwise I myself was next and to the left of me another woman, very young. Twenty? Short unkempt red curls, wind-blown, dishevelled. They say redheads are lustier. Loose V-neck sweater two numbers too large, blouse with sailing illustrations peeking around the corners, no jewellery; no watch; dark blue deck shoes with white stripes along the sides; flaring grey pants. The sailing type perhaps? I blushed.

Next, stuffed between her and the person in charge sat a big man, overweight, large bones, enormous ring on left middle finger. I couldn't focus on him and it confused me. He looked strangely familiar. Had I seen him before? Effeminate, I would say. Full lips. Powerful, broad hands with incongruous smooth feline gestures; puffy, oval face with dark brown locks curling down the sides; pouches under the eyes. The eyes! Radiant blue with an underlying mixture of curiosity, boredom, contempt and arrogance. Shabbily elegant, carefully-preserved fifty or more. Vest with chain and fob but too flat to hold pocket watch. Pretty Boy. Wore well-used brand-name casual shirt - could be John Palmer or such. Overdressed sleeveless two-tone silk sweater. Expensive Harry Rosen slacks; Bally loafers with run-down heels I speculated; no wristwatch. Could one perhaps detect a touch of make-up?

"Are you paying attention? Please, answer me. What did you see from where you sat?"

"The lady. I mean Miss, Miss..."

"Lynch."

"Miss Lynch. Yes, I remember. She seemed to muster me secretly. She had a laptop open. We didn't speak much."

"Why not?"

"I'm shy, that's why."

"You are shy?" The question came from the redhead next to me. "Explain that." She smiled.

"I don't usually look into ladies' eyes. Not in public. I think they dislike being looked at so directly."

"And yet you noticed that she studied you."

"Yes. Out of the corners of my eyes. Peripheral vision."

Am I by nature a coward, the doctor's secretary wanted to know.

"I don't really know. The occasion had never actually come up." I felt that I was blushing again. How embarrassing - it's always the same with inquisitive women.

She continued: "About the event, can you recall the last few seconds?" What was her name again? I had forgotten already. Damn memory is starting to play tricks on me.

"Missis..."

"Just Miss Hanna," she replied curtly. "I never married." For a second or so her gaze seemed to wander as her eyes searched something at the ceiling, but then she focused on me again and her smile returned. "What happened just before the event?"

"It was a bit jerky. It's usually a bit jerky over the Selkirks. Did you ever fly..."

"Of course. Did you sleep?"

I shook my head. "Dozed a bit. Had a rough two weeks behind me and was tired. Ordered a Scotch..."

"They serve alcohol now?"

"Yes, in Business Class they do. It's a bargain. Suddenly the bottom dropped off. That's really all I can remember."

"Were you badly hurt?" This question came from Pretty Boy. "I see you have a Band-Aid on your forehead, another one on your neck. And you have a ghastly limp."

Thank you for rescuing me. "I'm bruised everywhere but I'll get over it. Mostly just scratches."

The Significant Man spoke up again. "How did Miss Lynch treat you after the incident?"

"Well, Sir..., Sir..."

"Doctor Borelli." There was a slight emphasis on 'doctor'.

"I was hanging upside down from the double seat which was caught up in a bush or small tree. I don't know how she got off, but I was just hanging there. "

"Did she help you down?"

"No, not right away. In the end she did, but reluctantly. I even thought she might walk away and just leave me there."

"Was she friendly, helpful?"

"She eventually helped me down and I'll be forever grateful for that; but no, she wasn't."

"Wasn't what?"

"Friendly. She seemed angry. Irritated. It's not that I blame her. After all, we had just survived." I stopped. The council members looked at each other as if this disclosure was relevant.

Pretty Boy changed the subject. "If you could do anything you wanted in the near future, what would that be? You don't have to be specific or even adequately intelligent about it." He cocked his head as if to add 'we don't actually expect much from the likes of you', but then he continued. "And if you initially choose the wrong metier, as most do," stifling a yawn, "you can always change that later. Now, what would that be?" He rambled most of that without actually making eye contact with me, searching something just above my head. Only once, for the briefest of moments, I caught the man's contemptuous eyes. I renamed him on the spot: Shithead.

"I don't know," I answered. "What would be the point?"

"Indeed, what would be?" Shithead added gratuitously. "But surely, even a squatter must have secret wishes. Imagine you had suddenly discovered hidden talents, what would you want to do with them?"

"I would become a lounge pianist."

"You have musical endowment then?" Shithead's eyes lit up with mockery.

"None whatsoever."

"Why then?" He glanced at the other three council members, an unspoken 'see-what-I-mean?' on his face.

I protested. "May I remind you, Sir? The key word was 'imagine'. You asked me to imagine to have talents, not to actually possess them."

This time Shithead looked me straight in the eyes. "Yes, yes, of course I did. My humble apologies." His tone became somewhat more conciliatory. "Of course I'm prejudiced, but prejudice is so utterly comforting. So please tell us, why would you want to be a lounge pianist?"

"Dress well, play a few tunes, sing into a microphone, work from eight to midnight. Free meal. Flirt with your eyes. It's an easy life."

"The ease of existence is your primary aim, is it not?"

"Yes, the absence of stress." I became tired of this man's arrogance and turned my head towards the doctor again. Get this jerk off my back!

Doctor Borelli took the hint and came to my rescue. "There is no rush to work this out now." He looked at the other members, fetching their approval. Whispering to Miss Hanna just loud enough to be heard: "We should expect very few problems with him, I assume." Then, adding some explanation: "Some of the squatters come here who'll find the integration very taxing. Become terribly confused, jumpy even." Turning to me, "You show some promise, young man - perhaps it's your passivity, your youth. With your help we may be able to blend you in. How old do you think you are?"

"In real life?" This was an absurd question; besides, Max had cautioned me not to parade my past. It may lead to confusion or, worse, unleash strident argument.

Shithead spoke up again; now he was testy and irritated. "This is as real as it will ever get. This is the centre of all awareness, disappointing as it may seem to some of us. Get used to it, Kid." That numskull actually said 'kid'.

I said that I was estimated at being under twenty. "Who told you? Miss Lynch?"

"Max, her butler."

"The pugilist," Miss Hanna added.

I discreetly studied Shithead from the side, trying not to be obvious. A has-been newscaster, I guessed. Amateur actor. Vacuum cleaner demonstrator. Time-share condo agent. Did I perceive Oscar de la Renta after-shave lotion? And could one also notice a double chin? Underwear commercials are out of reach for you, baby! At best you'll do the late night weather report.

I spoke up, not addressing anyone in particular. "This is a mistake, right? I am a squatter, I understand. I want to register my objections. I'm not supposed to be here."

"Be where then," the Sailing Lass asked, raising her brows.

"Maybe there is a way…" I saw the discomfort on their faces and my voice faltered.

Doctor Borelli had the answer on hand. It often happens that squatters have a difficult time to fit in, he pontificated. They are so unfinished and come here in complete confusion, trying to upset the system. Don't really know where they belong. Some even try to escape. "Imagine," he repeated. "Escape! Escape to where? Be one more cadaver among in the wreckage? But then, who knows? Perhaps some day one can find a way out."

Shithead looked out the window to emphasize his boredom.

I felt cornered. "I don't mean escape, like from jail. Just that…"

Shithead interrupted me without even turning his head. "You are here forever, Boy. Forever and ever…"

Borelli came up with a solution. "Peer orientation," he said. "You need a counsellor at your side. Up close and personal. Somebody who teaches you the way."

"The correct way," Sailing Lass added, hinting that there are wrong ways to avoid at all cost.

The doctor circled the room with his index finger. "Pick yourself a companion mentor from among us here. Choose anyone with whom you feel comfortable, including myself."

Of course, I considered the doctor first. The man spoke with urgency and studied pomposity in unruffled tones and was the spokesman for this group, certain of his authority, steadfast in his position. A firm hand on the wheel. And yet, there was something indefinable, shifty. Whatever it was, something in his voice, in his bearings put me on guard.

I didn't like Miss Hanna with the big watch. She was obviously the bossy type and would just shove me around. Still, she might some day explain the mechanism of these bizarre dimensions and clarify the absurd. If there was one thing I needed more than anything else, it would be an explanation of what goes on here. She might chalk out my development on a big blackboard, mark the critical stops, advertise the dangers well ahead of time, nudge me onto the secure track whenever I would derail. I would not have to pretend to know the rules; she would explain them as we sauntered along. I should not discard her yet. Besides, she controls the purse strings.

The red-haired Sailing Lass! Just the consideration of it made me blush again; this angered me and I quickly put her out of my mind. Was I really a teenager again, having a crush on the first seductive maiden to cross my path? And would not everybody immediately know my motives?

Shithead didn't even direct his porcelain eyes in my direction; he was obviously tired of the whole affair. His demeanour advertised that he was drafted for this horseplay and didn't really want to be part of it.

"Well?" the Doctor asked, nervously drumming the table top with his fingers while adjusting his bow tie with the other hand. He was certain of being chosen.

I pointed my finger. "Shithead," I answered, and so became bundled with Sebastian Melmoth, former versifier, recluse and odd man out.

"Why did you select me?" Shithead asked when the others had left. "Anybody else in that group would have been more sympathetic. Surely you must have perceived by now that I am not a likable person. Furthermore, I can't stand you, and you know it. You reek of warm milk and latex. You have no trace of even the slightest graces, and look how you dress. Nothing fits, nothing matches, nothing is co-ordinated. You are an abomination. There is no suggestion of elegance, let alone artistic refinement. You are not only trivial but repugnant."

Suddenly I knew who that man was. Of course, I had seen his picture before, even remembered a few fragments of the man's writing. "It is only shallow people who do not judge by appearances. Right? You are Oscar Wilde, aren't you?"

CHAPTER FIVE

W e walked for some time through Gilbert Park only half a block from our meeting place. We did not speak, did not even glance at each other for some minutes. As we sat down on one of the benches, Melmoth finally repeated: "Why me?"

"Just a hunch, I guess. I remember you from High School. I enjoyed your plays."

"Cherish the art but not the artist. Let him toil in obscurity. And never, never address me with my old name. I do not appreciate familiarity. It stifles approbation. You should have followed your first instincts and go with Bernie. The redhead. I saw you blush. Only the lascivious blush. They have all the reasons."

I did not take the bait. "I don't know how to handle women. I'm shy. I try and cover it with a bit of studied showmanship."

Melmoth chuckled. "Your shyness, my boy, is a club. You wield it to bludgeon the unwary."

'My boy' angered me, but I let it slide. The dice had been cast and Melmoth was now my tutor to guide me through this labyrinth; instead I tried to ease the tension. "Still, Mister Melmoth, thank you for agreeing to counsel me."

He was not appeased. "You are lying. You are not the least bit thankful, not yet, but you will endure me." He chuckled. "Why? You must wrestle me down. This may, in the end, be one of your better decisions. How did you guess who I was?"

"I remember to have seen pictures of you. You haven't changed much. I almost expect to see you carrying a cane."

Melmoth's eyes lit up with a fleeting smile. "That certainly never was a cane, *mais un bâton de marche*, a sauntering wand meant for gracious strolls from the garden of Eros to the ladies' boudoir. Do you know my Garden of Eros? - No? But then how could you have known about my bâton? Indeed, I once possessed several, but one of them was my favourite. I had been quite fond of it, but I have now become accustomed to walking without its reassurance and comfort."

I studied the big man's walk – gliding, cat-like, stealthy. Why this arrogance? It seemed dramatised, an act. Was it a ruse to shield himself from personal involvement in the world around him? We would walk or sit for spells without speaking a word, ambling through many reveries, then suddenly Melmoth's big blue eyes would light up and the words would tumble out. "Why do you complain about being here? This may turn out to be the safest place yet. Furthermore, there is no escape anyway."

"Doctor Borelli seems to indicate..."

"Don't trust him. He's a faux farthing."

"And this 'squatter' tag. I'm not used to be merely some appendix of society. Makes me think of being an intruder or something. Could I not just wake up in bed? At home? After a terrible nightmare?"

"What, pray tell, would you want to wake up to? Sketch me the scene in big bold strokes. Charcoal will do."

"There would be my dog. The first thing I always see in the morning is my dog. He senses when I am ready to wake up, then he sits there and simply stares into my face. Unabashedly. My wife would be up already, brewing coffee."

"What's her name?"

Quick now: what's her name? How could I forget? "Laura. I think it's the aroma of fresh coffee which really ends my sleep. The dog knows that."

"What's his name?"

"Casper."

Melmoth laughed. "Casper? That means clown. Is he a clown?"

"All dogs are clowns. The original court jesters. Did you ever have a dog, Mister Melmoth?"

"Never. I'm not much of an animal person." He stroked his chin and appeared deep in far-away memories. "A friend of mine did, but not I. He claimed he could hold a conversation with him. Dogs are blessed; they can see their gods. - What else would wait for you if you could go back?"

I was eager to change the subject. "I don't really belong here. Everybody is watching me with suspicion. There's no one I know. I have a real job on the other... You know, the other side."

"Such as? A pre-stressed concrete inspector? I read your dossier, you know."

"I did other things as well. I'm an architect; used to design strip malls. Strings of little high-end stores with parking spaces in front."

"Were you good at that?"

My first instinct was to inflate my accomplishments. Yes, I was tempted to say, they were beautiful vistas of palmetto-lined boulevards with elegantly dressed shoppers strolling past the festively ornamented storefronts. At least one of the slender, long-necked ladies would lead a rhinestone-decked, coiffured poodle on the leash. I would close my eyes and recall what graphic artists had once dreamed up to wrap around my starkly geometric drawings, but then I thought better of it. "I brought my craft to a new level of vulgarity."

"No originality?"

"None was ever commissioned, none was delivered."

"Then I advise you not to radiate unbridled ecstasy. Learn to hide your mind. Agitate the least and demand the best. It simplifies life. Still, do not object to being here; that would be rather futile. Settle with this new reality. I have walked these streets for a hundred years with nothing achieved, nothing mastered, nothing to do. I came with vague ambitions, but there is no purpose to it. Ambition is the last refuge for those who failed. I suggest you minimise your career development, such as it is. It only gives you a label, nothing more. What is the current jargon? Handle; that's it. It gives you a handle." We walked in silence for a few minutes. "You must study something completely useless until you are an expert on a subject nobody cares about but which nourishes your vanity. That lends you social standing and they leave you alone. You coast. Of course, nothing worth knowing can ever be taught anyway."

"Study what, then?"

"Adhesives may be a good subject, especially if you get into its molecular structure. Nobody has yet figured out why sticky things stick. One can make fly paper but one can't explain how it works. It's rather humorous. If ever another glue master happens to come along, the two of you can seclude yourselves in some dark corner while you toast each other into oblivion. But don't show your hand too soon. Should you ever run into a real hostile expert - disasters happen, you know - you switch conversation to an unrelated subject. That's where you need a second set of flimflam. I would suggest *Racing Harness Design* or *Tire Profiles and Road Adherence*. Experts never focus on anything else besides their own narrow fields while sucking their thumbs."

Melmoth was a deliberate thinker; he remained silent again as we walked around the loop, then passed the old bandstand. At the corner of Duncan Street I bought us each an ice cream cone, and only after that Melmoth continued.

"Art is another jungle in which you can hide. It's at once surface and symbol."

"You had said that before," I reminded him.

"Of course, I'm repeating myself shamelessly. Everything has been said before; it now becomes a matter of fading memory. Art is a house of mirrors, the final sanctuary of the consummate impostor. The lure of deception is what drew me to the arts in the first place. Oh, you are a dangerous young man. You have opinions." He gripped my arm. "You must always hide them - look what happened to me. A little sincerity is a dangerous thing, and a great deal of it is absolutely fatal." He averted his face, but I sensed sadness behind that voice.

One more turn around the loop. "It pleased me when you called me Shithead. I congratulate you on your cleverness. Nothing is as flattering as a well-crafted insult. Don't waste it on your enemies."

"It was accidental."

"There is nothing accidental about the slip of the tongue."

I nodded: "Freud thought so too."

"Ho-ho! Now, there was a successful fraud. His vocation was already written into his name. *Nomen est omen*. Regretfully, I never met the man."

He stopped, looked at me as if he saw me for the first time, then continued. "You may want to attend the lectures of Professor Klonus. Of what I hear, he's disarmingly vulgar. It hides his motives. I know he wants to meet me, but I fear him. I fear them all. They are too clever for me. Just drop my name and he'll see you. I understand he occasionally quotes me. A few *bon mots*, that's all that's left of me now. Soon I'll be just an asterisk. Anyway, he teaches nothing useful - as expected. He may help you destroy any remnants of your belief system." Melmoth planted himself squarely in front of me, his eyes boring into mine. "How else could you grow up with all your hang-ups? He teaches Love and Dedication and Hope and Comparative Philosophies and such inanities. He claims to be a simple-minded country boy, but, oho, he's razor-sharp. The wit of a farmer, and that's the sharpest."

"Then, what do I learn?"

"Scepticism. The beginning of faith."

"Are you sure?"

"Of course I am not. I leave certitude to the pompous."

"If scepticism is such a prize, why should I believe anything you tell me?"

"Ah!" Melmoth chuckled. "There's a future for you yet." Turning contemplative again: "And one more thing. Flatter all with any droll platitude but despise those who relish in it."

We parted as the sun set. I drew Professor Klonus' address out of Melmoth and wished we could have talked more, but Melmoth merely winked me off. "Go home, Boy. I don't wear velvet knee breeches anymore."

※　　※　　※

A family moved into Ted's empty second floor apartment as I came back home. The man was a haggard-looking fellow with bushy moustache just like Doctor Borelli's, and thick black unkempt hair. I judged him to be in his late thirties. His wife was a thin-lipped blonde with big eyes, triangular face and pointy nose under heavy make-up and was plainly a few years older. They arrived with their ten-eleven year old son and moved in swiftly as all their possessions came in only a dozen carton boxes and one clothes hamper. I watched them in the dying lights of the day from the street-side window of my pad as they emptied their rusty old station wagon. Perhaps I should help, but then again I felt exhausted. An hour later they introduced themselves: Marlene, Joe and their son with the rubbery handshake, who giggled nervously and who's name I promptly forgot. I was still fatigued as I must have walked miles today. My thoughts lingered on this Melmoth, wondering who was really hiding behind that big face.

Next morning I found a pawnshop on Ricker Street where I bought some essentials including a wrist watch and a top-of-the-line Mont Blanc fountain pen which leaked constantly. Now I counted my money: so much in the bank, some in my pocket and a credit card to boot. The past seemed to thin out, blow away like fog, but I clearly remembered that in that previous reality I was worth more than a thousand times as much. For now this will have to do.

In the afternoon I searched out Professor Klonus' address, a third floor walk-up above a bank. The receptionist asked: "Investment or lectures?" Mister Melmoth had suggested to go for lectures, I replied. Ah, yes, she said, then excused herself and vanished into one of the doors in the back. When she returned two minutes later she smiled sweetly. Perhaps the Professor could take on just one more student if I would fill out the registration cards. That will be 50 loonies for two lectures.

I went through the selections offered: 'The Fountains of Righteousness' was one of them; another one: 'You Cannot Fill a Closed Fist', and for those who didn't get it, underneath in cursive letters 'You can only put riches into an open hand'. The next lecture promised big rewards through contemplation plus introspection, and the last one on the schedule was titled 'Being Good - What Does That Mean?' That one was to run next Monday; it may be costly but then again, what are credit cards for, eh?

Afterwards I took the bus to the university and registered for three courses: *Anthropology of Paper Roses, Low-Temperature Roller Bearings* and *New Approaches to Invisible Mending*. None of these subjects interested me in the least, but now I had my student pass which entitled me to eat in the cafeteria.

⚹ ⚹ ⚹

Joe and Marlene on the second floor had a clamorous argument in a foreign tongue long into the night, only to restart early Saturday morning. Ted came up just as I was making myself a breakfast. I was now quite well installed with a fridge comfortably stacked, the cupboards packed with a polyglot mixture of plates and cups and glasses - none of them matching - plus the crystal carafe and an unopened bottle of cheap Tawny Port. There was actually a brand new tablecloth hiding the ghastly sunflower-imprinted waxen cover underneath. I begged Ted to stay for scrambled eggs, toast, coffee. That done we went through the whole bottle of 18% fortified sugary libation mislabelled 'Port'. Afterwards we went down and tried to collect our thoughts in Ted's book-stuffed living room, played three games of chess, each of which I lost in minutes. I finally asked the questions which I had on my lips all this time but was not certain whom to ask: What exactly is this place here?

"This place?" Ted repeated rhetorically. "Well, the City of Crosley is mostly just a cesspool of freethinkers and heretics. We are a secular people here. Not just any but mostly an English-speaking, carnivorous, predominantly Caucasian, non-combative, humanistic society, typical of 19th century scepticism. I said Caucasian but I'm one of the few exceptions. See what I mean?"

"How come you are Russian? I've never seen an Afro-Russian before."

"Goes to show you how mixed-up this place is. Of course, there's overlap. That and the migrants and the visitors and those who got stuck with the wrong gender to begin with. There's even the occasional squatter like you. Just those. And of course we get some misfits, too. And musicians and poets. A few painters. One organ grinder. Not many others, though – and hardly any politicians or lawyers."

The commotion up in Joe's and Marlene's place above us had calmed down now and the tranquillity was a welcome relief. It didn't take long before we could hear the faint tinkle of the kid's glockenspiel seeping out from the hot air radiators.

"How do I get out of this place?" I asked without much hope of an answer.

Ted had some medication to chase the Port, namely a bottle of genuine Napoleon Brandy no less. Napoleon had absolutely nothing to do with what was done with his name behind his back, but minute by minute the Plimsoll mark sank till it hit the top of the label. A few drops of booze had spilled and Ted drew little wet circles on the wax cloth with his index finger.

"You don't," he finally replied, then topped off our glasses. "I had a hunch you would ask me this some day. Give it up, Tony. The days... the years go in circles - like these little rings here. It doesn't matter where you are, you are still racing around that ring. The sooner you make peace with it, the better off you are. In the end you might even like it here. For one thing, it's probably much safer here than on the other side."

There it was again, the rumour. "I heard from Max the butler, I heard from him something about the end of time..."

Ted interrupted me at once. "Yes, yes, there are hundreds of stories about the other side. It's just idle chatter. Pay no attention. Besides, what would a butler know about quantum theory anyway? Superstition, like all the others which have scared us. Concentrate on the here and now."

We raised our glasses and downed the firewater. Ted abruptly changed the subject, slurring his words slightly. "This town, Crosley... There must be a million places like this. Cities, towns, islands, villages - all of them in clumps of this and that. The sports people fit almost anywhere. You can't talk to them but one can observe them as they talk to each other. They wave their arms a lot. There must be whole cities for those types alone, all separated into many languages and funny little flags. Some say one can get used to it."

"Would that not create a terribly boring society?"

"That's the whole purpose of it." Ted chuckled. "No tension, no disputes, no life-style contests. No effort, no aspirations. It's an easy dream."

I pointed up. If we are all that much alike, why then does the couple up there dicker so much?

Why? Couldn't I tell? The man's a beer slinger; she's a hooker. He clears twenty, thirty bucks a day at most; she pulls in maybe a hundred. Sometimes he puts on a little show at the tavern by sneaker-wearers who can play the harmonica. Stand-up comics.

Tap dancers. Jugglers with five balls up in the air. That earns him a few extra loonies. On the other hand, on convention days she can double her take. They are always in competition.

Maybe there is some hidden ambition somewhere. After all, why else be concerned with making money? And wouldn't hookers deserve their own cities?

"Where exactly does the career expansion stop and the hooking start?" Ted asked rhetorically. "It's so hard to tell them apart."

"And why do they (I pointed up again) live in such tacky apartment?"

Ted puckered his lips and sucked in. "Drugs. Fags perhaps. That's probably all money is good for nowadays."

"What? Drugs here?"

Ted grunted: "Nicotine. The worst kind; but if not here, where then? Of course, that's much a matter of personal belief, but the faith industry had never taken deep roots here."

I had noticed already: never saw a church. Does nobody believe in a God anymore? We refilled our glasses after I popped that question.

"Gods?" he repeated. "Not here. Wouldn't have a chance, but up there, in the North, that's where the Snow People live."

He seemed uneasy for a few seconds but then he continued. "The Snow People, that's what they are. You know, everybody has a different idea but no one knows. Except the Snow People way up there in Novaya Semlya, they say they know how the universe was created."

We sipped slowly and I silently waited until Ted had collected his thoughts.

"I spent my mining years up there, so I have a pretty good notion of what they were all about. There once was this bunch of very friendly spirits, they say..."

Where? And how many?

In empty space, he said. Just floating around there - about a dozen, maybe. More like angels, the way Ted described them. Apparently very sociable spirits, by what I can figure out. Just floating around in empty space. By 'empty' they meant empty. No stars, no moons, no rocks, no nothing - except for this invisible energy hanging there. Imagine pure energy doing nothing; just being there.

"Have another?"

I nodded. We refilled our glasses.

"Anyway, the spirit boss - that's the old man in the family - one day he had a notion that things were not okay up there, that something was missing. This place was boring - sheer hell, I suppose. So one day... One millennium later he looked around and he finally had enough; so he said to the others: 'Let's fix up this joint, put a little pizzas into our lives. Do something!' He called for a general meeting... There, that's really nice." Ted was referring to the glockenspiel music which seemed to come out of the cold air return now. "I can almost make out a melody."

I edged him on.

There were perhaps only a dozen spirits or so, floating through that empty space, quite alone. He wasn't certain about it and I don't recall exactly how he phrased it as the Napoleon took its toll, but he talked about this spirit boss who speculated what they could do with all that energy just hanging there. So he consulted his favourite nephew, Beelze. He liked Beelze because he was the smartest of the bunch, and Beelze said 'since energy and matter are exactly the same stuff anyway, let's find out how one can convert one into the other. May things perk up after.' He was obviously itching for action, this nephew of his. They worked on it for a long time, but time was the one thing they had plenty of. - Another?"

Sure.

"One day they had done it - figured it out!" said Ted emphatically, slightly out of breath. "Beelze pushed that red button and - boom! - there was this big explosion, the biggest explosion ever in the whole universe, and it could be heard everywhere. And all that energy had now turned into bright light which they had never seen before, and it almost blinded them. Don't worry, said the nephew, I'll take care of it. And when the dust had settled there was all this galaxy-making stuff, rocks and gold and diamonds the size of goose eggs. And gas - lots and lots of gas."

We paused and thought deeply about it. "And then?"

'Wow' said the spirit boss and his nephew together, and 'wow' said all the others also, shielding their eyes from all that bright light. What do we do now? Well, they set to work as best as they knew at the time and that's what the universe is now."

The plimsoll mark hit the punt. "Wouldn't work here," said Ted. "at leasht not here in Croshley."

CHAPTER SIX

I felt dingy in my hastily collected clothes from Max, so early Monday I called Melmoth. He's still sleeping, his landlady said. He rarely gets up before noon. At noon I called again, and then we finally met at around three. Help me pick some clothes, I begged. Melmoth was an expert.

"Your shoes make the biggest statement. Never draw attention to your feet; that means absolutely no runners, no bright socks. Spend half of your budget just on shoes. Make your feet disappear, except for the subtle message that you are able to spend a fortune only to stand upright doing nothing. Besides, you spend more time in your shoes than in bed." Yes, he obviously knew his way around toggery.

By the time the stores closed I had blown most of my bank account and it was time to attend his first lecture with Professor Klonus. The Professor was a short, balding, rotund man with quick, sparkling eyes, rosy cheeks and the happiness of a chicken farmer on his face. He wore crumpled pants, a brown cardigan with leather-patched elbows, scuffed shoes and a ten-dollar Chinese wristwatch.

The classroom was filled with about thirty people all eager to find rapture outside of religion. The Professor paced up and down a couple of times, then intoned officiously: "Being Good - What Does That Mean?" He was an artist with his tongue, being able to put weight on every word. "Ask Yourself Again: What Does That Mean?" When it was absolutely still, and before anybody could sneeze or harrumph, he continued. "Goodness is its Own Reward.

And How Can We Be Good? How Can We Reward Ourselves? How Can We Reap the Bounty of Our Own Rectitude? How Can We Still the Craving Within us?" In contrast to his stern message, his round face gleamed with happy joviality.

I had already figured him out at the third sentence and long before the rumpled old man answered his own question. He was a master confidence trickster, through and through corrupt, playing on cheap emotions and bent on planting guilt in your mind before you could laugh.

An hour later I had changed my mind. That man up front was naive and, in spite of what Mr. Melmoth had said, perhaps a bit dense. He admitted as much when he said that nobody, he included, could ever say for certain what was good or bad. Everything is relative and forever changing, he preached. For instance, on one side of the ledger stood terrible global wars of another era in another world, yet on the other side stands technological progress, the invention of plastics, dignified justification for securing peace should such ever be desired, and for deflecting the course of history at great expense.

"If there had been no Boer War, we would not have barbed wire," he explained cheerfully. "Just think about that for a moment: no barbed wire! That means no cattle farming, no meat, no gelatine." It's an act of nobility even, laying down your life for the politicians of your fatherland, he explained. Fortunately, the victor always occupies the moral high ground right from the start. That proves once and for all that justice always comes to those who rightfully deserve it. How else could history ever been explained?

The Professor was a master of his craft but I soon became restless. My first impulse was to jump up and leave, and then I changed my mind. That guy should be told what a shabby windbag he is. Tell it to his face with the whole class looking on; humiliate him in front of his exploited students. If he doesn't know what goodness is, why then charge these exorbitant lecture fees?

The Professor seemed to have sensed my question. He himself had no pat answers, he admitted, looking straight at me. He could only vaguely point in the right direction. Anybody who felt disappointed with this uncertainty would get his money refunded and five loonies to boot to go out and buy a meal with a good bottle of wine. Nobody took him up on this offer; he had his audience in his palm. Then the Professor counted the stations along the road towards inner fulfilment and personal progress, the milestones of the evolution of all selves, the narrow paths they must travel in spite of the thousand illusions and disappointments. When after the lecture I went home through the darkened streets I knew that the man was an extremely clever swindler and as honest as a used camel dealer.

"How was the Professor?" Melmoth asked the next day. A pathetic old man, I replied, certifiably crazy. I learned nothing. Nothing?

And then it came to me. "I became a sceptic. Maybe it was even worth my fifty bucks, and there is one more sessions to come."

"He's a dangerous man. He has an agenda. Watch him. You learn only from your enemies; pick them carefully. From your friends you get nothing but flattery while they stab you in the front."

✳   ✳   ✳

Professor Klonus' next lecture started with the whole classroom decked out with about fifty colourful kid's balloons. "This," he said, holding one up as the audience waited in hushed expectation, "is your heart. It is big, full of hot air, lovely to look at, a great plaything for you and others. Some are full of helium; they float up." He let it go and its buoyancy made it stick to the ceiling. "Some fall down." The next one was full of plain air and fell on the floor.

I was sure the man would blow his cover now. What can one possibly say about these props? The Professor had painted himself into a corner and I perked up to find out how his other students would take it when they figured out that they had been hoodwinked? This time there was no mention of your money back plus five loonies for a meal and a carafe of Tawny Port.

"Put your hand on your heart," the Professor cajoled his audience. "Can you feel it beat? Is anybody here who has his heart on the right side?" Giggles, muttered negation. "See? We have our hearts all on the correct side so that we can touch it with our right hands. Now watch me!"

He pulled a pin out of his lapel. "This," he gratuitously explained, "is a common pin and the point is only a few molecules wide. Watch what happened when I bring my heart, as symbolised by this balloon, into contact with this pin which represents the barbs in our lives!"

'Puff' it went. The collapsed empty skin of the balloon was now a symbol of nothingness.

I couldn't believe it, but the audience still hung on his lips. "Go ahead," the lecturer coaxed his audience, "prick them. Those of you who need needles come and get them here." Puff, puff, puff it went all around.

"This," holding up the deflated rubber, "is your heart which was full of hot air and nothing more. And what is it now? It is not even worth one single penny. But, now watch me!"

From under his lectern the Professor pulled up a balloon filled with shiny new pennies and held it up for all to see.

"When I prick this balloon, one filled with true goodness and substance, filled with silver and gold, watch what happens."

Again he pricked the skin, then held up the now liberated contents, most of it fell on the floor and rolled around in all directions. "Look here, what do I have now? I still have all the gold and silver. My heart was filled with substance and goodness." His eyes sparkled like the coins rolling on the floor. "Now I will tell you how to get all this goodness into your heart, and how to preserve and benefit from it."

The Professor was a barefaced mountebank, but his admiring audience applauded him nevertheless.

After the show I lingered until the students had left and the cleaning crew came in with their yard-wide brooms to sweep up those shiny pennies and empty balloons. "Yes?" the lecturer said, looking at me over his glasses. "Are you not the squatter - ah, Mister Melmoth's companion?" My first impulse was to pitch him my full wrath for having been swindled, but then I decided on a different approach. I said that I wanted to help him, and could he use some assistance? What kind of help, the Professor wanted to know. Setting up his discourses, filling balloons, inventing effective new strategies, I proposed. "What did you make of my lecture?"

I took courage and dropped my pretence. "Outright swindle. Unadulterated shit, unless, of course, you are demented. That's a

Trojan Horse there, isn't it? What are you really trying to sneak into them?" Finally it was out.

The Professor looked at me for a long twenty seconds. "A Trojan Horse? You consider me to be a charlatan, don't you. I hate charlatans. They stand against everything I hold for sacred. I give you my assurance, young man, I wouldn't ever want to be one. - Unless, of course, there are no other options."

I now went straight for the jugular. "I don't really know where you want to go with this, Sir, but surely you must have had something more sensible in mind. You set yourself up to be ridiculed and that is not in the best interest of whatever you try to do. Agreed, it takes a great deal of courage to play the fool, but there must be better things to do. This lecture here... Any empty-headed bullshitter could have done a better job of it. This, Sir, is crap and it stinks."

"It stinks?"

I nodded. "To high heaven." I fully expected the Professor to throw me out at once, instead the man seemed amused. His eyes twinkled as it did just a few minutes ago with a hundred pennies rolling all over the floor.

"I'm delighted you caught on," he said. "Of course I have a hidden agenda, but what do you suspect? Go ahead. Tell me. Don't be shy now."

In spite of the blatant rip-off, I did not dislike the man for it. There was something disarmingly simple and lucid about him and I was convinced that he was purposely teasing his audience.

"You, Sir, are a thief. Your lecture was not even an attempt at teaching anything, regardless of how shallow. We should have pelted you with rotten eggs, if you ask me. So, what's your excuse for that?" I should have asked for my money back instead of ranting, but now it was too late for that anyway. The old rogue might as well learn the truth.

The little fat man sat down, his face lighting up with a broad grin. "Absolutely amazing. I had almost given up on this dumb routine until now. You are so refreshingly new. Come, my friend, let's sit down and talk about it. Indeed, you get more advice from a palm reader. But wisdom?" Professor Klonus reacted with mock surprise. "Wisdom you only get from failure. What am I trying to do? I want them to throw stinking eggs at me, just as you suggest.

Tomatoes, horse shit, anything. I try to shake them up. Revolt! Storm the Bastille, stomp your feet. Do something, for crying out loud! Look around you, young man. People everywhere are zombies. I want to kick their asses. It took me time to come up with something as stupid and as vapid as my lectures, but regardless of my obvious insanity, they still lap it up." Resigned he added: "I'm beating my brains out. What else could I possibly invent?"

I pondered the question. "Give them something new," I suggested. "Not a different lecture, give them something... Something like a fad instead."

"I've been here too long. Nothing comes to mind anymore. I'm an old man now and I've run out of inanities."

"For an old man you, Sir, have roving eyes. I saw you playing up to the young females in your audience."

For a second only, the Professor seemed to let down his guard. "The tragedy of old age is not that one is old, but that one is young. And those words are not mine - they come from that friend of yours, the poet. He fascinates me; a complex sapience in futile search of simplicity. He gives me much although we have never met. I hope that some day we will but there is nothing I can give him. I have little of what is new or of value inside me now. I have done it all."

"Surely there must be a thousand silly things one can invent."

"Any ideas? Quick, flash some scenes. Now!" The Professor was becoming increasingly impatient.

"A show. A tent meeting. A frenzy. Hocus-pocus. Mass mania." I was groping for words. "Something capricious. Have them roll in the aisles, Sir. Have them throw popcorn at each other; blow into noise makers. Have them wear silly hats; speak in tongues; sing rap."

"What's rap?"

"Inarticulate words set to absurd noises."

"That's it!" He slapped his knee. "Come with me," the lecturer beckoned. There was an unmarked freight elevator in the back; it connected with the underground garage where a chauffeured limousine was already waiting.

As we were driven to the airport the Professor took my hand and urged: "You know what is needed, don't you! You are so fresh, so illogical, so crazy."

"The world I come from is crazy."

"I need you. Where do you think we can go from here?"

"Start all over again. A new belief system." I rattled down disjointed words. "Something electrifying. New rules, dogmas, subjects, viewpoints, targets. The City of Crosley is a good place to start."

I had absolutely no idea where to go from here but the Professor nodded. "So full of faked reality and in need of a new Illusion," he added. Could I come up with an outline, he wanted to know. I admitted that I had no plans of any sort yet. The idea was only now fermenting in my mind.

"I knew it," the old man said. "I had always hoped that something useful might eventually come out of my penny act."

The limo rolled to a stop, two porters rushed to carry the luggage from the trunk, and as he stepped out he said: "Work out something." Then turning to the chauffeur: "Get this young man safely home. And give him back his fifty loonies."

✳   ✳   ✳

Ted was enthusiastic. Invent an original fad, a novelty act, a manifesto, a complete belief system even! Oh, what a challenge! We worked through the night to come up with some coherent new caprice. We agreed that the foundation must include inspiration other than hastily fabricated jingoistic slogans.

Ted put it this way: "We need to have something which comes from a bona fide virtuous source. I'm thinking of ancient scrolls, a wandering desert holy man or a bunch of angels who have descended from their starry lair to guide us mere mortals into their secrets. Well, we are mortals - sort of. Aren't we? Besides, who has evidence to the contrary?" Oh, what a brilliant mind.

How about something logical instead?

Ted was adamant. "Logical? You want to quantify the myth, the wonderment, the awe? Logic is for statisticians and others who want to fool you."

"Why not turn it upside down?," I suggested. "Why not just a joyful noise. How about something with tambourines? Ca-ching - ca-ching."

Ted loved them. "But who's the front person? We need a magician."

I suggested a woman, a banner-carrying Valkyrie along the lines of Jeanne d'Arc, the Gallic flag waver of Orleans. Aimee Semple McPherson, apparently, was just such a person. Not that she had actually invented new religious fads, but she managed to polish the tired old ones until they sparkled again. She certainly packed her admirers into that colossal circus tents which she always filled to capacity - and still many people had to stand outside and listen to the holler and ruckus through the canvas. Well, at least until that sex scandal closed her show. What a woman!

I added my own observation: "The Venice Beach House where she stayed between gigs still cash in on her fame. They charge a king's ransom to sleep in her bed. New sheets, though."

But where to carry out this extravagance? I came up with the old dance hall I had seen recently - Hertha Pavilion. Excellent, Ted said. What does it cost to fix up, he wondered. A million, two? More with electronics installed, I estimated.

The early morning light filtered through the curtains. We were both exhausted, excited, happy and simply worn out, so we broke to catch some shut-eye. It was close to noon when Ted banged on the door at the bottom of the stairs. "Someone's on the phone."

It was the Doctor from my guidance group. Could we have a short meeting today? Say at three?

✳   ✳   ✳

We found ourselves around the oval table again, that is all except for Melmoth who couldn't make it as he had some urgent personal contemplation to do.

"It had come to our attention," Borelli intoned, "that you had been seen to attend Professor Klonus' lectures. These are disturbing our peace. And, it may be worth pointing out, these homilies do not entirely comply with the statutes of the City of Crosley as they may lead to endangerment of personal morality values." Morality? Now comes the fine print on the back of the contract. The Doctor let the words sink in, then added: "Who put you up to it?"

I admitted that it had been suggested by Mr. Melmoth – but why would that be important? "It's not that we are spying on you,"

Miss Hanna injected, trying to blunt the point of the question. "We are merely interested to see you fit in. Duty over pleasure. You must adopt. Have you made any progress yet?"

Yes, I explained, I had adopted quite well. I feel now that I had never been older than nineteen.

"That's what I am driving at. You may be spending your money and time foolishly. All teens do. Your bank balance is near zero and your credit card is starting to amass… Well, it's not yet a big debit but we suggest you keep an eye on it. We all know that the Professor means well, don't we?" Miss Hanna wrinkled her forehead.

Sailing Lass pointed two index fingers in the air, closed her eyes, wiggled her shoulders and airily warbled 'Raa, raa, raa, money, money, money.' I kept her in the corners of my eyes.

Exactly what morality values does one endanger? I wanted to know. Miss Hanna continued: "You are here in this group as a - as a…"

"Squatter."

"Yes, thank you. I didn't want to be so rude about it. That requires that you adhere to our standards and use reason, logic, rationality and insight in your approach to appease the Eternal Enigma. The good Professor, it is said, has a tendency to hand out disturbing homilies, which, upon closer scrutiny, may or may not stand the test of intelligent judgement. Some even say he's an agitator although nobody has actual proof."

Borelli cut her short. "We are all witness of his generosity, though. So, what is your involvement with him? Are you prying into his investment schemes?"

Why was anybody interested? Should I bend the truth just a tiny bit, tell them that it was nothing, just a chance encounter? I decided to lay my cards on the table. "Yes, I saw him a couple of times, but I was mostly discussing the possible restoration of the Hertha Pavilion. I was to work out a feasibility study. After all, I'm an engineer. I was one, once."

Stunned silence for a couple of seconds; then Miss Hanna spoke up once more: "Why would he want that old dance hall?"

I explained: put up a show; tambourines and trumpets and dancing girls; very harmless stuff; no agitation, no corruption of morals - just some entertainment.

Miss Hanna seemed relieved and even Dr. Borelli leaned back in his chair. "Yes, yes, that's harmless enough. You must stay close to him, very close," he urged. "Tell us what goes on. Never be out of earshot. We would show our gratitude."

Before half an hour was up we all had reset our sails working out the details. At Doctor Borelli's insistence I even had my bank account topped off by a full thousand dollars. Miss Hanna seemed uncomfortable at this largess, but she bit her lips and hesitantly signed a cheque. After all, one needs to be properly attired to be a spy implant in the enemy's camp.

We broke up, shook hands and Sailing Lass whispered into my ear: "Got away with it this time." Damn, damn, damn - why are my ears heating up again?

On my way back home I passed Farmer Bill's Pre-Loved Car Emporium and bought a slightly used apple-red MG Midget. Cost: Sixteen hundred on plastic. Yes, I had been warned, but what the hell. All teenagers do such silly things.

There was nothing to do for the rest of the afternoon, so I cruised around the city, the suburbs, the shopping centres, Stanley's Amusement Park and then to the beach. There it was: 'ertha' and 'avil'. A million, two? A hundred million? Somebody give me some numbers!

※　　　※　　　※

On Wednesday I sashayed to the Professor's office in my tiny red Flivver and told the receptionist that I had worked out a framework as per request, and that I and my collaborator, Ted, were ready to submit our preliminary proposals. I was all pumped up and ready to go.

The phoned rang two hours later. Professor Klonus is expecting both of us for next Sunday, and would we kindly pick up our tickets at the airport.

CHAPTER SEVEN

Melmoth was furious when I told him what happened. And why did nobody think of him as the faddist guru, he insisted to know. Who but he had such stage presence, such aplomb, such style and grace? I answered that, honestly, I had never thought of him, but if I had proposed him to the Professor, would Melmoth have accepted?

"Of course not," he protested. "How can I, scion of stage and print and with my impeccable reputation, shill for a hippodrome? However, there is some honour in snubbing the unworthy, so at least give me the pleasure of turning you down."

Although Melmoth found the prospect of inventing the manifesto of a new doctrine terribly exciting in itself, he did not want to get involved. He is a literary man and Professor Klonus is a clown, a buffoon at best. Besides, there were too many sticky questions which needed to be cleared first. For instance, what should one call such brew? A secular or religious sect, a cult - what? Furthermore, what does one do with it when it is finished? Will it be financially self-sustaining; will it yield a profit? If so, what to do with all that money? Too many dumb questions.

I mentioned the tambourines and Melmoth admitted that this was inspirational. Add finger bells, he suggested. Make noise, shout it from the rafters. A scattering of burned-out rockers had moved in lately, perhaps some of them could cook up a fitting set.

"And furthermore, there is no trace of worthy promises. It used to be that you could sell Paradise and upon default nobody ever actually showed up to collect a refund. What can you sell now?"

I shrugged; I had never considered marketability being essential to faddist rituals. "In addition," Melmoth continued, "you would have to add truly disgusting practices. They are crucial to keep the flock together and to separate it from outsiders. Killing a lamb was once considered very stylish, then the offering was upgraded to oxen and from there it didn't take long until they skewered gladiators to great jubilation in Latin. That probably went over the top a bit, but for awhile they brought in the big gold aurei by the bucket."

What are gold aurei, I wanted to know. Melmoth looked at me askance. "You'd get a hundred gallons of wine for one aureus - and seven would buy you a virgin. A boy slave, though, costs more, and very much more yet for a fully trained, lithe young man servant. Females are for misers as they save cash. You might say it was parsimony which opened the floodgates of heterosexuality. Besides, it made public stoning so much more entertaining."

I tried to tone it down a bit. "Could we not just have one of the dancers bite off the head of a pigeon instead? A goose even? Just for very special festivals of course."

Melmoth chuckled. "The only creatures one may still kill unabashedly are insects and, except for some scarabs, these are not large enough to be seen from the back rows. All life is beautiful for the one who lives it. One must even imagine a cockroach happy."

"That's Sisyphus," I replied helpfully.

"I said cockroach. Anything wrong with that?" Melmoth reacted testily. I invited him to come along and meet Ted, offering him to share a bottle of Tawny Port with us to lubricate his golden tongue.

"Tawny Port on such a beautiful day as this? Are you mad, young fellow? Offer me Tawny Port when I have to see the dentist. That day is ruined anyway."

I drove him around a bit in my new car but Melmoth was a terrible passenger. Too fast, he complained, and he missed the clap-clap-clap of hooves. It was not his day to be happy.

On my way home I passed by the university and cancelled my registrations. Who needs to study paper roses now?

✼   ✼   ✼

Miss Lynch was home for a change. She had just come back from an assignment and looked worn out. She caught me talking to Max but was too exhausted to snarl at me. "Priests are the worst," she said to no one in particular. "They don't want to die. They cling onto their mattresses with their fingernails, scratching and swearing like buccaneers. What are they afraid of? The moment they talked about constantly has finally come. Why did they become priests to begin with? They wanted to get control over their childhood fear of death. They did it to accommodate only themselves and one day the curtain closes." The monologue burned off a bit of her tension.

Then, turning to her servant: "What does he want now? Whatever he wants, give it to him – then get rid of him. But please," looking directly at me, "please, don't come back. I had asked you before but here you are again. Is there no way I can finally get rid of you? You spell bad luck."

Max mentioned the used laptop in the attic. "Yes, yes. By all means, let him have it." She looked exhausted, resigned. "Just make sure it's re-formatted. I don't want to have any data leaking out. And after he's gone, lock the door." As she walked off she turned her head: "And keep it locked."

When we were alone, I asked: "Why is she so uptight? She hates my guts."

Max put the box of software down. "She's afraid of you. She loves you, but she fears you at the same time. I once met a man in the ring who was better than I. He was younger, he was stronger and I knew that he would knock me down, but I loved him nevertheless."

"I'm not in any ring with her, I'm not competing in any way."

"Not yet, but one day you will. She has a terrible job; puts herself on the line with every mission. You are a mighty embarrassment to her. She erred, and for that she knows that she will have to pay. She should have left you hanging there - nobody would have been any the wiser. But no, she had to stick her head out again."

I shrugged my shoulders. "You work for her; I couldn't."

"I couldn't work for anybody else. She's pure gold."

"Why doesn't she quit her job?"

"They don't let her. She was a dentist once."

✳   ✳   ✳

Ted and I worked feverishly for two more days on the manifesto, then we spiffed up smartly, took our beautifully bound proposals under our arms and went to the airport for a flight to see Professor Klonus. I voiced my reservations about taking a flight so soon after my crash but Ted did his very best to calm me, put his big arms around me in a symbolic protective gesture. Next he rattled statistics about safety and how many crashes per passenger/miles, but statistics only work as long as one is not among them. I would have gladly traded my misery for a couple of root canal operations by Miss Lynch personally if it had to be, but this choice was not open.

The black stretch limo was already waiting to take us to the airport. Two tickets Executive Class to Arakiri, a place neither of us had ever heard of. At Arakiri we changed into a small Bombardier business jet and an hour later we touched down on a dusty remote jungle airstrip. The people scurrying around us were clad in loose, airy cotton garb, 99-cent thongs and wide brimmed straw hats. Women in long black sarongs milled about, some with a child carried on their backs in slings. Decrepit old cars and trucks spun over dusty lanes, and even what was generously called the Airport Administration Building was nothing more than a frond-covered hut with a slight lean to the lee. Former pre-stressed concrete inspectors see such things.

In spite of their obvious poverty the people laughed a lot, were friendly to the visitors, offered us freshly squeezed pineapple juice and looked with a touch of reverence at Ted's bulk. They might not have seen such a hefty six-foot-and-two-incher before.

"Please, please," the driver begged us to get into the Hummer, a beat-up remnant from a war somewhere. Off we went. Winding road, rice paddies, thick-leafed waxen trees which neither of us had ever seen before, then swerving around the corner, through the stone arch. And there, before our very eyes a castle in gleaming marble and gold trim appeared from behind the tall royal palms as we motored around the gentle bend. The driver slowed down so that we might take in the many sights around them. Small bungalows were tucked in a semi-circle around the mansion like so many chicks around their mother hen amidst the manicured park-like expanse of at least fifty acres of sheer splendour which even African potentates would have envied. It included a big central fountain ringed by eight marble elephants which spewed coloured water high into the sky and over the loosely-clad maiden in their centre.

We entered timidly past the massive sky-high portals where three lovely young ladies took off our dusty shoes and replaced them with soft pearl-studded slippers, cooing and wooing endlessly. Then we were led over a marble floor inlaid with semi-precious stones towards the back gateway and out again. Before us a swimming pool, lounges, tables, sunshades, sweet-smelling flowers everywhere. Professor Klonus came towards us, hands outstretched. He wore an ankle-long mauve silk garb around his rotund frame and a broad smile on his face.

"So glad you could make it. You must be absolutely exhausted from the long journey." Of course he was kidding. We had flown luxury, not economy. Had he ever been squeezed into a 17-inch wide seat upholstered with shredded tires? Has he ever contorted himself to stretch his legs around the plastic shopping bag full of duty-free Cannabac? Has he ever eaten machine-packed semi-edibles from a plastic foam tray? Has he ever held a low-impact styrene fork in his hand and break off two of the tines? Has he ever, eh?

There was a hidden smile around the Professor's lips, which you could only detect if you looked into his eyes. "Oh well," he said, wiping the scene away with a brusque hand gesture. "Ubi bene ubi patria."

He raised a finger and two men came towards us, measuring tapes in hand. What are our favourite colours, one wanted to know. Dark blue and bright yellow.

We must first relax in these surroundings, he insisted. Take a shower, have a massage, loosen up. We would all meet in a couple of hours for a very informal tropical repast. And could we leave our proposal behind so he could just glance at it? It might give us a subject for a discussion later on.

The three slipper ladies led us towards one of the smaller bungalows surrounding the courtyard. I had seen many top dollar residences in my job, but these guesthouses were more than a truckload of two-by-fours with vinyl siding. The adjacent bathrooms to the bedrooms were nearly the size of Ted's entire attic rental suite, and the shower had three jets, each one about a foot in diameter. When returning reinvigorated to our quarters, I found a silk robe laid out on the bed, dark blue with bright yellow cuffs, lapels and waistband. Knock- knock. One of the slipper ladies stood before me. Would I like to have a massage? It refreshes, relaxes and cures seventeen different ailments.

Would I? Yes, oh yes. "No, thank you." For at least now I was too intimidated and overwhelmed to accept the gifts of Venus. Ted dropped in a moment later, wearing a bright yellow robe with dark blue cuffs and all that.

Dinner was a relatively quiet, unhurried affair and consisted mostly of fresh fruit, raw fish wrapped in black seaweeds and other stuff of uncertain parentage. That done we all retired to the adjacent library which, very much unlike the one in Ted's house, held no books of any sort. On the other hand, the walls clean around were hung with - I counted them - fifteen beautiful erotic calendars of a most beguiling nature. "Kama Sutra," Ted whispered. "The latest edition." They captivated his attention until the Professor started the conversation.

"I have thumbed through your proposal," he finally began as he slowly poured three Sherries, then congratulated us for the outstanding job we had done. "Gentlemen, I raise my glass as a toast to your genius."

We sipped slowly so as to savour the delicate bouquet.

"However, summa summarum, it's rubbish. You can't just fabricate yet another version of shamanism; we already have more of them than necessary. If that's what was needed, we could have warmed up any of the old ones. After all, there are hundreds of them. This is a secular society and religion is heresy. What we need is entertainment."

Ted and I gulped down the rest of our sherry.

The professor's fingers flipped through the pages, looking for the tie-ins. "I like those long Gabrielian trumpets. Love those tambourines, the finger bells, but where are the mementoes? You don't make money on tent shows, you make money on plastic things and candles and stuff made to collect dust. And we need to come up with a lot more illusion of happiness. Nobody really ever goes through unblemished happy times; only in retrospect it looks that way. And then lace those happy memories with aphorism and a light dusting of sex. Inject some melancholy and you can sell more nostalgia." He put the paper down and looked straight at me: "More money is being spent on wedding pictures than on education. We need more asininity, more levity, but always hide a tear behind your yarn. If you have a message to deliver, don't. Nobody wants to be lectured. That's right, gentlemen, there's a bundle to be made in folly and tears. Make it a package deal. And put somebody utterly pathetic on the stage. It stirs protective instincts."

We were crushed. Had we so entirely missed the ball? Did we totally misinterpret what the Professor really expected from us? We had worked so hard to reinvent a brand-new belief system, and this stunted fat man only wanted to sell us what in the end only amounted to a miniature wind-swept snow scene under a little plastic dome.

The Professor leafed through the pages, flipping forward, backward, then put the whole binder on the table. "We must get rid of any religious perspective. Tambourines are good, but we need more rabbit-out-of-the-hat stuff. Stage magic, sawing-a-lady-in-half. Funny guys on unicycles. Toot those long trumpets. The audience must be startled. Irritate them if this helps. One can easily forget a joke but one remembers most irritations. But afterwards, when they are home again, they must all laugh. Make sure it's funny, at least in retrospect. You have yet a lot to learn about showmanship."

The Professor excused himself for a moment, returned half an hour later dressed in baggy pants, his familiar brown cardigan with elbow patches and scuffed shoes. There he was again, strutting a hawker's pose as if he once more held that balloon full of shiny pennies in his hands.

"This, gentlemen, was a good start. You must be tired now, so I bid you good night. Stay for a few days if you enjoy my humble home. The driver will take you back whenever you are ready to leave. I've got a plane to catch." And with that and a barely perceptible nod of the head he left and was gone.

"Do you think what I think," Ted asked me after we heard the Hummer's cantankerous exhaust fading in the distance.

I was not ready yet to put our cards on the table. "Maybe he is changing the whole concept of our proposition. Maybe all he wants is a variety show. Song-and-dance. Stand-up comics."

"Yea," groaned Ted. "After all we've done for him. Changed his mind just like that! Maybe we pissed on the wrong tree."

We stayed for another three days, eventually accepting the attention of the feminine staff for relaxation and its cure for seventeen different ailments, including wiping away some of our disappointment and all those cobwebs on the brain.

CHAPTER EIGHT

The upstairs couple, Marlene and Joe, were fighting it out again, so this time I took my bottle of Tawny Port and knocked at their door. The boy with the rubber handshake opened. "Mom, that man is here again," then giggled nervously and turned his attention back to his toy glockenspiel.

I always find it difficult to cold-start a conversation, but Joe had no trouble with such hurdles and opened up with: "We wondered where you had gone." I replied we had accepted an invitation to somebody's cottage; it was wonderful.

And we came back by limo? Marlene asked suspiciously.

I lied, explained that the chauffeur was the guy with the cottage, and he merely dropped us off here on his way to work - and lets have a drink. Through the first half of the bottle neither of us spoke much but slowly the tension eased a bit until we started on rye with Coke.

They liked my little red car, and could they have a ride in it some day? Of course, they could - one at a time. How's theirs? Falling apart, they said. Needs brakes, tires, valve job. Steering is pretty loose as well but maybe it's worth saving as the floor boards are not yet rusted through. By now the rye was gone and we continued with dark rum and Pepsi.

Then, without preamble, Marlene suddenly burst out: "I wanna quit my job. I'm getting too old for this. I'm scared of the winter. High heels - snow up to here - what a drag!"

Can't she find something else? "Sure, but I need a decent wardrobe. You have to look classy. And I have no marketable skill. I have to go back to school, and that's not easy at thirty-nine."

"Forty-seven," said Joe, and then he suggested something about her working at Exxon Donuts, doing a little freelancing on the side. Marlene cried again.

"To think that I was a dancer once. Ballet. I can sing. Had lessons as a child, even studied with Miss Fishammer and sang at Christmas parties at the Greenpeace Legion." By the time the day was over I felt sorry for the whole family, but what can one do, eh?

✳   ✳   ✳

Autumn was slowly setting in and Melmoth was nowhere to be found. The trees in Gilbert Park defoliated branch by branch and Ted and I sat through many hours with strong coffee, undeterred by adversity and, in spite of instructions, continuing to invent brand new sins and their marketable expiation. Then came a phone call from one of Professor Klonus' secretaries: could we manage to see him briefly at his lecture hall?

He beamed broadly when we arrived. "Had some meetings with my management group. They suggested keeping this project separate and under wraps for now. I take it for granted that the two of you are willing to help me getting this thing onto the stage."

Of course we were; that is, as soon as we could focus on what he actually wanted. The Professor handed us a hefty binder. "Digest the information, point out which portions of it engage your obvious talents and then let's get to work. And have that poet friend of yours to help you. I must meet him some day." Where did this little fat man get such boundless energy?

There was very little of the original proposals left in the binder; instead the concept had been turned into a variety show and now contained several cost estimates, time tables, manpower requirements, advertising plans, sketches, costume designs and a hundred details we had never even thought of.

Could it still be rescued? And what might it all cost, I wondered. There were tooling expenses for plastic injection moulds, energy consumption contracts, logo designs, philosophical abstracts on thought control and even a legal brief on personal damage compensation. Ted, surely a master of a thousand disciplines himself, was overwhelmed by the sheer immensity of it all. What to pick?

It went well over my head, but I still felt that I should at least have some say in the rehabilitation of the Hertha Pavilion before everything slips out of my hands. Perhaps now was the time to scale down our proposal - if, indeed, anything at all could be rescued from our original concept.

And where would I fit in? Could there be a place for a person in charge of damage control, if nothing else? A hanger-on, a hack who drips smart advice now and then? With a meaningless title, such as *Director of Visual Conceptualization* or something else important-sounding but in reality quite superficial? I couldn't see myself sucked into a never ending spiral of weekly, daily drudgery regardless of how beautiful the overall show might be. The hallelujah angel was not buried yet but surely had its wings clipped. Ah well, one must learn to compromise on occasion.

Ted moaned and groaned and finally said that he wanted no longer to have any part of this business, regardless of what it may pay. Too shifty. One day it was this, the next it was something else. One could never rely on the Professor's erratic directives. Too unpredictable. Sorting books at the depository suited him just fine, thank you, even if it paid starvation wages. Books he loved, books he understood. Perhaps he could be a consultant on the side if it required no more than six hours a week. Well, make that eight hours - one day each week. That's all; no more!

We met with the Professor at the appointed time and had our say. If he was disappointed, he didn't let on. A day-a-week of Ted's input was OK with him, but he would pick the tasks. Ted reluctantly agreed. Yes, that'll be fine.

I had done some preliminary sketches of the new pavilion, which we showed the Professor who in turn replied that there would be engineers and architects and specialists on the job, so I would not get involved with the nitty-gritty of it. But someone would have to hover over the whole project just to make sure that things moved along. How would I like to have some input into the design of the theatre production? I could suit myself as to which pieces I might want to work on. There are choreographers on the job, and musicians and stage managers; I could link with all of them in a loose coalition of talents. I pointed out that I had absolutely no experience with show business but would very much like and try to fit in and to contribute what I could.

How about pay, Ted wanted to know. Glad you asked, the Professor said. "I used to pay my people good money and did not always get full value. Matter of fact, three of my companies went bankrupt. Mind you, I run none of these projects myself anymore. That's done by people who know their stuff. But I learned my lesson. I stopped paying salaries altogether. I do it differently now and it seems to work well. Nobody to my knowledge ever short-changed me. Why, I wonder, does nobody else follow my system?"

He handed us each a credit card and simply said: "Take as much out as you think is yours." And with that we were dismissed.

※　　※　　※

Finally I could reach Melmoth who sounded tired on the phone. May I invite him to meet Ted and have a really good meal? I have a hot proposition for Melmoth to consider: work on the Professor's cabaret production.

"Before I even consider this invasion of my privacy, is it Tawny Port again?"

"Your pick."

The little MG Midget could only hold one passenger, besides it was getting cold now and the car's heating system was a joke, so Ted and I took a cab to Gilbert Park where we met Melmoth who, unexpectedly and contrary to his usual tardiness, was already there. He looked outright dejected, crumpled, untidy and despondent. Only after we had taken our seats at the fashionable Trommer Restaurant did I dare ask if he was willing to work on that show.

"I only join you for the meal, nothing more. No, I'm not ready for such trivialities." Melmoth wetted his lips, took a long time looking at me and Ted, especially at Ted, and then said: "I can't. I just came out of rehab. Yes, it's nicotine again."

The waiter came with a bottle of refreshing Riesling, inched through the formality of uncorking and pouring it as if he was performing a wedding ceremony. Only after he had oiled himself clearly out of earshot again, I asked: "Why that stuff?"

Melmoth did not answer; we started our meal quietly, but towards the end during the second bottle of red full-bodied Bordeaux, Melmoth took on a bit of colour again and opened up. "Shit," he said, and nobody had ever heard him say 'shit' before; it was not his style. "Damn shit."

Ted looked up. He kept his mouth shut but I knew that he knew. Later when the waiter circled the table to stick me with the bill, I asked once more. "Why nicotine?"

"It helps me being a genius. Besides, a cigarette is the perfect type of perfect pleasure. It is exquisite and it leaves one unsatisfied; what more can one want?"

"Why can't you smoke Lucky Miss or Ganjada or even Ras Tafa Kings like everybody else? Why tobacco?"

"Can't stand the taste of rope. Even tried to chew Assassins Five. It doesn't do it for me. Every time I go in for detox I die a little. I wake up in the early morning hours bathed in sweat; my hands are shaking, and then I imagine to be on my cot in Reading Gaol again. I die a little more. It horrifies me and yet I must go on. - And the wild regrets, and the bloody sweats, none knew so well as I: For he who lives more lives than one, more deaths than one must die."

⁂ ⁂ ⁂

Talent Management Inc. opened its doors three days later, and that's when the whole project nearly came to an end. I had seen some poorly run jobs in my life, written scathing reports especially on bridge abutments only to be dressed down by those who were in charge of financing, but what I now encountered took the cake – candles and all.

'They' were in charge now, and although I was happy to get rid of the more mundane tasks, it seemed obvious to me that nobody had any clear understanding of what was required, where to get it, what it would cost or how to schedule the various interlinking phases of the project.

The calamities started with my office, a miserly cubby-hole with elbow-high partitions and boxes full of obsolete software which didn't even run on the old desktops. I dragged the laptop from Miss Lynch around, more for comfort than utility and finally got MS

Word running on it although it kept asking me for verification of legal ownership of the operating system. Everything was obsolete or in bad repair and the discouraging shabbiness of all depressed me. I felt being trapped in soul-destroying mediocrity.

A social dropout of unspecified gender and wrapped in a printed dress intercepted me as I rummaged through a cardboard box of staplers, trying to find one which matched the box of staples in my hand. "Those aren't for you," he let out as he saw my dreary loot. "Use paper clips instead. We have lots of them."

"And where is my chair?" I demanded. "And who are you?"

"I'm the Commander."

"Commander?"

"That's what some call me."

"In that outfit doing what?"

"In charge of everything. Name is Lauris. And you don't need a chair to sit on. You are supposed to run around and see that everything works as planned."

"Planned?" I laughed. "Nothing is planned. We don't even have proper staples."

"I'll get you a box of rubber bands..."

"And who is in charge of the Hertha Pavilion," I wanted to know, getting hot under my collar.

"Oh, that'll be Gus," he said. "Gus is good at that sort of thing. He's done it before."

"And where is Gus?"

Lauris shrugged his shoulders. "Find him yourself. No need to have a tantrum now."

It started to rain and I got soaking wet in my open flivver as I drove to the old dance hall. The nerve of everybody! Sure, I was just a teenager now, but did I not have thirty years of building experience under my belt? Not only did I lay out strip malls, but was I not also the experienced middle-age professional my company had sent here and there to fix things or to rattle some cages if necessary? Cool down now and let's first size up the job ahead.

The watchman came out of his tiny guardhouse and looked serious. "Hey, you there, you can't go in. Don't you see the sign? That included you." I told him who I was and he relented. "Be careful, some of the floorboards are missing. And don't use any of the washrooms. Have a nice day." He returned to the shelter of his sentry box.

The building appeared essentially sound although vandals had done a great deal of damage to the stairs and the balcony, and they had stolen most of the brass rails. The roof leaked badly near the bandstand area; this whole section must be renewed. The large adjacent kitchen was in truly wretched shape with most of the appliances ripped out, the walk-in freezer littered with garbage. The ceramic floor tiles had been torn out or were broken, a counter was cut in half with a chain saw and the large flow-through dishwasher had been smashed to bits and pieces.

From one of the offices along the West side a wrought iron spiral staircase led to a platform which once had a floor but was now a framework over open water. Two, three boats could have been lashed to this jetty. I craned my neck and peeked underneath to get an overall view of the substructure. The beams were a bit heftier then one builds nowadays and surprisingly intact. We need to get a diver down below to inspect the submerged steel and the concrete footings; even take some pictures. If the original builders had used big zinc anodes it might all still be salvageable, especially here in this fresh water lake. I knew my stuff.

A man with a moustache came up behind me. "Oui, I'm Gus. Had a look at that myself," he said. "We must build a caisson around it first, and that's where much of the money will go." He took off his glasses and polished them thoughtfully before pushing them back on his nose. "What shall it be, then? Not another dance hall, is it? Nobody's dancing any more."

It would be an auditorium to hold a thousand, I told him. What cost might we be looking at? About one point five to two for the steel alone, he said. Plus whatever sits on top. Could go up another two or three maybe, depending on how fancy. Two or three what? Million, of course, he said. Could he handle it? Ah oui, he said, he had done that before.

It was not until the next day that I dropped into the office – such as it was. My computer had suddenly been set up, with a comfortable chair in front and a flat bed plotter at the side.

I reported to Miss Pennsinger - everybody called her Miss Pennypincher behind her back. It'll be a hard grind, I pointed out. Miss Pennsinger was in charge of financing the whole project and you didn't kid around with her. Don't worry, she said. It'll all come together somehow.

There, my first official job was done and I was relieved that I got through it in some fashion. At least I was back in the loop again. Then I withdrew from the bank what I thought was mine: five hundred loonies.

CHAPTER NINE

Ted had received a phone call from Talents Management; would he kindly find out as much as he could about Egyptian Ceremonial Ships. He whined as I stepped in. "They say 'take your time, take your time.' They have absolutely no idea how long time can stretch out, especially here. It's not linear, you know. They didn't even mention which dynasty they wanted and I have only some Egyptian naval ships and fishing boats. I'd rather look into something Byzantine - unless, of course, they are talking about the battle of Actium. You know the one on September…"

I begged him to slow down as I couldn't understand much of what he babbled, but instead of easing up he carried on more eagerly than before.

"You know, the one which nearly got Cleopatra into deep shit. Of course, she was not the first Cleo – there were six others before her. Same name. Don't shrug your shoulders. Don't they teach you anything in school anymore? I think number six died as a kid, but I have no idea about the other five…"

"Ted!"

He was impatient that I had so little knowledge of things Egyptian. "She'd hardly made it back home, I mean Cleo number seven. And with the Roman navy hot on her tail and all… She had one of those huge things with a hundred rowers and lamps all over the deck and railings."

He continued rummaging and mumbling, mostly for his own benefit as I had no idea what he wanted. Then we both went into his basement searching through cartons and tote boxes of publications and other reference work.

Ted continued his ramblings. "Surely they don't mean King Khufu's ship. That was just a fad at the time; only a ceremonial vessel, if you know what I mean. Had eight rowers and two steering men. That's just a step up from their reed boats. Or do they perhaps mean those burial skiffs? Do they? If at least they had wanted something Byzantine, you know. There's a lot more we know about the Turks. Why don't you talk to me? Say something."

In the adjoining furnace room were a few more boxes. Tucked away in a dusty corner I discovered a number of woodworking tools, a table saw, router, plenty of hand tools, clamps. "Made lots of little things - bird feeders, doll houses, book ends. I loved working with wood, but now it's getting to be a bit of a drudge. My eyes, you know. Don't want to cut off a finger."

I told him to just sketch up something. Lots of glitter and stuff. A bunch of lamps - anything. Put a dragon or a lion at each end, the ones with their tongues sticking out, I suggested.

Ted was belligerent. "Are you mad? They didn't have dragons or lions. They had cats." Cats had the status of gods, he said. They kept the rats away, and with it the dreaded disease which had come all the way from Turkey and Greece. Not a single one of the cats ever stuck out its tongue. No, never. It's sacrilegious. "To any Egyptian this would be the worst possible insult, if you ask me. Perhaps I could plant a criosphinx at the bow. You know, like a sphinx but with the head of a goat instead. Very, very decorative. Tasteful like, and politically correct." He looked helpless for a moment, then his face lit up. "And one at the stern, too. They never had one at the stern before, so that'll be a novelty. And then - and then I'll have them spit Greek fire." Ted put his hands on his hips. "It wasn't just the Chinese who invented those firecrackers..."

What's Greek fire, I asked, and how do you make it?

Ted's eyes lit up. "Easy. You take kerosene and whip it up with egg yolk. They used crude oil back then but now we use kerosene instead. Egg yolk is the emulsifier, you know. Make it like mayonnaise. And then you pump it through an open flame and out of each nostril. It'll be exceptionally beautiful."

"Eggs?"

"About a dozen will do. With a little bit of salt; that makes the fire yellow."

"Did you say flamethrower?"

"Yep. Spectacular, eh? At bow and stern."

"And burn down the harbour? Are you crazy, Ted? Everybody will think a war broke out."

"Why always this militaristic jargon? Historically, it's been done just about that time, you know, when they had those boats. It's terribly authentic. The Minoans, I mean after they had rebuilt... Now that goes back a bit more..."

"No flamethrowers, Ted. Not in the bow, not in the stern. I forbid it." It was time I finally put my foot down. "Repeat after me: No flamethrowers."

"Maybe just little ones?"

"No flamethrowers, Ted. Say it: No flamethrowers."

"I can make them so that they don't dribble. They won't burn down the deck."

"Ted! None!"

"Okay then, no big..."

"None at all, Ted. Big or small. Understand?"

"Are you ever the bully!"

I walked out and slammed the door behind me.

✳   ✳   ✳

Check out Zelle's Dance Workshop, the note from the Professor read, so I wound up the Midget and went on my way. They were supposed to come up with erotic wardrobe and some spectacular routines oozing sexuality. I had expected to see a clutch of eager seamstresses stitching and gymnasts acting out various positions, but when I finally found the place behind a butcher shop I stepped into a small second-storey cluttered office which only promised dusty mediocrity. A girl in a big-collared school uniform greeted me. "Yes?"

"I came to see Mister Zelle."

"I'm Grietje. Can I help you?"

"Your - your dad, I assume. Is he around?"

She laughed. "It happened before. You probably came to see me."

"No, no. It's about some…" I felt uneasy. "Sex, that is."

Grietje laughed again, a very coquettish fou rire in stark contrast to her institutional uniform. She cocked her head slightly to the side, her long black curls framing the big, brown eyes. "I was expecting you."

"No, there's probably a little mix-up. You're a child. You are how old?"

"Thirteen. I'm a teenager, just like you. I know what you come for. I'm working on the sexual issue for Professor Klonus. For his show. You and I, we work on the same project."

"Grietje - it's Grietje, right? This is a subject not - well not really suited for…" I stalled. What a bloody dilemma.

"A child?" She turned the squeaky wooden office chair to fully face me and leaned back. "Kick that cat off the sofa there and sit down. I'm afraid you and I have to discuss our relationship a little further."

I gingerly stepped over two stacks of books and periodicals on the floor, shooed the cat off the green corduroy and stiffly sat down.

"Number one," she lectured me, "I could have been your great-great-aunt Gertrude. A hundred years old. So, get your age hang-up out of the way."

This was supposed to take the edge off the subject, but it didn't quite work. "How old, you know… when it happened, you know. I mean the Event."

"The termination? I was forty-one then. There, does that make you feel better now?" She shrugged her shoulders.

"Yes. No, not entirely. I still feel that this is, you know, a bit indecorous."

"Number two: don't for a minute think that - even if I were only thirteen - don't ever think that I would not know my way about sex. I'll tell you something, Mister…"

"It's Tony. Please, call me Tony."

"When I was thirteen, Tony, I knew all about sex although I was brought up in a convent. I knew about sex all my life. I knew about sex long before I actually had it, and when I married at age eighteen I had to teach my husband - who, incidentally was much older - I had to teach him all about sex. I had been a virgin until then and he had not, and still I had to teach him. Technically speaking, that is."

The cat jumped onto the window sill, Grietje got up, opened it and the cat vanished. There she stood, her silhouette framed against the bland whiteness of the muslin curtain. She is beautiful, came to my mind. Exotic, mysterious, tantalisingly out of reach and at the same time utterly familiar like the Jewel of the East - the gently scented trade winds of the Indian Ocean. No, I had never been there, never been out of the Americas, but my mind had wandered there since early childhood. Strange sounds, strange fragrances, exotic faces, bodies...

"Tony, are you listening?" I nodded; the child continued. "The question is: am I competent. I am supposed to design alluring costumes. Gauzy breasts and thighs. Lots of veils barely hiding nude bodies. Semi-transparent stuff. Very thin silks that float up in the Klieg lights. Makes them look like butterflies. I am not just relying on my own knowledge, I have been collecting an incredible amount of data and I'm now combing through it. The first distinction I shall make is between the two types of fantasized coition."

I tried half-heartedly to turn this embarrassment into a farce. "Only two? I would have thought there were hundreds."

Grietje remained deadly serious. "Just two, Tony. We are talking about either the mechanism of intercourse for the physical body or, conversely, the la Tour d'Argent of the boudoir for the mind. The mind, Tony, not the flesh." My own mind wandered, even as Grietje rattled off statistics and went on about the pros and cons of intercourse promotion versus prohibition, melange arrangements, group dynamics, covert eroticism or blatant in-your-face pornography and what was permissible on the stage. Her voice was still child-like, but the gestures which underlined her words had the smoothness of a ballerina, the feline gentleness of erotic imagination. She cut me short again. "Are you listening?"

"Yes, yes of course. The boudoir..."

"I was saying that members having found provisional serviceable mates on their own may cause some erogenous insouciance. So what would you suggest should be done about it?"

I had lost the thread. "I'd say, make them conform." That was the best I could think of right now. Please, somebody get me out of here...

Perhaps Grietje guessed what was on my mind. She closed the window and returned to her squeaking chair. "You're not paying much attention, are you? Here I am letting you peek behind the curtains of Eros and you... Where's your mind, Tony?"

"You should be a dancer yourself."

Grietje smiled. "Thank you. That's very kind of you to say that. I once was, you know. But it ended with a bang." She snapped her fingers. "Just like that."

CHAPTER TEN

Ted had come up with some sketches he assembled from what he could find and which included some fragmental scantlings of the 1717 Royal Water Music barge. Then he discarded all and started afresh by making a small model, a toy rowboat manned by eight little Styrofoam men with tongue depressors as oars. "And now I've run out of money."

"I thought you could cash as much as you wanted."

"I plumb forgot. You think a couple of hundred's too much?"

A phone call came in. Would I please see the co-ordinator of my integration council tomorrow? Meet him at his office at work.

Until now I had assumed Dr. Borelli to be a people's physician but he turned out to be a vet specialising in reptiles and simians at the zoo. His cramped quarters were smelly, overfilled with junk, papers no one ever read, dog-eared books and a small cage full of live mice.

"I know my offices are small," he apologised. "I once had a 20-room mansion in Lexington, and now this. Well, like the tides, fortunes come and go." He twirled his moustache, and, having just finished eating a home-made sandwich, removed his paper bib, rose and shook my hands. With his left he gripped my arm as if we had been friends for a long time as he pointed to a shelf with a dead turtle in a cheerily painted carapace. "Anyway, amazing creatures. Haven't changed a bit in two hundred million years and still as lively as ever. Come, let's just stroll around." Past the monkeys, the racoons, the white rabbits - future food for the boa constrictor - and past the funny little South American pigs with their long snouts.

He finally came to the point. "Work going well?" He acted superficially uninformed as if he had absolutely no idea what went on in my life. The Doctor obviously had asked me over to just pump me for information.

"Yes, they'll start putting up the caisson soon." What does he want?

"That's the old dance hall, isn't it? People don't dance anymore." Why these questions? Eventually he came out with it. "You are a nice kid - well, I should say young man. How old are you now?"

"Have been informed that I'll be twenty in a couple of weeks. It's in my dossier. Got it from Miss Hanna." Surely, he knows all these details. Again, what does he want?

"Out of the teens, that wonderful awkward age. You gave up on studying, then?"

I admitted: yes, for now at least. I really had my hands full.

"So I heard. What is this dance hall to be when it is finished?" I answered it would be an auditorium.

The doctor stopped and turned directly towards me. "For Professor - what's his name again?"

"Professor Klonus. You asked me yourself to stay close to him." He knows exactly what's going on. And why does he now pretend not to know the Professor's name?

"Right - Professor Klonus," the facilitator intoned slowly as if to chew on every single letter. "The dear old Professor. Do you know how old he is?"

I guessed he might be sixty-five, perhaps seventy. I had never asked him. Still going strong. Boundless energy.

"He is only forty-six years old. You didn't know that, did you?"

Then how come he looks twenty years older?

"Make-down. He made himself look old when he was - oh, in his late twenties. Operations; face drop; hair follicle removal; skin oxidisers; wart implants; vocal chords lengthened and more. And why? Do you know why?"

That's a silly question and I had absolutely no idea. Surely this man was just putting me on.

"He claims to be the son of Dabba. According to stories I've heard he quickly grabbed his old man's billions after he was murdered. Officially it's a secret, but word gets around."

This was unadulterated hokum and I didn't believe a word of it. Either there was a terrible mix-up somewhere or Borelli was making it up as he went along, inventing it out of thin air. Why? I had met the Professor... Well, how often now? At least half a dozen times. And why would he make up such an absurd story? People want to look younger, not older.

The Doctor continued. "Have you ever heard of Captain Wombat? Was on TV. Made himself look like fifty when he was still in his twenties. So he played that same role as a crusty old wayfarer throughout his entire working life. Smart career move. Now you wonder why I ask all these dumb questions. But our little discussion here must remain a secret between the two of us. You must first give me your solemn oath that you will keep this information constantly locked up. Will you promise? Say after me: 'I promise to never tell anybody. Nobody'."

"I never will."

"Say it, the whole thing."

"I will never tell anybody."

"You swear?"

"Yes, I do."

Looking around if anybody was in earshot: "When we have a private chat, I want you to call me Charlie. Like old friends. We are going to work together, so we might as well be comfortable with each other. How's your long-term memory right now? It will slowly erode. The pictures in your mind, fleeting snippets of a melody, the fragrance of perfume that you seem to have known so well - all of it will eventually fade. Even the knowledge of your skills will dim in time. In a year or two, if you are lucky, you'll be able to recall little. Just fragments, pieces here and there. It's better that way. Very much like a dream which seeps away with the early morning sun."

I was relieved that the Doctor wanted nothing from me except this little tete-a-tete. In spite of my suspicions, I would have liked to hug this gentle, wise man with his brush haircut and his big moustache, hug him for his concern, if for nothing else.

Without warning the doctor's banter took a U-turn. "What I will tell you now is a dangerous secret, and if you should leak it out in any which way it may cause you great harm. There are forces in play which we must not ignore. You might not know it yet, but you are sleep-walking under a black cloud."

I was taken aback - so, here it comes. A minute ago he offered his friendship, so what was the man driving at now? Did he not just warn me, order me to safe-keep a menacing secret? I said that I didn't want to know. I hate hazards. I'm a sissy.

Borelli drove the nail further down. "It's much too late for that now. In for a penny, in for a pound. This man, Klonus…"

"The Professor."

"Sure, let's call him the Professor then. Of course I know him. I was just testing you; trying to find out on which side you stand. He's dangerous. Wants to re-establish paganism. Rumours are going around everywhere. He is a fanatic." He stopped to let the weight of his words sink in. "You know what that means, Tony, don't you. Spookery is making a comeback. With wealth at his fingertips, his connections and the good men he has already assembled he might just be able to do it."

I was relieved. Was this a smoke screen for some other motives? After all, what's so bad about that?

Dr. Borelli continued. "Nevertheless, you must be on guard. You are in my care and I don't want anything happen to you. You are our implant. You must tell me exactly what he does. Every day, every hour. And you must keep your eyes on his money. Especially his money."

❊   ❊   ❊

I slept badly that night. I was being drawn into some conspiracy far beyond the original scope of my job. The activities of the Professor will create enormous tension between the forces of… Of what exactly? Money, power on one side, nothing but entertainment on the other, and I was in the middle of it all. Either Dr. Borelli was a barefaced liar, or there was danger lurking just out of plain sight, a tightly coiled catastrophe in the guise of an old man who claimed to be nothing more than a harmless rich fool. Could I become a prey to both sides?

I didn't fall asleep until six in the morning, and then stayed in bed most of the day. I wasn't physically sick but I wished I was and reacted accordingly. Escape, get away, was my first thought; far, far away. Get where? Anywhere. Move to another city, another country, anywhere. Surely there must be a refuge in the world. Whom to ask? Ted, of course. What would I give him as a reason? 'Ted,' I would say, 'help me get out of this one.' Ted would ask why and what would I reply? I was sick of this job now, sick of everybody, sick even of hearing the cackling on the second floor.

No, Ted would never believe me. Instead I confided to Melmoth. "You can't just get up and leave," he said. "Go where? I've been here forever it seems, and I should know. If ever somebody wanted to leave, surely it was I. This really is the gutter, but I see no stars."

It was never about religion, Melmoth explained. "Look at the crusades. The Bedouins had long nailed down the silk route to Cathay for themselves and charged a ransom for the spices and aromatic oils they brought from the Orient. European kingdoms went broke, all profits went to Damascus and Baghdad. So, how can you get an army together to challenge the Arabs? How do you recruit the poor fellows only to have them waste their lives? To fight for what? Cinnamon? Red peppers? Silk pyjamas?"

"Why not? We happily cut up countries for a barrel of oil."

"Surely you are jesting, my young friend. You need a consecrated purposes for war. Nobody would put himself in the line of fire for spices or a barrel of oil. You must have a loftier purpose before you can order your warriors to rip the infidels to pieces. Put a symbol on your banners and all will follow, even children. Yes, children. Just ask the Pied Piper of Hamlin. Those kids were never seen again. And all that for silk pyjamas."

Bah, Melmoth was just a hardened cynic. Perhaps he was researching this topic for another story, another sonnet, a dramatised joke for the stage He was supposed to write for the Professor. Was he now finally composing something on that subject? Was he? I could barely put a question mark behind my hint.

Melmoth squirmed, trying to evade the issue. Finally he admitted: "I don't create much anymore. Lack of readership, you know. No platform, no outlet for my poems. I think I have forgotten how. My inkwell has dried up. I often swore to myself to start again

- some day. Besides, I could find use for one of those flat electric writing machines. Those... those things you call laptops."

I changed the conversation and came out with a surprise I had hidden in the trunk of my car. When passing my favourite pawnshop on Ricker Street I had just dropped in - only looking. No, nothing I actually wanted. Tucked away in some dusty corner I had spied an armful of walking canes including one with a big round grip. The old pawnbroker saw my look and pulled it out of the bundle. I took it in my hand; a gorgeous red ebony cane wrapped by a silver snake coiling itself twice around it, its head touching an elaborate silver knob cradled in ivory claws at the top. The knob was the right size for a big hand.

"Look here," the pawnbroker had pointed out, reaching for a magnifier. "Look at the artwork on the knob. It's terribly damaged from many years of abuse, but you can still make out the golden tiger wending its way around the base. See the tiger's eyes? The platinum hinges are broken now, but once you could prick the eyes and the lid would spring open." The lid was a delicately framed round piece of ordinary coloured glass the size of a goose egg.

"What was it meant to hide?"

The man shrugged. "Anything." Seeing my puzzlement he continued. "This piece of glass? According to the Fabergé catalogue it was originally an opal but it must have gotten lost - or stolen or sold."

"Is the cane valuable?"

"It was. This is a genuine *bâton de marche*. Only six of these were ever made for the Imperial Russian Court, but it is in such bad disrepair right now that I wouldn't know its value. Why do you ask?"

"I might know the man who once owned one just like it. Is it for sale?"

"Of course, but I truly would not know what to charge. I paid the poor man only... - Yes, here it is. I paid one hundred and twenty loonies for it, but it may easily be worth ten times that to a collector, even in this pathetic state."

I weighted it in my hand. "Amazingly light for its size. How much?"

The pawnbroker looked alternately at the bâton, then at me; finally he said: "I should be a very rich man now if it wasn't for my dogged sentimentality. Tell you what. Give me what I paid. No, make that one hundred and forty. If it's not his, will you bring it back to me?"

"Yes, I will."

"Say you swear you will."

"I swear I will bring it back. On my honour."

This was the second time in only a week that I had uttered an oath.

I now approached Mr. Melmoth. "I have found a little something I want to give to you. Would you be annoyed if I did?"

He mustered me from the side. "I will only consider bribes from my enemies because I cannot afford to insult my friends. I don't have enough of them to waste."

"Then you must know that I am your worst nightmare, that I'm the most disgusting adversary you can imagine."

I opened the car trunk, took out the bâton and handed it over. It was the first time I saw him taken aback. Melmoth reached out slowly, took the cane and turned away from me as if to inspect it in better light. I could only see his Adam's apple move up and down a couple of times; then Melmoth turned back towards me. "How beautiful it is. I once owned a similar one - cherished it for all those precious years. This is not the one." He handed it back. "But I am forever grateful for your gesture. Thank you, Kid."

I didn't take it back. "You must keep it. A cheap substitute for the one you lost. If the right one ever turns up again you give it back to me, hm?"

Melmoth closed his hand firmly over this old bâton and his knuckles whitened. "Very well, I'll keep it for awhile."

"Promise to give it back if you don't need it anymore?"

"Promise."

CHAPTER ELEVEN

The Professor was jovial as usual. "I'm glad you came. Great job," he beamed. "Let's walk." We ambled around the block and my flapping nerves slowly calmed.

"Heard you got along fine with Grietje Zelle. Just let her muddle on, disorganized as she may be. She once suffered great injustice but she had given away nothing. It was a trumped-up charge. Gallic jealousy."

Eager to change the subject and still with Borelli's words in my ears, I had a question on my mind. "You said once that you went bankrupt three times in a row. How did that happen?" I hoped my query sounded innocent enough not to put the Professor on guard.

"I never failed personally, but three of my companies did. I have enough to get me over the humps." Prompted he continued. "My first business was based entirely on my invention of the Rockapussy. That's an electric toilet seat which gives you a power massage while you sit. Just because there was this minor short circuit and the lady got zapped a bit was no reason to take the product off the market. No reason at all. The improved model ran on twelve innocent, non-lethal volts, but the inspectors were over-officious. Even after we renamed it Buzzabum. Nobody ever got cremated on scant twelve volts. You don't even know you're sitting on it."

"I talked to a vet and he thinks you are a fraud."

"You must have been talking to Borelli. But the next brainwave was an obvious winner. I could see it from a thousand miles away. There was our alphabet which I noticed never had been patented. I wanted to see at least a 'Patent Pending' label attached to it. There was absolutely no trace of ownership anywhere, and I searched back as far as the cuneiform. I intended to lease it cheaply. For a newspaper - oh, say fifty bucks per annum. It's not worth fighting over in court, you know. For individual users: one loonie per lifetime. I'd make a fortune on that one alone. But this was when I still paid salaries which made my staff lazy. Lost my shirt again. Was in all the papers."

I finally had a chance to interrupt him. "Is the alphabet still patentable," I asked, making sure that he would detect my doubts. Besides, why would it be important for him to make money? Surely, with his wealth he could have bought a hockey team and live with the losses. Money is just a hobby for him.

He laughed. "Why all that? Of course, it isn't patentable, but it would have cost a fortune in legal expenses alone to assert this fact. Shows you how money can be wasted." And as for the profits? He actually didn't need any, he had enough.

"Look at me," he said. "I am a walking cartoon, that's what I am. The only opportunity I have to get a bit of self-respect is to do something, anything, and be successful at it. Only make it spectacular and make a profit at it. How much profit? I don't care. That's a value judgement. A single penny is quite enough. It's a strange thing, what money does. It buys me both the luxury and the agony of failing."

We walked silently for a while. Finally I carried on: "What was the third failure?"

"Publishing. Have you any idea how difficult it is to publish anything? I was in calendars and greeting cards. I had these fine artists - all of them enormously talented. Well, you've seen some of my calendars at my home recently. Beautiful stuff. Soon we added a new line, books, and that was a great success. We named the first one 'I Forgot', and underneath: 'The Audacious Bathroom Reader'."

"Why 'I Forgot'?"

Barely detectable the Professor smiled. "First of all, it was a good collection of all sorts of events and titbits throughout the past year, good reading in small portions, stuff everybody forgets. I had hopes that I might cash in on the forgetfulness of my older customers. And I was right!" He paused to let the impact sink in.

"How right were you, Professor?" Did I detect that smile?

"The way I figured it out, this slight haze of confusion and amnesia contributed more than seventeen percent to the bottom line and I was suddenly in the black. Many came to buy a cookbook or some other tome on self-improvement, and many left with 'I Forgot' under their arm instead. For years I made a profit, that is, until we diversified and went into memory pills. And that knocked the wind right out of my bathroom reader. Cookbooks went straight up again. Ah - and yet, it was such a beauty. In one of the many, many radiant chapters I placed some of my own homilies. I really loved to transform them into exciting new stuff such as 'never give a sucker another chance'.

I corrected him. "It's 'an even break'."

"What is?"

"Never give a sucker an even break. So, what happened then with your memory pill business?"

"People forgot to take them."

I finally realised that I had been hoodwinked. The Professor not only set me up for a joke, he was toying with me like a cat playing with a stuffed mouse, but his next words comforted me again. "Just having a bit of fun with you, that's all. But it's true; I was in calendar and greeting card publishing. Don't ask me why. Sometimes one does outright stupid things for no visible reason. Haven't you ever done something just for the hell of it? Your birthday is coming up, isn't it? Tell you what: I'll throw you a little party. Invite a few guests. Have a bash now and then. Don't always be so stubbornly serious. But why are you interested in my money?"

I decided to let the cat out of the sack. "Doctor Borelli put me up to it. I can't figure out what he wants."

We had rounded the block twice, now the Professor invited me to his office, third floor, taking the freight elevator in the back. "He once was an investment banker. Did he tell you that? No, of course not. Things didn't work out well. He'll want you to find out the tipping point. Just agree to whatever he wants. - Now, let's talk about the show you and your friend are putting together. What's the name of it now?" The elevator had stopped and we stepped into the Professor's little office above the bank.

"Trumpets of Joy," I answered.

The Professor handed me a beer. "Yes, that one might do for now. The Trumpets of Joy. Does that fit across the pavilion? Write me a playbill of sorts."

I had reservations. "It has already changed a great deal since I first mentioned it to you. Miss Zelle is working out a sexy dance with only transparent gauze over all that nakedness. She's just a kid, you know."

The Professor chortled. "See, that's why I need you. Keep this sex dance in place for now, but shape it, give it form, model it, make it look less scandalous. And don't ever call it sex. That's so, well, naked. Invent a new phrase, one with 'nature' and 'innocent' in it. Who was this erotic ancient lady with the long neck?"

"Venus."

"The other one."

"Aphrodite? She's dangerous. She helped start the Trojan War. She also had another name: Cytherea."

"Anything you can do with that?"

"Not a thing."

"Then leave that dancing in there until you can come up with something risk-free. Stuff from the classics which gives them a certain license of legitimacy. Take most of the tacky nudity out of it; except let one breast show. That image has been sanctified in antiquity. Drape the dancers in sybaritic gowns instead. Voile perhaps. It'll be a lot more erotic that way, believe me. Then add dramatic staging, something with smoke."

"We can duct clouds of laughing gas under the seats."

"That's overkill, don't you think? Come up with material that feeds the brain deep down. Euphoria, sacrifice, guilt, satisfaction, impulses of all shapes and stripes. Make it colourful, especially if it's green. Mesmerism, anxieties, tears - stuff like that. The sort of emotions that make you put your hand on your chest where the heart is and make you give all you have. I mean not just money. Not just."

It would go over my head, I objected. I'm not a stage master.

"Of course you are," the Professor insisted. "We all are - one way or another. Say, do you earn enough money working for me? Take all you can use. One never knows how long all that may last."

I brought up Melmoth. "He's a nobody, really. Has no money, no women, perhaps not very many friends even."

"Oh, you must invite him to your birthday party. I have always hoped to meet him, but he's such recluse. I must tell him how much I admire his acerbic wit. He hasn't written anything since he came here, I understand. Perhaps a change of scenery might rekindle his ambitions. You'll come to my home and stay for awhile. If I'm not there every day, the servants will look after you. They get antsy if they have no one to pamper."

We finished our beer and the meeting seemed to be over. How can one tell the end of a chinwag exactly? One more minute of small talk? Looking at your watch is outright insulting. The best way is to softly say "well" and just let it hang there in mid-air. But don't wait until the other asks "well what?" That's one second too late. Just before this moment, get up and beam.

In the elevator down I weighed the evidence against the man. Could he possibly be a fanatic, an evil man as the monkey doctor claims? Sly he is, oh, he's sly all right, and razor-sharp. No doubt. Weird he is, also. Matter of fact, that's much of his charm. Endlessly fascinating, spellbinding. Memory pills! I actually fell for it. What a clown. Gotta watch this guy. He'll pull the wool over your eyes just for the sport of it. What is this tight-ass vet in the zoo talking about, and what's wrong with inventing a spectacular show in the first place, eh?

CHAPTER TWELVE

On my way home I passed the Inuvik Dance and Ballet Studio. DANCERS & SINGERS WANTED the cardboard sign at the door advertised. A Mr. Busby was in charge of training some fifty very young lads dressed in gym clothes. They slithered across the stage, kicked their heels, threw out their arms, turned their heads right, left, up, down, wiggled, smiled and did everything required to earn a meagre living. Mr. Busby harshly bellowed some orders, a young lad was crying, somebody led him off - sheer madness. I had a hunch this might be some dance routine for a school conviviality of sorts in some remote picnic ground. The way it looked it wouldn't amount to very much. Ah well, teenagers. Soon I would be twenty and out of this uncomfortable age.

Mr. Busby was the unfriendly type. "Yea?" he shouted from his high bar stool. "No visitors." He waved me off as if I was an intrusive vermin. I gave him my card. "Oh yea, I've heard of you. And?" I shrugged my shoulder. "Well?" the instructor insisted nervously.

I asked him if he needed more of those little dancers and singers. Not that I knew any, but I wanted to appear like a friendly sort of chap. "No more of these. I hate kids. I need women. The more mature types," he bellowed and looked me up and down. "So?"

Nothing. I left without a trace of sociability. What a unsavoury character. And the man chewed gum to boot. How disgusting. There ought to be a law.

I went straight home, but passing the second floor tenants I knocked at their door. Their snickering son opened. "Mom, the man is here again."

I stuck in my head. "I have a job for you," I lied to Marlene. "They are looking for dancers and singers. Here's the address. But don't tell the guy I sent you."

⁂　⁂　⁂

I was up at seven as the sun was just beginning to colour the horizon. Coffee, strong black coffee. I paced up and down my two rooms and tossed the next challenge around in my head. How could I, an insignificant student who doesn't even study, a squatter who rents the attic of a half-blind unemployed oil rigger, he who lives above a hooker and who's only real friends are his landlord and a has-been rhyme smith who is an addicted nicotine user... How can I tie so many ends together?

From the floor below came a lot of banging noises - ca-thump - ca-thump - ca-thump - rat-tat-tat. What the hell is going on now? Knocking on their door, Marlene stood before me in leotards, slippers, her thinning blond hair falling over her brows, sweaty beads on her forehead. She threw her arms around me and I noticed that she was wet through and through. "Got a job," she shouted. "Got to dance and sing. Dance and sing! Come in, please. Oh, I'm so out of shape, you know. Have to limber up, lose at least ten pounds. And you know what they pay me? Have you any idea?"

She rushed to her coat and pulled out a credit card. "This! Can you imagine? This here. And no limit. This is unbelievable. I can draw out as much as I want. Just imagine, as much as I want. Took out a thousand. Nobody stopped me. You must be a very important man."

I straightened up and grew an inch taller right there on the spot, then went down to see Ted who was in the basement rummaging through more books. "Damn," Ted grumbled, "can't find much more." He had set up a sturdy poker table heaped with some twenty books dealing with naval subjects. "Had a call this morning from a Doctor What's-his-Name. Appointment for tomorrow - my eyes, you know. They need looking after. Any idea why that man called me out of the blue?" I suggested it must have been somebody from the Professor's retinue. He's got lots of connections.

I left but seemed lost. Were they not ready to start the caisson today? Or was that yesterday? My little red MG Midget got me to the site in minutes. I could spot the floating crane already from afar. Starting with the first corrugated steel panel on dry land, two more interlocking units had by this time been pile-driven into the lake bottom. Everything is going well, said the man in charge. "No problems so far; we should be ready for the pumps in four or five days unless we hit rock below. Not likely, though; sounding the bottom had not brought up anything unexpected."

The construction boss climbed up from the scaffolding. There were more small problems, including the sewer outflow, which they'll just cut up and remove, he said. "They won't let us get away with dumping the waste straight into the water anyway. Regulations, you know. Have you seen the preliminaries for the superstructure?" Of course not. Too busy.

On my way back home I passed my office, peeked into my cubicle, checked my e-mail, rifled through some unimportant flyers and memos, said a fleeting 'hello' to Miss Pennsinger, but she nailed me on the spot.

"Have you seen the sketches of the superstructure yet?" I had not. I didn't even know I was still in the circle of decision makers. "Well, come into my office, I have copies." She actually had a real office with walls all the way up to the ceiling. I glanced at five E-size blueprints but my mind wasn't entirely on it. "What's happening in what was the kitchen before?" I wanted to know.

"The TV production stuff." Going on the air, blowing big bucks, doing it from the top down. Well, the boss has loads of money, why not. Your size is measured by the price of your toys, and these here run into millions. Did Borelli not say the Professor had his hands on a fortune? Billions, and each one of them is one thousand millions. He wouldn't miss a hundred of them. As hard as I tried, I couldn't wrap my mind around such staggering sums. Suddenly I felt tired and looked it because Miss Pennsinger said: "Are you OK?"

"Just tired."

"Go home. You're of no use in that state."

I shook my head. "I have loads of work to do."

"We all have. Go home."

Perhaps I had a cold coming. Pennypincher slipped the plans under my arm and I was gone. Back at home I glanced at them. Hydraulically lifted orchestra pit and proscenium, rotating working stage, two backstage sections, dressing rooms, mechanical facilities including light and sound control, everything was clearly marked but, being unfamiliar with stage or theatre construction, not much of it made sense to me. The balcony seemed to have been eliminated, replaced by office space. I had asked for a long jetty alongside the whole building, where was it? With a black marker I drew in the pier and added a bold arrow: "Festive Barge here - permanent mooring". Next I widened the opening past the dressing rooms and connected it directly with the wings of the stage. Why? I had no idea. Just wanted to be nasty and throw my weight around, that's all. Let Gus figure out how he could wrap it up.

Then I went to the zoo to see Charles Borelli, to tell him that he was wrong, that the good old Professor was not inventing a new religion, just a show with exotic dancers with one breast exposed. I should know, I was the one putting the agenda together and there's nothing holy, divine, sanctified or even idolatrous anywhere in it.

"Be careful, Tony, be very careful. He'll fool us all. One must know on which side of the fence one wants to fall." With that the man vanished into his smelly cubby-hole again. I decided to call him Doctor Borelli again from now on; our short-lived friendship was over. And I better start keeping an eye on him from now on. There's something fishy about the man.

Next day Ted was gone for hours, and when he came back he wore an eye patch. I saw him enter the house from my street-side window, so I went down. "Accident?" I asked apprehensively.

"Nah, little operation. Have to put these drops in. Gotta take it easy for a week. And after that it's the left eye. Cataracts; getting new lens implants." If it hurt he didn't say. He never complained. He's a Russian.

Melmoth was home when I phoned; we fixed a time to meet again in Gilbert Park as usual. I invited him to that birthday clambake and did my best to persuade him to venture out to this strange land. "You should see the fountain in the court yard. There are these eight elephants, this big, and they hold their trunks up in the air, and they spout orange water high up against this beautiful image. It's a young woman in a tight clinging negligee holding a slim booklet in her raised right hand…"

"What kind of book?"

"How would I know? A book."

"A bank book or what? A paperback?"

I became impatient. "Could be anything. Maybe a passport. How the hell would I know? Anyway, these eight elephants… They're all sculptured from white marble. They spout water from their raised trunks directly over the head of this heavenly creature. I say heavenly because of her wet nighty which makes it cling to her naked body. That's on account of the eight elephants, you know. By the way, she is made from red marble."

Melmoth was cynical. "Is that's what is commonly known as the golden shower?"

I carried on unperturbed. "There are motion detectors all around, and as soon as anybody approaches the court or only wiggles an ear the fountain starts automatically. The elephants have powerful lamps hidden in their open jaws. At night they shine right into this spray from below. Really, you must see this."

Melmoth said he would and he had almost forgotten just how juvenile his friend still was. He tapped his bâton three times on the ground. "I emphatically agree. I must see those red elephants myself."

CHAPTER THIRTEEN

In spite of my reservations, the second white-knuckle flight to Professor Klonus' hideout was uneventful. Melmoth had to check his bâton at the gate where it was duly labelled and marked to be returned to him at the point of destination. Absolutely no canes, crutches, baseball bats or other sticks on airplanes - even here on Level Two. "What are they afraid of," he asked rhetorically. "Militants? Then they should fix the cause, not the effect. What are you afraid of?"

"Flying in airplanes. How about you?"

"That some day I might need a nurse to help me pee."

He didn't appear too impressed by the executive jet, even a bit bored it seemed, but I suspected he was merely hiding his amazement. The Professor picked us up at the jungle airstrip himself. I had told him earlier that I did not want a big bash as I didn't know very many people yet and, besides, Ted was not coming on account of his eye patch.

We turned the last curve, the driver slowed down to a crawl to heighten the impact. I kept an eye on Melmoth. Would he freeze in utter amazement?

"Impressive!" Melmoth muttered under his breath. "I don't believe it."

The driver stopped to let the impact sink in. I grinned ear to ear, that is, until Melmoth moaned: "Disneyland on steroids!"

The Professor who sat up front turned around and faced Melmoth. "I had in mind to change the white elephants for green frogs, but it was too late to have it done before your visit. Frogs are so kissable."

"Only for a princess."

My face dropped. There's simply no accounting for taste and a tiny bit of my birthday spirits had just drained away.

The staff had aligned itself in front of the main entrance under an overhead bamboo trellis which spelled out the number 20 in big tropical flowers. As we sat down the Professor inspected Melmoth's bâton.

"This is an unusual piece. It looks like an original Fabergé. Pity the opal is lost. Opals come from here - do you know that? There is a small lapidary workshop in town which had done exquisite work for me before. May I send one of my people there with this? I assure you it will be back before the day is out."

One of the servants picked up the cane and left. The Professor and Melmoth bantered with polite niceties, carefully avoiding any meaningful exchange of ideas. Was he, the poet who once entertained potentates, bored, annoyed or simply angered? How could he be so indifferent in this sumptuous place in the sun with the palm trees slowly swaying their fronds in the gentle breeze? The Professor seemed not to notice as he continued. "What do you make of horse racing, the sport of kings?"

"Kings they may be, but sport this is not. True, in the end you breed better horses, but to what ultimate purpose? Still the same number of them will end up as dog food."

"Indeed, they will. At the cost of about three hundred loonies per pound." The Professor smiled disarmingly, and even Melmoth suppressed some of his brittleness and had a little tic on the corners of his lips. Suddenly I knew: he was playing a role, his role, his very own, the role of the cynical guest which probably underwrote the invitations to many a sententious gathering where the host had summoned this poet to insult his guests by proxy.

"Still, you might want to inspect my stables," the Professor continued, unperturbed. "I have the jitney waiting for you, and I shall take this opportunity to talk to my young friend here about many things that concern only the two of us." Before Melmoth could utter any intelligent protest he was hustled away, out of sight and sound.

"Now we can talk. You have made rapid progress since your arrival here."

To me it seemed more than years.

The Professor nodded. "Time is a strange continuum. It comes in little portions, like fine sand. You can build a whole castle with it and yet it's only dust." A servant came and refreshed our cool drinks. After he had left silently, the Professor continued. "Only death stops the clock."

"Death?"

"You melt away, become the substance from which you had been made. You are no longer needed." He raised his glass, took a slow sip, then continued. "Have you ever heard about the seeders?"

I had never heard this expression before and shook my head. "What do they seed?"

"Life, my young friend. It doesn't get around the universe without help, you know. Why do we look into the sky when we contemplate eternity? What is our attraction to other stars? Do we instinctively recognise our obligations? Do we realise that we are the shopkeepers who eventually must hand down the business to those coming after us?" He stopped, his eyes observing a butterfly dancing through the tropical air. Seeing my eyes following his, he continued. "They are so fragile and yet they can fly a thousand miles. What guides them? What guides us? Perhaps some day we'll know."

Was he one of the seeders? And how much does he want to cultivate? The whole universe or just one planet?

"Just one at a time, but design it with intelligence. No more platypus. We all carry the future on our shoulders. We must. It's our job."

But isn't the universe far too big to do any seeding? Would it not take thousands of years to reach the next liveable planet, even if we would send machines to do our bidding? How would we know that we have succeeded?

"We wouldn't. And what is time? I assure you, time is one thing the universe has in abundance. There will still be infinite amounts of it long after our own sun is gone." The Professor now appeared uncomfortable and eager to change the topic. "How is your Integration Council these days? I mean specifically your friend Borelli?"

This question threw me for a loop. How should I answer? I loved my boss and my new job, regardless of how often he changed his mind, and now I was determined to stay on the good side of the Professor.

"He warned me about you. He wants me to spy on you. He considers you to be very dangerous. And crazy." I added the proper emphasis to the last word.

"This good doctor is absolutely right. He might not even know how crazy I may yet turn out to be. Are you worried?"

I shook my head. "No, not about him. It's something else which has been on my mind ever since I came here." If ever there was a time, an opportunity to discuss the subject, it was now. "There's a secret nobody wants to discuss. Heard it from a butler." Could I continue?

The Professor anticipated my question and took direct aim. "Still thinking about escape from here? To wake up on the other side and in a hospital bed somewhere? Forget it. Surely, I'm the master of the quick exit, and if ever there was one, I would have found it."

I told him of the rumour that time itself may end.

"You don't mean this superstition about the Mayan calendar, do you? What did they know about atoms and such things? They had not even invented the wheel yet, so what makes you think their calculations were correct?"

"So far they have been proven accurate."

"That calendar... It's not what it seems. It's a monument, left by others who want to tell us that they had been here. They are the ancient travellers, the ones who came before. The ones we must follow. They were our gods, and some future time we must become the gods of others. - Oh, there comes our friend."

At this moment they could hear the jitney pull into the courtyard as the fountains were triggered to spew coloured water on the lady with her bank book held high. Melmoth appeared flushed and happy, but before he drew to within earshot the Professor said in hushed tone: "Stay with the Doctor. Humour him and keep me informed."

When finally Melmoth returned, he was overjoyed. "I had the most exhilarating ride in my life," Melmoth shouted from afar. "You, Sir, have the absolutely finest collection of equines anywhere."

"So the stable master let you mount one of them?"

"A mare, and she was very gentle with me. She must have sensed that I am not an accomplished rider, but the way she moved her rippling muscles, her gait... It seemed as if I could talk to her."

The Professor was pleased. "You could and you probably did. Do you realise, Mr. Melmoth, that some animals can read human minds? It is true. We may not be able to read theirs, but they have us all figured out. It's no wonder that so many of them are afraid of us."

During the informal dinner very little conversation went around the table, but afterwards the Professor held a short birthday speech in my honour. "This young man here has become my idea generator. I let him go wild as it behoves his youth, and I would gladly let him cross the Gobi on stilts, but I myself may travel more slowly on foot as it suits my age. Still, I have a little birthday present for you, young man. Open it."

It was an envelope, sealed in the old-fashioned way with shellac and an imprint done by a ring with two crossed trumpets on its face. The seal cracked and rather than expecting joy I had a premonition of something unpleasant coming towards me. At first I wasn't sure of what I pulled out of the envelope. The Professor helped.

"It's the ownership certificate of your new residence." This, I knew by the address, was the ritzy side of the city where you never saw people in the streets because they would pull into their triple and quadruple garages and simply vanish from the face of the earth.

I turned the document with the embossed golden paper seal around in my hands a few times as if it could metamorphose into something else. Finally I came out with it. "Thank you, but I cannot accept."

"And why not?" Disappointment mirrored in my mentor's eyes, even in his voice.

"I love where I am. I know it sounds stupid; a half-blind landlord - and frankly, sometimes he doesn't shave for weeks. And that strange couple up there with their idiot son. Always quarrelling. And my primitive, poorly furnished dump of an apartment. But I would miss Ted and his house with all the books and the basement with more books. And Joe and Marlene - even that weird kid hammering away on his glockenspiel. I would miss it all."

If the Professor was displeased he recovered quickly. He said he understood, and jumping milieu isn't everybody's enjoyment, and it was true: there (tapping on the document) are no people on the streets. But if I should ever change my mind...

He beckoned one of the attendants who came with a long, narrow wooden box. The Professor handed it to Melmoth. "I promised it would be back by tonight. Go, open it."

The ebony *bâton de marche* looked brand new. Scrapes and dings in the coiled snake removed, the enamel renewed where is had been chipped and worn down, the golden tiger reworked in its original bold beauty and the glass top was now replaced by a dazzling smoky opal on platinum hinges. "Careful now," the Professor advised. "The tiger's emerald eyes work again and I took the liberty to have its contents replenished as well." Replenished with what was never revealed, but Melmoth was absolutely speechless. Not a word, not a quip, not even a 'thank you'. Not a single, solitary moan.

On the short walk to our habitation Melmoth swung his Fabergé cane with joyous abandon. The Disneyland fountain in the blackness of the night had an almost magical charm under gushing millions of golden beads high up in the air. Melmoth finally found his voice again: "I understand what you meant by not wanting to leave your cold water tenement. Life doesn't happen within four walls of a dwelling; it does so within your cranium and the walls you set up yourself. If you become too comfortable with the pre-packaged plastic boundaries of affluence you might not want to break them down. You would stay there forever. You would mummify - albeit in a magnificent, glossy sarcophagus."

The ladies who greeted us at our bungalow were even lovelier than I remembered them. Before he fell asleep Melmoth knocked on my door and stuck in his head. "Thanks, Kid."

CHAPTER FOURTEEN

The last of the piles of the caisson had been driven in and the pumps started to drain the now enclosed body of water. I wanted some lightweight tasks on my plate right now and immerse myself in nothing of grave consequence. The office was no kinder. Only some memos loitering in my in-basket, none of them of any importance. Miss Pennypincher sped by me a couple of times, barely acknowledging me standing in the middle of her runway.

I left again and made a slight detour to drop into the Inuvik Dance and Ballet Studio. The Rockettes could hardly have done better. There, all dressed in orange jump suits stretched the chorus line of some twenty women kicking up a storm. Studying the group more closely I noticed that, unlike the dancers in Radio City Music Hall, these ladies appeared all to be around forty years old. Superannuated sex kittens. I expected Marlene to be among them but could not find her under the industrial-strength make-up and wigs. Mr. Busby barked his belligerent orders, the line stopped, the lone piano player craned his neck, a bell rang somewhere, a resigned 'from the top, one more time,' and then it went tap-tap-whomp again until I quietly stole myself away.

Suddenly it hit me. Now was the time to escape, run off with the circus, get lost, vanish… Some clouds had drifted in, so I attached the side windows on my MG but left the top open. I had a foreboding of something indefinable when I saw Crosley shrink in the rear view mirror, leaving me alone on a deserted rural road.

The asphalt turned into tarred gravel, then narrowed down to a mere two-lane dirt road leading straight north. To the left of me the blue haze of far-away mountains, to my right the rolling prairies, in front of me the endless expanse of grassland. The few farms I saw on the way seemed far away, secluded. It surprised me to find the highway system in such poor shape; but then again, I might have taken the wrong turn to begin with. Wherever it leads to is most likely as good a place as any. I might end up in a small village, a friendly dude ranch perhaps, an out-of-the-way Nirvana, anything just as long I could put some physical distance between me and my life in Crosley.

The crunch of the loose gravel under my tires, the spread of green, the wind tussling my hair, the stillness except for the gentle murmur of the pint-sized engine calmed my jangled nerves. I had altogether too much agitation around me recently and felt drained of energy. In the far distance to my right I spied a clump of trees, so I turned towards it. I had been driving for some three hours now and my gas was getting low.

The grouping of trees opened up to a broken-down ghost village, yet one lonely service station with an old-fashion gravity pump was still in business. A fat woman waddled out. "Come from Crosley?" she wanted to know. I nodded. "There ain't many comin' from Crosley no more," she continued as she unscrewed the tank cap. "Guess too dangerous now."

"So what's the danger?" I wanted to know.

She started pumping. "What with them riots and I heard there was another lynching. Where? Where you're goin'. In Vesper, that's where."

"Is Vesper straight ahead?"

"You can't hardly go anywheres other'n Vesper from here, Honey. It's Vesper or back to Crosley where ye come from."

No, she didn't accept credit cards but I had plenty of money in my pocket to pay her and leave a fair tip to boot. "That's awful sweet of you, Honey, but my advice is you turn right back and be home before dark."

"Are there no hotels in Vesper?" I asked, somewhat irritated.

"Oh yea, hotels there are plenty; it might just be that they won't let the likes of you in. You know what I mean. Coming from Crosley and all that." I wanted to ask more questions, but she waddled off, letting the screened door slap shut behind her.

It took another two hours before I could see the skyline of my target city: High-rises, a spindly tall tower with a fat bulbous head, polished office spires reflecting the golden rays of the setting sun, a faint brown haze covering it all. Even from the distance I could make it out to be a big cosmopolitan city of well over a million people.

The dirt road widened to blacktop, then concrete, again stretching to four lanes, centre divider, feed-ins, six lanes, eight...

The maelstrom of dense traffic sucked me along through monolithic cloverleaves, over bridges, across other roadways which in turn crossed more highways themselves, down in spirals narrowing to one-way streets in canyons of glass steeples. Not a single spot to park my car anywhere.

I hung right, circling nine blocks, then dipped into the basement garage of the downtown Sleep-Easy Hotel where I pulled the parking ticket out of the machine, found a small stall, put up the ragtop to secure the ticket on the dashboard, and looked for the elevator. Big cities have their own rhythm, their own orchestration of routines and cacophony, their own opaque rituals. The elevator door shut right before my nose and the couple inside made no attempt to hit the OPEN button to let me in. I ran up the one flight of stairs and entered the lobby just as the two came out of the elevator and headed straight for the reception desk.

The man behind the counter greeted the couple with a broad, toothy grin. I could overhear a few fragments of their conversation. "... quiet or rather on the street side? We have this lovely..."

The liveried doorman circled through the rotating door, slowed down to scrutinise me, rotated out again, then cycled through the same routine once more. The two were still negotiating the type of room they wanted, not too pricey, please. "... with a view of the skyline? Beautiful at night..."

I waited my turn, looking at my reflection in the polished marble of the centre column. Scuffed shoes, baggy jeans, wrinkled windbreaker. I looked a mess and felt uncomfortable.

"... fourteenth or seventeenth floor? You'll have a better view..." The couple giggled, a porter picked up their small overnighter, and it was now my turn. Before I had an opportunity to state my want, the desk clerk said: "I'm sorry, but we are all sold out."

"I just overheard you offering several..."

He cut me short. "Yes, but they had a reservation. Now we are all sold out."

His demeanour irritated me. "How can that be? There was nobody else ahead of me." I fumbled and pulled out my credit card in case I did not look creditworthy or respectable enough. The clerk raised two fingers, the outside doorman suddenly stood right beside us, elbowing his way in, his hand on my left upper arm the better to hustle me out of there should the need arise.

I protested. "Just a minute! I have parked my car in your garage, I have money, I may not be dressed properly for your uppity house and I might not have any luggage, but I assure you..."

"Anything the matter?" A portly starched-collar-and-matching-tie chap with a carnation in his lapel now stood next to us three. "Merely a small misunderstanding," the deskman muttered. "The gentleman is just leaving."

"I am not leaving," I interjected emphatically. The portly man, obviously the boss on this floor, took my credit card, studied it for a moment, looked at me again, then quietly said: "Just follow me."

We went towards the back, through a door labelled STAFF ONLY, past carts with dirty dishes, past folded tables and stacked chairs, through two more doors and into a padded service elevator which took us up two floors. A door with the numerals XII opened into a small sparsely furnished room overlooking the refuse containers below.

"May I suggest you'll stay in your part of town in future? It shall spare us all embarrassment and unnecessary tension. We will not charge you for this room, but be out of it by six in the morning. You are from Crosley, aren't you? It will be a lot safer if next time you would just stay in Wallsdorp." He never directly looked at me, but he must still have noticed my puzzlement; so he added, "Wallsdorp - that is north-east of here, an hour drive at best. Trust me, it's better for all of us."

With that he left and I found myself alone, looking down onto two kitchen helpers noisily dumping a load of rubbish into the iron garbage bin.

CHAPTER FIFTEEN

The banging on the door woke me up. A uniformed policeman planted himself in front of me, his right hand at his side as if to pull a taser gun any second now. "You the one with that sports car?"

I glanced at my watch: twenty past five. This man undoubtedly was sent to make sure I was out of the hotel well before other guests may rise and notice me. "Yes."

"Didn't you see that sign: Small Passenger Car Only?" The cop was single-minded about his task.

Of course I did. I can read.

"Don't sass me, boy. Well, do you have a small passenger car?" The man was openly belligerent and I was ready to slam the door in his face. Instead I nodded. The uniform continued: "That's not a passenger car you have, that's a sports car. It says nothing about sports cars on that sign, doesn't it now?. You are lucky that it was I who found out, others might have taken a dim view of your parking violation. That's a twenty-loonie fine. Pay now in cash and we won't have to lock you up until court."

He handed the ticket to me; I couldn't believe what just went on. This was the most outrageous shake-down I had ever heard of, and I was not going to let this liveried monkey here roll me. The police man looked straight into my face; any moment now he'll break out in boisterous laughter, say something funny such as 'April fool's day', and that would be the end of the joke. Instead, he held out his hand. "That'll be cash, and I take no credit cards. - Hurry, Boy."

I was still seething about the outright hostile reception last night, but this man was not going to get away with it. "I refuse to pay, and furthermore I shall lodge my complaint against this hotel as well as against you and whoever you work for. Most likely, your own pocket."

There, I actually said that! Before I realised what happened, I was pinned against the wall barefoot and half-naked, shackled, jostled into that padded service elevator, pushed into a waiting patrol car and hustled to the local police station. I did not even have the time or opportunity to put on my socks but had my naked feet chafing in my boots. Surely, I must resemble some known gangster. Maybe there had recently been a bank job and I looked like the man on the poster. A child molester. A heinous monster of some sort. A terrorist. A cigarette smoker. Whatever, but stay calm at any price. Just stay calm.

They did not remove the handcuffs until after I had been photographed, and only when it came to the fingerprinting did somebody reluctantly free my hands. Without a word I was taken to a small cell where I waited for some three hours. Somebody walked past and threw a bundle into the cell: my clothes and socks from the servant's room in the hotel.

Finally a guard took me to a tiny room with a table and four chairs where I waited for another half an hour. Two men entered, suited, smiling. "Sorry about the inconvenience," the first one started. The second man read out aloud from a printed sheet of paper in his hand: "Illegal parking, refusal to pay parking fine, resisting arrest by a peace officer, attempt to batter same officer, having no visible means of support, indecent attire, vagrancy." He looked up from his paper. "That's a lot of charges in only one short day."

I protested. "You guys are crazy. You are absolutely crazy. I come for a friendly visit, I park my little car in the corner where it says for small cars only, and then I can't rent a room. What do I get instead? Some stinking cubby-hole - for free because they didn't dare taking money from me after their shabby treatment ..."

Number One interrupted me: "Did you pay for the room?"

It was free. - Yes, but did I pay the taxes on it? - No, of course not.

Number One turned to number Two: "Add theft and tax evasion."

These were trumped-up charges and the men knew it. My hope that it might still turn out to be a party prank ebbed away. Exhausted I said: "Okay, what's the game. All this is bullshit, and you know it. What do you want from me?"

Number One turned a chair around, the backrest facing me, sat on it spread-legged, looking into my eyes. "You know, Boy, we don't want your kind here. You're from Crosley and you are here exactly for what reason?"

Number Two added: "Have you ever had your knuckles rapped? Hm? In something like that," pointing to the steel-clad door.

Now they were threatening me with physical harm for a crime I could neither determine nor even guess; damn me for a wholly fabricated offence as I saw it.

In a sudden display of anger number One slammed his hand hard on the table: "Tell me, Boy! Tell me!"

I knew that I had to declare something or they would beat me up right here on the spot. "I just drove out, away from Crosley, for a bit of serenity, a bit of quietude. I didn't know that I was not welcome."

Now number Two took over. "This was a peaceful city before you people came. We left our houses open and unattended, we left our car keys in the ignition, we trusted you with our children, we even grew tobacco for you, and now see what has happened to us. Just look around you. The stench and the corruption, the garbage, the cigarettes, the bombs, the fires, the crime. Babies dying, new diseases everywhere. We can't even drink our water anymore. And you dare to come here with your dirt and disease and filth, and you complain that you are not being loved? We hate you, we despise you with a passion. This is war, Boy."

Number One opened the door. "Get out of here. Get out and never come back. And if you do, we have your number. I'll handle you myself personally."

With that I was on the street, but no taxi would pick me up. How can they tell, I wondered. How do I look different from other people on the street? Well, it's true, I'm not professionally dressed, have no tie, carry no attaché case under my left arm, but that in itself should not be significant in any way. Do I smell differently, do

I walk differently, do I look differently? Perhaps a little bit of each, and, come to think of it, my work boots were indeed scuffed.

I had not eaten since leaving Crosley, and that was twenty-four hours ago. With the imminent danger gone at least temporarily I became aware of my hunger. Would they throw me out of a proper restaurant? How about a junk-food joint? Or the Nortel Pizza Parlour right there?

As I stepped over the doorsill, the short curly-haired pizza chef just wagged his index finger. Some patrons looked in my direction and drew away a smidgen as if I had the pox. From a vending machine I pulled some candy bars until I ran out of change. People I asked on the street didn't want to give me directions. I knew I had come north from Crosley, so I must head for the south quadrant of Vesper. I pointed the hour hand of my watch towards the afternoon sun, halved the angle between it and the number 12 and set out in that direction, walking, walking, walking straight south.

It was near evening when I reached the hotel again. My car was gone, 'collected for contravening published parking regulations', as the note said. Where did it go? It will cost me a twenty-loonie overdue parking charge before they tell me. After I had peeled off the required funds I could neither get a taxicab to drive me to the pound, nor could I phone them to have them bring the car to me as I had long ago exhausted my pocketful of change.

By now it was night again and my hunger had subsided, worn away with fatigue, tiredness and anger. First I tried to stay awake, then I found a bench near the river, only to be rudely awakened by some vigilante patrol that chased me out of the park. I counted my cash: one hundred and forty loonies and eleven cents in my pocket.

It was in the morning when finally a taxi stopped, the driver rolled down the window and stuck out his bald head: "Need a ride? Got any money?" I ran over, jumped in, slammed the door shut and sank into the rear seat as the cab driver continued: "You are from Crosley - I can tell."

"How can you tell?"

"Look the way you dress, the way you walk, you speak different, you smell different and there ain't no place other'n Crosley you could've come from."

"So why did you stop to pick me up?"

"I ain't 'fraid of you. Got this big stick here, see? And if you 'tack me I can take care of myself. And some of you guys ain't all that bad. You tip well. I got tolerance, see? One's gotta have tolerance."

The cab fare came to thirty-two loonies and I gave him forty to keep. The car pound was fenced-in, and to get inside you first have to enter the clapboard office shack. "Yes?" The man behind the counter was a giant with tattoos on both arms.

I explained why I came and which car it was; the tattoo man leafed through some loose sheets, then said: "Right, here it is. MG Midget. That'll be - let's see now. Pick-up is sixty, parking fine twenty, storage forty - that'll be a hundred and twenty."

I said I had already paid the parking fine, and besides, I have only a hundred left and still have to get back home and buy gas and what-have-you. "Better talk to Charlie," muscle man said. He paged him over the PA system, and a couple of minutes later Charlie entered. He could have been a twin brother except for his tattoos, which were higher up his arms and larger yet.

I explained to Charlie that I had paid the parking fine, Charlie said the attendant there had gypped me and pocketed the money, then looked at the same piece of paper and turned to the other guy. "Ain't that the one which slipped off the hook?" The other man nodded.

Charlie turned back to me. "Okay," he said. "I'll let you have it for the hundred because I want to get rid of that piece of shit." I handed him the last two fifty loonie bills, got the sheet stamped PAID and was permitted to enter the pound through the rear door of the shack. Some thirty cars of all descriptions and stages of neglect lingered on the gravelled ground. Around the corner - there it was: my MG Midget. The soft-top had been slashed several times, the whole right side was stowed in, the front squashed down and the hood flattened. One wheel was missing altogether, the other bent at an angle of 15 degrees. "There," tattoo man said. "Fell off the hook. Gravel truck ran into it." He tried hard to suppress a chortle.

It was at this very moment that I lost my cool. Lost it completely. I stormed back into the office shack, picked up the heavy Underwood typewriter and threw it straight through the plate glass window.

Both men instantly and soundly thrashed me. An hour later I was back in jail.

Number One was waiting for me. "Wondered when you'd come back. Your type always does, never fails." He twiddled with some papers, made a short phone call, then continued: "I guess I don't have to kill you now. Got enough charges against you to lock you up for seven years, but you'll be outa here in six weeks. In a body bag. By the way, you have one free phone call. We always observe the rules here. Always." He forced himself to a grimaced smile.

I called Melmoth. "Get me out of here," I begged. "Just get me out of this hell."

It was not until early next morning that the Professor's limo pulled up and Melmoth emerged. "Dammit," he said, "I was in such haste, even forgot my bâton." He had a brief conversation with the deskman and I was out of his cell in seconds. As I slumped into the back seat I broke down and cried.

"Why are they so paranoid?" I sobbed. "Why do they hate us instead of loving us?"

Melmoth put his arm around my shoulder. "Is it not as sweet to hate as it is to love?"

CHAPTER SIXTEEN

The Woodcrest Hospital patched me up, a couple of stitches here, a few there, four to close the gash in my lips. They kept me there 'for further observation', but next morning I was released and delivered to my home, third floor. Ted, eye patch on the other side now, was already waiting. "I heard. They told me all about it. Why on earth did you drive to Vesper? Didn't anybody tell you?"

I wished Ted would go away and let me sleep - sleep - sleep. Instead Ted sat at my bedside for an hour. The people in Vesper are evil, he told me. Ever since some fanatical revolutionary group blew up their Capilano Bay Bridge about five years ago they blamed the community of Crosley who, in one fashion or the other, appeared to have had a hand in it. At least that's what the local politicians kept saying. Nothing was ever proven but agitators in Vesper used this opportunity to stir up a wave of hatred, which they used for their own nefarious ends. Buildings occasionally burned on both sides of the war zone, people were killed, they said, were mutilated, even vanished without a trace. It was clear right from the very beginning of the hostilities that Vesper was a depraved federation which set out to destroy the Crosleyans, as the Crosleyans were clearly out to humiliate them. Problem was, the Vesperians were far more powerful militarily and had an incredible arsenal of weapons of destruction which the Crosleyans claimed would be unleashed against them any day now. On the other hand, the Crosleyans looked upon the Vesperians as uncultured, steeped in meaningless rituals, oblivious to any rationality or reason, blindly following the calls of their masters. They had no history of open debate, of the push and pull which is the foundation of any healthy society. For the Crosleyans, the others were the truly evil ones, hiding behind the ramparts of their front men, evading serious questions and answering to none.

I stayed in my walk-up flat for three solid days until the stitches were removed, my swollen lips had flattened and the bandages were taken off when Dr. Borelli appeared without warning.

He had been informed about my predicament but did not want to disturb my recuperation earlier, he claimed. Had he not warned me? His group had solid evidence that the Professor was the secret driving force of the hostilities between the two desert cities. He played both sides of the game, and it was his influence which not only started the tension between these two cities but this scheme was repeated in at least a couple of dozen other places. The total human costs now ran well into high numbers on all sides, not even counting the loss of prestige.

I tried to defend the Professor, but Dr. Borelli cut me short. "I understand your loyalty, but sooner or later he will bring you all into jeopardy. Yes, we know all about him. He has groomed you to become one of his inside officers, and if it wasn't so advantageous to them, they would already have dealt with you in Vesper. But we need you here as our inside informant. Do you know what that means?" His question hung in the air like the sword of Damocles. I nodded wearily.

The Doctor pulled up a chair and sat down. "I will level with you," he began. "There is a secret I had not yet revealed to you, but now that you are one of us, our trusted inside man, I have decided that you should know the whole truth. The Professor is our... Well, he is our front man for a pecuniary scientific implementation which... But first, you must swear secrecy. Nobody must ever know what I am going to tell you now. Do I have your word for it?"

"Why?"

"For your own safety, my Boy."

I objected. "But I don't want to hear. I want nothing to do with whatever..."

"Too late for that. Listen me out and then decide for yourself. He is... The Professor is... Well, I don't actually trust him, but he is the front man of a great number of industries, although he doesn't run any of them himself. He has professionals for that.

I'm certain you already knew that. But what you did not know is
this: he is operating a meticulous new investment system which
guarantees extraordinary profits for those who participate. The
money goes mostly to fund the many businesses which benefit from
the capital of the investors. And what is this scientific system? You
are looking at the inventor himself. Yes, it is I, Charles Borelli, who
has worked out the algorithm which makes all this possible. After a
couple of false starts it took a lifetime to perfect but now it works
flawlessly. Mind you, there had been a few setbacks earlier, but
now the system is perfect. I will reveal something to you which is
a deep secret. Needless to emphasize that you may not reveal this
to anybody. Is that clear? I am the Chairman of a secret society, the
Security Exchange Company. Have you ever heard of it? - No? - Of
course not. That's because it's secret. This is how it works."

Borelli wiped the beads off his forehead, twirled his moustache
and carried on. "You invest in this structured entity, and in only
six months you'll double your money. It is guaranteed and written
into the contract. If you are happy with the system and don't cash
in on the spot, so much the better. If you cash in you'll have to wait
your turn again until there is an opening. That can take a year,
depending on demand. If you stay, your investment then doubles
again. Endlessly and without fail. And that's what turns the wheels
of industry."

I was not convinced. "How is that possible?"

Borelli leaned back with a satisfied smile on his face. "That's how
my system differs from other investment schemes. You are just the
man to help make it work flawlessly. There comes a critical moment,
the tipping point, when the books close and the investments turn
into corporate shares. Mind you, although investors won't get their
money back, by now all the many enterprises are well established
and most are already churning out a profit. Day after day after
day the money keeps rolling in. It is a win-win-win situation. Of
course, I cannot reveal the details to you, but to maximise profits
we will pull out our capital which by then will have more than
quadrupled, and we'll still enjoy the benefits of being shareholders
of all that business. That, my friend, is how it works. As I said, it's
sheer genius. - Did I mention that it was I who invented it? One day
it will be known as the Borelli scheme."

The Doctor looked exhausted, but I was not quite finished yet. What would be my role? Would I participate in the rewards?

"You, my Boy, will earn my eternal gratitude. Plus, of course, our standard one-tenth of one percent finder's fee. Of course, should the Professor ever learn about your role he would be quite upset, but the only way he could find out is from you yourself." Left unsaid but palpably hanging in the air was what would happen to me should things not work out as planned. The Doctor shrugged his shoulder ominously. Nothing personal, no bad feelings, but the stakes are high.

The vet sensed that I was not satisfied with that answer. "Anything else?"

It was my old dilemma. "I want to get out of here. Back to my own life as I had it before. That's all that matters. If you have these connections…"

The vet spun around, his smile wiped away. "Yes, yes, it can be arranged. What's that worth to you?"

'Everything,' I was tempted to say. I could leave this place this very moment, sell anybody's secret to the highest bidder and send everybody to hell, if that's what it would take. The Professor, Melmoth, Max the butler, Ted and Miss Lynch… Especially Miss Lynch. I could imagine to wake up in a hard, cold, rattling hospital bed, a nurse would look into my eyes, then say 'He's coming around.' A man in scrubs would draw into view, pull down my lower eyelids and nod. 'Yes,' that man would say, 'he made it. Amazing. Keep him on that drip.' And then my wife would emerge out of nowhere, my wife… What was her name?

"But they say that's not do-able," I finally let out. "I heard rumours."

Borelli nearly exploded with anger. "Rumours, that's all one hears lately! What kind? The end-of-time yarn again? The universe collapsing? Atoms colliding? The black hole? Bacteria taking over? Oceans boiling away? Which one? All of them unfounded superstitions. Why does everybody have to cling to these old wife's tales? Do you want to know the latest? You'll split laughing when you hear it. They say the last living thing on the other side will be a radio-active cockroach. A radio-active cockroach! I can only laugh."

I did not think this was funny. There was obviously something substantial going on but I could not put my finger on it right now. Not yet, anyway. Perhaps the Doctor was crazy – perhaps he was a genius. All I needed now in my misery was some screwball from the zoo to come here and hint at dire consequences - even threaten me.

I walked over to the window, turning my back to the vet as a gesture that I wished this conversation to be over. Parked on the street below, where my old MG Midget used to stand was a brand new tomato-red MGA. It must have been out of production for a very long time now, had become a classic in its own right, and yet there it stood; most certainly restored at enormous expense from the ground up. I turned back to the doctor.

"Did you come in that one down there?" Pointing my finger downwards.

The Doctor calmed down, put his right hand on my shoulder. "It's probably the classiest sports car ever built, don't you think? That, my friend, is a gift for you from us. For what you have done for us already, and for what you'll do for us in future." He then pointed at the car. "She's a beauty, isn't she? Under-powered as they all were in those days. They required skill and dexterity to handle. Driving was more than merely a matter of transportation. Perhaps one day we'll rediscover all those delights." He turned towards the door, indicating that he was ready to leave. "Just one more thing," he continued. "Do you have an affair with Miss Robinson? Yes, the redhead from our first meetings. I must warn you. She's a psychopath. Oh yes, don't play innocent with me. I saw you blush. She will ruin you as she ruins all men."

It was true; I had once or twice thought about her but that's as far as it ever went. There was no one I felt comfortable asking so I put away this juvenile notion until an opportunity might present itself.

Dr. Borelli walked towards the door, turned to face me and quietly said: "Enjoy your car." With that he left.

I waited until I heard the front door slam shut, then hurried downstairs as fast as my still aching muscles permitted, and there, in the car's open cockpit lay a black plaque with the engraved words 'Thank you - The Security Exchange Company'. The keys dangled provocatively in the ignition as if to say 'don't even think about it.'

✳   ✳   ✳

It was more than a week later when I had the first opportunity to talk to the Professor who said something about the remarkable recovery after such beatings, and that he had heard about the car.

"I was glad that I could send Mister Melmoth. It was just a small misunderstanding. They thought... Now, you must listen to this: they suspected you to be a provocateur or some other kind of snake in the grass. I merely told them the facts, and furthermore I personally vouched for your character. As your employer this was the least I could do for you."

We stared at each other for awhile in total silence. Finally the Professor asked: "There's more, isn't it?"

I spilled the beans, told him all about Dr. Borelli's bribery attempts, his membership in the secret society, the tipping point he wants me to find, and his threats and warnings. I even mentioned the gift of the MG, and then, trying to leave a bit of a positive notion hanging in the air, said that, if it came right down to it, I would rather trust him, the Professor, than the Doctor. "At least you have a sense of humour – the Doctor doesn't and he lies a lot."

"Humour?" the Professor asked in return. "It's the wit of a simpleton. And lies? What is truth? Is a long list of facts the truth? Can a fable in one's own mind not be just as true? The truth can be suffocated by facts; any court of law will attest to that. We have two court systems in this land; one builds upon facts, the other, the durbar on impressions which may indeed be lies, but which are culled from the stories everybody openly contributes. These stories are the real truth although they may not actually be fact."

What's the Professor's story? There was obviously some undercurrent I could not penetrate.

"My story? Oh, there are so many of them. Here is just one. Besides you, very few people know anything about it, and they never might. As it so happens, I come from the Barbary Coast and my ancestors have all been abbas going back hundreds of years. 'Abba' in Barbary means pirates. Now you might think that such outlaws live a life of lawlessness, but that is not so. My upbringing was strict, our social customs were austere and often demanding, and my schooling was grounded in sciences, languages and philosophy. The fact that we were abbas never entered our consciousness any more than the kids of bankers and stock brokers think of themselves as being the progeny of thieves."

He walked to the window and gazed out for a moment, as if to gather his thoughts. Then he sat down again, looking straight at me as I listened with great attention.

"My mother died before I even knew she was my mother. I was not yet three years old, my dabba – that means father – my dabba lived for five more years until a rival gang murdered him on his honeymoon with his second wife. It was headline in all our papers at the time as the 'Abba Dabba Honeymoon Murders'. Prosperous uncles brought me up, and when I was still very young I inherited great wealth. At first I thought to become a playboy, but just look at me. I am short, fat, pasty-faced and hardly reach to your shoulder. Could I ever be the good time Charlie? I am simply not that type. But even if I had been, that sort of life could not ever have attracted me. Sure, I could have lived on my yacht forever, have a hundred servants around, women galore, every little hint of a wish instantly fulfilled. Luxury in every respect, never ending, for a whole life. I didn't think I was tough enough for that style of existence. As a wealthy person I would have never experienced frankness because every sycophant would tell me only what I might want to hear. No preparation could have readied me to handle such relentless fortune, so I planned to evade my responsibilities altogether."

He sauntered to the small hidden bar, poured Armagnac into two snifters, then handed me one and sat down again. I kept quiet the whole time.

"I became a buffoon. Grew a goatee. Can you imagine me with a goatee? But I did. Let's not underestimate the social attraction of buffoonery. Changed my name even. I tried to be like an idol of mine. Have you ever heard of an ancient jester by the name of Eulenspiegel? No? You must. He was and still is my icon, but he was tall and lanky with a pointed chin and nose. I have a moon face. He also was dirt-poor and had to work his way across the lands from marketplace to marketplace so he could both irritate and astound and move the people. He thought it would wake them up from their tedious grind. Farming then was an endless string of monotony and hard work. I came from the parlour, he came from the land. Putting this show together is something he would have loved, but he was always broke. But then, why not I? Why can I not afford to buy my own audience so to speak, and tell them my own Eulenspiegel yarns? And as this strange man never left his listeners without making them think about themselves, perhaps so can I. Everybody might learn something."

The libation was exquisite and lingered in the very back of my nose for a long time. The Professor carried on: "Some are mistrustful of me because they fear I might want to reintroduce superstition. Nonsense. They think I have the power to stir up trouble everywhere. That's plain applesauce. I've been around for a very long time, and money speaks. But I never let it scream, never." He took a slow sip. "Those people in Vesper? Yes, they are angry with us, but they have ample reason as they see it from their side. They know me and they trust me. Indeed, my power is money, but I dare not to let it overpower me." He bent towards me in a conspiratorial gesture, adding in hushed voice: "And I have the very best people who can do things."

I felt a boulder had been lifted off my chest. Of course, deep down I had always thought so, too, had always trusted him. Yes, the Professor is a bit nutty, but had I grown up in such riches myself, would I have stirred a finger for anything at all? Would I not just have let myself be pampered from all sides until this blessed money was all gone?

✳   ✳   ✳

The new car gave me great pleasure and soon I had bulldozed my misadventures into the darkest corners of my mind. True, the Vesperians were a bunch of hoodlums and roughnecks, but this lay in the distant past now. Didn't it? Could I some day go back there again under totally different circumstances? And once there, what would I do? Would I want to rub their noses in their own vomit, or would I try and fix whatever bugs them?

Back in the office, Miss Pennsinger handed me the drawings of the auditorium, sheet 11, Front Elevation. There it was spelled out in bold blue, red and yellow calligraphy: Trumpets of Joy.

I crossed it out and replaced it with 'Eulenspiegel Hall'.

Eulenspiegel, the wise owl recognising its own reflection. Would Professor Klonus accept these changes? Miss Pennsinger was sceptical. How big did I want it on the building? I said it should cover the entire front. She stalled; Pontiac Neon might have already started the job, she said, and besides, she would want to have official clearance first. That woman was a real nuisance and could drive you to utter distraction.

In the evening I dressed smartly but casually for the occasion and invited Melmoth out to dinner as a small gesture for having rescued me. Melmoth asked me if I would permit him to select the fare for the evening to which I thankfully agreed. I could live on hot dogs and a beer if it came to it, but my older friend had much higher expectations of what might constitute a proper meal. We started out with roasted pigeons in aspic and a chilled rosé wine.

The entrée went silently, but then the conversation lit up. "Have you ever heard of an Eulenspiegel," I asked. The type of restaurant and the chosen meal with the long pauses between the dishes was designed for muted conversation. I didn't keep count of the number of courses, but all together there must have been perhaps a dozen of them, all spaced apart by long breaks of chat over free-flowing libation.

"Till Eulenspiegel," Melmoth slowly repeated. "Of course, I have. Fourteenth century guy. He was a thief, a shrewd trickster with dubious taste dispensing vulgar jokes. A scandalous character. Comes from somewhere up in North Germany." The waiter refilled our glasses and silently removed some utensils and empty plates. "A real rascal, as I see him. Yet, at the same time he was infinitely fascinating. His stage was the many fairgrounds in the pastoral farming regions, and there were reports that he had visited other countries as well. It was said that he spoke several languages, but that may just be a legend. He would play up to the simple-minded rural people with practical jokes, insulting gestures and humiliating antics. His audience was infuriated by his foolishness and the indignities he inflicted on everybody. He always got away at the last moment. If they had caught him they surely would have soundly trashed if not even hang him. Yet he also was a philosopher of sorts. He usually drove home his point by charades that were crudely satirical of the current mores of the time, and he most certainly did not spare the arrogant social classes. It often seemed that he was bent on bringing down the rich and powerful. He was quite a handful. What brings up this obscure clown of the Middle Ages?"

I told him that I had changed the name of the new auditorium to Eulenspiegel Hall. Melmoth leaned back in his chair, rested his chin on his fist as I had seen him do so many times before, and said: "That is utter genius. A reincarnated Eulenspiegel. And a rich one this time."

Nearing the end of the meal, I whispered barely audible: "Do you know anything about a certain Security Exchange Company?"

Melmoth dropped the desert fork. Looking around if anybody was in earshot, he asked behind his serviette: "Who told you?"

Equally furtively I replied: "Borelli."

"Did he actually tell you?"

"He said he was a member himself."

Melmoth closed his eyes, sighed with relief and said: "For a moment you scared me. They are supposed to be capitalistic terrorists, but that's just a rumour. Nobody knows, and nobody will ever admit to being a member. Forget it, it's a hoax."

Suddenly he leaned over the table, crushed his napkin and whispered: "You must call me by my first name." Looking around to see if the waiter was watching us, he added: "Do you know my first name?"

"Of course I do. It's Sebastian."

"Rubbish."

"It's Oscar then."

"See? You don't know the first thing about me, do you? You simply don't care about your friends, pay no attention, disregard them with utter insolence. It always amazes me how people can ignore their closest, dearest friends. Of course, my name is not Oscar. The temerity!"

The waiter came to circle the table. Melmoth kept him in the corner of his eyes, and only when he was two tables away again he continued. "What makes you think my name was Oscar?"

I didn't have an answer ready, couldn't even invent one on the spot, so I stuttered: "It's not Sebastian, it's not Oscar, what is it then?"

"Knuckles."

"What?"

"Knuckles. And I have not yet decided if it's my first or family name." He let his answer sink in.

I stared into the deep red of the Malaga to gain time, then asked: "Why Knuckles? That's not even a proper name."

Melmoth seemed irritated. "Why not? I'm tired of Melmoth. A dark ghost hangs over that moniker and I am no longer Oscar. Haven't been for a century." He slowly sipped his drink. "Nobody will remember me for what I say, for what I write, for what I think. Not anymore. But Knuckles - that everybody will remember. Trust me, Kid. But speaking of sobriquets, I always meant to ask you: what's yours?"

CHAPTER SEVENTEEN

The early six o'clock news had just started on CKKK Radio when the tomato-red almost brand new MGA exploded into a mangled mess of shredded sheet metal, tattered leather, twisted bits of frame, shards of glass and pieces of this and that. I had just gotten up, had taken a shower and readied myself to start a busy day. The explosion shattered several windows in Ted's as well as some neighbour's houses. On the still dark city streets lay a light dusting of early-winter snow, as yet undisturbed by many footprints. Ted hit the street even before I could put on my boots and run downstairs, nearly colliding with Joe and his weird son from the floor below.

Quickly the street filled with the curious, the rubberneckers, hastily clad angry neighbours, a woman screaming hysterically, a few kids grinning in joyful excitement not quite comprehending the enormity of the devastation; to kids even bombs are exciting playthings. Within three minutes more than fifty people had gathered; most of them staying a respectable distance away while waiting for a second explosion which never came.

Ted was fully dressed, wearing a canvas apron powdered with sawdust as he had obviously already been working in his basement wood shop. "What the hell is going on here?" he confronted me. "Is that your doing? Look at the mess! My window - look at the door. What did you do to your car?"

I was equally stunned and had no answer. Ted intermittently shrugged his shoulders, shook his head and stuttered verbal incoherency.

At this moment the bright headlights of a street cleanup truck with rotating steel brushes rumbled around the corner, followed by a service truck from Imperial Mirror and Glass, one from Home and Castle Improvement and another one with the logo YOU BREAK IT - WE FIX IT blazoned on its side. Ted intercepted the cleanup truck and had a short lively exchange with the driver.

"What did he say?" I asked.

"He said he had been prepaid to be here at exactly fifteen minutes after six and clean the streets."

"Prepaid by whom?"

"He didn't know. Cash transaction. Big bonus. - Wait, I'll ask that man." Ted went over to one of the Imperial Mirror and Glass people and had another short discussion. I came close to catch a few words and could make out enough to confirm that they, too, had been prepaid in cash; a substantial gratuity and no questions asked.

A saleslady handed Ted her card: KFC Development and Real Estate. "I can imagine how shocked you are at this time, Mister Ramelov, but I want you to keep this card in case you decide to sell your property to us. We are allowed to pay fifteen percent above market value..."

"Get out of here," Ted snarled. "Have you no shame? Look at my place - just look. Does that look to you as if I want to sell my house?"

She was insistent. "I fully understand your present frame of mind..."

"And how come you are here this early in the morning? It's still dark, dammit. Who ordered you to be here? Who is behind all this?"

The lady momentarily stepped out of her studied sales approach. "I don't know myself, Mister Ramelov. I swear, I don't know. I received a cash incentive to be here at six-thirty, exact to the very minute. I am sorry if I have approached you at this most inconvenient moment."

Just at this time several more service trucks lined up, headlights blazing. One of them dispensed hot coffee and buns to the crowd; a tow truck hooked onto the wreck and pulled it away. Ted motioned me to follow him inside the house. Before we reached the badly damaged door a tradesman from Home and Castle Improvement intercepted us.

"Mister Ramelov, just one minute please." He held up a catalogue. "Which of these doors would you..."

Ted was furious. "Get the hell out of my way. Do whatever you want but leave me out of it. Clean up this mess and then get out of my life."

Finally reaching the basement workshop, away from the animated crowd of gawkers, tradesmen, street sweepers, cleanup crews, window repairers, painters, carpenters and assorted folks of vague purpose and motives, Ted turned to me. "That was meant for you. That was the best-orchestrated terror attack I have ever experienced. What did you do, and to whom?"

I was still too agitated to have any coherent thoughts. Perhaps the vet at the zoo, I suggested. He said he was connected with the Security Exchange Company.

Ted was obviously shaken. "Are you linked with them?"

"Perhaps we both are, you and I."

Somebody entered the house, shouting. "Mister Ramelov? Taddeus Ramelov? Are you in the building?" The voice drew closer. "Ah, there you are." A man in police uniform came halfway down the basement steps, holding onto the handrail. "I just want to get a statement from you and the owner of the car, if I may. You are the owner? Any idea what's behind this?"

Ted answered for both of us. "Give us just a few minutes to discuss this between us, will you? We'll be out shortly. Just leave us alone for a moment, okay?"

The policeman nodded. "Of course, take your time. You must both be terribly shaken." He climbed the stairs and out of sight.

With him safely gone, Ted put his finger on his lips to indicate absolute silence, but said loud and clear: "Tony, that's nothing to worry about. You can afford another car now, I'm sure." He sneaked to the handrail the uniformed man had clutched, looked under, motioned to me to come and see, and there, stuck underneath, we both found a loonie-sized metallic disc not much thicker than a hearing aid battery.

Ted nodded. "Don't know where all this gunk comes from. Gotta wash my hands. You, too, better clean up." With that we both walked up the stairs, chatting innocuous small talk. As we reached the bathroom and let the water run, Ted whispered: "They are on to us. Let's walk and talk."

We hastily dressed against the cold. On the street a different policeman asked for our statements. No, no, they know nothing, hooligans no doubt; happens almost every day. Yes, yes, the cities are restless but we know nothing. Maybe somebody dislikes sports cars.

Once we reached the park, Ted continued. "Unless one of our parkas is wired, we are safe here. What do we do now?"

We walked for several minutes until I suggested to better move out of his house. If indeed I am the target I'll get him into trouble as well. The demolition was perfectly well organised, planned in detail with precision and pinpoint accuracy. It was not meant to kill me; that they could have done far cheaper. It was meant to scare the dickens out of me. It was to show me how well they are organised, how thoroughly they have infiltrated our city, and how malignant they are. It was a show of force.

Ted mulled it over. "No, you don't move out. If anything, we are better off to stick together. I'm in it as well, you know. Don't forget they blew out my windows. And only last year I repainted that door. Did you see what the blast did? Ripped the bloody hinges right off. Wonder nobody got killed. Damn city-states. When did it all start?"

I tried to explain it. Venice, Hamburg, Hong Kong, and now even Crosley. In another world, another time, city states were commonplace. "Perhaps I should do as I was told when I first came here: study, learn something, anything, and be useful to our society. And keep low profile. I could get back into engineering before I completely forget what I once knew."

What is the Professor really up to? Ted wanted to know. "He's kissing your ass."

Slowly the darkness gave way to a grey morning with light snow falling. We turned into Duncan Street and ordered a solid breakfast at the cafeteria. The waitress was chatty. "Heard about the explosion?" she asked. "Just four blocks from here. Blew up a car. Wonder if anybody got killed. Must be the Vesperians again. Why don't we just move in and level that place." It was a rhetorical questions; everybody knew they had twice the army and three times the budget.

She refilled our cups. "Why don't we, eh?" she coaxed.

"They may have the dirty bomb, we only have anthrax and pox. They laugh at us," Ted answered resignedly. Then, turning to me: "Damn the torpedoes. We carry on as if nothing happened. I dare them."

Not wanting to return home on account of the commotion there, we decided to walk the streets. Although the thermometer settled just below the freezing mark, Ted felt good about getting some fresh air after he had spent so much time fiddling around in his basement shop. I was curious. "What are you doing there?"

"I'm building a model. I need some tiny, tiny little lamps. Any idea where I can get them?"

I had an idea. "How about those little Christmas lights?

"We don't much celebrate Christmas here. You should know better than to ask a dumb question like that."

I mentioned the pawn shop not far from here. Harmless old man. Fifteen minutes, twenty at most.

Ted said 'let's go', but, after having a fresh coffee and parking the old one, it was almost an hour before we entered Ricker Street. Dingel-lingel-ling went the tiny bell over the door.

"Christmas lights?" the old man behind the counter asked perfunctorily. "Yes, of course I have Christmas lights. It's a bestseller at this time, but I keep them under the counter. Have to respect the sensitivities of my patrons."

He brought forth a boxed string of a hundred little bulbs, all attached to a white cord, ready to decorate a contraband tree in somebody's recreation room.

"Aren't you a Jew?" Ted asked the man. "How come a Jew is selling Christmas lights?"

"Yes, I am Jewish. And why should I not sell Christmas lights? Is it not to celebrate the birth of another Jew?"

I had this question burning on my mind for a long time, and here was the opportunity to finally ask: "Could your name be Fagin?"

The shopkeeper flinched almost imperceptibly, then smiled vaguely. "No, no. Surely you mistake me for somebody else. I'm actually a shoemaker, but in my restless years I became a stage magician. Here, this is my card. Ahasverus Pre-owned Treasures at Bargain Prices, 27 Ricker Street. But I don't do parlour tricks anymore."

"Do you have a first name?"

"This is my first name. Some have called me The Wanderer. - Did your friend enjoy the bâton you bought for him?"

I told him he absolutely loves it, cherishes it, uses it constantly. Now I can hear him coming half a block away. Tap-tap-tap. I thanked him for his generosity. "That lovely cane is completely restored now, even has a newly rebuilt top."

"Is it an opal? The original was a magnificent opal."

As he paid, Ted said: "I see, you two know each other."

Ahasverus pushed his glasses back up the bridge of his nose. He smiled. "Yes, we do. This young man here, and I, this old man, we both must fit into this society which may not have been especially made for either of us."

He put the carton of Christmas lights into a plain brown bag and handed it over to Ted. "I bid you both to have a prosperous day. Be careful now; there had been a bomb blast early this morning. I hope nothing happened where you live."

As we left, I turned around and said: "Thank you, Mister Ahasverus. Thank you for your kindness."

"You are very welcome, Mister Parker." Somehow I was not even surprised that he knew my name.

As we reached home in the afternoon, just as the winter sun was about to vanish behind Crosley's rooftops, the last of the many service trucks was about to leave. The street looked transformed. Many porch railings had been replaced or at a minimum painted despite the cold. Some were far away from the explosion or even around the corner and could not possibly have suffered the slightest damage, yet they now were beautified anyway. They counted seven brand new front doors on neighbour's houses, three bay windows that replaced their ho-hum older flat varieties, and Ted had a magnificent new stained-glass entrance door with polished brass hardware. His front window had been transformed into deep, tile-lined fenestration with crank-operated sidelights and electric-powered shutters.

"Just look at that," Ted said quietly. "What a windfall for so many. They now have a hundred new friends and only one enemy: you. And they get respect."

It was never expressed just who 'they' were, but every city, every village felt under siege mentality, and 'they' were always behind everything.

CHAPTER EIGHTEEN

I obviously needed a vehicle, but my love affair with cars had now died of betrayal and disappointment. I took the bus to Farmer Bill's Used Car Emporium, walked around the lot of a hundred cars until a salesman appeared from behind an invisible broomstick.

"Sell me a comfortable, big, gas-hungry reliable whatever."

"Right this way, Sir."

What we found was a 10-year old red limousine with the nameplate *dillac* attached to the trunk lid, leather upholstery, and "...barely two hundred thousand klicks on it. These cars can live for fifty years if properly looked after. They never wear out." I bought it on the spot, without haggling, without questions, without forcing the commissioned salesman to lower his dignity and humbly beg for a trade.

I pointed my new old car directly towards 27 Ricker Street and reached the pawnshop near closing time.

"Mister Parker, how absolutely wonderful that you came back. Somehow I knew you would. I think you want to talk. Come, we'll sit in the back." With that he locked the shop's entry door, turned the CLOSED side of the sign towards the street and turned off most lights. "What can the two of us have in common? you ask. You are a young man and I am an old one. And yet, in spite of all this difference, there is more semblance between us than one might assume."

We shuffled past a few cartons on the floor, around a corner, past a Grandfather clock, through a narrow corridor that opened up to a comfortable old-fashioned living room with old-fashioned bookshelves crammed with old-fashioned books.

"I always enjoy a glass of tea at this time. May I brew us a cup?"

He shuffled off, and as his voice faded off in the distance I looked around. Into which kind of a society had I fallen? Everybody, it seems, had lots of books; that is, except for the Professor and the family on the first floor. Melmoth will probably have a very large library all to his own - he's so, well, scholastic.

Big, tall, leather-bound editions of art reproductions: Renoir, Manet, Monet, a hefty German book of ink drawings with rhymed two-liners under each, comic book-style, by a satirist named Busch. Gauguin, Erotic Art of the Masters, Post-Impressionism, together with an ancient edition of *Spacio de la bestia trionfante*, Occult Sciences, Des Knaben Wunderhorn. The out-of-sight clock struck the sixth hour, its slow, measured tick-tock faintly audible.

"Being old is not a bad position to be in. One becomes detached and more observant. Do you prefer lemon, cream, sugar? I myself like a tot of rum and a piece of rock candy in my tea. May I prepare the same for you?" Ahasverus had returned with a large pot of tea and placed it on an electric warming tray. "Yes, by all means, look at my art collections. Monet, one of my favourites. For the longest time I couldn't tell the difference between a Monet and a Manet although it's quite obvious, isn't it? Look at the transparency of light on the haystack. That's Monet, luminous, short brush strokes, and here by comparison Manet who was actually the first of... But I see, I'm boring you."

"Of course not, Mister Ahasverus."

"You seem to be a concerned young man. Is it because somebody blew up your car? Word gets around here so fast, we don't need the news on television." He poured a tot of rum into each glass, 'just for the flavour, you know', added a lump of rock candy and waited for the tea to steep. "So tell me, what's on your mind."

For one thing, I didn't really understand all goings-on here. Ahasverus stood unmoved, looking straight into my eyes and I was certain that he knew much more than he let on. I prompted him: "Why city states, for instance?"

Ahasverus returned the tea pot to the warming tray. "Instead of independent countries, right? Well, it actually is one country now; everything is one huge unlimited gigantic country."

What's the name of this country?

"The name, young man... yes, what's the name. It's The Global Democratic Federation of Bata. We are all so very angry at our country; we never speak its name. It's a corporate entity. Everything from horizon to horizon clear around the globe belongs to Bata. That is, with very few exceptions such as the Andorras and the Liechtensteins of this world so to speak, and the powerful city states like Paris, Sevastopol, Shenyang and Moncton. And some fifty others. Then there is the Tim Horten's Chain and of course the many independent islands such as Helgoland, Saltspring and Sardinia. Sardinia, that's where the little fish come from."

Can that structure not be fixed?

"What can we do?" he asked rhetorically. They have no weapons to fight for their own state. There are none of any kind anywhere, except for some dynamite one can easily cook up in the basement, or a new disease that may flare up. The state is everywhere and nowhere. Crosley has reciprocal trade and political deals of one kind or another with something like eight hundred other cities across the world; it has artistic cross licensing with three or four hundred others, sometime the same, often not. And that changes almost by the year, the month, even the hour. A real jungle and nobody seems to actually be in charge.

"And right here in what some might call the cultural, commercial and artistic backwater of the Prairies, there's Crosley. And everybody owns a part of the government. Would you prefer to have old-fashioned wars again?"

No, of course not. Nobody gains from wars; except the Swiss, of course.

"But that's not really why you came here, is it?"

"Yesterday I called you Mister Fagin and you seem to have reacted to that name. Were you indeed once a Fagin?"

"Now, that's a silly question. How could I be Fagin, hm? He's a fictional character. I'm just a puppeteer. I also did some small illusions such as pulling a kreutzer out of someone's ear. It's just a bit of misdirection. Small country fare trickery, that's all. - Bit more tea?"

I sat uneasily. There was still something on my mind but I dared not to come right out with it. "I heard rumours…" I began, not finishing my sentence.

Ahasverus started pouring the tea, eyeing me askance. "Rumours?"

"Somebody hinted at the end of time. Is there such a thing?"

He did not answer directly. "The same question had bothered me all my life. You hear the clock in the hallway ticking? It cuts our time into small portions, each one of them a measured bit of eternity. Will time ever run out, I wondered. And then, one day…"

He slowly sipped the hot beverage before he continued. "When playing the fairgrounds in Germany a long time ago I met a man who became my dearest friend. He thought time and the universe were unlimited. According to him, all started an infinity ago, it goes into more infinity, and everything is unbounded. The universe has no limits and neither has time, he maintained. It goes on and on and on and forever. There are an unlimited number of Parkers sitting with an unlimited number of pawnbrokers just like me, drinking tea. Imagine everything you see here exactly duplicated an unlimited number of times. And we all speak exactly the same words. Hard to imagine, isn't it?"

"Yes. I deal in structures all of which have a precise numerical limit somewhere."

"Nobody could imagine it, not then, not now. Neither could the pope of that time, but then again, he had his own interests to protect."

So what happened to his friend?

"They threw him into one of the many ghoulish dungeons of the Roman Inquisition. Most prisoners could not endure these dark, dank, rat-infested holes for more than perhaps a couple of months before they died of starvation, disease or torture. Il Nolano survived for seven years. How?"

Ahasverus did not answer his own question but slowly shook his head. Finally he continued in barely a whisper. "Then they executed him. The servants of the holy inquisition drove a long iron spike through his left cheek and out through his right. He could speak those heretical words no longer. Next they pulled his tongue out with crude pliers and drove another spike vertically down through his tongue, out behind his chin and into his larynx. That stopped his moaning. Then they carted him drenched in his blood to his stake in the Field of Flowers, past the barbarous, cajoling crowd, and then tied him to the post with thick ropes and lit the fagot, which lit the kindling, which lit the logs."

"Could they not have executed him swiftly and with as little pain as possible?"

Ahasverus shook his head. "On the contrary. They did not even sprinkle the wood which would have granted him a quick death by asphyxiation, instead they used dry wood to singe his flesh slowly and make him suffer the most. Soon the sweet stench of burning flesh wafted over the large crowd. A priest held up a cross but my friend turned his head away. He knew that the death sentence had already been cast long before he was taken prisoner in Venice. After his body had turned into a scorched heap of charcoal they smashed his bones with hammers and threw his ashes into the wind." He silently refilled the cups, then added: "So died my beloved friend Il Nolano on the eighteenth of February in the year sixteen hundred. This, as it turned out, was the dawn of the modern era and the first spark of light after a thousand years of darkness."

There was a long pause hanging cloyingly in the room. Except for the faint tick-tock of the clock it was deadly still. We silently sipped our tea.

"How could such tragedy have happened?"

Ahasverus carefully blotted one drop of tea glistening on the spout. "Two tectonic plates colliding with each other, namely the black Middle Ages and the promising renaissance with its quest for knowledge and invention. And a stubborn monk between them to make it happen."

How does he know all this?

"He told me so himself. But that still does not fully answer your question, does it. Let us for a moment assume that he was wrong, that both time and the universe are finite, where then is the end? Are they bundled together? Or does one end before the other? And which event would terminate either? This, my friend, we will never know. Unless, of course, someone foolishly collapses an atom."

I had to smile. A single, solitary atom? Why would that matter? There are quadrillions of them in a single speck of dust. "Who would miss one atom?"

Ahasverus was slow to answer. "That, Anthony, would create a tiny black hole. It would be so small and heavy that it would fall through everything we know, fall immediately towards the centre of the earth through all the other stuff in-between, and in its passing it would collide with at least one other atom which in turn would collapse. Now you have two of them, and both might not even have moved one millimetre so far. But it would carry on, double speed. Now you have four collapsed atoms, one-millionth second later eight, then sixteen, thirty-two and so on. It would be a chain reaction and within seconds all atoms and molecules would have collapsed and the earth, with the empty space in-between the atomic particles removed, would be reduced to the size of a beach ball. With all matter now compacted, this super-heavy ball... Yes, it would still be the weight of the whole earth but only the size of a beach ball, and this would attract first the moon and then the other planets including the sun itself. It would be so heavy and have such strong gravity that nothing would escape, not even light. That then would be the end of time, but only for this one solar system."

The clock in the hallway struck eight with seven long pauses between each.

Suddenly, changing the topic, he asked: "How is your friend the poet? You must look after him. He needs your help."

✳   ✳   ✳

It was unusually late for a visit, but I went on to drop into Melmoth's rented flat in the old cobblestone part of the city. I was now a man on a mission and he greeted me excitedly. "My dear boy, I am so glad to see you, however late. I heard about the explosion and I knew it had to do with you. It was you, wasn't it? Simply had to be you, nobody else got himself into trouble so fast, so deeply and so vulnerably. Missis Wanger - Missis Wanger! Be a dear. Could you please make us a spot of tea?"

I objected. "You Brits drink far too much of this - yuck - this tea."

"Missis Wanger, could you please make it coffee this time? Yes, that's right. Coffee. Please?" Books, books, books. Everybody has so many books - that is, everybody except the Professor. He does not seem to have a single one. "I'm not even certain my landlady has coffee in the house. She's from Manchester, you know. Never lost her dialect. I want to talk to you about Professor Klonus. You must, you absolutely must arrange for me to work on his stage routine. Before you say no, let me remind you that I am experienced, both as a writer and a stage presence. Do you think you might be able to arrange this?"

What does he have in mind?

"My dear fellow, I must preserve my artistic integrity and not prematurely reveal a single word of any of my brilliant ideas. There is such profundity of them; they almost overwhelm even me. Besides, my inventions have neither matured nor been fully conceived yet. But may I first point you to the character of Eulenspiegel himself. In many ways, he was very much a product of his time, coarse, vulgar, mischievous and occasionally spiteful. So is the Professor, with the exception that he has money to better conceal his malice. The Professor, as you call him, is also a huckster, a grassroots philosopher, a swindler, a genius although I am not yet certain in which field. And, last not least, this facsimile of Eulenspiegel is in search of the befitting venue for massaging his audience. This venue, my dear boy, he found thanks to you."

"He says he wants to touch the stars - or whatever. I don't believe this gives me any leverage but I will ask. On the other hand, perhaps there is something you could do for me."

"Yes, yes? Out with it now."

"I had in mind to ask you before, but I didn't have the nerve till now. Introduce me to that young lass from the meetings we had. The one with the short red curls who sat between us." There! I finally had come out with it.

"Bernadette Robinson. Bernie? There, you blush again."

"Borelli said she was a psychopath."

"My dear Boy, today it's a sin not to be one. Let's phone her and find out."

CHAPTER NINETEEN

" What did she say, what did she say?" I drove slowly so as to wring all important information out of Melmoth who took a certain pleasure to dribble the salient parts of their short phone conversation a word at a time.

She had just come home, took off her combat boots, is tired but needs a good laugh of such nature as can only be cultivated in the tension of sympathetic opposites. And yes, come on over for an hour, she had said. Of course she remembers me. She has only that one charge to look after, so how could she forget?

"She's working late?"

Melmoth had held his eyes transfixed on the road ahead, but now he turned fully towards me. "Don't you know Crosley has an army? It is true, we have a citizens army. Every city has one."

"How big?"

"We have two tanks, two helicopters, that is, if you include the V3, some vehicles and other left-over stuff. Guns have never occupied the fulcrum of my own interests."

"How long have you known each other?"

"This goes back - oh, I seem to have known her even before we actually met."

"But she's barely twenty."

"Fools you, doesn't it? She is - lets see now, she must be twenty-four if my numbers are accurate. She might have been your own great-grandmother once but here she's twenty-four. Arithmetic has never been one among my many remarkable talents, besides, time here is measured so erratically."

"How did you meet?"

"That, my young friend, is a very long story. The day may dawn when I might tell you. Now she's an army officer. A tank commander no less."

"An Amazon?"

"Once you stuff them into trousers, all women are. We men are assigned to the soapbox, being discarded on account of our martial instincts. Men cannot be trusted with weapons in their hands, they say. Now it's even worse, if such is possible. The ladies have a bad hair day and right away it becomes a crisis for us all and there go their firecrackers again."

"Who exactly are our enemies?"

Melmoth had to think it over for a few seconds. "Enemies? One doesn't really need enemies to have an army. At least not if you have a fully functional propaganda industry on your payroll. You can always find adequate reason to fight the battles of righteousness; just make up the rules as their need pops into your head. But now it's called a peacekeeping army. Fewer guns with smaller calibres. There are no more big wars, just skirmishes. For what? For monkey food, essentially. Hardly anybody ever gets killed fighting over peanuts." They walked towards the house. "Of course, you must flirt with her," Melmoth insisted. "Any superficiality will do. She has social graces, so she wouldn't believe a word you say. But your attention will please her."

A tidy suburb, tree-lined streets, ticky-tacky little boxes both sides, garbage cans out for the truck in the morning; lawns and hedges trimmed; injection-moulded plastic flower baskets hanging on imitation iron hooks; automatic porch lights instantly destroying the sheltering darkness as one approaches the front door.

"Sebastian!" She threw her arms around Melmoth. "How good of you to come. I haven't seen you in…"

"Must be a thick slice of eternity now, my dear." Turning to me: "This, my young friend, is Colonel Bernadette Robinson, Peacemaker, tank commander. Of course you remember."

She blew her tousled hair out of her face. "Parker, yes. Anthony, isn't it? Last time we met you blushed. That was so sweet."

"It's just Tony, even if Knuckles here insists on forgetting my name."

"He does that on purpose. Come in, come in. So he told you his secret name too? You must be good friends then. He calls me Lillie in his sleep. And forgive me for still being in uniform. Just got off my duty cycle. But please take your shoes off - the carpet, you know."

The room was stylish in a professional interior decorating style with not a speck of dust, no tattered newspapers, no ashes in the gas-fired genuine fake fireplace, no magazines, no empty cup, not a thumb print to be seen anywhere. I had the impression of having stepped into a show home, what with the profusion of Rockwellian graphics on the walls and the untouched look of the place. The absence of any traces of human habitation, the aseptic ambiance, the lovely piano which nobody seemed to play, the soul-destroying aggressive tidiness made the place look like a picture lifted straight out of some no-money-down catalogue.

"Now that you two are here, let me quickly take a shower and finally do away with my fatigues. Sebastian, my Love, you know where things are." And with a swoosh she was gone.

"Unlike most other women, there's more to her than what you see," Melmoth said softly as he served three cognacs in snifters. "Aside from being a chocolate addict."

He explained: The Aztecs called it xocoatl and they prized it highly as a medicine. "Don't ever give her any chocolate, only the cocoa-less variety, you know, this yellow candy stuff with artificial flavouring. She cannot help herself but when she goes on a cocoa binge it can last for days and get her entirely out of control. Anyway, she's quite a personality in many other ways. Three times a year she has to go on a short peace-keeping tour, active duty. Otherwise she runs the Sovereign Bank corner Klein and Third."

"That's a big bank."

"Egad, she's a big girl. But don't ever call her a girl. It annoys her mightily."

We sat in silence until she came back, dressed in a loose-hanging polychrome muumuu, her short red curls still moist and uncombed. "Thank you, dear, I do need that drink. - That was a rough stint this time. Dust, and then we had that windstorm. We had to do without skyhook support, and the kids are getting meaner each day. They use slingshots again. Heaven knows where they get those rubber bands with the embargo and all. Had to close my hatch practically all the time." Turning towards me she explained. "It's hot inside the Tiger. The kids fling small rocks at us. That can really hurt somebody. The other day we had to evacuate a casualty as she was hit right between her eyes. Could have blinded her permanently."

"What's with the kids," I wanted to know.

"Oh well, they have so many of them. They'll breed us out of existence if we let them. If the hostilities continue like what it has become lately we'll have to shoot with gummy bears again. Of course, we try not to harm any of them and usually fire over their heads, but accidents happen. Why don't these people understand that we bring them freedom, democracy and justice? But I suppose once a Hutterite, always a Hutterite. No amount of education and enlightenment will ever throw off their bondage and liberate them from their mindless superstition." To me this sounded just a little bit too studied, too propagandistic.

"So, why are they so angry?"

"It's really nothing. The City of Crosley and incorporated areas have now... What is it exactly, Sebastian?"

"One-point-three."

"Some one-point-three million people and it's still not stabilised. Of course we need the land in case we want to expand, but will they move? They claim it was handed down to them by their elders, as if that was a reason! Stubborn as mules. Ah, that's a good drink. Thank you, Darling."

I was only half listening, wondering how she might feel in my arms. Dammit. Melmoth observed both of us with obvious relish and a mocking little smile around the corners of his lips.

She continued. "So, what brings you here so late?"

"Bernie dear, as you might have long suspected, this young fellow is spellbound by you and he wanted to meet you privately and in person."

"He could have chosen me as his companion mentor when he had the chance. Instead he picked you, but even I must admit that you were the better choice. All I could give him would be sex; from you he gets class." Turning fully towards me: "That's so darling of you to have come at this late hour. I take it as a compliment. Did I hear that you want to return to the other side? That's only possible if you are one of the super rich and go in for cloning. At least, that's what Nostradamus said - but then again, he's made mistakes before."

I was eager to change the topic and gave a brief outline of the Professor's ambitions, the work-in-progress, the renovations and my own recent harassment in Vesper. "Yes, Vesper," said the delightful young redhead in her colourful muumuu. "We should have taken care of them when we still had all our tanks."

✳   ✳   ✳

The day came when Ted was ready to show off his model of the festive barge. An indoor swimming pool had been rented for the early morning hours; Professor Klonus was finally in town and standing by. The model was carefully wrapped in blankets and transported to the pool. On the day of the spring equinox, at four o'clock in the morning, the mock-up was launched under the watchful eyes of the Professor, Miss Pennypincher, me, Gus the construction guy, Marlene the hooker and Joe the bartender, plus Sebastian Melmoth and Grietje Zelle, that child from the dusty sex office. Even Mr. Busby attended as he was conscripted to think up an entrance number fitting for the planned occasion which now was only a little more than three months away. By the time the model barge was launched another dozen people had drifted in to rubberneck. When the overhead sodium vapour lights were switched off and the barge floated with all its forty-eight tiny lamps reflecting from the gunwales and railings on the water's ripples, it was absolutely still in the usually deafening swimming pool.

Ted jockeyed his barge model with the skill of a juggler on a high wire, letting it do full circles, even move sideways to gently touch the top rung of the basin's ladder with search lights blazing in bow and stern. "Side thrusters," he explained. "Important in getting the thing into and out of tight spaces." There it floated in all its Christmas glory, sixteen little cardboard natives behind sixteen little plastic jock straps pumping their sixteen little tongue depressor paddles as if their sixteen little electric lives depended on it. Ahs and ohs from the attentive crowd. Somebody sniffled as if to suppress a tear.

Demonstration finished, the overhead lighting crackled on again, the Professor crumpled his hankie, appreciative applause from all, the magic was over. I joined Melmoth and Bernie. "Wanted to call you," she addressed me. "Had in mind to invite you, if you can spare the time. You must have been very busy arranging all this."

It was all Ted's work, I explained, but yes, I would really love to see her again. Any time, any place, any adventure. I hoped my enthusiasm wouldn't show and I tried to sound casual with my heart in my throat.

Before the gathering broke up the Professor addressed the meeting. "Do we have anybody here with shipbuilding experience?" Ted, still glowing with excitement, hair dishevelled, shook his head. "Just an amateur model maker."

"Anybody?" the Professor repeated.

Joe answered from the back. "I once worked in a shipyard."

"Very well, you are my new ship builder. Build me that barge. You have sixty days."

"I'm not sure I can." Joe looked around the group, begging for help.

The Professor was adamant. "Of course you can. Anybody can - there's absolutely nothing to building ships. You have a new title: naval architect. And watch the spelling; I don't want you to start designing belly buttons now. Go and build me that barge. And you, Ted, you are in charge of strategic planning. How is your eyesight?"

"Perfect, absolutely perfect."

"Then why do you still wear those god-awful glasses?"

"Habit mostly. Different lenses. Bit of astigmatism. I need something on my nose."

"Ted, I now promote you to be my barge captain. You are a genius. And don't you dare and disappoint me." Facing Miss Pennsinger: "See to it that Joe gets a card." With that he turned and quickly left.

CHAPTER TWENTY

It was only days later when I had finally gathered enough confidence to pay her a visit. "So sweet of you to come. White Kallé Beau Chocolates." Bernie shrieked with delight. "How exceptionally cavalier."

"Open the box and look inside. I had them specially made for you."

Bernie tore off the PVC wrap and there they were right in front of her very eyes: twelve perfectly shaped identical little ivory-coloured ersatz chocolate Tiger Five tanks, each one not much larger than a bar of soap. "And so delightfully corny. Come on in, Dear."

I shrugged my shoulders with an it's-nothing gesture. "Only white imitation. No cocoa inside."

"Sebastian must have told you. He's such a sweetheart. I couldn't sin properly without him. Please, Dear, take off your shoes and let's squat down right in front of the fireplace. It's Tony, isn't it?"

How could she be so rattle-brained? I had been thinking of her every day for the past week, but she had forgotten my name. Or did she just pretend? We crouched down on the deep-pile stain-resistant white carpet next to the non-functional decorative fireplace tools with the fake onyx handles, but the conversation did not really take off until after we had feasted on ice cream doused in Great Marnier and generously sprinkled with pecans.

"Tell me about the army."

"Best career move I ever made. Used to be wild on a Boeing forty-nine, you know, the scooter, but when they spread the lure of the army before me, I simply couldn't resist. First basic training. Three months. You've no idea how that gets you into shape. I used to slouch; walked with a dowager's hump at age nineteen, but the army surely straightened me out in a hurry. Look at my gait now. I glide like a queen."

She got up, walked around the room twice, then hunkered down again.

"See what I mean? Worked at the bank then as a teller. I love to be close to money, but tellers are nobodies and most of them have long been replaced by those wicked machines. Of course, the bank had to keep my job till my stint was over, but, honestly Dear, who needs it? Suddenly, out of the blue one of the directors called me in and asked if I had previous banking experience."

"Did you?"

"Imagine that: I was a Quaker! Of course, that left me terribly immature when I left Level One, so when I finally got here as a six year old kid I was bowled over. Suddenly I had a real human family. Instantly I had toys and playthings which I'd never owned before. I had liberties of which I could only dream. Even today I still need all my gadgets, my tanks, people to play with, but I never had my own house. I now rent. I need mobility. You can't take it with you when you move."

"No, you can't. Well, you know I'm a squatter."

"Of course; that's how we met in the first place. That must be awfully tough on you. What did you have to leave behind?"

I had to think for a few seconds. "Not all that much, I guess. I start to forget. My dog, Casper. A BMW. A house. Will you believe it? There's still a mortgage on it - runs for another three years. And of course my wife. It's been nearly a year, you know. I, too, didn't take anything with me. It can't be done."

"Let's not be hasty on that one." Anyway, she continued, this guy, the director, he had his eyes on her for some time already. Now that she had straightened out and cut her hair, how would she like to go into management training when she came back out of the service in a couple of years? "Of course, I said 'yes' right away. Changed my first name to Bernadette. I have short curly red hair and no other name seems to fit. Could you imagine me to be a Miranda? Or a Mary? Tell me honestly."

I thought her name suited her admirably. But how did she get into tanks?

Knowing about her love of the Boeing scooters they first upgraded her skills to driving the big Hogs with sidecars, and from there to tanks was just another rung up the career ladder. When they learned about the scheduled bank management training, they wanted to beat the bank to it and promoted Bernie through the army ranks so fast that she couldn't sew on all the gold tassels quickly enough. "And here I am an officer on both sides. It's strange how they all tear themselves apart to get at you in such a hurry where before they couldn't have cared less. - So, what are you doing? I shouldn't ask, being one of your guides into our society, you know, but, frankly my Dear, I had my hands full with other issues."

I admitted that I was actually nothing, just a feral alley cat meandering past the trashcans of society. I was an idea man, but what exactly is that? Vacillating between Ted, the Professor, Pennypincher, the monkey doctor, Ahasverus and Gus the construction guy, and on and on. Who really am I?

"You are their juggler," Bernie suggested. "You entertain them while having three balls in the air. There's one like you in every organisation. They don't actually do anything, they are just there to get the coffee and to flatter everybody - and let's face it, that's what drives the industry. Anybody needs encouragement, even from a corporate hobo. Other than that, you're a transient."

I protested lamely. "I had the original idea."

"Ideas are cheap, Dear. How do you think patent lawyers get so rich, hm? For every marketable product there are at least a thousand ideas which lead to nothing but fat retainers for the patent law industry. You are the pebble which caused an avalanche. You are not the avalanche, Honey, you are just the pebble."

"Ever heard of Rockapussy? Buzzabum?"

She laughed. "Of course, and the Professor wanted to get funding from us. He said he needs to make a profit for his self-esteem. Of course, he was just joking. And now he's loaded with all the construction he handles, and his - well, his investment schemes and that. But back to you. What do you plan to do with the rest of eternity?"

"That's impossible to say. Eternity lasts such a long time."

"What would you want to do right now?" I wanted to hold her in my arms, but there simply was no polite way to express my sentiments so openly. We freshened up on spiked ice cream again. Indeed, she walked as if she wore in-line skates under her floor-length skirt.

"Tell you what," she continued as she raised the licking gas flames around her fireproof asbestos log replicas. "Why don't you take a six-weeker?"

She laid out the details of the abridged military training, the many benefits (actually none), the pay (practically zero), the free dental care (I didn't need any) and the Government Issue clothing (drab army olive combat togs).

"The best part is what it does to you personally. It gives you the satisfaction of doing good in the world. You are helping these poor creatures and finally open their eyes, make them aware of their oppression by their tyrannical overlords, their mind-twisting superstitions, their singing in German."

The ice cream was scrumptious, and when we had ladled off the orange liquor we refilled the bowls to the brim once more.

"Not only that." She was now unstoppable. "You should see their little babies laugh when you give them lollipops. Horsley bars, man, they go goggle-eyed over Horsley bars. Of course, I can't eat any of them myself."

I opened the box of white chocolate Tiger Five tanks, but they looked so cuddly nestled in their vacuum-formed plastic tray that neither of us dared to bite off a turret.

"There's just one little drawback. We don't have very many young men among us. You may get heckled a bit. You know how horny these young chicks are but we try to catch them in the act, figuratively speaking, and weed them out. No blow jobs in my army."

"I think I could adjust to that."

"Fortunately I can pull rank. I could perhaps even get you into my tank as a loader. Mostly just for the training, you know, but if we're lucky we might get to collect taxes and see some action."

"A loader of what?"

"Ordnance, of course. Artillery shells. But don't worry, we rarely shoot anymore. It's mostly now a battle for their hearts and minds, not so much against their tractors and road graders anymore. Are you thinking of sex with me now?"

⁂   ⁂   ⁂

Professor Klonus had no objections. "Six weeks? Of course. Tie up some loose ends before you leave, that's all." He seemed entirely unconcerned.

Ted and Joe were busy searching for a used barge among the jetsam and flotsam of the harbour mayhem. They found three possible candidates; one of them had first hauled coal and later gravel for the construction industries and was in pitiful shape. It was now destined to carry the city's garbage all the way down to Leadbridge, which had a trash disposal treaty with Crosley. There was good money to be made in garbage, and Leadbridge had it all: a payola system which barely left bookkeeping traces, a valley on the other side of the watershed, high unemployment and, best of all, Tammany Pub and a mayor who was a drunk.

The second barge was much newer. It was self-propelled with a modest 6-cylinder Maypond diesel but it had most of its portside gunwale stowed in. The barge was still afloat next to the dry dock but had not yet been cleared by the insurance processors. Repairs, once they could be started, would be slow and expensive.

Number three had been hauled onto dry land; it also had an inboard engine and would have been a honey of a ship if it would still have had the keel which it lost a year ago when it ran aground in some backwaters in the Coral Seas.

Ted thought that number one was the best. Wrap the whole damn thing in Arborite, he suggested, and nobody will ever know what's underneath. Open two moon pools through the planking and lower a couple of the biggest outboard motors you could find. For side thrusters in both bow and stern connect port and starboard with a lateral tube below the waterline and fit it with a hydraulic drive unit and a tunnel prop. For crying out loud, the finished barge eventually has to cover only five nautical miles. What's so tough about that?

Joe leaned more towards number three, and since he now had officially become a naval architect, the decision went his way if for no other reason than parading his professional rank. A couple of days later I talked to the guys at Polar Drilling who owned the wreck and were only too happy to get rid of it. We finally bought the whole bundle for the price of the engine alone, under the condition that the Majestic, as it was now called, would vacate the middle management parking lot when repaired and never comes back. That was OK with Joe as he already had extended the jetty alongside Eulenspiegel Hall for its permanent moorage. Polar Drilling even agreed to lease them three of their own shipbuilders who actually knew what they were doing.

Dr. Charles Borelli was very happy to see me leave the Professor, even if only temporarily. "The Military will do you a lot of good, believe me. You'll learn so many valuable lessons: how to get up at five in the morning, how to handle Uzis and grenades, how to take out any human stone thrower at a hundred yards and how to hog-tie your prisoners. They'll teach you to march all through the night on an empty stomach, to move in robotic unison, to crawl under booby-trapped barbed wire, rifle in hand, to jump from up high into an overflowing cesspool and have spit-polished boots again the next morning."

"At five o'clock?" It was supposed to sound funny but it didn't.

"You will deal with being shot at with live ammo, you will scratch up personnel mines with your bayonet or even with your bare fingers, take cover in the open field against overhead shrapnel. You'll run a hundred yards while wearing a bio-mask, dig your own manhole with your hands in two minutes flat and eat sand-sprinkled army rations out of a tin cup. You will learn to soundlessly crush your enemy's vertebra and even draw a bead when wearing infrared night goggles. It's a very rewarding existence and you'll never forget what you've learned. These are life-enriching experiences which will nourish you forever. You go in as useless trash, you come out a hero."

Melmoth was much more understanding. "A sticky wicket, my friend. Are you really that desperate? Go for it then. Remember that those six weeks will pass regardless of what you do with them, or where you are and how miserably you may have to live. Six weeks are gone either this way or that, and when they are finally over you'll still have the Colonel to schmooze. That is, if she sticks with you. Don't forget she has many more recruits to sign up. If she eventually makes one more promotion the bank will have to give her at least a directorship. It's a comfortable life."

Ahasverus the pawnbroker was even less enthusiastic. "Wars, big ones or little ones or even tiny little skirmishes, they have never decided anything. You go in a mensch; you come out an untermensch, a subhuman. You learn nothing you need to know, you unlearn all the good things in you. The army will rip out your soul and replace it with blind obedience. You will become a hollow person, or, worse yet, they'll stuff you like a turkey."

"With bread crumbs?" I tried to lighten the issue; it wasn't my day for jokes. Besides, all this was getting too goddamn personal.

"Don't be such a schlemiel. And don't try and hornswoggle an old man like me. They'll stuff you with slogans and patriotism and allegiance to symbols and flags. They will desensitise you so you can go out and kill, kill, kill. It takes a lifetime to become accountable to your own inner self, it only takes six weeks to turn you back into the monster you were when you were born. Yes, yes, babies are born as monsters; they grow into savage children, and those grow up to become selfish and reckless young oafs, and only the abrasive tumble through the grit of life may - just may - polish you into a mensch."

A woman entered the store. The pawnbroker recognised her immediately. "You are Missis Kimmelbaum, right?"

The woman nodded. "You remember."

"I still have your departed husband's beautiful overcoat here. Nobody bought it yet. I can sell it back to you. Half price for what I paid you. As you can see, I need the space."

Mrs.. Kimmelbaum shook her head and carefully unwrapped a beautiful old gold pocket watch. "Emil's," she murmured quietly. "He had inherited it when he was still a young man. I didn't want to sell it earlier..." Her voice trailed off.

The pawnbroker studied it at length under his jeweller's loupe. "It has no manufacturer's hallmark, but look here. See that little micro balance spring adjustment? Right there? That's the mark of a very expensive watch. I would say it's a Glasshütte. I could give you only a hundred for it, but it's worth much more. Do you really need the money, Dear?" The woman nodded again.

"Here is what I propose," Ahasverus continued. "I will send it to Beijing by express courier. I know a very good auctioneer there; I have done business with him a hundred times and he specialises in these. If this is what I think it is, it may fetch - well, let's see… Yes, it may get as much as four, five thousand. Would you like me to do that?" Mrs. Kimmelbaum nodded again.

"He will charge you fifteen percent of what it fetches for him, and I will charge you another fifteen percent for my part on what's left, and there are the shipping costs and the insurance. And we all have to pay taxes, but even then I would think that you can still get about twenty-five hundred out of it. Would that be satisfactory?"

The woman nodded once more. The pawnbroker filled out a short form and handed it to the customer. "Just sign here, my Dear."

She quietly put her name to the bottom of the document. "From now it will take about a month to six weeks, so you must be patient. In the meantime, this will tide you over." With that he handed her two fifty-loonie notes and she quickly left the store.

Returning to me: "If my hunch is right, the watch might even get as much as twelve thousand. Didn't want to get her hopes up too high, but it seems to be an extremely rare Glasshütte from the Biedermeier era. Needs a bit of work on the crown, though. The poor woman, she really has use for the money. She may be a very rich old lady in a couple of months."

I was dissatisfied with the advice I received from him, secretly hoping to find approval for my recruitment although I suspected that everybody knew what I really wanted. My true objective was pretty transparent and appeared to be a lot closer to the commander than the command. I should talk to Max, but I had not contacted him for nearly a year now on account of Miss Lynch.

"Who?"

"Tony Parker. You know, the squatter."

"I cannot talk to you, Tony. You know, Miss Lynch… I don't think you should come here any more."

"I have to make a decision and I hoped you could advise me."

"I know which decision you are talking about. It's about your military training."

"How did you know about it?"

"Miss Lynch. She secretly keeps track of you. She's worried you'll get yourself into a mess. It could all come crashing down on her head. She saved your life, now she's responsible for you. She could have walked away from you, you know."

"Yes, I'm aware of that. So, what am I going to do?"

"Talk to Hanna. You know, from your integration meeting. The one who doles out your money. She looked after me when I was in similar situations. I know what you are going through, but I can't talk to you." Click, he hung up.

Miss Hanna came in her canary-yellow sedan and parked on the Eulenspiegel Hall lot near the bus loop. "How can you go around asking everybody if you should take a six-weeker? Can't you make up your own mind? When you came I had hopes that you might be a person with integrity but you turn out just like all the others. Forget your duty, forget why you are here, betray those who only have your welfare in mind. You can't think on your own for a minute, always recycling the opinions of others."

We watched a flatbed deliver a load of construction beams, the forklifts weaving their dance, the people scurrying about in their assigned tasks.

"There," she continued. "They know what to do. They build you a big convention hall, just as you had wanted. That's when I still had hopes. But now you have become a simpering milquetoast. If you can't sort out what to do for the next six weeks, stay in bed."

I said that I had to get out of here; it's growing over my head. I started something and I didn't have the end in mind.

"Yes, and now you are stuck with new responsibilities which you wanted to avoid. You bit off more than you could handle, didn't you? Still thinking you are the engineer of a former life, but you have forgotten most of it now, haven't you?"

Why did I forget it all?

"Babies are born with their memories intact," she said. "They even remember being in the womb, being born, seeing light for the first time, and yet, in only a couple of months they have forgotten it all. Their heads are now filled with other adventures. Perhaps a six-weeker is good for you after all," she added.

⁂   ⁂   ⁂

On the fifth of July I signed up for a six-week military training course with the Armoured Division of the Liberation Forces of the City of Crosley.

CHAPTER TWENTY-ONE

"Taaan - shen!" Her eyes were as grey and as hard as the gravel under her feet. In her left she cupped a six weeks old snow-white Samoyed puppy. Fourteen young women and I, the only man, in front of her tried our best to come to some semblance of order.

"At ease." She scanned the people lined up. "I am Sergeant Primrose, your drill instructor. In one hour you will be issued your uniforms and gear. There will be no talking, no whistling, no hand signals between you. You there, what's your name?"

"Evelyn. Evelyn Duncan."

"You will snap to attention and answer with "Recruit Duncan, Sir. You will answer with a loud clear voice. Who are you?"

"Evelyn Duncan, Sir."

"Who?"

"Recruit Duncan, Sir."

"Recruit Duncan, come here." The young lass quickly stepped forward. "While you are in front of me you will stand at attention. Attention! Recruit Duncan, you will hold this puppy in your hands for one minute. You will touch it and stroke it, and if it licks your hand you will lick its nose in return. Is that understood?"

"Yes."

"You will reply in a clear and loud voice: 'Yes, Sir, that is clear!' Is that clear."

"Yes, Sir."

"Is that clear!"

"Yes, Sir, that is clear."

The Sergeant handed the small dog to Recruit Duncan. "In one minute you will give this puppy to the person on your left who will do the same. Then hand it to the next until each recruit has held this dog for one minute. The last one brings it back to me. Is that clear?"

"Yes, Sir. That is clear."

Recruit Duncan stepped back into her line cuddling the pup. Sergeant Primrose continued to outline the duties of her new charge, explained the locations of the washrooms, the mess hall, the meal times and other details of institutional submission. Finally I, being the last one in line, returned the dog to the drill instructor where it sat quietly on the ground beside her polished boots.

The Sergeant continued: "We are a modern peacekeeping unit and we have a long history of humane treatment of our recruits. For example, whoever steps out of line will no longer be punished with extra duty or other disciplines. Instead, she will take the dog into the puppy trauma room behind the mess hall where she will find a long whip." Pause. "A HORSEWHIP." She spit out the syllables as if she was now whipping that horse's ass personally, then waited five seconds to measure the impact and came to the point: "And with this HORSEWHIP she will dole out as many lashes to the dog as the charge calls for. Here are some of the penalties: failing to get out of the sack in the morning within ten seconds of the bugle call: three lashes on the dog. Disobeying a direct order during training: six lashes on the dog. Cowardice during peacekeeping duties: you will have to strangle the pup personally with your bare hands until it is dead. As the dog grows up and becomes more ferocious, so will your physical strength. Is that clear?" Barely concealed grumbling from the group.

"Is that clear?" She was now on attack.

"Yes, Sir, that is clear."

"Louder. Is that clear?" So ended drill number one and I wondered if I had made the right decision.

✳   ✳   ✳

Nobody had tipped me off that there was no furlough for the first four weeks of military service. When I finally held my day pass in hand, the allocated time was between twelve noon and seventeen hundred hours exactly, and those are banking hours during which I could not communicate with Bernie. I took the base bus into town, but neither Ted nor Melmoth nor Professor Klonus were to be found anywhere, nor did I want to see the pawnbroker and most certainly not Dr. Borelli or Miss Hanna. In passing by the old Hertha Pavilion I watched for a while as the work crew hoisted the heavy 'Hall' part of the huge sign into position, the 'piegel' and the 'Eulens' sections of it still lying under wraps on the truck bed. The building looked good, larger than I had thought, but suddenly I felt strangely out of the loop. Events had passed me by and nobody asked for my opinion any more. Finally I decided to get into my old office, see Miss Pennsinger at Talents Management to find out what's going on, but she was in a meeting with Mr. Busby from the dancing school and several other people I had never heard of before.

"Where's my office?" Lauris filled me in: he had divided my cubicle, installed himself in one section and put someone else in the other. "But we kept all your data," he added cheerfully. "Just in case. Are you coming back?" The scent was Chanel 49 Spray; I was certain.

I returned to the base an hour ahead of time. The army had assigned me a four-bed dorm behind the power transformers, which hummed all night, but I was the only occupant. Things are not going well. It was now clear that Bernie had stiffed me. She was probably recruiting other suckers and dish out little favours here and there, up and down and clean around. Damn women!

And what about Eulenspiegel Hall? I had, in some fashion at least, always thought that I was the guiding light behind all this. Now I had to find out that there was no longer a need for an idea man, that my suggestions had long been appropriated by professionals in the field, and that the Professor could get along very well without me, thank you. I could see it clearly now: I was out of a job. Damn women.

Not just that, I was out of friends! Everyone I knew had a role, a target, a berth. Everybody was busy being happy, productive, important. I had touched the lives of so many people and they all profited from me, all of them but I now had nothing for myself. Now I was in the army, stripped of all dignity and self-esteem and unable to just walk away from it all. I felt like punching Sergeant

Primrose right in her obnoxious face, punch her with all the anger I had bottled up - and hang the consequences. And then I would take that white pup, take it into its trauma room - oh, what a word! - and strangle it with my bare hands until it stopped quivering. Damn women.

There was a special section on the base, the Family Consultation Facility as it was officially called; it dealt mostly with PMS and split ends. Nobody could console the only male on the post who had the blues: me. I suddenly found myself alone in the world, forgotten, dishonoured, rejected, abandoned. Discounted merchandise left over from a Boxing Day sale. Tomorrow starts the training on actual tanks and I was to become a gun loader. Women will learn to drive, reconnoitre, command; they will decide on strategy, procedure, action. And where am I? I will sit in that cramped hole down in the bottom of the tank, see nothing, hear nothing, do nothing but stick shells into the breach of a gun which somebody else will aim and fire. Damn women.

I was dog-tired but could not fall asleep until early next morning, and then I nearly overslept as the canned bugle blasted reveille from the loudspeakers.

✳   ✳   ✳

"Recruit Parker, to the commandant's office," blared the outdoor bullhorns. I dropped a track link and straightened up. "Recruit Parker, to the commandant's office. On the double."

It was only a hundred and fifty yards but it gave me time enough to wonder what I might have done to be called into the commando zone. Nobody had ever gone in and come out looking the same. It could only be one of two things: I was to be reprimanded for who-knows-what, in which case I might be asked to take that snow white Samoyed...

I would flatly refuse, and to hell with the penalty. They could do no more than throw me in the stockade and eventually give me a dishonourable discharge. Or I was being canned for health issues or some other specious reason. Only three weeks ago a recruit was discharged after they discovered that she was a practising Catholic.

The desk sergeant merely moved her head in the direction of the commandant's office, and when I entered and stood at attention, Colonel Bernadette Robinson got up from her seat behind her desk, kicked the door shut, put her arms around me and kissed me squarely on the mouth. "I have good news for both of us."

She then went back behind her desk. "Recruit Parker, at ease. And sit down. Sit! I managed to snare this assignment for myself, so that's why I'm on duty right now. We have a five-day window and imagine what I have arranged for both of us."

I sat stiffly upright on the visitor's chair, uncertain as how to act or what to say.

"This is your last week in the service and I see here in your two-oh-one file that you have been doing well. This assignment is for volunteers only and I trust that you will…"

I interrupted her. To hell with the whole damn army and everything, I shouted at her. Look at my hands! The blisters, the scratches. The broken fingernails, the cuts and bruises. And don't wink me off like that. I've done every damn thing you people ordered me to do, and if you court martial me for insubordination, to hell with all of you, to hell with the army and to hell with the City of Crosley.

"My, my, the language! I had expected to hear 'I love you' or some such endearments. Here I am, planning an adventure for us, looking forward to next week when we can both be civilians again, and all I hear from you are complaints. Relax! That's an order."

I told her what the drill sergeant had planned for the white puppy, but Bernie only laughed.

"So it's a white puppy now, is it?" she laughed. "Couple of months ago it was a little Persian kitten and the microwave." There is no trauma room, she insisted, no horsewhip, nothing of the sort. That's just Primmie's way of getting attention. There had never been an animal hurt or killed or harmed in any way. We have two cats, a goat, two rabbits, a budgie and now this puppy, she claimed, and they are all happy and healthy and spoiled rotten. Did I really think for a moment she would send me into trouble?

"Colonel… Do I address you as Colonel?"

She smiled and it was this innocent, childlike face, which had attracted me way back when I first saw her at the initial meeting. How long ago that was.

"The door is safely shut. You can call me Bernie, or just 'Darling'. This is private now. For the last time, relax."

I felt somewhat relieved. Of course, she meant no harm to come to me. After all, we were lovers now, weren't we? Well, weren't we?

"These Hutterites," she started as her subordinate served some coffee, "we love them. We love their kids, even if they are weird and dress funny. But there are still pockets of resistance hidden deep inside their innermost power structure. Paramilitary groups which want to fight us. You had your headache with Vesper, so you know. Or take the Mennonites. Just because they still use horse-drawn buggies doesn't mean they can't be outright dangerous. How dangerous, you ask? I'll tell you how dangerous. For instance, they refuse to pay their taxes. They use our highways, but they refuse to pay the silicon tax. We don't even force them to buy the gas but just the tax on what they would have used on machines instead of horses. Pay up as if they were regular people like the rest of us."

"Well, if they don't use gas, why should they..."

"Tony, Darling. Those metal-rimmed wheels can really chew up the gravel roads. They leave ruts which have to be filled. With what, you ask. With tar and gravel. Sticky tar and hard, crunchy bits of silicon, Tony. Grey, rock-hard silicon."

Bernie let the words sink in, took a sip of coffee, then continued. "These people are a nuisance on the highway, if you ask me, always driving on the soft shoulders which have to be kept in serviceable condition. But do they pay their fair share? Oh no, they don't. So, once in awhile we go in and we re-educate them; show them our loving and reasonable ways; explain to them their civil duties and obligations; teach them basic math. We do that with lots of charm and dignity. We go by the book, you know. We may sort of accidentally run over a barn here and there, but we always make sure that there are no children inside, especially females under ten. That would give us a bad press. Should that ever happen, that's would be unfortunate collateral damage and can't be helped. Now, does that sound like cruelty to you?"

She was certain that her explanation would allay my panic. I was somewhat more at ease now, so we both just stirred our coffee again before she carried on.

"The Hutterites are a different problem. They make lots of money from their land but they never pay Rural Development Fees as per schedule. They claim they develop their land themselves, they even maintain their own roads which connect with public highways. As if that would make any difference. No RDF they say. They obviously don't want peace. And all of them, the Hutterites, the Amish, the Mennonites, they all sing in German. Now, don't tell me that they don't exchange secret messages that way, or not incite their members to who knows what kind of conspiracies. I tell you, Tony, these people need to be constantly liberated."

We stirred our coffee once more; I cleared my throat. "Why not just leave them alone?"

"Tony, Tony. my dear friend, what would happen if we just turned away from their problems - ignored their plight? We have a moral duty to come to their rescue. Do you know what these people eat? They eat only what they grow themselves, what comes off their land for which they haven't even paid their RDF. No trace of culinary adventure. They cook their own instead of going out for a McFraser. We tried and tried. Where would the global economy go if we'd just look after ourselves instead of helping our fellow citizen? Just a year ago we built these highly decorated McFraser Spud Mobiles which we dispatched to their colonies. We offered them deep-fried turnips with pumpkin pie and a free diet cola float, and you know what they did to us? They let out this big Black Lab, you know, one of these huge dogs. The ones with those big teeth. And they were probably trained to intimidate us. Do you know what they did? These dogs, I mean? They pissed on the Spud Mobile's wheels. There, now I said it. The indignity of it. Does that look as if they'd love us?"

"Why do we need to be loved in the first place?"

The Colonel ignored my question. "Not so long ago there was this Operation Tenderness. We went all the way out, bought them DVD players, HDTV sets, satellite dishes, distribution amplifiers, even Readdimaker's Popcorn for the microwave. We hired experts and installed it all for them in their mess halls, even supplied them with free - mind you, free! - movies such as 'Sex in the Country', 'Queer and Happy' and 'The Pregnant Nun', all of them with German subtitles. Do you know what they did with all this?"

I ventured a guess. "They trashed it?"

"How did you know? You are uncanny. Yes, they did. We come as friends and that's how they treat us." The fire seemed to go out of the Colonel and we quietly continued to slurp our coffee before she carried on.

"I have a plan but you must never tell anybody." She laid out her strategy to raid a farm for the RDF back taxes in the form of three hundred and eighty-four fattened geese. The goose transport truck was already fitted out, the G-snatchers had been issued their bolas and the SPCA was standing by in case there should be undue feather loss during the liberation campaign. Why me, I wanted to know.

"Darling, that's a good question. This is a voluntary action, as you know. We started off with five likely candidates; however one of them was marginal so that left us only four active bodies. Of these, three showed real promise because they had two good contenders between them. You won."

"A Pyrrhic victory."

"My Dear, there are many kinds of victory and they are all glorious and sweet, even if the booty is small."

At the end Colonel B. H. Robinson agreed that I would be granted twenty-four hours to decide if I would volunteer for this peacekeeping glory or regretfully decline the privilege. I would still get my honourable discharge, but no medal. And, implied, no amorous dalliance either.

CHAPTER TWENTY-TWO

Ted looked up from his job. "You're off your rocker." He raised the flap of his welding guard, wiped the sweat from his brow with his sleeve, put down the long-handled tongues and moistened his cracked lips. "Is that dame really worth all that much? If it's just a matter of getting a chick into your sack, even I can line up something for you. What do you need? Another redhead?" Something else must have been irritating him to speak in such rude manner. Perhaps he can't handle the pressure now, which is drowning him in toil and sweat.

"That's not the point. The assignment is a short deployment, one day only and perhaps we really have to liberate those people. They are still terribly religious, you know."

"Tony, you are such an imbecile. Do you actually believe all this shit? The Hutterites are happy just huttering. You can't break up their - their... What is it this time? Piglets again?"

"Geese, but I'm not supposed to tell anyone."

"We do that nearly every year and it really pisses them off. Did you know they closed their farmers' market? Used to be that you could get their apples and cherries and all their wonderful butchered meat and that out-of-this-world Westphalian smoked ham at their market. It was lean and completely organic. You know what they do now? They freeze it and they package it under the Saint Augustine brand name and it goes straight into the boxcars and off to the export brokers. They are mighty tired of getting jerked around by us and I don't blame them one bit."

What I really wanted to hear was some encouragement, but Ted was no help at all. Melmoth showed a bit more sympathy. "My dear boy, war is not what I do well myself. I am actually quite useless to society, if you want to be pedantic about it, but war is even further from my mind than another visit to Paris."

"What's wrong with Paris?"

"I don't like their wallpaper. Of course this is a war of sorts. Don't get sucked in by this liberation farce. It's a trumped-up thing just so we can bully somebody around again. We, that is the City of Crosley, we are bigger than they, but do we ever stop and reflect for a moment what we are stirring up? Why do you think some bridge suddenly falls down every time after we have stolen the Hutterites' pigs?"

"It's geese."

"Let's face it, it's Bernie plain and simple, isn't it? This whole thing is testosterone-driven. I know what you are going through, just take my word for it."

"Were you ever in love with her?"

Melmoth evaded the question. "If you really must roll Bernie in the hay, go ahead and steal pigs."

"Geese."

And that's as far as it went with Melmoth. There was no use in calling either Max or Miss Hanna as both of them clearly did not want to hear from me, but my luck held out when I found the Professor in his headquarters. "How come I have not seen you for such a long time," he wanted to know. When I filled in all the details the Professor was pensive.

"Let me tell you a little story about stealing geese. I heard it from someone who's parents were very poor. Their house was small; they only had one cow, two horses, four pigs and five beautiful white geese which were trained to guard their property. Almost within reach of their front door was this one great, big old linden tree growing on the square next to them. The tree was more than a hundred years old and had a big, wide bench all around where many would gather in those warm summer evenings and smoke their pipe, drink cider and talk. One day some vagabonds came and asked to stay in their barn overnight. The parents agreed, and so these strangers settled in; first only the one family, then came another wagon, and then three more. Soon the barn was filled with many, and they ate and made music on all their fiddles and lutes and things they had, and they sang in wonderful harmony even though nobody could understand their language. They danced and laughed and were very happy, and all the people sitting on the bench around the tree got up and danced and many more villagers came to take part, and in the end all sang together and had a wonderful time under the full moon. The next morning the vagabonds were gone, and so was one of the geese. The little boy's father was very angry. He wanted to saddle up and go after the thieves, but his wife said: 'My dear husband, is all the happiness these people had brought to us last night not worth one old goose? Just leave them be, let them enjoy it and hope that some day they may come back.' And it was at that moment that the five year old boy learned the difference between stealing and collecting what was morally due to them, because they had entertained a whole village and asked for nothing in return, except for only one tough old goose."

The Professor stopped as if his mind was entangled in some childhood memories. Finally I broke the spell: "Does that mean I should help collecting the RDF?"

"What, what? - Son, I cannot answer your question with a 'yes' or a 'no', you must do that for yourself. Should the Hutterites pay those taxes in the first place? After all, they use our roads, our water out of the river, our city and our markets. Are we so poor and destitute that we must collect their hard-earned money? This will only make the farmers increase the price of what they grow for us and in the end we all have to pay the taxes as they are hidden in the cost of the food we eat. Or are we merely harassing these people because they are different from us? You must figure this out all on your own. But it's the woman, right? The redhead army commander. The one who's also the big shot in that bank. I tried to get some money out of her once but she's as hard as flint stone. How can you possibly have a thing for her?"

I felt that my commanding officer was under attack by my employer, and that slowly made me angry. "How come I'm no longer part of your organisation? My desk is gone, my cubicle is divided up between strangers, nobody asks me any questions. Why have I been pushed into the sidelines? The army wants me to do something. I don't give a damn what it is, but they find me useful, they need my help, they ask for my input and here in your damn outfit I am nothing. Nobody gives a shit any more." I was really steamed up.

That said I walked to the small fridge, reached for two cans of beer, threw one to the Professor and opened the other for myself which I emptied in one long thirsty draw.

The Professor looked at me with big, round eyes and said nothing for a long time. He gingerly opened his own can, poured the content into a tumbler and slowly took a couple of tiny sips. Finally he spoke up again, quietly hiding his exasperation.

"Tony, my young friend. You see me fooling the people, take money from them for some of my silly little acts, and you think I am ripping them off. Right? Yes, I do. But I not only entertain them, I try and make them think of me, an old confidence trickster, a harmless old man who swindles them out of a few loonies. But when they go next day and buy a car or a house or just a new suit they will think 'does that salesman there swindle me like the old professor did?' Hm? When I do this ridiculous balloon thing with the pennies, nobody comes right out and says 'Hey, you old geyser, you ripped me off". They are too proud to admit that a little old man with a pouch has bamboozled them, a guy who's almost bald and not even speaking English very good. They say nothing and maybe they think there must be great wisdom behind all that, how else would everybody spend so much money on it. But it's like the emperor's new clothes. Nobody wants to be first to speak up. After that they think maybe they have been deceived. Right? Did you not think that yourself? And when you walked away from my lecture, what did you do next?"

"I saw Mister Melmoth."

"Ah yes, your friend the poet. He is a very wise man, this poet. Then when he asked you - I am absolutely certain that he asked you. When he asked you if my lecture had changed you, what did you say?"

"I told him I had become a sceptic."

Professor Klonus drew a long gulp out of the glass. "You became a sceptic. That is all I wanted from you, and that is exactly what became of you. Many refuse to become sceptics for some idolised reasons for which they must suffer all their lives. Most others must buy scepticism on the open market for which they pay huge sums, sometimes their entire life's savings. They are victims of romance, superstition and advertising. Don't underrate the power of slogans, especially the patriotic variety. Salute the flag and walk straight into battle only to be killed. That makes you worthless to yourself, to the society you live in, even worthless to your own ideals because you are much too dead to have any. You paid how much for my lecture?"

"Fifty loonies, but your chauffeur paid it back"

"In the long run you will save fifty thousand. And, don't forget, you were also entertained."

"So, what has that got to do with stealing pigs? Geese?"

"Everything. You collect if it is yours; you leave it if it is not. Unless, of course, it had entertainment or philosophical or utilitarian value. That's all. Now go and figure it out yourself."

Ahasverus, the pawnbroker, had a different angle. "Young lad," he said in the back room over a glass of steaming tea, "theft can be just another form of wealth redistribution. Don't we steal every day in a thousand different ways? Taking from the rich to give to the poorer, especially if you are one of the poor, is no sin. Of course, it is against the law, but the law has been made up by the powerful to protect themselves. But to steal from the poor and give to the rich is a sin. That's called capitalism and is legal."

The telephone rang in the shop and Ahasverus answered it out of earshot. When he returned his face glistened with radiant joy. "Such coincidence. Do you remember that Missis Kimmelbaum, the old woman with the gold watch? I have just now received news from Beijing and it was a Glasshütte after all, just as I had suspected. It brought in eleven thousand loonies. That leaves that dear old woman..." His fingers tapped the calculator, "...seven thousand seven hundred and thirty loonies and seventy-five cents. If I were poor I might be tempted to shave another thousand off and slip it into my own pocket. I would be a thousand loonies richer and she would still be just as happy although, unknown to her, I would have stolen her money. Would I not have provided a superior service for my charge? As the money goes through my hands I should entitle myself to take a handful each time I see the coins rolling past my nose. That's just what the bank does. Of course, now that I am a fairly prosperous man myself that would be theft, plain and simple. Instead I will give that dear old woman every cent she deserves, exact to the penny. Guess why."

I ventured a notion. "Because you are honourable?"

"Because I can afford the luxury of it. This is the greatest indulgence your money can buy. It's such a pity that the greedy have never discovered this simple truth. Chasing wealth is a race to the bottom. You must excuse me, I have this urgent call to make."

Again he vanished into his store and I strained my ears to catch some one-sided fragments of the dialogue. "... sitting down? ... and yes, in about three or four days... and seventy-five cents..."

When he returned he deeply inhaled the aroma of the tea. "Please be still for just one minute." He leaned back, closed his eyes and smiled. When he opened them again he softly added: "That, my lad, was a thousand-loonie smile. Such a bargain."

CHAPTER TWENTY-THREE

E vents progressed at such breakneck speed that I later had difficulties remembering everything in detail. Two tanks were lined up, together with one multi-level goose transporter, a self-propelled fowl harvester the size of a combine, two Hummers with enormous bullhorns affixed to their roofs and an ambulance on tires from two different manufacturers. Aside stood a troop carrier loaded with twelve female soldiers with grim faces, in full battle dress and armed to the teeth; all in all twenty-six women and one man - me. We jumped off and lined up smartly in front of our commanding officer, Colonel Bernadette H. Robinson, who addressed her combat forces.

"Women…" She looked around, caught sight of me at the very end of the line, then added: "…and man. This is not a raid. We are going to liberate our brothers. They have never enjoyed a moment of unbridled liberty in their lives. We shall come as strangers and we shall leave as friends, and anybody who thinks differently is disqualified to join us on this mission. Is that understood?"

"Yes, Sir, Colonel Robinson." A resounding approval of her battle-painted fighting troops.

"This Hutterite cell, called the Dariusleut, has fallen behind their RDFs and we shall go in and help with the bookkeeping." She paused and waited for polite giggles. "Unless under direct assault by insurgent stone throwers we will not fire our weapons. We brought grenade launchers, machine guns, artillery shells, flame throwers and rifles loaded with gummy bears, but these are only show pieces. We will not fire any of them unless we are forced to fight for our lives or until so ordered by me personally. Especially the flame throwers will be handled with utmost care as there is usually much combustible material around. Is that clear?"

"Yes, Sir, Colonel Robinson."

There was a one-minute pause as she looked into every warrior's eyes, double portion for me. Now comes the devotional part. "We are all volunteers," she finally continued, stirring the patriotic mood. "We are fully aware what that means. Our peace-consulting duties lie in the disputed Vesper Area of Political Interest. It means that some of us may never return to our mothers and fathers again, to our sweethearts of either gender, to all the people we so dearly love." Her tone now had a solemn timbre while her eyes seemed to alternately search for distinct pebbles on the ground or phantoms in the clouds. "It means that she will be left out on the lonely, wind-swept battlefield, dead, stiff and cold, and with only black ravens as her chattering companions." From the ranks of her commandos came one lonely muffled sob. "You will not have given your young life in vain. You'll die knowing that you may have saved one person or more from fanaticism and bondage, that you have helped to break the mould which has for hundreds of years held these primitives in enslavement and servitude. You will know that you have paid the highest price, your own life, for the highest goal, namely democracy for all, under the benign umbrella of the highest moral authority, The Global Federation of Bata. Let us go in boldly and raise our flag. Rah, rah, rah."

"Rah, rah, rah," echoed the chorus.

"We will collect three hundred and eighty seven geese, three of which will be appropriated for our own consumption, the rest of them to be handed over to the City of Crosley for further processing. We will now have a weapons check. Take your positions!"

The troops scurried back to their vehicles, swiftly moved behind the steering wheels, the machine guns and flame-throwers and into their appointed stations inside the Tiger Fives. When the dust had settled, the Colonel commanded through her megaphone: "Let me hear the recorded battle hymn, the German version first."

Hummer number one, the vehicle with the semi-German slogan 'Wir sint Eure Fraind und Bruder' peppered on the side banners was the first in line. The bullhorn blared 'Üb' immer Treu und Redlichkeit, bis in dein kühles Grab,' sung slightly off-key, Hawaiian style with delicate Japanese accent.

The colonel winked off. "Now the English version." Hummer number two wrapped in the translated slogan 'We are Your Friends and Brothers' now blared out the approximate version for those intransigent Dariusleut who pretend to know only German but secretly watch TV and are fluent in English: 'Serve always faith and honesty until you're in your grave.' The singer was the same and obviously did his lick phonetically. The commander was satisfied. She climbed into her tank, donned her Kevlar helmet, raised her hand, commanded "Forward, roll" and pulled the bio-proofed goggles over her eyes. Our commando rumbled off Wal-Mart's parking lot and onto the highway.

※   ※   ※

It was 11:49 hours when we arrived. Half a mile in front of us lay the farm buildings in tan and red and white, embedded in a huge orchard nestled against the mountain range in the backdrop. There was no sign of life anywhere except for the fifteen cows in the nearby pasture craning their necks to study the invaders. Our desert armada came to a full stop and we let the dust settle in its wake.

At 12:03 hours the colonel dispatched five scouts who threw themselves bodily into the gravel road and crawled forward towards the enemy, one pebble at a time. At 13:17 they returned, reporting: "We heard singing." - "In German?" - "Yes Sir, in German." - "I suspected as much." Bernie shook her head with sadness.

At 13:28 hours the Hummers cagily moved forward, followed in safe distance by the rest of the invasion forces. We stopped within a hundred yards, then shut off the engines and observed absolute silence. At 13:39 we turned on our PA systems and played the battle hymn through the bullhorns, first in German, then in English. A boy peeked out of the mess hall door and quickly vanished again. I could see nothing at all from the bowels of the tank, but Bernie gave us a running description over the intercom.

At 13:47 two men emerged, one with a long white beard wearing a baseball cap, the younger one clean-shaven and under an

- 153 -

enormous black Stetson. They walked right up to the tank with the Colonel sticking out. "Yes," the beard said, "can we help you?"

"We came to liberate you and to collect the RDF. We are your friends and we bring peace, good will to all and a stack of application forms for those of you who wish to be liberated and join our benevolent community, the City of Crosley."

The Beard and the Stetson held a small conference. At 13:53 they had reached a reply. "What is RDF?"

"That is the Rural Development Fee which, according to our city bylaws number eleven forty-nine, applies to those agricultural units which show an annual profit."

Beard and Stetson held another conference. "We have a contract with Vesper," the beard said. "We pay them."

"But the Vesperians are eye rollers. Do you want to unite with those?"

"We have no cash money here."

"In that case we shall collect your geese."

"How much money do you need?"

"We want four thousand and eight loonies, in cash or credit card."

"Ach du liebe Güte, das ist too much. No credit cards. Our money is held at the bank in Vesper. You came at the wrong time. This is not the goose season. There are fourteen geese for breeding stock only. We are now into smoked ham, sausages and cheese."

"When do you have geese?"

"Come back in December. You want apple cider? Very good, very powerful. Then come back in October. Are you hungry? We have enough food for all of you."

"We are the liberation forces. We cannot fraternise with you."

Now the Stetson spoke up. "Ve haf much good bratwurst und yellow potatoes und ve make our own beer that is very strong. Ja?"

"We came for the taxes or your geese."

"Will you take some cows instead," the beard asked.

"You owe the City of Crosley four thousand and eight loonies."

"Take six cows and a good bull then."

I could hear the Colonel's exasperation in my headphone. "Damn Army Secret Intelligence again. Can't we talk this over?"

"Come down from there, come in and take a rest; all of you. Then maybe we talk."

At exactly 14:01 hours the communal mess hall was cleared of all Hutterites, and instead one army commander, twenty-six soldiers, female, entered, sat down and ate bratwurst mit brot und bier. I, as the lone male, was segregated and had to sit by myself at a long table on the other side but I was served more of everything, especially home-brew.

✳   ✳   ✳

It must have been around three PM or thereabouts - nobody recorded the exact time - when the conference began. For this purpose the negotiators settled at the Mannestisch, the men's table where I still nursed my beer; first the Beard, next to him the Stetson and next to him two men in porkpie hats who never spoke a word out loud. Included was also Bernie, or, if I have to use her proper address, Colonel Robinson, having been promoted to temporary male status on account of her military rank. The topic of discussion returned to the shortfall in RDF moneys. "How much cash do you have," Bernie asked the Beard. He in turn asked the Stetson who asked porkpie number one who whispered to porkpie number two who was the treasurer. Porkpie number two whispered the answer to porkpie number one who whispered to the Stetson, the Stetson to the Beard. "Two hundred fifteen and some coins," he replied.

"Not nearly enough," Bernie said. "Is this all the money you have in this commune?"

This question was relayed again down the line to the treasurer; however, the answer came back in four staggered nods. Yes.

"Do any of your members have cash money on hand," was her next question. This time the answer came back in quadruple shoulder shrugs.

"Can you get at your money in the Bank?"

"Oh no," Beard answered without first going through the vetting process. "It's all invested in Vatican Airlines."

I suggested addressing the people over the intercom regarding anybody's contraband loose cash, which then was promptly done.

All eighty-nine adults over the age of thirteen were assembled in the mess hall where they emptied their pockets and shoeboxes. This added another seventy-three loonies.

Still not enough. Porkpies, Stetson, Beard and Bernie looked expectantly at me, hoping that I might be able to come up with a better solution. Would the courageous and fearless soldiers be interested in emptying their own pockets of all cash, I allowed myself to query.

Next the soldiers who were still sitting at their Frauentisch, the women's table, cleaned out their own pockets as well and the total on the table now stood at one thousand and thirteen loonies.

"We are still short nearly three thousand loonies," Bernie intoned sternly after consulting her calculator.

"That's a lot of loonies," the Stetson said. "Now vhat do ve do?"

A boy came running into the mess hall. "Telephone for the leader. Come with me, in the Schreibstube."

I followed Bernie to the commune's office which was just around the corner of the mess hall and turned out to be an amazingly modern facility with fully integrated electronics and communication devices, including a two-way satellite hook-up. "General Nellie Smith of the Vesper Liberation Forces here," the husky, gin-soaked voice at the other end of the wire intoned.

"Commander Colonel Robinson of the Crosley Freedom Fighters here. What can I do for you, General?"

"If you don't pull your god-damned Tinker Toys out of that Hutterite farm within ten minutes I shall dispatch two of my gun ships and wipe out the whole bloody lot of you. Is that understood?"

"Do you imply an armed retaliatory thread, General?" She put her hand over the mouthpiece, whispering to me: "The bitch is probably soused again."

"If you don't get your ass out of there immediately, I'll come over personally, and this time I wouldn't just shoot over your heads. Is that understood?"

"You know as well as I do, General, that this is disputed territory which the adjudication committee..."

"Shit, don't talk to me about the adjudication committee. They are nothing but a bunch of thugs. I said get the hell out of there or I'm on my way. End of message." Click.

"I've run into her before," Bernie said pensively as she hung up the phone. "She means it."

Back in the mess hall the money lay untouched on the table, all staring at the mound of loonies. "General Smith and I had an affable discussion," Bernie fibbed, "and we both agreed that we must come to a quick decision." The messenger boy reappeared and handed Bernie a small floppy. "Copy of the transcript in MP3," he said, upon which she hastily slipped it into one of her fourteen army battle dress pockets.

How to make up the shortfall?

The four wise men of the colony got up, moved out of earshot and stuck their heads together. After a long, wasteful four-minute conference they returned. Beard spoke up again: "We will pray."

"Soldiers," Bernie addressed her troops, "at your battle stations." The Amazons who had respectfully remained in the background and now fortified and lubricated scurried through the door and into their vehicles. Turning towards the four wise men Bernie sternly advised them: "We will take this money, apply it to your outstanding RDF charges, and trash your hen house with our tanks. This action of charitable compensation will be carried out under the provisions of the Crosley Military Peace Accords, section B13, paragraph nine, which states the terms for abrogated dignified negotiations. Please, assure that no female children are hiding inside, as they may get crushed by our Tiger Fives."

Now it was high time for my intervention. "Hold it," I said. "This is insane. Here is my credit card. Put the whole lot on it, and return that money there from where it came." It was, after all, the Professor's money, and if my credit card gets accepted, then so be it.

"Gott hat uns erhört," said the beard, comforted that their as yet unspoken prayers had already worked.

The funds were transferred via satellite from the Sovereign Bank of Crosley to the account of the Hutterite colony in the International Bank of Vesper, and from there again to the Treasurer of the City of Crosley. A soldier reported breathlessly that two gun ships of the Vesper Liberation Forces were approaching. As Bernie and I ran towards, reached and climbed into our tank, we could already spot them coming over the mountains and out of the blazing afternoon sun.

The land was flat, the orchard offered scant shelter and there was no place to run to and hide. Commander Bernie, being a person of great courage and short temper, ordered her driver to aim straight for the barn, crashing through the closed doors, over the rutabaga shredder, the cream separator and into the milking machine. The second Tiger Five followed within seconds, then came the two Hummers, the ambulance and the goose transporter. Only the fowl-picker the size of a combine didn't make it in time. It got wasted on the second and third airborne attacks, well after its crew had rapidly evacuated their contrivance. That done, the choppers left as quickly as they had appeared.

Everybody spent the next hours to help and clean up the mess. The damage to the barn and farm implements was quickly settled. The City of Crosley paid compensation to the Hutterite community in the amount of nearly four thousand loonies in addition to the full return of the RDF. The goose picker was abandoned as unsalvageable in front of the outhouses where it had been shredded by the gun ships. Soon the night tip-toed in and the Crosley Liberation Forces rolled into the headlight-illuminated dust cloud of our convoy after leaving behind a stack of application forms for all those who wished to be liberated and join the democratic community of the City of Crosley.

Colonel Robinson got on the inter-municipal battle phone and called General Smith. "I get you for this, Nellie," she shouted loud enough for me to hear in my earphones and over the engine and track noise of the rolling tank. "You have my solemn oath, I get you for this."

"Fuck you, Bernie," the General replied with hoarse laughter because she grew up an orphan and had no manners.

CHAPTER TWENTY-FOUR

The story was all over the local newspapers the next day. There were staged pictures under headline banners which, depending on political persuasion, read either 'Commander Abandons Battlefield' or 'Peacekeepers Fight to Last Bullet'. Stand-up comics had new gigs along the lines of 'something funny happened on our way to the goose farm,' Heineken International News transmitted a re-enactment on Global TV and T-shirt manufacturers increased their exports manifold by cartooning what everybody perceived as great military embarrassment. Vesper officially named a doggie poop park in their city the Nellie Smith Canine Relief Range which soon became known in common parlance as the Smith Shitter. In twenty-four hours the whole incident was forgotten, replaced by a subway hijack in a city nobody had ever heard of and no newscaster could pronounce.

Tranquillity returned, except for Colonel Bernadette H. Robinson who, having had her fifteen minutes of fame, was busted back to Captain. The Sovereign Bank of Crosley took her off the management development list and transferred her to the subterranean mimeograph department. I completed my six-week stint in the army with this footnote in my two-oh-one dossier: 'Embezzled funds from employer to pay delinquent tax of rural religious community'.

The worst part came about a week after the event when, in a misguided effort of reconciliation, I appeared at Bernie's condo, box of white ersatz chocolate Tiger Fives in hand. My hopes for rapprochement were quickly dashed as she flung the box in my face, stomped on all twelve miniatures in their plastic cradles and assaulted me with vociferous language the likes of which I had not only never heard before but would not have expected to come from between the sweet lips of such young Quaker-educated lady.

✳   ✳   ✳

Eulenspiegel Hall was coming close to its completion date. The work crew fitted row on row of seating and technicians installed rooftop parabolic dish antennas. Delivery vans opened their cornucopias and disgorged boxes of wonderful gadgets and gimmicks, souvenirs and picture postcards, fridge magnets and underarm deodorants, shoe horns, tambourines and millions of paper match books with application forms printed on the inside to join the Eulenspiegel Social Club at a one-time 45% discount. I oversaw much of the final preparations only to notice that practically all of my original ideas had vanished somewhere in the morass of organisational efficiency. Somebody had turned the sex liberation theme into a slim picture-loaded booklet titled The Eulen Sutra which did not require the athletic contortions as prescribed in the original version but which instead suggested even greater pleasures yet for far less effort. I had the numb feeling that my primary objectives had been warped out of recognition.

"He never wore those," the Professor remarked as he stepped out of the shadows, pointing at Eulenspiegel's polychrome fool's cap on the booklet's cover. "He never advertised his arrival beforehand, he always showed up when absolutely nobody expected him. Just look at that ghastly picture! Three disgustingly noisy little brass bells - how undignified."

"How do you know all this?" I asked.

The Professor didn't answer. "But look here!" he called out, holding up a pair of miniature nickel-plated die-cast zinc Eulenspiegel boots of uncommon ugliness. "Salt's in the left one, pepper in the right. Of course, he never wore fancy boots like this but one can't get a lot of salt into a loafer."

"What happened to all our lofty ideas, our issues of unbridled lust, our new moralities? We were to have new ideological fads, break the old mould of uniformity and stagnation. What happened?" I was crushed but tried not to let on.

Professor Klonus sat down on a crate of Eulen Chewies. "This is where the idealist meets the public fairground. Do you think any of this had escaped me? What we have worked out on paper still goes, but we have to slip in the message unnoticed, undercover so to speak. You get from here to there in very thin slices, not in thick jaw-breaking slabs. First you must entertain the public. You have to reintroduce them to laughter and joviality. Then, and only when they are disarmed, only then can you begin to slip in your message. That's their moment of vulnerability when they have an open heart, an open mind, an open wallet. Oh, you have a lot to learn yet. Do you know how democracy evolved? No, not from parliaments. It came from the fairground, from the Punch-and-Judy show, that's where. The Prince of Darkness - did he not wear a paper crown and had a nose just like the king's? Liberating thoughts never emerged from the pulpit or out of the mouths of politicians and ministers. The people speak from behind the black curtain of the Kasperle Theatre."

I wondered out loud what his own presentation would be.

"That, my friend, is still a deep secret. I trust Mister Melmoth is on top of it, yet I have not heard from him in a very long time. Is he actually working? Do me the favour and find out." He tore open a pouch of Eulen Chips and tasted one. "Phooey, garlic."

Melmoth was wary to see me. "So much happened! They had your name in the papers, and of course Bernie's. But have you read this?" He handed me the front page of the Vesper Herald. Accident at Ammo Dump the headlines read on page three The picture of a huge bomb crater accompanied the story which gave details of the old but now destroyed armoury in the rival city and sketches of the apartment blocks which may replace it. Page five had the actual interview with the commanding officer, General N. Smith, which rambled on about safety being the first order of the day, and stored ammunition can be so volatile. And no, there are no suspects yet, but - and here I had to read the sentence again and again: '...but if we ever find out what caused it, I'll kill the bitch.'

I changed the topic. "How's the program for the Professor coming along?"

"Oh, get off my back, will you? It's all in my mind. I only have to put the words on paper. The rest is crystal clear. Tell him it's coming along fine."

Bernie could not be located by phone, neither at the bank nor at her home, nor even at her army post. Answers were evasive, improvised, so we both decided to go and find out personally what happened. First to her place which had a For Rent sign rammed into the manicured lawn.

The army headquarters were usually off-limits to non-military personnel, but Admiral So-and-so made an exception. "She has resigned her commission," she said, playing with the gold tassels of her epaulets. "Out of the blue, she threw down her whatchamacallit things..."

"Bars," I assisted.

"...her bars, said 'I'm gonna get this villain'. She didn't exactly say 'villain'. She also called me some very unbecoming names the likes of which I had not heard since finishing school. Such pity. She could have advanced and we would have become rank equals."

The new bank manager was outright suspicious. "Why would it concern you? I cannot say more than that she quit. She said some very original things before she dumped the coffee grinds on my promotion certificate. She said 'I'm going to get all you bastards'. We are very happy that she finally left, after she had humiliated herself, our brave army and our great city!"

Evening was settling in Gilbert Park, and we sat down on our old familiar bench as the sun's last warm rays filtered through the leaves.

Melmoth took a couple of minutes before he finally came out with it. "Revenge, that's what it is. The strongest and lowest of all motivations, yet it once liberated me. That was... yes, that was another time. Time stands still here for me, but there it passed all too swiftly. I was... I then was..."

"You were Oscar Wilde." There! Somebody had to say it openly.

Melmoth nodded. "Still in my twenties, not yet married - that came two years later. I liked the ladies, they liked me, and I took full advantage of my celebrity status as a wit, a poetic writer, a glib charmer who could coin amusing bon mots at the drop of a lady's fan. What made my life within the social class of London such an easy game was the skill I had with words, an uncanny ability to stitch them together, to twist phrases inside out and make them reappear wrapped around most unexpected verity. And yet, much of it was a sham. Inside myself I was timid, insecure, frightened of my own fame. People frightened me, the stage frightened me, even my friends frightened me. I had to overplay my hand, overcompensate for my agony of constant dismay and insecurity. Yet nobody could tell from the outside. Famous for my self-importance, I was much too smart to be detected."

"Some can sing, some can draw, some know where the fish bite. You knew words." I hoped this would nudge him over his melancholy.

Melmoth nodded. "Finally it was arranged that I go to America. It gave me an opportunity to be among actors. I always liked their company. They are so eager to please, so hungry for compliments, so utterly insecure and thus such easy prey. Of course, they are all egomaniacs, pumped up with hubris, but some can fake humility better than others. Do you like actors?"

"I never had the chance to find out."

"Pity. Of course, I also wanted to earn money, not just spread my colourful plumage. Don't forget, I already was somebody important back home, yet underneath I was a quivering bundle of raw nerves. The Statue of Liberty had not yet been built, but approaching the Big Apple through the Narrows, the immensity of the city was, at least for me, a frightful portrait of power and possible humiliation. New York - ever been there?"

"I loved it."

"I spent nearly a year in that great big boisterous wonderful inferno. Ever seen the Chester Arthur statue in Madison Square Park? That's just off East 26th Street. There's a bench where I used to sit and feed the pigeons. Are they still there?"

"Probably. They tried to kill them, but you know pigeons."

"An old woman, poorly attired... She was not yet fifty but looked much older, haggard, indigent, ugly even. In painful contrast, I used to dress extravagantly in those days. Yards of silk and velvet. This old woman and I somehow started a conversation. Her name was Henrietta, a very melodious name, don't you agree?"

I thought it had sound and rhythm.

"My lectures started badly; the critics ate me alive. One day she said: 'You are that Irish lad they talk about in the papers, aren't you.' In spite of her destitution she appeared unusually well educated so I assumed that her family must have fallen on hard times. Once I invited her for a repast to my hotel, the Grand Hotel... Does it still exist?"

"I don't know."

"She declined most vehemently. She said she could not be seen in such an elegant place. She had been married for fifteen years and had two children. People talk, she said. Mainly she objected, she said, because people might think she'd put on fancy airs and strangers might harass her. Instead, she unwrapped her sandwiches which were greased with nothing but margarine. That devil's lubricant had just been invented, you know. With it she drank water from that little bronze fountain right behind the statue."

What did he like about her, I wanted to know.

Melmoth drew circles in the ground with the tip of his bâton. "I'm not sure, even today. It was almost as if I wanted her to discover the real me inside myself. To stop playing games, if just for an hour. I was not this flamboyant stand-up comic as the world saw me, but a frightened boy. What harm could this old woman do to me? She was a nobody; one of the faceless poor of a big city. I was certain that she and my friends and audiences would never meet, so I released all my tensions, all my guile and my artifices. Often we would sit and hardly talk. I felt no longer obliged to trump every one of her sentences with a witty repartee. With Hetty - I called her Hetty - with her I could remain absolutely still and not fear that some smart ass emerged from the shrubs to steal my thunder."

The Piggy Ice Cream cart rolled by and I bought two cones of maple fudge. We enjoyed it silently, then got up and washed our sticky fingers at the fountain a few paces up the walkway.

"Ah these wonderful minutes *entre chiens et loups*. How still the park becomes when it gets dark."

Finally I begged: "Is there more?"

"She asked me why I was so insecure, and I told her that being fascinating earned me no permanent income. My lectures went badly because my fame was mostly built on illusions and on the fact that I pretended to be wealthy, which I never was in spite of my fabulous income from my plays. I spent money lavishly on my friends and fans, on iced champagne and caviar, on festive meals and exotic adventures, and if a friend was in need, which actually was quite often, I gave unstintingly and without malice. Nobody knew that I was always near bankruptcy. It was my imaginary wealth regardless of pretence that helped me each day to walk erect and face five hundred faces all at once."

How did she react to his confession?

Melmoth did not directly respond to that question; instead he continued his reminiscence. "Will you believe that I fell in love with her? An old dowdy hag, twenty years my senior, and yet she was the mother I've never had, the companion I've never met in polite circles. She was the maternal friend this scared boy had always needed. She was my confidant and my sorrow, my joy and my conscience; she was the only audience I never had to pervert. She made me see the world through other eyes. I eventually decided that fearing my audience was a luxury I could no longer afford, not here, not in New York, so I rewrote much of my delivery and finally the Big Apple became my triumphant conquest." He paused for a few seconds, then continued: "Mind you, it's not that she had no sense of humour. I always suspected that there was always a trifle of a mischievous child in her, but she kept that well hidden."

"Did she ever tell much about herself?"

"Yes, by and by she did, but she was always guarded and never let me look deep into her affairs. But once she told me about a love affair she had as a young lady before she was orphaned. This man was arrogant, wealthy and came from a most prominent Boston family of merchants and bankers. Boston then was the paradise of prigs, you know. Hetty was certain that the two would marry but events turned out differently. Although her family had once been quite well off, as she claimed - and judging by her obvious good education I had no reason to doubt her - he laughed in her face. 'Marry an ugly wench like you?' he once sneered. 'Some day I will inherit great wealth and I can buy the likes of you by the bushel on the Hay Market.' She told me that this so enraged her that she swore to get even with him, to humiliate and ruin him, to buy out his bank, destroy it and grind him underfoot. She would from then on only live for revenge." He paused deep in thought for a moment, then added: "For some, hatred is no other but unresolved love."

"Did she succeed?"

"She never told me, but someone else had once remarked about this wealthy Bostonian banker who had lost all, became a pauper and finally committed suicide. Hetty and I never saw each other again. Instead, the day before my brief departure for... I forgot. I think it was for Chicago, or perhaps Philadelphia. That evening, I was just ready to get on stage and face my audience; at that very moment a small parcel was delivered to me. I opened it and inside I found a hand-written note: 'My dearest Oscar, take this to help you become famous forever and ever. Love, Hetty'. And in the parcel were one hundred thousand American dollars."

CHAPTER TWENTY-FIVE

The launch of the Majestic was an unmitigated disaster even for Crosley. Appearing at the launch site well ahead of time I found Ted, Joe, Gus the construction foreman, the dancing instructor Mr. Busby, Miss Pennypincher accompanied by Lauris the cross dresser, and Grietje the juvenile sex expert already present. For the occasion they had by now imbibed most of the contents of a keg of Mountain Red, and when that was gone I ordered another. All except Grietje were deep into the sauce, addressing me with slurred words and fourteen bleary eyes. A piano and a drum kit had been hoisted on deck, which was freshly painted a fog-piercing mauve. Four stout lines were attached each to dockside mooring rings and ending in neatly coiled ropes on deck. The barge itself rested on two robust wheeled carts on railroad tracks which vanished into the shallow water at an angle of some ten degrees. One wheel of the carts was blocked with a solid wooden wedge. A heavy two-inch hawser went from the clove hitch on a deck-side cleat to an apple tree halfway up the bank some thirty yards inland at the edge of the Middle Management parking lot.

Joe and Ted explained it all, spelled it out in gesticulation and verbal fragments which, if one stitched it all together, laid out the launching procedure about as follows.

Big kitchen knife in hand, Lauris was supposed to stand behind the hawser on dry land somewhere half-way between the Majestic and the apple tree, exact placement inconsequential. Ted, Joe, Gus and Mr. Busby were to climb on deck, each holding the end of one mooring line so that, after the launch, the barge would not float away into the bay. Pennypincher was to explain to the press and multimedia the purpose and procedure while casually dropping hints of coming attractions at Eulenspiegel Hall. Grietje was expected to fill the plastic tumblers of reporters and spectators with libation and pose attractively if cameras were trained on her. She was dressed in smart sailing outfit complete with khaki captain's cap and pictures of nautical knots printed all over her short-sleeved jacket. Yes, she would grow up to be a dancer all right.

I ordered yet another keg of wine but hid it until it would actually be needed to lubricate dry throats and promote the effusion of appreciative ahs and ohs. I myself was told to maintain a low profile as it was thought that my verbal expression might be too dialectal for this particular audience and thereby disturb the ambiance of public awe and admiration. All was now set for the big event.

The four musicians - a bass player, a trombonist, the pianist and the drummer - were the first hands to show up. There was yet enough of the Mountain Red to get them each a couple of good belts. Next arrived the Professor and his chauffeur plus a couple of very photogenic ladies in Hawaiian style high-density polyethylene mock grass skirts who looked deceptively like two of the hospitality maidens from the Professor's private retreat. Then the reporters and camera operators and interviewers showed up. Safely out of the inner ring and noticing the gathering crowd, I quickly ordered yet one more jug of wine. Just in case. A hot dog vendor showed up with his pushcart, about a dozen onlookers dropped in, and the launch began.

Joe, Gus, Mr. Busby, the four musicians and the two hula dancers smartly took their positions on the deck as per game plan. Ted grasped a sledgehammer since, as a former miner, he was the most trusted hammer operator in the crew; he knocked out the wooden wedge in front of one of the wheels. Both carts with the Majestic on top leaped forward by about a yard and the lashed tree up the bank bent dangerously in direction of the lake. Everybody stopped breathing for a moment. The tree held; cautious moans of appreciation. Ted scrambled aboard, triumph written all over his face.

Lauris, under fresh make-up and high-gloss lipstick, took his place behind the hawser, kitchen knife in hand. The band struck up Hello Dolly and the dancers gyrated their limbs more or less synchronised with the beat. Ted shouted "Now!" and Lauris began to hack away at the thick rope which didn't show any signs of releasing its hold on the wheeled carts under the Majestic.

Video cameras rolled, reporters spoke into their microphones, still camera's fill-in flashes lit patches of the scene here and there, someone who didn't know what went on applauded and the spectators shouted 'go, go, go' in unison. However, Lauris could not hack through the rope and the apple tree began to emit some memorable creaks.

I was close enough for immediate rescue, so I leaped forward, relieved the exhausted rope cutter and began to whack into the strands of sisal until a muffled growl from within its core advertised its readiness to part.

"Faster, faster," Ted shouted, the band struck up Tishomingo Blues and the hospitality maidens rotated their tanned limbs again. He turned around to face Joe: "Did you close the scuttle cock?"

"What scuttle cock?" Joe, the Naval Architect asked.

"Shit," said Ted the Captain.

With a loud snap which could be clearly heard by all present, the hawser finally parted, one end whipping in direction of the Majestic and knocking out Lauris who erroneously believed to have planted himself safely out of harm's way. The now released apple tree whipped the other way, hurling its fifty rock-hard apples into the parked cars and news vans, redirecting at least one of the roof-mounted parabolic antennas to face a different star in the universe. So, under the drum roll of green missiles, the wheeled carts supporting the barge began to roll into the water, and roll even more until they submerged, whereupon the Majestic, now in its natural element, floated away into the bay with Ted shouting from the top of his lungs to hold on.

Reporters were unanimous later in praising the deck crew for their dedication and steadfast determination to hold back the barge. As it turned out, they held on just a moment too long and all four of them, Ted, Gus, Joe and Mr. Busby were pulled clean off the deck and into the water while the proud Majestic irrevocably drifted another fifty yards into the lake with musicians banging out Swanee and the dancing girls twirling.

From their vantage point on deck the remaining six passengers could not clearly perceive the totality themselves, but we on shore watched with great admiration as the Majestic slowly sank and where it finally came to rest on the bottom, the deck still a foot above the water. The musicians struck up Sobbin' Blues. The same guy from before clapped his hands again, and since it was not entirely clear if this spectacle before our eyes had rolled off as scripted or not, all bystanders joined in and applauded first tentatively, then enthusiastically while the four wet rope handlers scrambled out of the water. I attended to Lauris who just now came around again. "Wow," he said. "Some launch, eh?"

✳   ✳   ✳

I had adopted the habit of visiting Ahasverus the pawnbroker on Thursday evenings, usually clutching the old laptop computer from Miss Lynch to make notes of this and that. I appreciated the pot of tea with a tot of rum, the musty smell of old furniture and knick-knack drifting in from the store, and especially the companionship of the wise old man who had rubbed shoulders with kings and beggars, saints and scoundrels. One day I broached the subject myself.

"You had mentioned Il Nolano some time ago, did he have a name?"

"Of course, and he still does. Giordano Bruno. We are the best of friends, even today, but I have not seen him for, oh, so many years now. Occasionally I get some mail from him, nothing more. He used to travel a great deal, living here, teaching there, writing a book somewhere else yet and running from inquisitive eyes everywhere, but mostly he stays home now."

"Where is his home?"

"London. He said only the people there can understand him."

"Is he a fanatic?"

"That is very difficult to say. He's a bully and he is arrogant. His big fight was with all those who blindly follow any dictum, especially the assertions of Aristotle. That's the Greek who said that all things under the heavens are made from only four elements. Giordano said 'nonsense, all things everywhere are made from atoms.' I would say he cracked the shell of ignorance, which eventually led the world out of the dark ages. It's dangerous to be right in a world which is wrong."

"My friend the poet could have said that."

"He did; I was merely quoting him."

We drank our tea in silence. Tick-tock went the old clock in the parlour.

Finally I broke the silence. "What was the last message from him?"

"I still have it." Ahasverus got up and walked out of the room and came back a few minutes later, holding a yellowed letter in his hand. "This is the last message from him, and it only says: 'Nathan my dear friend; Aristotle was almost right. He only had the symbols wrong. Giordano.' That's all. I should have asked him about some details, but I simply did not have the courage."

"Why would that require courage?"

"He exhausts me. His mind is not just miles ahead, it's somewhere else altogether. He has the only brain that comprehends infinity. Besides, he's so pig-headed. Stubborn as an ox. Perhaps that alone would have been enough to get him into trouble with the authorities. Who knows."

"And yet, he's your friend."

"The dearest I've ever had."

※   ※   ※

I had finally been given my own little office right in the former balcony section of the new Eulenspiegel Hall. Several facilities had been installed there, including a most agreeable corner section with a Lilliputian palm tree for the Professor. Now I had my own private hide-away, one with a door and a window from where I could see most of Crosley's waterfront. The very best part was the red leather couch squeezed between the inner wall and the corner of my desk. With that and the washrooms downstairs and the use of the Professor's shower - that is, as long as he was away - one could easily spend a night here. Maybe two. And if one can stow a bit of clothing and stuff under the desk, one could even stretch it to three. Directly above me was the rooftop helipad; however, nobody could foresee any use for it at present.

I found a note in my mail: "Please let us meet. It is of utmost importance for both of us. Let me know when or where. Charles Borelli." Strange; the message started with the word 'please'. No title in the signature, no set time frame, no demands as to locality. This was no command, no threat, not even a hint of disapproval. It sounded almost like a plea for help.

We met at noon in the Tacky Chime Pub where we could submerge into the office lunch crowd. I spoke up first: "Thanks for blowing up my beautiful sports car."

"That sad hunk of scrap? It was the Vespians who did it. I don't do violent stuff, besides, that thing was theirs to begin with. It made a lot of petty thieves happy and bought tons of good-will."

"And where's the Commander, Miss Bernadette?" I tried to hide my anxiety yet I expected the Doctor to somehow sense my tension.

"I knew you would get involved with her. In the end she'll kill you. Remember that I warned you."

I insisted. "Where is she?"

"Perhaps she jumped a broomstick and flew into the full moon. And even if I'd knew, what makes you think I would tell you?"

We sat down at the lunch counter and ordered sandwiches. "So, what do you want from me?"

The Doctor evaded a direct reply. "First of all we need to get one thing straight: I am not here to ask you for a favour. I am here because you and I need each other, so shut up and listen."

He looked around to make certain nobody was leaning in our direction listening in. The place was crowded with mostly the young, but the patrons were far too preoccupied with their food trays, their small talk and their rampant disinterest on all topics. The veterinarian leaned forward and spoke in a tone barely audible above the background noise.

"What I have to tell you now is first and foremost self-serving. I don't give a rat's ass for your well-being, understand that clearly, but this one time you and I must work out something together." We blew imaginary steam off our lukewarm coffee before the Doctor continued. "I have damaging information which must be kept absolutely secret. If ever a single word of it leaks out we know that this could only have come from you. We, that is I and some members of the Security Exchange Company, we have some investments - well, let's call them business interests in the Klonus enterprise."

The waitress served Montreal Smoked Beef sandwiches, the dill pickle bayoneted with toothpicks, but the Doctor did not continue until she was safely out of earshot again. "Philosophically speaking, you and I may stand on opposite sides, but if even the Hutterites can hitch their wagon to Vatican Airlines, what the hell... In the end, it's all about money."

"How much of your funds are tied up there?"

The Doctor did not answer the question. The sandwich was delicious. I insisted. "How much?"

"A great deal. But let me come to the point. We have just now received hard evidence which forces us to the conclusion that Klonus, your Professor, is nearing the tipping point. Why have we not heard from you?"

I shrugged my shoulders. How would I know? I'm not that close to the action.

"You better get close, Boy. If you screw up I'll personally see to it that you hang with the others. After all, you're only a squatter. Who would protect you? Who would care?"

We ate our sandwiches in silence while I frantically searched for an escape hatch. How could I now stand up against this schemer? One would have to try either the direct frontal line of attack or appeal to his humanity. A side-glance indicated to me that either was futile. Perhaps some rudeness could pry loose a few relevant titbits.

"You are nuts, you know? First of all, why should I care what you want? You have been nothing but an irritation since..." How long had I been here? Only eight months? I paused, slurped a couple of sips from my cup, then continued. "I tell you what bugs you. It bugs you that his companies are prosperous. This Eulenspiegel stuff, that's just his toy. Let him. Are you afraid he may pull your leg? Oh yea, these court jesters are a dangerous lot. Even kings could not shake them off. But look what he really carries out. His companies build modern clean houses where slums existed, and shopping centres and libraries and schools, and they make tons of money on all of them. It bugs you that he saves eighteen percent of all capital flowing in and out by eliminating the bookkeepers and the accountants and the lawyers and the whole overhead industry.

Go ahead and check this out. What he pays you in dividends is chicken feed. He really found a dumb sucker when he found you." There! I said all that in a menacing tone, hoping it would shake something out of the man.

"You insolent little bastard. I'm not sure where you learned your arithmetic, but we had forensic accountants on his tail and he is going down. The money he claims he has? The guy's flat broke. The castle he claims he owns? He's just the caretaker for an absentee landholder who has to hide out somewhere near Baghdad. And we want our money back."

"Take it out then and leave me alone."

Charles Borelli smiled acidly. "That only shows how little you know about economics. We can't. All eyes are on us, and if we take out only one loonie, other investors would want to cash in and the whole house of cards will collapse. We'll get nothing and end up owing the bank millions. No, we can't let go of the tiger's tail. The only ace we have up our sleeve is you, and you better deliver. Frankly, I wouldn't want to be in your shoes. But this is the deal. Listen me out, goddammit. You have been your Professor's... What do you call yourself?"

"The idea man."

"Your Professor's idea man." He chewed the words. "You can hack his data base, and if you fail, I assure you, we'll know where to find you."

"Why me?"

The Doctor pushed his plate away, half his sandwich yet uneaten. "Because, my young man, this is the way I want it."

"What data base? He rarely uses a computer. He's scared of those damn things."

Borelli's tone softened. "Think for a moment. He pays no salaries, right?"

"Right. We take what we want. Most people take less than what they could have gotten on the open market. With that system nobody needs a bank account. The credit card is for life."

"Of course," emphasised Dr. Borelli, "but how does he handle chiselers? Surely, you'll have chiselers now and then."

"Anybody stealing outright, or anyone who double-dibs..."

The Doctor completed my sentence. "... gets found out, right? Where does his organisation get this information? Don't you think that some agency, some accounting system doesn't have a quiet little program running in the background somewhere perhaps, adding up all services and all costs and all expenses? Did you really think anybody could fleece him? You must be terribly naive if you believe that."

Dr. Borelli wiped his chin and signalled that the conversation was over. He got up, walked halfway out of the restaurant, then returned and leaned his head over my shoulder. "She's at number six Merklin Street, Vesper." I paid for the sandwiches.

CHAPTER TWENTY-SIX

"One-and-two-and-one... No, no, Mister Parker, chest out, head up, don't look at your feet, keep your eyes straight forward and faster. Back to your spot and once more. One-and-two-and... That's much better. Don't wiggle your shoulders; never ever wiggle! Do you know, Mister Parker, that the way a person moves reveals more about him than his handwriting? Do you know that you can spot someone by gait faster than by facial recognition? And once more. One-and-two... Very good. Do it six times around the gym now and then see me in my office."

I had broken out in a sweat trying the typical Vesper walk: nervous, hasty, pushy, close contact. Unlike the New York gait which is mainly dodging and dipping although equally fast; the Vesper gait was martial. The Londoner uses his brolly as his weapon, the Vesperian his attitude. They have developed a mode of gait whereby they never look at anybody; instead they use their noses to part the ocean of humanity before them like Moses parted the Red Sea. They only perceive their surroundings by peripheral vision, yet in spite of the urban density they never collide. Crosleyans, on the other hand, look at people, step out of each other's way, walk in a slow, leisurely pace, more as if sauntering from nowhere to nowhere, and still bump into each other occasionally. A Crosleyan can be spotted in Vesper just like that. At least that was Mrs. Carnegie's opinion, and she should know, having successfully run her famous Carnegie Social Integration Courses for some thirty years now.

Knock, knock. "Come in, come in. You are doing very well, Mister Parker, and I think two more lessons should be adequate. We must soon start on your speech correction, though. The clipping of vowels. Like so: la - la - la. Short. Not lah - lah. I know what you are thinking; 'she's a regular professor Higgins now', but you are not a flower seller. Enunciation will be Thursday's lessons, but before that we have to correct your mannerism. The way you hold your hands, the way you eat, the way you pay your bills."

How can one pay differently?

"In Vesper you put your money on the tray, and your change comes back on the tray. You never touch anybody, nobody ever touches you. Here? You put the money directly into the cashier's hand, and she will put the change back into yours. These differences may at first appear very subtle to you, but when I point out the fine distinctions you'll be amazed how much information the slightest gestures contain. This is especially true when it comes to ritualistic gestures. We don't have many here in Crosley, but I've taught all sorts of body, hand and finger movements, from imitating the power-nodders, the chest-beaters, the knee-walkers, the finger folders, the carpet-kissers, to the hand wringers and even the wad-chewers. Tomorrow we'll get into the eye-rollers."

Can she give me a hint?

Mrs. Carnegie closed her eyes, folded her hands behind her neck and said: "Spirits to the left, spirits to the right. Spirits above and below. Here you open your eyes," she opened them, "and you say: ...'and spirits all around.' At this point you roll your eyes clockwise. Women roll counter-clockwise. Three times clean around." She rolled her eyes until nearly only the white was visible. "Anyway, we'll study that tomorrow. Such devotional opportunity might never come up but you must be prepared."

The lesson for the day was over and I decided to check on the fitting-out of the barge. The superstructure had been pre-assembled by some affiliate furniture manufacturer and, now completed, was lifted onto the deck. It suddenly gave the Majestic a totally different appearance. Instead an old tar-coated barge which for years had carried nothing but sand and gravel, it now had become a stately imperial ceremonial vessel with gilded fittings, floral embellishment with vaguely Egyptian motifs and four pompous pillars supporting a fringed red baldachin with golden tassels. Bow and stern sported each a proud cat with its tongue sticking out.

Ted came up. "Don't talk to me about history, OK? I know the Egyptians never had them with their tongues exposed. Not like the Chinese. The Egyptians considered tongues to be too intimate an organ to show off. To them it's like mooning. But why can't one be a bit inventive now and then, eh? I like cats with their foot-long tongues hanging out. It's almost elegant - in a non-sexual concept, of course."

Joe was below in the engine room, installing a demand valve for the hydraulic side thrusters. I opened the conversation. "How's Marlene? Haven't seen her in ages."

The newly-minted naval architect put down his wrench. "I dunno. I haven't seen her... I rarely see her at all. When she comes home she sinks into her bed and is gone. Dog-tired. She snores now, you know."

"What is she doing all day?"

"She's taking dancing lessons again, and more singing. She has a lovely alto voice - you should hear her some time. She and the kid are going to the piano teacher again. She used to play, did you know that? She said she was fairly good at it once, but how could I tell now? Hadn't played in years. Maybe I should get her a keyboard or something. One day I'll marry her."

"When?"

Joe shrugged . "She said she wasn't ready yet. Forty-seven and a kid and not ready yet. Women!"

On my way to see Melmoth, I made a little detour through the Old City, as the section of town with cobblestone streets and horse-drawn carriages was known. At Sparrow Keyboards a little old lady in a plain black dress greeted me. A piano to play what style, the lady asked with a slight nasal accent. I said I didn't know but it was for a lady who rediscovers her love of music.

Mrs. Sparrow took her cane and slowly walked to a baby grand. "Is she a classical player?" she asked, sat down and played something utterly unfamiliar and on a twelve-tone scale to boot. "That was from Beerbohm. I'm sure you never heard of him. He was my first husband. - Or is the lady more in tune with this."

She ambled over to a brand new apartment-size upright. "Listen to the softness of this one. This is the kind of music that goes well with this instrument. The tune is called 'The Honey and the Bee'."

I was totally unaware that different pianos were built for different musical styles, so I added: "This lady, wife of a friend of mine - well, it's just a little surprise gift for her. She's more into cabaret stuff I think."

"Ah, honky-tonk." Another piano. "This one has barrel house ambiance, it's carefully restored, centre strings de-tuned ten Hertz. It's a beauty. Very aggressive." Out came a piano roll number of great volume and spirit.

"More like a quiet dinner piano, I would say."

Mrs. Sparrow went to the opposite corner. "This one here is a very old instrument, a Holtzen. Of course it has been in many hands, very careful hands I might add, but we have completely refurbished the exterior and the action. Its touch is feather-light, tender, warm. You merely look at it and it goes off almost all by itself with the touch of an angel. Expressive without being overwhelming. Just listen how lovely it sounds."

I bought it on the spot and had it delivered to Marlene's address the next day.

Melmoth was amused. "Bought her a piano? You don't even know if she can play a sequence of only five notes."

"What does that matter? She obviously loves a piano because she and her son are taking lessons. Just forget about it, all right? How's the stuff for the show coming? I see nothing on the table."

"You have no appreciation how difficult it is to fold your hands and do nothing. And why should it be your concern. Besides, you couldn't read it anyway. It's in longhand."

"I've gotten you that mechanical typewriter and I want to hear click-clack-click-clack."

"That's not how it goes. I have to think."

"May I remind you that you swore by the beard of King Edward the Fifth..."

"The Seventh."

"... the Seventh that it will be done on time? There's hell to pay if you don't produce."

"Tell him I guarantee success. Tell him I stand behind my art."

"That's like selling grave stones with life-time warranty."

Melmoth protested angrily. "It's always the same with you pedestrians, isn't it? Always push, push. Never a pause to let the genius think."

"Geniuses are not allowed to think, they are supposed to write. For crying out loud, it's only words to string together! Do as you always do: wrap platitudes in lofty phrases. So sit down and start wrapping!" I turned on my heels and left without uttering another word, slamming the door behind me.

CHAPTER TWENTY-SEVEN

Number six Merklin Street in Vesper was shoehorned between warehouses, tool rental shops and a synthetic vanilla factory. The house had a simple little plaque next to its door, GM Diaper Service; other than that the district showed no signs of habitation. I searched for a doorbell to ring, a knocker, any means of communication. Except for a sputtering lone mercury vapour lamp on the corner casting its cold blue light, the street lay abandoned in darkness. Uncertain what to do next, I contemplated climbing over the wrought iron gate with its treacherous barbed wire intertwined with sinister spikes when suddenly the door opened, a hand grabbed my windbreaker and I was swiftly pulled inside.

"Are you completely mad? Someone could have spotted you. Who gave you my address?" Bernie was obviously enraged with her unexpected visitor. "And who permitted you to come? What are you trying to do to me? Trip me up?"

"Don't worry, I took the course."

As we quietly climbed up the steep stairs, I briefly outlined my conversation with Borelli. The room at the top was small and unventilated as there was no window, no opening to the outside, no relief from the stifling heat which had not found an exhaust vent. On one wall were three TV monitors.

"How did you get here?" Her anger was slowly subsiding.

"Rental car - Vesper plates. Lauris checked it out - no beacon transmitter. Parked four blocks down. You were the one behind the ammo dump, right?"

"What's in your attaché case?"

I stalled. "A sandwich and something I… Well, last time you stomped on them so I had them make me another set."

"A set of what?"

"Tiger Fives. You know, the chocolate ersatz variety."

Bernie squeaked. "Oh Tony, Honey, that's so extravagantly tasteless."

I opened the briefcase and handed her the wrapped box. "I thought if I came with yet another peace offering…"

"How sweet of you, Darling. No, no, don't open it. I like it just as it is, wrapped in Christmas paper. How lovely - if not exactly timely."

"You're not going to eat any?"

The ex-Commander didn't answer but just shook her head. Instead she poured us a mug of coffee. I continued: "Why are you still here? Let me take you back to Crosley. Tonight. Now."

"You are crazy", she replied. "We'll get caught within minutes. Cops are all over the place."

"So what are you still doing here"

"Unfinished business," she said smilingly. "Pure, clean, germ-free settling of scores. I must get even with that bitch. Will you help me? Of course, they have more troops, more weapons, more of everything. But we have pepper spray. Figuratively speaking."

"Like what?"

"Like you and me, Dear. You cost me my commission, you cost me my job, so you better do as I tell you. You should be lucky that I talk to you at all."

"I came out of concern for you and you do nothing but chew me out. I might not even be in the mood to help you. Help you do what?"

"Tony, Dear, help me prevent that next war."

"What war?"

"The one I'll start if she doesn't agree…"

"How can you start a war? Just like that? For no reason at all."

"Oh, my innocent little man. That's easy. You don't need a reason to start a war. You just go ahead and have one."

Like how, I wanted to know.

Bernie had her answer ready. "First you demonise them…"

"But they have done nothing wrong."

"What does that matter? You just point out how perverted your foes are. How they roll their eyes the wrong way. How they treat their goldfish. Anything. But I don't want to discuss international diplomacy with you. We've got to be up early and look sharp, so now you go there and sleep. You have five hours."

I stared into the silent monitor screens and wondered what brought me here. It's a complete waste of time. Before I finally fell asleep I had just one more question: "Ever heard about the Professor's investment scheme?"

Bernie must have been wide-awake because she answered immediately in a clear voice. "Of course. Is that what Borelli discussed with you?"

✳   ✳   ✳

"I said just you and me. Who's the kid?" General Smith was a plump fifty-ish, out of uniform and into jeans and denim shirt.

"My incidental lover. He's just a squatter. He's the one who paid off the Hutterites. I'll send him away if you want me to. He brought you a personal gift. Smuggled it in."

Nellie Smith studied me for awhile. "What's in that attaché case?"

"The gift. Here…" I handed it over.

"Where do you camp? GM Diapers again?"

Bernie nodded. "That's just between us."

The General visually searched the nearby knoll, the floral clock, the parking lot in the distance. "Anybody else?"

"No, just the two of us."

"Any wires?"

"Nellie, do you really think I would do that? Search us if you like, but I give you my word of honour."

"All right, all right." She stepped closer. "Let's talk then. There, on those things."

We three sat down on kiddie swings. General Smith unwrapped the gift at once, stared at the twelve Tiger Fives in their vacuum-formed cradles, took one out as if to bite off the 75mm gun but then changed her mind and replaced it intact in the box.

"Ricin?" she asked, looking sideways at Bernie.

"Nellie, Dear, if I wanted to kill you I wouldn't do it with poison. I would have enjoyed blowing your head off a thousand times, but not this way."

"And you. What's your name again?"

"Tony."

"Thank you, Tony. That's the nicest gift anybody ever gave me. Really." She carefully re-wrapped the box in the Santa Claus paper, then addressed Bernie: "It was you, wasn't it?"

"I did you a favour, Nellie. You wanted to buy that land for condos anyway, didn't you?"

"To blow up the whole damn thing. That wasn't called for. You could've killed somebody."

"Not after you pulled back your guards. And we carefully watched."

"How many of you were there?"

"Nellie, it's just me and one of your own body guards."

"How much did you have to pay her?"

"That's a military secret."

We swung for a minute until General Smith continued. "We sure creamed you at the farm."

"Yes, you did, Nellie. You got us all right."

"Did we hurt anybody? Please notice that we didn't shoot until you all were safely in that barn."

"Nobody got hurt."

"Good. Lost your command, didn't you?"

"I want it back, and I want you to give it back to me."

Bernadette Robinson, former second highest ranking officer of the Crosley military might, unfolded her plan. The Vesper armed forces had four Tiger tanks versus only two for Crosley, but the Vesper tanks were the older type Four models with shorter gun barrels and minus night vision equipment. Not that anybody had actually found any use for either, still, General Smith had begged for years to be upgraded. It's a prestige thing, but to no avail. Replacement only comes down from headquarters when the old weapons have been destroyed in combat, and there was no reason to believe that any such armed conflict lay in the near future. What to do?

"Nellie, listen to me. We, that is Tony here and I and nobody else, we'll blow up two of your tanks. You shout 'bloody murder', then lob some missiles into the Sovereign Bank corner Klein and Third."

"They are the ones that fired you, right?"

"They didn't fire me, I quit."

"Sure."

"You must flatten them. Then you go and blow up the small transformer station near Gibson Bridge. That's where they store the back-up data. Here are the co-ordinates." She handed over a slip of paper.

"That would cost me at least four missiles, the expensive ones. And then?"

"Then, Nellie, you blame me for the loss of your tanks upon which I'll get my commission back, you declare victory for breaking our banking system and you'll receive your new hardware. That done, the three of us, see?" She circled our threesome with her index finger. "We'll fly to Paris for a whole week and help ourselves to all the champagne and caviar we can lay our hands on."

"Can I bring Bessie? That's my mom."

"Of course."

"Dammit, Bernie, you're a bloody genius; I'll give you that much. Who else knows about it? Does Borelli know?"

"Nobody knows. This is between you and me and Tony here; nobody else. And Tony is as silent as a wooden lamp post."

"Suppose anything goes wrong, then what? Tell me, Bernie. What'll we do then?"

"Then we blame it on him," pointing over her shoulder at me. "He's our guy." Turning her head: "Aren't you, Honey?"

"Why me?"

"Because, Dear, there's nobody else around and you already look guilty. Doesn't he, Nellie?"

Of course she was joking, but I squirmed nevertheless. "Would I have to go to jail for it? I mean, if they catch us."

"Catch you, Sweetheart? No, probably not. We'll get you a sympathetic judge and you have plenty of good friends who will vouch for you, and with that and good behaviour I'd say two at most. Perhaps just a year and a half. That's the worst case scenario." She was joking. – Wasn't she?

General Smith nodded. "Two at most. And much of that at a halfway house. OK, Bernie, you're on. Give me a week to set it up. And for heaven's sake, get a decent haircut."

⁂   ⁂   ⁂

There was an air of excitement about the city of Crosley now. Placards wherever one looked, and the public was invited to attend the Grand Opening of Eulenspiegel Hall, now only nine days away. Except for the Styrofoam motorised rowers, Ted's Egyptian-plus barge was nearly completed and even had survived a couple of trial runs in the harbour. A whole lot of people were suddenly milling about, carting this, painting that, hauling a piano, delivering soft drinks and crates of balloons, and moving underfoot wherever one stepped. From my small office on the balcony level I watched in bewilderment the avalanche of action I had caused, all of which had started with me believing that the Professor was building a Trojan Horse so he could dip into the people's pockets. I was ready to help him even then, but I also believed that, in addition, the Professor had a secret agenda, and that by some hidden lever he wanted to manipulate his audience. Now it became clear; the little rotund bald man only wanted to generate laughter, nothing more. He had always been what he claimed right from the start, a jokester who needed an audience hanging on his lips. Everybody wants to be a sage regardless of sagacity.

Trouble was, the more the opening day of the show advanced, the less I was required for anything. I tried to contact Ted, to chat with Melmoth, with Joe, and where the hell was everybody anyway? I hadn't seen Marlene for a month or more, and her dumb kid was sent away to some camp or whatever. The Professor was hiding out on his retreat.

Ahasverus from the pawn shop had a great deal of sympathy for me.

"You, young man, were the nucleus once. You are no longer needed now. You have done your job and your baby will be delivered without your support. It happens that way to most fathers. I know it doesn't do much good to tell you, but you must ease up a bit. You are burning with a thousand fires inside you."

"How can you tell after only one glance?"

The old man smiled. "Experience. Running this store here means being a good judge of human nature. And, of course, having computers. Anonymity is the first thing we trade away with these machines. Nothing is hidden away anymore, all is in the open. I can get you to any place anywhere, find out anything, communicate with anybody and be home again unseen, unnoticed in ten keystrokes or less. Do you think I haven't heard about you visiting that young lady, Miss Robinson, in Vesper? Car rental account books, ledgers, credit card tracers, it's all there for the hacking."

"You? A hacker? You are much too old to be into this sort of stuff."

"You have no idea, Anthony, how close wise old age and callous youth are to each other. They practically rub shoulders." He poured the tea, as always. "Besides, there is one thing you must learn: if you never stop questioning, new knowledge comes easy. Would you believe I could become a - a - well, name something."

"Anthropologist."

"Very well, an anthropologist. There is so much information already dumped into my cranial cells, all I need to do is rearrange the data a bit and perhaps add just another ten percent new material. I could be an anthropologist complete with diploma in less than a year. It's only the inactive who get left behind. But that alone is not enough; it's too passive. You must cultivate a questioning mind. Retaining new information is the easy part. The mind is like a child; it needs to play with toys, with stuff within its reach, so give it toys to play with. Give yourself pictures for the inner eye, melodies to wash through your dreams, opposing opinions so you can contradict yourself, viewpoints which change with the seasons, sermons from the mountaintops and propaganda from the bowels of hell. The innocence of a child has a voracious appetite and immense storage capacity which, in a whole lifetime, cannot ever be only half filled. And there is quite a bonus: your dreams will come in colour."

"How do you know all that?"

"I learned this and much more from my friend, Giordano."

"Il Nolano?"

The pawnbroker nodded, but suddenly he jumped up. "Almost forgot. Yes, it's true, I'm a bit absent-minded but look." He held up a bronze medal of unknown origin. "Missis Kimmelbaum - do you remember her? She was the dear old lady with the Glasshütte…"

"Her dead husband's expensive pocket watch? Yes, I remember quite well."

"See how easy it is? She said it was his only treasure and maybe you were her good luck charm and she wants you to have it."

"Is it valuable?"

"That's hardly the point. Yes, it is valuable. No, it has no cash value. A loonie at best. You know what your friend the poet would say to you now?"

"He would say that I was a man who knew the price of everything and the value of nothing. Thank you, Mister Ahasverus. Tell that dear old lady that I'll cherish her generosity but I can't accept it. I did not earn it. Do you know what it was given for?"

"Some long forgotten war in some jungle somewhere; who knows exactly. The bigger the medal, the more dead bodies are left to the maggots. It's the badge of state-organised mass murder. A sad ornament only for those who might come out of it alive."

"Thank her for me, but please, give it back to her. I'm no hero."

CHAPTER TWENTY-EIGHT

The message on my laptop read: 'Don't forget our date next Saturday at 15:00 hours (that's three PM for you civilians). I'll pick you up at your office. Love, Bernie.' The directive flew in like ever so much junk mail and there was a fake return e-mail address, no hint as to how I could reach her any which way.

Saturday was completely unsuitable for me as the Grand Opening of Eulenspiegel Hall was set for the same day, a date I could not and would not miss. There was yet so very much to do, so many picayune details to look after. Big Idea Man had slowly been reduced to a 'go-for-this-and-that-and-hurry-up' person, a nobody of limited prominence but one who is nevertheless the grease that once lubricated the squeaking wheels. I had now become the same appendage as Lauris, the cross-dressing factotum.

But Lauris had many dimensions. The first thing he taught me was the difference between him and a transvestite. "A transvestite is a woman inadvertently cast into a male body, a cross-dresser is a refined male of exquisite taste who likes to feel the luxury of Italian silk on his ass."

Lauris was the most resourceful person I had ever met. He knew where to get what, often buying it, if he had to buy it at all, for a fraction of the cost others have to pay. He knew where to dig up the strangest contraptions, where to get the best discounts, have the most Green Stamps or even those new Air Clicks. Lauris knew how to fix a leaking tap for free (plumbers charge you just for limo fare), how to purge a room of secret listening devices, or, of greater value yet, how to plant them somewhere else and not be found out. Lauris knew whom to ask for whatever gadget you needed and have it done on time and to perfection. Most important of all, he knew how to find people. He never told anybody just how he did it, but you ask him to get the CEO of Such-and-such Company and in less than an hour that person would be on the line. Lauris was indispensable, and the fact that he dipped a little deeper into the slush funds than anybody else on his status level was easily overlooked because he needed attire for two genders. He knew how to deal with everyone, overcame all obstacles with diplomacy and sheer willpower, and we all knew that he saved the company far more than he cost.

Best of all, Lauris was the confidence keeper of a thousand secrets. You told him your problems, he would see you through and never a single word would leave his lips. He was as still as the grave of Barbarossa and never took credit for anything himself.

"Get me Miss Robinson, the former Commander of our municipal army," I had asked him.

"Bernie, the one from the bank?"

In forty minutes she was on the phone. "How did you find me," were her first words.

"Lauris."

"The Commander?"

"I don't know how he does it and I'm scared to ask. Saturday is out."

Bernie's voice left no doubt that she meant business. "Saturday is the exact right time, all eyes are on Crosley. The action has already been set up. This Eulenspiegel thing is being played big on all channels. Saturday you're either on or dead."

"Why don't you drop the whole issue?" There was no answer. 'Click' the phone went. I turned around. "Lauris, on Saturday - can you cover for me?"

"You going back to Vesper?"

"Nonsense. What gives you that idea?"

"Just a hunch. Ammo dump going up, and you and the lady… Just a hunch. Yea, sure. How long do you want me to cover for you?"

I had absolutely no idea. I might not be back before late, I said. And I had not the vaguest notion what problems might arise or how to handle them.

The Commander did. "Here's how it plays. I'll do whatever needs to be done, and I tell them the order came directly from you. They'll never find out."

I was relieved. "Lauris, I could kiss you."

"You forgot lesson number one already, haven't you. I'm a cross-dresser, not a transvestite."

✳   ✳   ✳

Ted had problems with his Styrofoam rowers, eight on starboard, eight on portside. The first set was shredded by the over-cranked actuating arms causing the plastic bits and pieces to break up and float away into the harbour. Ted and Joe paddled their inflatable Vinyl dinghy energetically to collect the debris; however, they got only as far as the old coal harbour where they gently bumped into one of the barnacle-encrusted dock piles. The dinghy sank in less than twenty seconds, not only dumping the crew into the drink but also releasing the carefully collected bits and pieces of flotsam which now slowly drifted out into the lake.

The second set of oarsmen fared only marginally better. In order to make the action look more lifelike, not just the arms of the rowers but also their whole bodies faked a slight forward motion with each oar stroke. The problem turned out to be the lower pivot point, a glued-on wooden bushing rotating on a short dowel. With the speed of the action now geared down to a realistic 12 strokes per minute the broomstick-sized dowels broke off one at a time. "It's the torque," Joe said, and as he was the naval architect his opinion trumped Ted's who said it was the speed. With only three days to go there was no time to dicker. They called for the Commander.

"I can fix it," Lauris said, and when he finally returned in the afternoon he brought back sixteen Viking plywood shields in the bed of his pick-up. They were quickly affixed to the gunwales of the Egyptian ceremonial vessel, mercifully covering many sins of previous beautification attempts. The one thing Lauris was not was a historian.

The Professor came for inspection. "That's how it must have looked when Norsemen were in that area," he said. "Didn't it?"

"Heard they went as far as Egypt and halfway up the Nile," I added helpfully. "Even made it into the Persian Gulf." I hoped it would clarify matters.

"How did they get from the Mediterranean to the Red Sea," the Professor asked rhetorically, but then he quickly answered himself. "Of course, they must have dragged their ships over the dunes."

"They were pretty tough guys," I added. It seemed that nobody wanted to critically investigate the annals of Viking conquests at this particular moment.

When we inspected Eulenspiegel Hall we found the 'Eul' part of the neon sign to flicker, hiss and crackle. "Condensation," said Lauris. Off he was, but soon he returned with a hair dryer, and in another fifteen minutes the sign lit up evenly and perfectly.

"I like your dress," said the Professor.

"Thank you, Sir. It's a good copy of a Chanel."

"Put it on my bill."

"Thank you, Sir. I already have."

※　　　※　　　※

I drove with Bernie to the little shack in the country. We arrived at a small farm just outside the city limits where the sign HR Flying School had directed us. Now I gingerly stepped up to that scary contraption right in front of me, fingering it here, touching that.

"This here? Of course you are joking." That was not only the first, it was the only thought that came to my mind. "In that thing?"

"It's a gyroplane," Bernie explained. She walked up to a tiny wingless aircraft with V3 in foot-high letters flaunted on the sides. She gave the single vertical rotor a push with her hand. "See? It's freewheeling. No power needed."

"What keeps it up?"

"Not much. But it does have a bit of an engine," pointing to the forward horizontal propeller. "Twenty-five horses VW."

"And it flies? It has no wings. Nothing."

"Yes, it flies amazingly well, actually. A bit unstable in cross winds, but even when the engine quits or you run out of gas, it usually comes down rather gently. One usually survives. Have done it hundreds of times."

"What is it for?"

"It's an assault aircraft. Imagine hundreds of them, each with two armed combatants. Very cheap. Aluminium tubing, some plastic film, Velcro."

"Is that thing yours?"

Bernie laughed. "No, Dummy. It belongs to Miss Hanna. She taught me."

"She can fly?"

"Rockets to the moon, if the chance ever came up. Told me all I know; she's the best."

"And all that on just three bicycle wheels?"

"You don't really want to drag a lot of empty rubber around, would you now?"

I rounded it a couple of times. "No way. That's just made from bed sheets."

"Don't be so childish. Once all airplanes were like that. Besides, it's varnished." When she read the panic in my eyes she added: "Makes them almost airtight."

"You actually want me to get into this - this... I can't get it across my lips. And where is the runway?"

"You're standing on it, Honey. This driveway. It's all we need. Now, don't be so infantile and get in. You sit in the back and I'm right in front of you. At least try the seat and see if it's adjusted right."

"What, on that banana seat? I had a bigger one on my Schwinn. And where would I put my feet?" Looking inside and down. "There's not even a floor in there. Just a foot rest."

"That's where you keep them, or, swoosh, you fall right through. That probably hurts – for a man. And use a seat belt or you'll fall out. Where would you be then without a parachute, hm?"

"What? No parachute?"

"They only hang up in trees and electric wires, Dear. Now get in or I have to shoot you."

"You wouldn't do that. Would you?"

Of course she wouldn't. Highly unlikely.

Bernie started the engine by pulling a rope, hand-cranked the pusher prop and two minutes later we took off. Shah - shah - shah went the overhead rotor. I didn't dare open my eyes, instead I slung my arms around Bernie and held on for dear life. What had ever gotten into me to agree to this disastrous adventure? Certain suicide, that's all there's to it. Sheer madness. Only a brainless cretin like me would fall into such a hopeless trap. How many broken bones would I have, assuming I'd survive at all. If not, what then? Where does one go from here? Is there a Level Three, one with yet another bizarre reality? Don't some mystics claim there are many of them? Why do they call it a Level to begin with? Nothing here is very level; everything seems slanted. Has nobody heard of purgatory yet? Or the Elysian waiting room? Furthermore, another air crash in less than a year would be far too much for even the stoutest heart. Oh, Bernadette, what have you done to me?

There was this tiniest little bump in the air, a micro-bump really, but I let go of Bernie and clutched the sides of the cockpit instead. I also opened my eyes.

We were flying rather low, just above the treetops. The landscape undulated in front of us in gentle waves of green pasture, clumps of bushes, a patch of forest. Bernie avoided going over the hilltops but stayed in the dales instead. She turned her head.

"You OK, Honey? First time I have a passenger. Wasn't sure if we had enough lift." And then she pointed her nose forward again. I looked at my watch: Almost four now. The party was beginning in Crosley and I wasn't there to celebrate with the others.

At four-thirty I tentatively began to enjoy the flight. We spotted a truck way up in the distance. Another one. Two cars. A hundred cows or more. There, was that not the Hutterite colony? I tipped my fingers on Bernie's shoulder. "Is that the farm?"

She nodded, took a thirty-degree turn to port and flew straight towards it. Nobody heard or saw us coming, so we circled a couple of times until we could see the white of their faces. Bernie waved her hand; I cautiously let go of the thin aluminium railing and also waved. Some waved back. The new barn door was painted international distress orange. Then we went back on our old compass heading: straight north.

I tipped Bernie's shoulder again and put my lips close to her ears.

"You're quite a gal," I shouted over the gushing air noise.

She turned around. "You're quite a guy." I felt pretty good at that.

At 17:37 hours we sat down in the lone ghost town I had visited about half a year ago. Bernie landed right on the dusty road close to the gas pump.

"Hello, Commander," the fat woman greeted her. "Flying that old V3 again? Why don't you get a real one, you know, one with wings? I know you can afford it."

"It's Miss Hanna's. It's her favourite toy."

"Has she finally cooled down? Should find herself a husband or something. It's no good for a woman like her to be alone all the time. Makes them snarly. Can you come a bit closer, my hose isn't quite reaching."

We got out, stretched our limbs, then pulled the amazingly light craft right up to the pump.

"What time are ye comin' back?" the woman inquired.

"About seven-thirty. If all goes to plan."

The woman chuckled. "It usually does, Bernie. It usually does."

We took off again and soon one could spot the City of Vesper in the hazy distance. Bernie banked her craft slightly to the left and lowered the altitude until we almost touched the fences. She held up her hand, showing five and five and five fingers. "Fifteen minutes", she shouted. I repeated the planned action in my mind and went through the details once more. It was all arranged, Bernie had said. General Smith is in on it, only two guards watch over the compound. They, too, have been instructed and paid accordingly. The tanks are lined up behind the main building, the anti-tank mines are in the ammo cabinet which is locked. Fortunately the fire alarm box holds a pickaxe on pegs behind the glass door, and a heavy dictionary to break the glass lies nearby. 'Nothing will go wrong,' I repeated the mantra, and then Bernie held up ten fingers.

I contemplated the exercise once more: Tape up the guards, get their keys, open the rear doors, run across the parade ground to the ammo bunker, get inside and take two igniters on rack two, second shelf, then set igniters to four minutes. Next take the axe, knock off the security bar, grab two of the mines - easy now, they weigh eighteen kilos each - and run towards the main building around the corner while we screw in the igniters. Climb aboard the Tigers, pull the beaded cord; we now have two hundred and forty seconds. Open the hatches, gently deposit the mines, one in each, close the hatches, jump off...

Three fingers.

...and then run, run, run.

In front of us the compound. High concrete walls, iron-studded entrance doors, deserted pillboxes to the left and right. Bernie pulled up on the stick, effortlessly hopped over the ramparts and set down on the other side right in the middle of the exercise ground. The time was exactly 18:16 hours.

The two guards were watching TV as we burst in, shouting 'bang, bang' and cocking the fingers of our empty hands. "Oh no," one of them cried, "can't you wait a few minutes? Look, a wedding."

The screen showed Crosley's Egyptian festive barge with Viking shields over their gunwales, slowly pulling past a huge audience on the beach. In the distance behind a fireboat gushed a rainbow of scintillating water, lending the ceremony the required official merriment. As the camera swung around one could see the whole lakefront crowded with thousands and banners flying everywhere.

"Look, look," one of the guards shouted excitedly. "Those big cats with their tongues... Look at that fire shooting out. Oh, how beautiful."

"Both front and rear," the other one added. "Isn't that stunning? How do they do that?"

"With eggs," I added helpfully. Damn, damn; I'm going to have words with Ted.

A roll of duct tape was found right on top of the guardhouse TV set - such coincidence - and the two young ladies in uniform were quickly wrapped against their high-back office chairs. Bernie thoughtfully turned her captives towards the TV set so that they might not miss a single word.

"... the lovely couple and their adopted son..." And there, illuminated by the early evening low-angled sun, stood Joe and his bride, Marlene, all dressed in white, and both smiling broadly into the cameras. The point-of-view changed to an onboard camera. The back of a man came into view. Even before he spoke I knew that it was Taddeus Ramelov, Master of the Majestic, all dressed up in a dark blue uniform with yards and yards of gold everywhere. "As the captain of this ship..."

"What are you doing there," Bernie hissed. "We come here and you watch reality TV?"

There was not a minute to lose although we were on schedule, but the moment we broke the glass of the emergency fire alarm box a red light started flashing and a Klaxon outside screamed bloody murder. "Oh shit," said Bernie. "It was supposed to be deactivated."

I ran back, turned up the volume on the TV set so that the tied-up prisoners could still hear the ceremony above the alarm. "Thank you," moaned one of the guards from behind the duct tape over her mouth.

The destruction of the two Tigers ran pretty much as planned. Whoom - whoom went the muffled sounds of the explosions inside, and only thin trails of yellow smoke curling out of the cracks indicated anything amiss. The real surprise came when Bernie suddenly ran back and returned with one more mine. "Let's make that three," she said and another whoom signalled her success.

We hurried back to the guard's office to check on the soldiers. They nodded their heads: all was well. I glanced at the screen. The rituals in Crosley were over; glasses were raised; the new couple kissed; the fireboat in the background doused a burning rowboat. The camera panned over to the small band dressed in white long tails, and there, in the midst of it all, sitting right in front of the piano and belting it out as if there was no tomorrow, was Marlene's and Joe's strange kid. I'll be damned...

Now it was high time to leave. We jumped into our flying machine, such as it was, and as we lifted off Bernie checked her watch. She held up four fingers and drew a horizontal line in the air. "Four minutes late," she shouted, but it sounded very much like laughter.

CHAPTER TWENTY-NINE

I t was pitch dark when Bernie dropped the V3 onto the helipad atop Eulenspiegel Hall directly above my office. It was an awful tight fit for the craft and the procedure would have been a masterpiece of airmanship even in broad daylight, but now darkness had fallen with only a thin strip of orange still visible in the West. Matter of fact, it wasn't even a landing as per manual - more like a thumping free drop from four feet straight up.

"Darling, you have been an absolutely wonderful terrorist. Are you sick, Sweetie?" She threw her arms around me, and I needed a few seconds to collect myself.

I shook my head. "Just a minute, please. I've been through a lot today. How will you ever get this thing off from here?"

"I have no idea, Honey. Why not just leave it there? It's good advertising."

We cocked our ears. From the inside of the auditorium below came laughing and singing, trumpet blows and the clapping of tambourines, and then an amplified voice I knew instantly belonged to Marlene, the newly-wed bride. She sang and the whole audience fell into her refrain and it was a boisterously swinging ruckus the likes of which I had not expected to ever hear in sleepy Crosley.

We lashed down the gyroplane so that a sudden wind gust would not tip it overboard and into the lake. She brushed her red curls aside, laughing. "That's music for dancing. Just listen to that."

The way down from the upper deck was via rebar rungs welded on the outside, connecting the roof to the landing jetty where the

Majestic was lashed to her dockside cleats. Ted was still aboard. Here at the jetty the laughter and singing and toots and tambourine slapping from within sounded now louder, more infectious even. Why was he not inside there?

Ted grinned from ear to ear. "Why? This is my home port. Right here, this is where the Majestic is now moored. This is where it shall remain until the next voyage, and I'll be the Master again. I've been in and out there a dozen times but I always come running back here again. You know, I couldn't just leave my ship unattended. This is the first important job I've ever had in my life. From the coal mines to a floating palace. Just look at me, I'm a real captain. Look, gold buttons, my epaulets, the sash, the belt, and get a load of my patent leather boots. Like a tribal king, eh? Man, I'm telling you, I wouldn't let go of this moment for a million. And did you see that kid of theirs? What bloody luck that I was rarely home the last few months. That piano banging would have driven me to drink."

"Captain, may we come aboard?" Bernie always knew just the right thing to say.

"Are you gonna ream me out for the flamethrowers?"

I had a change of heart. "Nonsense, Ted. They were beautiful, the best I've ever seen. We come to shake your hand."

"Come, come. Oh, thank you. You honour me. Yes, you do. Oh, what a day." Ted leaned back and let the events of the day float through his mind once more. "The best part for me was when we sailed along the whole waterfront to bring the Professor here. There he was, looking just like a fat little Liberace in this glittering outfit, and with all the sequins and the baubles. His hat, man, you should have seen that big thing with all those feathers and jewels and stuff. Of course, it also hides his baldness. Man, he alone was worth the ticket price. He stood there on deck, proud and as happy as a puppy. The cameras probably didn't pick it up, but that man was actually crying. Very quietly, and still he grinned and waved and blew kisses to the people on shore all the time, but the tears were rolling down his cheeks. I've never felt so happy in all my life."

How's the gig going, Bernie wanted to know.

"Those side thrusters. Man, how it worked. Touched the jetty as gently as a feather. - What? The gig? Of course, it started with a disaster. Melmoth didn't show up. They sent Lauris after him but he came back empty-handed. You know, if even the Commander..."

"Yes, yes. So how did it go then?"

"The Professor - it didn't faze him the least bit. He must have expected it. Ad-libbed the whole show as if he had done it a hundred times before. Didn't faze him at all. Of course, I didn't see everything right from the start. Had to watch my ship, you know, but I tell you, five minutes after it started they were all laughing already. Could hear it out here as if I was in the audience, and every few minutes I ran there behind the stage, you know, at the sides. And there was Joe, running around like a chicken with his head cut off."

"Why?"

"Well, he practically ran the whole production from behind all those plywood cut-outs. And that without a plan or anything. He'd just point the finger at this guy and that one, and he said 'you're next', the guys on their tricycles, or the clowns, or this or that. And every fifteen minutes he'd send out Marlene again and she just told the band what's next and B flat or something, and then she let loose. She had them in the palm of her hand. Just like that. The audience went crazy. You must have heard it in Vesper. After maybe an hours the musicians were all worn out, so they took a short break. And Marlene announced a song for her new hubby. I couldn't hear it clearly from here, but it sounded as if she stood there all alone, middle of the stage. It was a very slow number, about 'set 'em up, Joe'. And one was for her baby and one for the road or something. That's on account of Joe being a bartender, you know. She started off all by herself, but then I heard a piano sort of sliding in underneath. Very softly, elegantly. Had a real touch. I had to see that, so I quickly ran in again. And you know who was playing it? Her idiot son was. Could hardly reach those levers down there..."

"The pedals."

"Couldn't reach them and still he played like a genius. I swear. I couldn't make that up now, could I? Man, what a day. I am completely exhausted."

"Happiness is a full time job," said Bernie. "If you do it right it's a mighty powerful work-out. Pity it comes so rarely. Projectorially,

I mean." Then turning to me: "I must use the phone. Can we get into your office from here?"

It was down the end of the jetty, through a door on the left, up the inside stairs, straight on, at the end turn right, then left again and you're there. Marlene was still belting it out below but we closed the office door behind us.

She dialled the number. "Nellie, Nellie? This is..." Pause. I could only hear her half of the conversation, but it sounded bad.

"Now, don't say that, Nellie."

Crrch – crrch - pop was all I could perceive for fifteen seconds, and then Bernie's voice filled in the blanks on her side again. "Nellie, Nellie my dear friend, I have done this as a favour..." Pause.

"I know that, but don't do anything irrational now. I beg of you, don't." Apprehensive pause.

"What do you give them, Nellie?" Pause, then: "That's not enough. Have a heart. Make it at least an hour." Pause. "Nellie? Nellie!" Turning to me: "She hung up."

We listened to exuberant applause faintly filtering through the door. Quietude for a few seconds, then laughter in the audience. Perhaps a clown act.

"She gave us only half an hour." Bernie cocked her head. "And they are already on their way. There..." Mixed in with the hilarity from below we could now hear the distinct wail of far-away air raid sirens coming through the window. "Quick, to the roof."

Ted had also heard it and, for the first time today, totally abandoned his ship and followed Bernie and me on the welded rebars to the rooftop.

From here we could see a wide sweep of the beach along the city, but high-rise buildings barred the view of the downtown area corner Klein and Third.

"How do you know where to look?" asked Ted.

"My bank."

"How come you know?"

"Military secret." Still the distant sirens blared, mixed with the laughter from the stage below. I looked at my watch. "Fifteen minutes." We waited. Flashing lights were now visible speeding towards the inner city. Ambulances, fire engines, emergency vehicles, traffic controllers, the full mobilisation from a city crew that had experience in these kinds of disturbances. All people in the targeted section, plus those in the surrounding eight blocks would now have been evacuated.

"Should we not have warned those in the hall?" I asked.

"Don't create a panic," Bernie warned. "They are safe down there. It's just a local thing."

"Three minutes more." The laughter from downstairs stopped, instead a band was striking up some Dixieland toe-tappers.

"There, there." Ted saw them first. The missiles came in pairs about four seconds apart, and when the first pair had passed, the second followed shortly after and in a slightly different trajectory so that it soon vanished from sight. We saw the reflection of the first flashes in the tall buildings, the audible whoom, whoom came a good time later.

"All mine now," Bernie whispered to herself, then out loud: "Think nothing of it. These tiffs happen almost every year. Bata Transcontinental Assurance doesn't mind losing money on occasion. It's cheaper than war."

We stood and watched until the all-clear sirens blared. The spook is over, close the books. "Damn electricity," said Ted. "They can take out something as small as a trash can nowadays, and it's all done with damn electricity."

Suddenly it was quiet. "Oh, the Professor. I must hear his closing speech. Anybody coming with me?"

Bernie and Ted followed me as we hurried down to the lower level again, past the dressing rooms and into the wings of the stage from where we could see Professor Klonus address his audience. Some other dancers and performers were milling about, out of sight of the audience, straining to hear what he had to say.

The audio system had been arranged to minimise feedback; as a result it was difficult to understand the Professor from their position. "What did he say - what did he say?"

"He said he was now coming to the end," someone closer to the proscenium answered.

Two or three minutes must have passed already and now the Professor's monologue was almost over. He paused. We could see little beads on his forehead. The audience applauded again.

"He said he will now have to leave this city... all the friends he has here..."

I could faintly listen into a whispered conversation between a female dancer and the young lad with his unicycle. Dancer: "Who was that new one? The one who sang? She's a sensation."

Whispered answer from the cyclist: "I heard she'd been a star once."

Joe pushed his way forward and I clearly heard him add in hushed voice: "She'll be again. A big one."

"What did he say now?" somebody inquired about the Professor.

"He said this was his happiest time ever, or something like that. And he's not the least bit sorry."

"What does that mean, 'was'?"

Marlene joined them in the wings, slowly working her way from the back to me, waiting for her cue. She was dressed in long black trousers and tails, cylinder hat, white gloves, high heels and holding a walking cane with a big silver knob not totally unlike Melmoth's. "What's going on?" she whispered in my ears.

"I'm not sure. Can't make it out clearly, but someone heard he was quitting."

"Quit the show?" She grabbed my arm. "Did he actually say that?"

"Shhh," the one up front shushed them. "He said, he's going home."

Suddenly the Professor turned his full face towards us, the twenty or so people in the wings. "You there, all of you. Come join me on this stage. Come out and take a bow. Ladies and Gentlemen, friends. This is my family."

Tentatively the performers stepped into the light, one by one. Five dancers, a unicyclist with his wheel, two clowns, a prop guy wearing a baseball cap, Bernie, Joe in old jeans and sandals, Ted in his magnificent captain's uniform, seven or eight others, myself included. We walked on stage, slowly, hesitatingly, blinded momentarily as we advanced into the bright footlights. Everybody was greeted by the audience with a hearty applause, and when Marlene stepped onto the boards which again meant the world for her, the audience got up on its feet and the hand-clapping didn't want to end. Finally the Professor waved his arms and silenced the crowd, which reluctantly sat down again.

"These and many more are the ones who did it all. Look after them," he commanded. Marlene stepped forward and sang *Falling in Love*. All walked off the stage, and just before the curtain fell we all saw a man and a woman in police uniforms handcuffing the Professor and leading him away.

⁂   ⁂   ⁂

The following morning Marlene, Joe and Ted and I held a conference in my under-furnished third floor lodging. The front door slammed noisily and, huffing and puffing, Melmoth appeared, throwing a stack of newspapers on the table.

"They can't make up their minds what the biggest headline is," he shouted. "Here, a local paper. Get this one: PORTFOLIO PANDER PINCHED. It goes on: 'A massive scandal hit Crosley last night when the city's largest financial manipulator, a self-promoted professor of the humanities... and it goes on and on about a stock swindle. But it gets even better. On page three there's this: Business Bank Damaged. And it reads: The Sovereign Bank corners Klein and Third Avenue was heavily damaged and may have to be torn down. Blah, bah, blah, and then: ...the cause is still under investigation. Natural gas leak is suspected. The bank carried full insurance. And on page - wait a minute - page 17: Transformer substation burns down, and in the article it talks about overload and part of town was blacked out for almost two hours until the load was switched to another power grid, and so on and so on."

"Does any paper refer to tanks in Vesper?"

"Sure does. This paper here, way back on page twenty-three. It reads: Three obsolete Tiger tanks of the Municipality of Vesper were taken out of active duty. Nothing about foreign invasion or such. But page one has this headline: OPENING A ROUSING SUCCESS."

"Let me see that," Marlene asked. She read quietly for a minute, then out loud: "Listen to this: The greatest surprise was the performance of a new star, Marlene. She kept the audience spellbound with dancing, singing and just being herself. We shall undoubtedly hear more from her in the future. On one occasion

Marlene was accompanied solo by her 12-year old son Wolfgang Amadeus at the piano, another star in the making."

Ted: "What about the Professor?"

Melmoth read out: "This paper here. EULENSPIEGEL KAPUT. Dah, dah, dah… packed house - here, at the end. Although the performance at the newly refurbished Hertha Pavilion under its new name Eulenspiegel Hall was sold out, it could be heading for financial difficulties as, according to reliable sources, its funding may have been overextended. The new management of the Sovereign Bank may negotiate bridging funds… And on and on. Now that we are on the subject, I have the latest information on this. Hang on now. Bernadette Robinson is the new CEO of that bank. It's true, I talked to her earlier. Apparently, their data bank had broken down and only Bernie could fix it. They had to give her the job or it would have been curtains for all of them. And between you and me, I'm not surprised."

"How about the Professor," Marlene insisted to know. "Is there anything we can do?"

Ted vanished for a minute, then came back with a gallon of Mountain Red and a stack of plastic tumblers. "You know where I got this one, eh? It was hidden under the tracks of the launching platform. You know, when we launched the Majestic."

"What about the Professor," Marlene kept asking. "What did they do to him?"

I had the answer. "He's under house arrest. They let him stay in his office suite at Eulenspiegel Hall. He phoned me late last night. He wants to see me this afternoon."

"The best one I have saved till now." Melmoth pulled another newspaper out of his pocket. "Here, read this: Eulenspiegel's Arrest Staged. And it carries on like this. Da, da, da, …the two peace officers which led him off the stage had been hired by one of his employees, a certain Miss Lauris. The two actors, in uniforms which resembled those of our Metropolitan Peace Officers, are members of Talents Management Inc. and were a part of the stage show. They could not be reached for comments and were last reported having been spotted at the airport waiting to depart for the town of Arakiri."

"Mountain Red anyone?" Ted asked.

CHAPTER THIRTY

"Sit down, Son, sit down."

I was concerned. "Do they treat you well?"

The Professor was upbeat. "I've done it! I have actually pulled the rug out from under them. They didn't even see it coming." His radiant face lit up the room. "Yes! I have done it again. Never trick an old trickster – you loose every time."

I had to smile at the Professor's exuberance, but I was anxious about his well-being. "Can you move freely, Professor?"

"Yes, yes, they treat me quite well. These cops here are real, you know. I have all the upper floor and the washrooms downstairs. They pretty well leave me alone as they decide what to do with me now. They are going to charge me with fraud, and you know how emphatic these people are regarding property rights. The ones who have it all don't want to share it with those who have very little. They hang you for theft but slap your wrist for character assassination. It's become a very strange world." His grin widened again and his eyes radiated elation. "But I've done it again. Yes, yes, they'll try and give me a hard time, but something will come to mind. It always does."

"Would it help you if I moved into my own office next door? Just for the transition, I mean."

"I don't know if they would let you." Professor Klonus' confidence was now visibly fading. "Of course, it was Borelli who is laying charges. I expected it."

"They lost a great deal of money, didn't they?" I was not sure, but the Professor did not seem to be sorry about it. "What will you do next?"

The Professor walked over to the window and looked out, mulling over the options still open to him. "My alternatives are very few," he finally admitted. "Instead of facing a court I would like to go through the durbar. Can you help me?"

"What's a durbar?"

"It comes from India, but it has been changed in many ways. Instead of a court, this is an audience chamber where no lawyers are allowed. There are so few of them here anyway. Should the reason for my crime be based on mitigating circumstances, I can be sent into treatment or whatever measures may be prescribed. To set up the durbar requires an amanuensis." Noticing the question mark written all over my face, he continued. "He is the arranger of things. I may not set up my own affairs; instead I have to make use of a go-between, a messenger of sorts, one who in turn must find a podesta, and that's somebody who is completely uninvolved in the matter. Then the amanuensis must assemble a ring of ten people who know me, have had contact with me and are somehow aware of my offence."

What exactly is he accused of?

"They have not yet specified the charges, but it will be for investment swindle. As the facts here are crystal clear I would not stand the chance of a light sentence in a regular court. The durbar gives me hope. A reprimand, perhaps a year in some re-education ranch, a chance to make good, but not behind bars forever. I could not take forever. Will you do that for me? Will you be my amanuensis and try and organise the affairs for me?"

"Why me?"

"The moment we met I knew that you would be the person. I anticipated this day with a certain pleasure, even knowing how it had to end. You came just in time. - Will you?"

It sounded like an immensely complicated task but I nodded agreement. I will try, I will do my very best. I'll be the best damn amanuensis the Professor ever had. "But please tell me, why did you do it? You are a wealthy man."

The Professor laughed. "I am? You know, Tony, I don't have a cent. I never had. That castle? I happened to be a guest there just when the owner had to flee. He asked me to look after it while he was gone, and that I did. I kept it in perfect shape, as you know yourself. He left a sizeable bank account, which pays for all upkeep and the servants and maybe a bit more. I am a poor man, but I have never pocketed a single penny, not a single one. Never just for myself. I'm that poor farmer's boy whose goose was stolen. The old cardigan and the baggy pants you see me wearing? These are my own. Still, I have assembled the best crews to build things; I left my traces all over the world. Do you know why I got you out of Vesper so easily? They have a big library there, a big, beautiful opera house and a budget to run it for eight more years. Two public swimming pools and a bird sanctuary. Somebody has to pay for all that, and I figured the Borellis of this world should be the ones to do it. They are thieves anyway, and it's so easy to steal from thieves. Now go, my friend, get me that durbar."

✳   ✳   ✳

Bernie's temporary office was a cramped trailer in the parking garage of a minor sub-branch of the Sovereign Bank at Twenty-eighth and Hamilton. A million organisational tasks distracted her and I was uncertain if I could thoroughly explain the situation, or if she was even the slightest bit interested in the Professor's fate. "Sit there," she said, "and don't move." I sat down, then stood up, ready to leave. "Sit!" she commanded, pointing me back to the small chair near the door.

I sat quietly as Bernie did this and that and more, and the minutes ticked by, people came with questions and went with instructions, the phone rang constantly and she hardly ever looked at me during this time. Finally she was free and I told her of my job to get a durbar together, without, however, mentioning the Professor's pecuniary realities.

"Borelli," she mused, and a smile lifted the corners of her lips. "He'll be the obstacle. Let's go and see him now."

We met him in the conference room of the *du Barry Club*, third floor, next to the Mason's headquarters. There was no hello, no handshake, no friendly greeting. Right from the start it was clear that this was going to be a nasty bit of one-upmanship. I opened the encounter and asked for change of venue for the Professor from court to durbar, Dr. Borelli vehemently opposed this suggestion, and Bernie just sat back in one of those fat red leather chairs that can live a hundred years and still look elegant and important.

"I told you," Borelli addressed me. "Durbar is out. Absolutely and definitely out. And after I am finished with this huckster…"

"The Professor."

"… this huckster you call professor, after that I'm going for you, my friend, and I'm going to cremate you. Take my word for it. You knew damn well what was going on; you were supposed to get me the tipping point, but instead of working with me you undermined me, you betrayed me, you caused me colossal grief. Don't for a moment forget that."

Bernie's voice was too sweet to show genuine sympathy. "There was no tipping point. The Professor turned himself in. Everything was staged; he fooled us all. And then he informed the real police afterwards. He wanted to fail and he wanted the world as a witness. How much did you lose, Charlie?"

He whipped around to face her. "You viper. You knew all along what was going on and you didn't warn me. How could you?"

"But Charlie, you were in on it. I could see it from a mile away. If there is one thing you should have learned, it's to stay away from investment schemes. The likes of you always get caught. For how much did he get you?"

"A lot." How much? "It's not just my money, it's for the Security Exchange Company. I'm finished. They'll not only kick me out, they'll bar me from even coming to this club here. And nobody has ever been fired from here before." For a moment I thought he would break down and cry.

Bernie smiled so disarmingly that one could easily fall into her trap. She always smiled this way when she moved in for the kill, and the gorier the better. It seemed to give her immense pleasure.

"Charlie, listen me out. I run the bank now, you know that. We lost all data in the accident. Copies were safely hidden away but they got to that place also. Now think for a moment, just a very brief moment. Why do you think I am the CEO there now, hm? In case you can't figure this out all by yourself, I'll tell you why. It's because I hold all the trump cards. No, I didn't say I could doctor them, I merely said I hold them. How? Banking secrets. Now, Charlie, it so happens that you do your banking through my bank, right? And a lot of the Security Exchange Company funds, as well. Right? Charlie, it would be a shame if all that got lost, don't you agree? One day you wake up and all is gone. All of it, except for the mortgage on your house and the money you borrowed."

"It's been long paid off."

"Not according to my records. Not according to mine. And I am sitting on a mountain of money and can easily drag this issue through the courts for at least five more years. I can now buy better judges than you can. But listen me out, Charlie. I have a proposition for you. You let my friend here go ahead with getting the durbar organised and he will include you in the Ring of Ten. As a direct result of your, say, generosity this will do many things for you. Let me add them up. First, you will look less vindictive. Gives you the aura of impartiality. Fake, mind you, but aura is aura. Next, you can have your input in the Ring as one of its fully qualified members, and if the group agrees with you, which they very well might, you'll have it your way regardless. And thirdly..."

She smiled even lovelier that ever. "Thirdly, my dear Charles, you may then find your credit ratings and your accounts safe and intact. It's such a miracle."

"That's outright blackmail."

She shrugged. "Sure is. You decide."

Dr. Borelli bored his eyes into mine. "I want him. He started it all."

"But Charlie, what would you want to do with him? He's just a penny-less squatter. But ask him yourself if he agrees." She turned to face me. "What do you say, Honey?"

I nodded, uncertain as to what I just agreed to. It sounded like a shell game and I couldn't figure out where the peanut was. "Okay."

Charles Borelli knew he had limited choices, but he was prepared to launch his last missile. "I agree only if I am in the Ring."

I weighed the proposition. If it actually came to it and I let Bernie be my own amanuensis to set up my durbar I could hope that I might walk free, even with Dr. Borelli in the Ring of Ten. Otherwise the Professor would have to face the full court and the evidence against him was irrefutable. He would admit all and there were no other options. Borelli looked at the bank CEO: "But know that I agree under protest." His bushy moustache quivered with rage.

"It's all settled then. Men can be so thick-headed at times." Bernie's face lit up and her eyes sparkled like diamonds.

CHAPTER THIRTY-ONE

Ahasverus the pawnbroker opened his door when I banged on the window, hoping the old man would hear me. "The hour is late," he said, "but sometimes people come in the middle of the night when they have an emergency. I should have a night bell some day. Come in, young man. You must be in great distress to visit me at this time."

It was just past nine PM, or twenty-one-hundred-oh-seven hours as Bernie would have put it, and I felt badly about invading his privacy. I searched for excuses, but the pawnbroker cut me off.

"Oh, think nothing of it, Anthony. My door is always open for my friends, any time day or night. Tell me all about it."

It took me some time until I had unravelled it all, explained the details of the raid in Vesper, the premiere and last performance of the production, the Professor's fate and now my own problem of having accepted the duties of an amanuensis and setting up the durbar. Ahasverus stroked his thin white beard and thought it over for a minute.

"The way I see it, your biggest problem will be to find a fitting podesta. Although it's not a tightly regimented court session, it would still be an advantage if he had some experience in court matters. I know the right person, but he may be too old now to accept this honourable duty and take the long trip to here. It is my friend Il Nolano. He hasn't travelled much in past years. Must be ancient now."

"How old are you, Mister Ahasverus?"

"Time here is not at all the same as it was once. If I were a mathematician I might say that here the quanta come in irregular lumps. Which measure is the correct one? I don't know; nobody does. But I'm much older than Il Nolano. We came here together, he when he was in his early fifties. I was perhaps just thirty-five Planck years then, but I was already an antique, an itinerant conjurer. How old am I now? I have lost track."

"He lives in London, right? If he is willing to come, may I go there myself and accompany him back here? I would take great care of him."

"Yes, you would, I'm sure. I am very hesitant to ask him. I owe him so much; he owes me nothing. But you are right, I must send him a message."

After a glass of tea we composed this letter: 'My dearest friend Giordano; The news from here are too insignificant to have reached you in London town, but a young friend of mine has accepted the duties of an amanuensis and is now looking for a podesta. I have suggested that you may lend your distinction to this venerable task. However, knowing how frail you might be now, I am very hesitant to ask you for this favour. This young lad, Anthony Parker by name, would be very happy to come to London town and accompany you personally here to Crosley; that is, if you are still able to travel long distances. I assure you he would take great care of you.

'I must also admit to a secret agenda of mine. I have hoped day by day that we might meet again. Your room upstairs is in readiness for you as it has been all these many years. For one thing, you must explain to me why you now think Aristotle was almost right but had the symbols wrong. I am burning with curiosity.

'For ever your faithful friend and disciple, Ahasverus.'

"How long have you been friends?" I asked.

"In my wandering years Il Nolano and I met for the first time in a little town near Lübeck where he changed my name to Ahasverus the Magician. - There now, all we can do is wait." With that the pawnbroker clicked the 'send' icon.

*   *   *

I temporarily moved into my small office in Eulenspiegel Hall near the Professor's abode. A hastily scribbled message waited for me, which read: "We must talk. Tell me when. Sebastian." It was highly irregular to see it signed with his first name, so I immediately called back only to learn that Mr. Melmoth was already on his way to see me in person. "He was very agitated," Mrs. Wanger remarked. "He said something about a scribe. No, I really don't know what he meant."

An hour later Melmoth showed up in person. "Anthony," he shouted from the end of the corridor, tapping his bâton fervently. "Have you picked the scribe yet?" He hurried closer. "Really!" he bellowed as he entered my office and studied the cramped room. "You actually live here? Don't they even give you a suitable bed to sleep in? The indignity - and on a leather sofa!" He sat down on it, out of breath. "Hard like a tomb stone. - Yes, a scribe. You need one for the records. Believe me, I'm certainly the most competent of all the scribes you can find anywhere. I have experience in both the courts and the writing, and I assure you that my spelling will be perfect. It always has been."

I objected. Didn't Melmoth know what a disaster he had been? Unreliable, useless and incompetent. Besides, a scribe was neither called for nor necessary. How long has it been since he wrote his last line?

"Over a hundred years, literally. I know, Tony, but what harm can it do to let me try? Please, Tony, I beg you."

It broke my heart but I had to decline the offer. "No, I cannot do it. You have a bad track record, Mister Melmoth, and you nearly screwed up the show."

"I know, I know. Would it help if I got on my knees? Right here in front of you? Ask the podesta. Ask the Professor. His liberty may be at stake but my soul is dying. What harm could come of it? You have a court recorder anyway, and I'll be back there in the farthest corner and out of harm's way. At least say that you might reconsider; grant me that much."

I protested. "You are not trustworthy. Much had gone wrong on account of you."

"I would blame myself, but then I would disallow you the privilege of doing so. When the gods want to punish us, they answer our prayers."

"There you go again. You have nothing new to contribute."

"Tony, my friend, the Professor is a dreamer. They'll crucify him. Society forgives the sinner; it never forgives the dreamer. Let me help. At least ask."

In the end I did not have the heart to deny him that small favour. "No, but I will reconsider. I will ask the Professor and I will ask the podesta, and if they both agree... It's against my grain but I grant you that much. It will most certainly still turn out to be a 'no' anyway."

Melmoth jumped up and hugged me so hard that I had trouble breathing. "Oh, thank you. You are so gracious. Have you found your podesta yet? Tell me, Tony, have you?" I told him what was planned. "Who?" he insisted to know. "You must tell me, who?"

"It is a former monk. He is called the Nolan."

Melmoth sat down on the leather sofa again and stared at me with wide-open eyes. "You mean Giordano Bruno? But he is a saint."

"Do you know him?"

"Everybody knows something about everybody here. We've all been around for such a long time. No, I have never met him but I have heard stories. He saved a man's soul once, they say. It's an old legend, and you know how unreliable legends are. Most of them are poetic claptrap."

"Tell me the story, Mister Melmoth." I rolled up the big leather chair from behind the desk and sat down directly in front of my visitor. "Now you owe me that much."

"Yes, yes, I do. First, do you mind if I smoke?" I nodded, Melmoth delicately pricked the tiger's emerald eyes to open the cane's opal lid and offered me one of the five Black Russian cigarettes hidden in his walking cane. I declined, and only after my visitor had lit up and inhaled a few puffs did he continue.

"The story begins in Germany at the end of the sixteenth century where this Dominican monk, who was called... I'm so overjoyed, I can hardly focus my thoughts. Let me hug you." He jumped up, squeezed me once more and then sat down again and continued. "Anyway, this monk had written a book on magic. The title, I think, was *De Magia*. He was on the run from church authorities in Italy because he constantly collided with their dogmas. The pope and cardinals would have liked nothing better than to throw him into the dungeon where he would probably have died of neglect or starvation or disease within a few months. That would get rid of this pest once and for all."

What specifically angered the pope? I bent forward as not to miss a single word.

"For one thing, Il Nolano - that's what he was called - he asserted that the world was round and that it turns on its own axis and circles around the sun. The church dogma was still locked into the old Aristotelian credo that the world is a flat plate and the sky, complete with all heavenly bodies in it, is more or less a broad canvas covering it all. Copernicus had come up with the new arrangement of the solar system some fifty years earlier already, but his heliocentric calculations were not yet widely known. And of course Columbus had already sailed to the Americas on nothing more than a rumour. A round world circling the sun? Millions of other suns visible to the naked eye, and probably millions of planets just like earth full of people and monkeys and who-knows-what? And all that coming from a Dominican monk? If at least he had been a Jesuit. Well, that simply put a bee in the pope's bonnet."

I wondered. "So, this monk - was he a mathematician himself?"

Melmoth took another drag and inhaled deeply. "That and more. He was a bloody genius by all accounts. He wrote I don't know how many books on a dozen subjects, on memory, cosmology, on infinity. I think he even wrote a play. Incredible man. Magic, though, was his favourite interest."

"The slight-of-hand stuff?"

"That also, at least as entertainment, but mostly the type which invokes the supernatural. And of course, it was also fashionable then that one tried to make gold from lead. So it happened that he searched out a man he had heard about. This man was a conjurer earning a modest living with a Punch-and-Judy show in market places around the little towns and villages between Hamburg and Lübeck. Naturally, the two were drawn together and became friends the moment they met. Magic in those days was equated with witchcraft and sorcery and superstition, all of it in direct opposition of the Church. Christians who were suspected of performing wizardry were hauled before the inquisition from which very few ever returned. - So you will ask him, will you?"

"Yes, Mister Melmoth, I'll ask the Professor; I promise. Please, carry on."

"The people were so terrified of the inquisition in those days that they did not even dare having cats. Those had been symbols of mysticism in Egypt and hence were suspect of being instruments of Beelzebub. As a result of this the rat population exploded, and with it came the plague which killed half the population of what was then the Western World."

Melmoth nervously flicked the ashes off his cigarette.

"But I'm drifting. That region of Germany was already Lutheran and he was safely out of the pope's reach. The two men spent a lot of time in each other's company. Did the monk learn from the puppeteer, or did the puppeteer learn from the monk? I don't know. They certainly influenced and benefited each other. - Are you going to ask him today? I mean, the Professor? When can you let me know?"

"I'll ask him today, and I'll let you know immediately. OK? Now, go on."

"Oh yes. Here the legend really begins. That puppeteer said he was the Wandering Jew who, as the myth goes, was cursed by Jesus personally for having slammed a door in his face when he was on his way to his crucifixion on Mount Golgotha. The man - he was actually a shoemaker by trade - he was damned to wander for all eternity, or at least until Jesus came back. Jesus, of course, didn't, and the poor man kept wandering. That's as far as the myth goes, and it was said that only someone who could understand eternity and infinity could free him from this curse of vagabondage and to deliver him from his endless state of vagrancy. That person was Giordano Bruno, the man from Nola. But there was a terrible condition he, the monk that is, had to agree to. The condition was that he voluntarily return to Italy where he knew the cardinals were already honing their daggers."

Melmoth inhaled another drag deeply before continuing. "Yes, the monk actually returned on his own free will. Deliberately. Why? Nobody could ever explain this, but he went back to Venice knowing what awaited him. This was the worst thing he could have done to himself and he knew it. Some thought that he had fallen prey to a schemer by the name of Giovanni Mocenigo, a man who pretended to be his friend and then betrayed him to the authorities, but in essence Il Nolano returned on his own volition. He wanted to see the pope personally, he said. Of course, he was arrested, incarcerated and after eight years of torture burned at the stake. With the death of Giordano Bruno, at that very hour, the nightmare of a thousand years ended and the modern Western culture began. - Do you mind if I smoke another one? - Go. Go ask him now."

✳   ✳   ✳

It took me nine frightful hours to fly to London where I rented a small resting chamber directly at the airport. There I relaxed for five hours and then waited at the VIP entrance until the white limousine drew into sight. The pawnbroker had arranged everything beforehand, the first class tickets, the limo, even the nurse who accompanied Il Nolano on the plane to make sure that he did not suffer undue stress. The monk looked amazingly hale for his age. He greeted me with a hearty handshake and a wide-open smile. "So you are the youngster to take care of me?" he laughed. "May I call you Antonio? You look just a little pale to me. Maybe I should take care of you?"

"I would be delighted if you'd call me Antonio. It gives me the illusion of being a light-footed Italian instead of a heavy-booted Canadian. I had some bad experience with airplanes lately, so forgive me for not running in circles to catch my own tail. I am, however, absolutely delighted to meet you personally, Sir. I have heard so much about you."

Il Nolano winked me off. "Young man, I have absolutely no intention to live up to whatever you may have heard. Do not judge me by what you believe to know, judge me by what you actually learn from your own observation. Better yet, tell me all about yourself. We have a long flight ahead of us and you look like a person with a story to tell. I heard that you are a squatter and desire to return to the previous reality."

I had mulled this question over in my mind lately without coming to a conclusion, but suddenly I knew. "Not any longer. I don't remember much of my life there anymore. I have now settled here. I love to be here now."

It was nearing midnight when the monk Giordano Bruno and Ahasverus the Magician finally faced each other. The clock in the parlour divided eternity into countless measured portions, it's tempered tick-tock permeating the stillness and making the seconds gently float away in all directions. They did not speak a single word, they both stretched their arms towards each other, walked the few steps which now separated them, and then quietly hugged for a long time; two old men embracing each other in undying devotion.

CHAPTER THIRTY-TWO

"May we all come to rest?" Il Nolano greeted the assembled members of the Ring as we sat at the horseshoe-shaped table. "We shall first introduce ourselves to each other, and let me begin by myself. I have accepted the honour of being the podesta for this durbar. I am called a podesta because in former times I would sit just a little higher than everybody else, but that has long been done away with. If there are any questions, please interrupt me and speak up. Are there any questions now?"

He looked around the table at the five people sitting to his right, the five sitting to his left and the Professor in front of him at his own small desk. At the rear to his left and right the recorder and the scribe respectively, both at their individual escritoires at the sides. In addition there were about fifteen people in the gallery overhead.

"Nobody? Very well then, let me carry on. I am a monk and I come from Nola, a little town in Italy where I was born in the year of fifteen hundred and forty-eight. My full name is Giordano Bruno and you may address me as Father Giordano. Or just Giordano, if you prefer."

He scanned his Ring. There we were, looking like ordinary people, yet we had to decide what was real, what was an emotional issue, what was best forgiven if not forgotten, and what was needed to be amended. He was not here to judge, he was here to help and find out who, if anybody, was answerable to what.

"Look upon me as the gendarme who directs the street traffic, but, unlike in an adversarial court, I do not have the authority to jail any driver I dislike. Our resolutions will be final as it will be born out of mutual understanding and respect, and no appeal will be entertained. I shall have no vote unless required to break a deadlock, and I shall be allowed to ask any question, which, at least in my mind, may shed some light on this event. Are there any questions now?"

He made eye contact with each of us but there were none. Father Giordano continued: "I now ask our person of interest if he agrees to the proceedings as they are now constituted. Are you, Professor Klonus, satisfied with the makeup of this durbar, and are you prepared to live with the outcome of these proceedings?"

The Professor voiced clear and distinct agreement. "Yes, Father Giordano, I agree."

"Then would you kindly introduce yourself to all of us."

"I am Till Eulenspiegel. I was born on the first day of April, in the year one thousand two hundred and ninety-one at Kneitlingen near Braunschweig. That's just a little south of Hamburg. I died on the first day of April in the year of one thousand three hundred and thirty, and my bones are buried in the cemetery of the Church of St. Nicholas in the town of Mölln. They say I fooled a lot of people. The first day of April has since then been known as the Fool's Day."

"Would you please tell us where the town of Mölln is located?"

"Mölln lies between the city-states of Lübeck and Hamburg in what later became the country of Germany."

How would he like to be addressed?

"I have always wanted to be addressed as Till. It is the name my dear parents gave me."

Father Giordano smiled. "I know the town of Mölln well. Next to this church is a tiny market place where I once purchased a jar of that wonderful dark heather honey which you can only obtain in Mölln and nowhere else. I also had met a man there, a puppeteer who later became my dearest friend. The two of us had stood at your grave and wondered who you may have been, you, the jester who entertained and upset so many. I bow my head to you, Sir, in admiration and affection. Before we deal with the allegations against you..."

"Whatever you may say, it is true."

"We are not investigating the validity of charges; we are dealing with the underlying motivation so that we may form an opinion of our own. Matter of fact, we assume the evidence of your culpability to be true but we shall each try our best to establish the reasons of your motives." He looked around to make certain that everybody had clearly heard his words. Then he continued: "May I direct my next question to the person sitting at this table the farthest away from me to my right?"

Joe cleared his throat. "My name is Joseph. I have a full name but if the durbar allows me to maintain my anonymity, I would prefer to be called simply Joe. I am... I was an employee of Mister Till and I am ready to testify."

"Thank you, Joe. Yes, you may remain incognito. The person sitting to your left, please."

It was now Bernie's turn. "My name is Henrietta Robinson. I married Edward Green and so became Hetty Green. Some called me the Witch of Wall Street on account of my clever trading at the stock market, which brought me one true friend and many enemies. At the time I was the wealthiest woman in the world, but I lost it all."

"Would you mind to tell us how?"

"Making it was easy, but I did not spend it wisely. Spending is an art form I never learned. I let others waste it."

"How would you like to be addressed, Missis Green?"

"Please, call me Bernie. All my friends do."

Il Nolano nodded. "Thank you, Bernie. The person to your left, please. You and I have met a few days ago, but please state your particulars for the record."

It was now my turn and my throat was dry. "I am Anthony Parker." I looked around; a million eyes hanging on my lips, but there was nothing more to tell. I was ready to sit down again, but then added: "I am a squatter."

"You have shown great skill in assembling this durbar, and I thank you for your efforts. You are also a very considerate young man who accompanied me from London town to this meeting. Now the woman to your left."

"Eulalia Pennsinger. I'm used to being called Miss Pennypincher behind my back. I smile at that because it signifies my exactness in money matters. I am an accountant. I was also the financial confidant of the Professor. I mean, Master Till."

"Thank you. Now the man directly at my right, please."

"Doctor Borelli, veterinarian. I work at the zoo."

Father Giordano looked at him quizzically. "Have we ever met before?"

"Impossible. I come from Lugo in beautiful Italia…"

"Right, but your face… Did you not have another name?"

"Impossible. I swear on the grave of my dear, beloved…"

"Be careful with that, Doctor Borelli. Were you not also known under the name of Charles Ponzi?"

"Only temporarily, your Honour. I had several names, and one of them might have been Ponzi. I am the originator of a scientific wealth management system, a system which results in a cornucopia of monetary abundance from which we have all benefited. There is no laundering of any kind. The funds are clean and sanitary. You are talking about a methodically constructed instrument for the rapid transfer of wealth. Out of the savings accounts - right into the heart of all our industries. I am its inventor and promoter."

"Are you not also a member of the secret society known as the Security Exchange Company?"

"I trust it will not disqualify me."

"On the contrary, Doctor Borelli. All of us, especially myself, are interested in the workings of secret societies. The more we know about them, the better we can deal with this curse. Now to the child at the extreme of my left, please."

"I am Margarete Zelle. I would like to be considered an adversarial witness because…"

Il Nolano interrupted her. "First of all, my dear child, this is not an adversarial court but an audience chamber where we shall find out the underlying causes of our conflict. We shall hear your opinions at the proper time. For now it suffices if you will merely state your preference of address."

"In Dutch it's Grietje."

"Is that your original name?"

"Yes, I didn't change it. I'm not ashamed of it."

"Nor should you be. Were you not an exotic dancer once?"

"Yes, but my career was abruptly terminated."

"Thank you, Grietje. Or may I call you by your nom de guerre, Mata Hari? I now direct my question to the young person sitting to the right of Grietje. I see you dressed as a woman but I believe you to be a man?"

"Yes, Father Giordano, I am male. My name is Lauris. I'm the factotum here. They call me the Commander, but that's a red herring. I command nothing. Other than my dress code, there is absolutely nothing remarkable about me. I am not certain of my cosmic age, how or why I came here, or what my past might have been. Nothing at all. I am not even certain of my full name, that is, if I have one."

Il Nolano focused on Lauris, then said: "If you had a choice, what name would you like to have?"

"I really don't know."

"You look Nordic. You are actually much too broad-shouldered for a woman. Could you stand up, please?" Lauris stood at attention, straight up and chest out. "And your hips - my goodness. They could never bear a child. May I suggest your name to be, say, Norstad? It seems to have just the right timbre."

"I would love it."

Il Nolano looked around, addressing the entire group. "Does anyone here have any objections to give this young man the name of Lauris Norstad? Hm? Hm? You up there, in the galleries, any objections? - I see only head-shaking. Very well, Lauris, you are now Mister Lauris Norstad. How would you like to be addressed?"

"I would like to be addressed as Mister Norstad. I love that name."

"Thank you, Mister Norstad. Now the person at your right, please."

"I am known only as Busby, but my full name is William Berkeley Enos. I am a choreographer and I had my hand in many motion picture productions. Call me anything you want but don't call me before noon."

Il Nolano smiled. "That is very humorous. You may have borrowed that pun from the inventor of the life jacket. What was her name again? - Mae West."

Busby shook his head. "No, this joke is my own. In spite of my usual acerbic disposition I have occasional funny streaks. And Mae

West did not actually invent the life jacket, it was merely named after her on account of her hourglass figure."

"Thank you for enlightening me, Mister Busby. One never really stops learning, does one? The man sitting on the right of Mister Busby? Please."

"I am Gus. I am a civil engineer and some of my work is well known, such as one very tall tower in Paris."

"You are Monsieur Gustave Eiffel, then?"

"Yes, I am. You may also know that I had built the structure under the Stature of Liberty."

"Were you not also known as the Magician of Iron on account of the many bridges you built?"

"Yes, I was, Father. I am now retired. Please, just call me Gus."

"Thank you, Monsieur Eiffel. I am honoured to see you in this durbar. Now to the lady directly on my left, please."

"I am Marlene and I would like to be addressed as Marlene. My past is my secret."

Il Nolano placed his hand over hers. "And so it shall remain, Miss Marlene. Your secrets are safe with me." Turning towards the recorder sitting in the far back towards his left: "You are the recorder, and you need not introduce yourself to us." He then turned his head slightly to the right. "And you. Yes, you, the scribe."

"I am known as Sebastian Melmoth. I had adopted this name when I moved from London to Paris after my misadventure."

"You need not reply, but if you do, what would you say was the root cause of your misfortune."

"Everybody knows that now. The whole world knows it."

"Of course, it does. But do you know?"

"Arrogance, Sir. Nothing but uninhibited hubris."

The monk closed his eyes for a few seconds, then continued as if the question had been irrelevant all along. "How would you like to be addressed, Mister Melmoth?"

"I hate and despise my name and would like to be Oscar Wilde again. I beg my friends never to call me Sebastian nor my ridiculous nickname of Knuckles, and certainly never as Melmoth."

"What exactly does a scribe do, Mister Wilde?"

"Nothing of any import, Sir. I invented this post on my own."

"How delightful. Why are you here then?"

"To interpret the proceedings in my own fashion which may differ from the verbatim transcript of the recorder."

"Please, give us a demonstration, Mister Wilde. Tell us how you interpret what Miss Marlene had just answered."

Wilde cleared his throat, scribbled on his note pad, took the bâton in his hand, got up and walked towards the open centre of the horseshoe table between Eulenspiegel and the monk. We all focused our eyes on him as he imagined for a moment to have been transformed back to a free-spirited Berlin when the Cabaret ruled the boards. Twirling his bâton over his shoulder as if it were a parasol, he gyrated to his imaginary mark. There could not have been a greater physical difference between him and Marlene, but his hip movements, his gestures, his eyes, his pinched, mocking lips, the way he held his head and the style in which he minced his steps caricatured Marlene with the deftness of the consummate mime. In spite of the artistic exaggeration the total impression of his impersonation was at the same time a loving tribute to her stage presence and charm.

"I am Marlene," he said, copying her soft, accentuated alto voice, paused, slowly looked at each member of the durbar with raised brow, then added. "Nothing else needs to be said." As he languorously walked back to his escritoire applause broke out.

Il Nolano stood up and bowed towards the poet. "Mister Wilde, I am impressed and delighted by your exquisite little performance. I now fully understand your magnetism and your wit which once enchanted a whole world." Sitting down again, he continued. "Having introduced ourselves to each other, we shall break early today. Are there any questions from my panel?"

Bernie raised her hand and stated her petition. "Father Bruno, I have an important meeting tomorrow for which I require time off. It is a political matter for which I also require the presence of Tony Parker as a witness - that is, if he agrees."

I nodded. "Yes, yes, of course."

The monk looked around. "Any objections? Very well, tomorrow is a holiday for all of us. Personally I would like to add that I am looking forward to some rest myself. It was a long flight and I am an old man who needs to catch his breath more often now than in former years. We shall resume our panel on Monday morning, ten o'clock."

✳   ✳   ✳

We took off in the Sovereign Bank's newly purchased executive ultra-light fixed-wing aircraft at eight in the morning. "You absolutely must help me with this one," Bernie instructed me. "Nellie Smith will be suspicious of our intentions, so I need you to set things right." Reading my mind she continued. "What are my intentions? Tony, Dear, they are entirely honourable. We want to get some of their money." How? "By making peace with them."

"So, why don't you just come out with it? Everybody wants peace."

"Sweetheart, that's a crock. Nobody wants peace. It interrupts career development."

Bernie was flying this plane with the joyful abandon she had already exhibited in childhood when she first strapped on her ice skates. I sat white-knuckled next to her, staring intermittently out of the plastic side windows and calculating our chances of survival should the engine stall and we were forced to an emergency landing anywhere in this ocean of wheat and canola and tall prairie grass.

"Can you sort of slow down a bit? My stomach, you know."

"Honey, why? Did you have sardines for breakfast?" She had that damn infectious smile again. "I can show you how to fly a loop." My grip tightened even more. "Just kidding, Darling."

I forced myself to be calm. The weight of the aircraft, the fuel, the passengers, even the picnic stuff in the back, divided by the total area of all load-lifting surfaces... I crunched the numbers in his mind. "Bernie, I just figured it out. You and I have each about the size of a handkerchief of wing area to hold us up in the air."

"See, Love, that's why I can't slow down much more. Now, if I could go faster we wouldn't need much more lift than from a postage stamp. For each of us, of course."

I closed my eyes and invoked the picture of an aquarium filled with lackadaisical zebra fish to get myself in control again.

Bernie gave me peace-making instructions. "You will agree to everything I say, even if, on the surface, it seems to be dumb or false. It's called 'tactical diversion'. You echo the voice of the public and I trust that you'll always nod and perhaps say something fitting now and then, such as 'it is common knowledge' or 'it's in all the papers'. You have to ad-lip as we go along. By the way, we'll land in less than an hour." She tried to calm my anxiety, and soon it was "just another twenty minutes," and finally "let's find a spot here somewhere."

Under us now rolling grassland, a fence here and there, cows and buffaloes and llamas, lots of llamas. "That's Vesper territory," she explained. "They have all the high-priced cardigan business and we just make their buttons. Something needs to be done about it."

We sat down near a tree-enclosed creek and quickly unpacked our load consisting of a folding picnic table, four chairs, two lounges, baskets of food, a tub of crushed ice with five bottles of champagne sticking out their banderoled necks. In addition there also was a flower vase with six rare black roses, linen table cloth and real cutlery as Bernie could not stand the sight of plastic utensils. Then she read our position from the GPS and made a short phone call from the cockpit. When she returned, I was laying out the table for four in the shade of a mighty maple tree; she laughed. "They already spotted us from a satellite. They'll be here in half an hour. Wanna skinny dip?"

CHAPTER THIRTY-THREE

Hastily dressed and still soaking wet we watched their helicopter land next to our ultra-light. Nellie Smith and her dark-brown pilot, a heavy-set matron well past retirement age, debarked fully dressed in battle gear. "Who's your chocolate bunny there," Bernie greeted Nellie, pointing to the old aviator at her side.

General Smith replied. "You cheese faces better be nice to her. She's a storm trooper and one sour remark from any one of you and she'll lay you flat before you can fart. - This is Captain Smith, my mom." Whispering conspiratorially: "I'm adopted."

This broke the ice and we greeted each other with the affection of old enemies who had been undercover friends for years. "Nelly, take that damn uniform off, and you too, Missis Smith."

"Call me Bessie like everybody else," the Captain replied. "I'll call you Bernie, if you don't mind."

"Thank you, Bessie. I have a hunch we'll get along just fine. Let's all sit down for a nice, slow picnic and talk. I have a big list of what we should discuss, but first let's have a glass of iced champagne to celebrate. And thank you for coming."

"I know what you have in mind," Nellie Smith said. "You want to drink us under the table and then..."

"Nelly, how could I out-drink any of you. Especially you. I grew up a Quaker, for crying out loud. Quakers don't drink. Maybe nowadays they sip a little bit, but that's all they do. - How about you, Bessie?"

"Oh, I can hold my liquor okay. Gimme some gin and I'll sing you the blues."

Within minutes the two newcomers had changed into light leisure outfits which, in an amazing sense of premonition, they had safely packed into their chopper, then we finished the first bottle of champagne and everybody relaxed. Preliminaries over, Bernie launched her opening bid. "The reasons I asked you... I begged you to get together with us are manifold. First the tanks. I'm not in the army anymore. I now run the bank, and that's a completely different game. But let's get over this tank business first. We have too many. Isn't that true, Sweetheart?"

"Absolutely," I replied, nodding with emphasis. "It's in all the papers."

"What papers?" Nellie inquired.

"You know, newspapers. Like the Transvaal Guardian," I floundered.

Heading off certain disaster, Bernie quickly intervened. "If you like, I could arrange it so that we give you one of ours. If you feel better about it we can stage some sort of a rumble and then make a skilful switch."

General Smith was not convinced. "What are you driving at, Bernie? What do you want?"

"For one thing, we need more industry. Look around here, you've got all those little camels..."

"They are llamas."

"... those cute little llama babies and I would like to trade with you. I'll give you the Hutterites."

"They don't make us money, and they are ours anyway."

"No, Nellie, they are not and you know it. We can waste our time fighting over them for another hundred years, but I am here to see what we can arrange between the two of us. Just you and me, Nellie. And your mom, of course. There must be something we can do for all of us."

"You've got Doctor Scholl's."

Bernie shook her head. "You can't get rich on insoles."

"You have Universal Velcro and Buttons."

"Want to trade? Give me the camels."

"Llamas."

"Give me the damn llamas and you can have Doctor Scholl's and shoelaces and arch support and the whole lot. Tony, dear, what did you tell me yesterday?"

I was ready. "People want top quality cardigans everywhere. There is a crying need and Crosley really wants them very badly. Besides, we have lots of empty manufacturing..."

"I mean about Doctor Scholl's."

"Everybody is craving for them. Insoles and all that. With so many flat feet around nowadays, this is a gold mine."

Somehow I felt this was the wrong approach, so I quickly got up to evade further questioning, refilled the glasses and the second bottle was finished. We nibbled on shrimp salad and jellied eel, on fresh strawberries with whipped cream, and on soft cheese on Melba toast and caviar on ice, and when bottle number three was emptied our real trading resumed.

"I don't want Doctor Scholl's. It hasn't got any romance."

"Doctor Scholl's has lots of romance. Tony, Darling, doesn't Doctor Scholl's have a lot of romance?"

"It's chock-full of it."

"How?" General Smith was sceptical.

I nodded fervently. "It's common knowledge. There's something in their commercials that attracts public attention. The style, I guess, the colour, the script. The format. The whole sanity of it."

"See, Nellie, even Tony can see the romance in it. The name lends certain weight to it."

"Then why trade it away?"

"Tony, Dear, why do we want to trade Doctor Scholl's?"

I took a deep breath. "Bookkeeping. We don't have good bookkeepers, that's why we lose money on that stuff. Vesper could be set up for streamlining the overhead, what with all their laptops and accountants. Unless, of course, we keep the factories and just farm out the management. Put the headquarters where they rightfully belong. Build you a new command centre right in downtown Vesper where all those talented CEOs operate. We can keep the noisy, stinking factories. And if we let those TV commercial producers at Vesper do all the global advertising we could even double our output, make more money yet and divide the loot among the two cities. Fifty-fifty." There, what a tour de force!

"Incredible," said Bernie.

I was just warming up. "And after we've gotten rid of Doctor Scholl's..."

"Tony, Dear," Bernie interrupted me. "We are clean out of champagne again. Please, be an angel and touch up our glasses." Turning to Bessie, "Drink up, dear. There's so much more of it."

Bessie cleared her throat and sang a few notes. "Gimme a pig foot and a bottle o'beer…"

Bernie was puzzled. "Beer? Do we have beer, Tony Darling?"

Nellie interrupted. "That's just an old tune she keeps bringing up." Then addressing her mother: "Hush, Mom. We'll have our reefer later."

In the end Crosley kept Doctor Scholl's and Universal Velcro & Buttons. Instead we traded the llamas and the high-priced cardigans against the Hutterites which were an endless source of friction anyway. Then Bernie added a sentence which almost brought this impromptu conference to a grinding halt.

"And after that's done, let's build a proper six-lane highway between the cities, and a monorail, and gas and oil and water pipelines, and electric…"

"Stop right there!" Nellie Smith interrupted her. "What's all this talk about trade and peace? What would I do for a living? And how about poor mom? Flying these things is all she knows. She's no good doing anything else. She can't even boil an egg. What would you like her to do? Become a hash slinger at Xeller's? We have a vested interest. You can't suddenly have peace break out, just like that, without warning."

"But Nellie, what we have done so far is nothing more than a game. Like football or hockey or something. We've not been at a real war for - what is that now? A hundred years or so? Face it, Nellie, wars are getting out of fashion."

"Bernie, can't we just have it sort of peter out? Slowly, I mean."

"It's petered out a long time ago, Nellie. War is dead. I'm in banking now, and I would like to try something different."

"Oh Bernie, you are at your old tricks again. What you want to do is sneak in capitalism again. It didn't work before, what makes you think it does now? Gave us nothing but billionaires and people underfoot who sleep on sidewalks. If you do that you'll really have me pissed off."

Vesper desperately needs water, which Crosley has in great abundance, Crosley needs oil and gas and electricity which Vesper has to sell. Both need trade and commerce and elimination of duplication of services. Finally Bernie played her trump card. "I'll give you Eulenspiegel Hall."

Nellie was stunned. "You would? How - how could you move that?"

No, we can't move that one, Bernie explained, but we can build you a brand new one. "We have all the best engineers on our side, we have all the talents, we not only have the show, we even make those trumpets and tambourines in our own factories. Look at your city. What do they manufacture, if anything? You can't even come up with a good cardigan without using our buttons. You have nothing but accountants and lawyers and underwriters and real estate agents and useless bank managers. There isn't a single solitary genius among the whole bloody lot of you. You guys are always running around, stiff, noses in the air, serious, deadpan, humourless, laptops under your left arms. Look at us, Nellie. We have them all, poets and builders and inventors and lots of crackpots. We Crosleyans may be a dysfunctional society, but we are dynamic, artistic, lively and productive. Isn't that true, Tony?"

"Absolutely. They are all talking about it."

Nellie was sceptical. "You are all so poor."

"Yes, we sometimes run out of cash. We have less than you, but for some reason we have never considered ourselves to be poor. And now we have rediscovered something we thought we had lost - just like you. We are laughing again."

"I understand the Professor who started it is under investigation."

Bernie shook her head. "I'll lay you ten to one that he'll get off with just a little slap on his wrist. Just ask Tony."

I was ready. "Yes, he'll get off. I'll personally make sure that he does. It's all set up."

"And Tony should know. He's so close to the Professor, he could be his son. Tony's the genius behind it all. What is it worth to you if we send him to Vesper? Him and Gus and Ted and the Professor; that's all you need. Think about it. We'll build you a brand new Eulenspiegel Hall, supervised by the originator of it all, Master Till himself. And there's another thing, Nellie. How would you like to be in charge of the combined Crosley-Vesper Military

Force of Peace Consultants, and Bessie, you'll be in charge of your own airline. Would you like that?"

"You mean forever?"

The General added: "Till them eagles grin, Mama."

Captain Smith did not have to think for very long. "Yes, I would like a desk job for a change. Look at my hips. I put on a few pounds and those seats are getting to be awfully tight now. They were made for men with narrow asses. And the seat belts are too short to get around me. And I have a hell-of-a-time getting on board. That first step is a real son-of-a-bitch."

"But Mom, flying is all you know. You'll be so lost with memo pads and staplers."

"Hush, Nellie. I would love to sit behind a broad shiny desk, in a very wide, deep, Burgundy-red leather chair."

Bernie agreed. "You'll have the best chair there is."

"With five wheels under."

"Yes, Captain, with five wheels under."

The General was still uncommitted. "What's in it for you, Bernie?"

Bernie didn't have to think; she had been waiting for this question. "I want to be the richest woman again."

"That's the part which scares me about you, Bernie. Your single-mindedness. Have you no other dreams?"

"I want to put my cards on the table. I want my bank to move into Vesper. I'll build the headquarters there. Mind you, the accounting and paperwork will still remain in Crosley for now, but I'll build a new banking high-rise, taller than your Vesper Tower."

Nellie protested. "You can't do that, Bernie. Not taller. You'll insult us all if you do that. At least have the decency to stay, say, five storeys lower."

"Done, Nellie. And one more thing. How would you like to have the world's largest shopping plaza, one with a thousand stores, and an indoor lake, and dolphins, and half a dozen submarines, and a roller coaster and a huge merry-go-round with painted horses and gilded angels in the rafters? All of that under one roof, eh? My bank will lend you the money."

"Bata will never let us do that."

"Oh yes, they will. We'll stand up to them, and if they give us the least amount of trouble…"

"Then what, Bernie! Declare war against them?"

"Much better. We laugh at them. They have one Achilles' heel, and that's their lack of humour. We'll ridicule them in all the Eulenspiegel Halls everywhere, and in print, on the net, on the air waves, on satellites, in the movies we show on our own airline. They better start to laugh with us or the whole world will laugh at them. They couldn't take that."

It was time for bottle number four. The sun was now at it zenith and all of us took a skinny dip. "And you, Bernie," Nellie asked while treading water, "what will you do?"

"I?" Bernie laughed, "I'll be sitting on a stack of money again. It's only a numbers game, like the score on a pinball machine. I have no secret agenda."

"And how can all this be accomplished?"

"A million here, a million there, you have no idea what money can do. It buys you presidents and their vices and Prime Ministers, city hall and public opinion. I know how to use leverage."

"How would you get your hands on so much money?"

"With Tony here. He's a real genius. Aren't you, Honey?" I only nodded. What can one add to something so obvious?

Indecision seemed to falter the meeting. Trying to be helpful, I suggested putting this issue to a referendum, a democratic plebiscite perhaps. The women looked at each other, then at me. Bessie broke the silence. "What's voting got to do with democracy? We're just discussing how it's going to be done, that's all. Voting just makes waves."

Men! They are such sticklers for details. "Well," Nellie returned to the topic, "let's go for it then. Anybody got a towel?"

CHAPTER THIRTY-FOUR

"Mister Wilde, would you kindly hand over your cane? Pardon, I mean your bâton."

"Father Bruno, under normal conditions I would be disconcertingly reluctant to lend it to anybody or for any occasion. This is the only luxury to which I am enslaved. However, in this case I shall be absolutely delighted to make an exception." Oscar Wilde carried his bâton directly to the monk.

"Thank you, Mister Wilde. It shall be returned intact." Facing the entire group: "This is the Talking Wand. Only the person who holds it may speak. Master Till and I are exceptions to this rule. While you hold Mister Wilde's bâton, please admire the beautiful artisanship. I believe it to be one of the last from Fabergé. Am I right, Mister Wilde."

"Yes, you are right, Sir It was restored to its original beauty.`"

"I see, Mister Wilde, that you had scribbled something in your notebook. Could it be your interpretation of what just occurred? Please, read out aloud what you wrote."

"You might not want to hear…"

The monk showed his impatience. "On the contrary. Don't underrate the curiosity of an old monk. We are all eager to hear every delightful word."

"Only if you insist." He briefly scanned his audience. "All right then, here it goes. 'He sat there, aware of his powers yet under a fake egalitarian patina which fooled no one, not even himself. Although he should have drawn my apparent fondness for my bâton out of nothing more or less than my subtle gestures alone, he still used this precious item - now pay attention! - as a Talking Wand. Not a Talking Toothbrush nor a Talking Hairpiece - that one would at least be mildly amusing - no, it had to be a Talking Wand. In the end, my bâton was reduced to a common stick and so elected by a majority of one over zero.' Shall I proceed?"

"Thank you, Mister Wilde. I am delighted that you finally found your voice again. Your wit had always enchanted me with its quirkiness; now I know about its directness as well. You must forgive me for exploiting this situation for my own selfish wants."

The rules of the durbar were quickly laid out, and the first person to speak was Grietje.

"I am certain everybody will praise him," pointing to Eulenspiegel, "but think of the cost."

Il Nolano studied her quizzically. "Such as?"

"I'm not talking about the money he admits stealing, that's really not my business here, but the way he exploited me." So much study went into her research trying to account for the romantic desires of the public, so many exotic gowns were designed and sewn, so many veils, shoes, baubles and beads for the dancers fabricated. New scores were composed, dances choreographed, and where did it all end up?

"And for what!" she ended her tantrum. "Not only did I practically have to work around the clock, but in the end I had to throw it all into the dustbin. Just like that. I worked my heart out and he just took his felt marker and crossed me out of his life. I had worked up so much enthusiasm, and then it was all undone in less than one single second. I was not even worth the meagre pay I drew out. Let him answer to that!"

Grietje sat down. There was a pause where everybody assessed his own experiences, and how much of her story was the truth? Not just the facts; facts can't explain the truth. Indeed, I also had put my heart and my time and energy into my tasks, some of them pretty knotty ones. I, too, never drew out a lot of money, at least not for myself, but there was a monumental difference. I worked for the sheer love of just doing it. Frustrations? You bet, but they were long forgotten. I raised my hand but Busby's was up a little faster and Il Nolano had him holding the Talking Wand.

"Mister Busby - yes?"

"Before Master Till answers to this challenge, I would like to ask if Grietje fears to be short-changed of public acclaim for a job well done. She needs to be applauded, that's her style. I understand her completely. I have confronted the same problems in my own jobs, and often what didn't work on one production worked on some other. Or it ended up in my biography, which always gives one's own life a bit of superficial polish. In the end I always got my applause. If her job was well done in the first place, the body of it can be reworked into an anthropological study. Or a self-help book: 'Eroticism in new Makeup'. If nothing else, the data could be used to try and discover the motivations why people buy what kind of soap, or whatever. She's still very young, a mere child, and new opportunities will come up. The work will have public recognition somewhere in the future, unless, of course, the efforts were rubbish to begin with."

The monk looked directly at Eulenspiegel. "What's your view on this?"

Eulenspiegel closed his eyes, stroked his thin hair and was deep in thought for a while. "Yes, Grietje is right. I was misled by her age. It did not occur to me - or to anybody else on my staff either - but her efforts should not have been entirely wasted. The problems with the work done by her was simply too detached from what was needed for the show. Not that it was wrong, but it was only half finished; however, I was negligent for not thinking of other options. And Parker here - it was his job to catch these glitches, but he sat on his derriere a lot and tried to push everybody in the wrong direction."

I looked at Eulenspiegel, my much-adored Professor, and our eyes briefly met. Was that a tiny, nearly unrecognisable wink in his left eye? If so, only Bernie and Joe could have seen it also, and neither of them would talk. "Yes, I should have paid more attention," I admitted.

"Ah, young Mister Parker here is eager to talk. Please give him the Wand."

How could I respond? How could I tell this group that I cherished the old man as if he was my own father, but this man was also often a terribly distracting, superficial, demanding monster of a boss. "Grietje is right. We had worked out a brand new belief system complete with rules, regulations, structure and symbols.

What has he done with our efforts? He wasted all of it. Nothing of what we accomplished in this short time was ever used. What did he do instead? He put on a variety show. Ordinary, run-of-the-mill entertainment. Tap dancers. Unicycles. He fooled us. He lied to us. He said he wanted one thing, and when we delivered he just trashed it all. A variety show..."

"What did you expect?" Eulenspiegel interrupted me. "Of course I fooled you all. That's what I do. That's my job. I'm a jester, a buffoon. And don't forget, I kept the tambourines and trumpets in the game plan. You want depth? Go, drill for gas."

I addressed my adored Professor directly. "You robbed us of our efforts. They say you stole money. What you did to us was far worse; you stole our contributions in sweat, labour and dedication." Turning towards the podesta I added: "All around, he drove me nuts almost daily. He wants this and he wants that, and it all has to be put together by Monday morning, and the terrible pressure... He isn't even aware of the demands he puts on everybody. I suppose he's just too expeditious to get into details."

I looked around the circle, trying to fetch agreement from the group. Only Grietje nodded, all others turned their faces away. Catching Eulenspiegel's eyes I saw the hurt I just caused. No, I did not want it to come out this way, I did not intend to complain, to harass this little fat man whom I loved with all my heart. How could I explain in a few words that, in spite of my personal disappointment of having wasted so much of my efforts, I loved working for him, with him, against him even, if that got the job done faster.

"But the strangest thing is that we all loved our jobs and we did it. All these tasks were plainly over our heads but nobody here ever failed. That's the strangest thing: nobody ever failed. We simply didn't permit to let each other go down. We all came out a lot larger than we went in. For my part, he made me feel proud of what I could accomplish, proud of what I have become."

Nobody spoke for awhile. Finally the monk said: "I begin to understand who this man really is. But we must hear other voices. You, Mister Lauris Norstad, what would you say?"

Lauris was dressed in unisex sport apparel, yet he would never be mistaken for a woman again. "Sir," he began, "I still don't quite know on which side of the fence I shall fall. I love him, but Master

Till was most certainly also a vexation. Nothing this man ever touched worked out right. At least not the way he had in mind. You had to hover over each one of his moves, and you take your eyes away for a second, just one lousy second, and I'll swear he'd push the wrong button. Sometimes I thought he took delight in pushing the wrong buttons. All the same, he had a touch of genius. Whatever he did, whenever he seemed to fall on his nose there was always somebody around to catch him, to set him upright again. And yet, he had such canny wisdom that it may take us a long time to understand it all. He could see through us and challenged us to our utmost. And in the end he was always right."

"How long did you work for him?" Il Nolano asked.

"Five years. I started with him at age sixteen or thereabouts, right out of school where I learned very little. I quit high school early to get my hands on a few loonies, so I became something like his gopher. Soon I had to remember telephone numbers. He could never remember anything. Then he made me read the whole encyclopaedia - twice. From cover to cover. And then this and then that and I would have to stretch my memory into a million obscure corners, trying to remember where to get this, whom to talk to there, and there was no end to it."

"How did you do that?"

"I invented my own system. For instance, I mostly transformed numbers into symbols which I could remember. Five-seven-nine would become 'a handful of weeks is one short of the perfect ten'. I don't know why it worked, and often enough it didn't, but if you screwed up he never even mentioned it. It's almost as if he had fun seeing someone goof occasionally and then watch you come up with a thousand tricks to straighten it out again. He sure gave me lots of rope."

The monk smiled. "I understand that you are considered to be some sort of a mental genius. It just so happens that I am one of the very first experts involved in the training and mastery of memory. What you did was to control memory and combine it with your native intellect and spontaneity. Could it be that he intentionally did all this to you so that you could develop your own inborn capacities?"

"He practically made me memorise his whole telephone book."

"Exactly. Are you not proud that you can do that now? Where would you have been otherwise."

"I'd be a gopher, maybe."

Il Nolano nodded, then looked around, his eyes hanging on Miss Pennsinger. "You were the accountant. What have you to report?"

Miss Pennsinger rose and delivered her say standing up straight. "I was in on the scam. I was the only one who actually tabulated the results. I did it not for personal profit, but I wanted this little chubby man there to succeed. Sometimes I even thought that it was I who dreamed up the whole scheme by myself, but that was not entirely so. I merely let it happen. With his meagre knowledge of accountancy I suspect that he didn't know what went on. His sense of bookkeeping was in step with the Middle Ages, but I'm not sure he was actually aware of what went on right in front of his nose."

Till Eulenspiegel raised his hand and responded. "Thank you, Miss Pennsinger, but I would rather be considered to be a thief than an ignoramus. I often shudder when I see you all running in circles, but I urged you to muddle on. And my heart leaps with joy when I see how you all managed to evade my many traps."

"I have a complaint," Dr. Borelli shouted out. Given the Talking Wand he laid out his claim. "I don't want to cuddle up to this swindler and bathe him in saccharine sweetness. Our investors, and I am one of them, they have been robbed of a great deal of money. We either want it back or we want other compensation."

The Doctor laid out his loss statement. How much? A great deal. Millions? More. Much more. "I don't want to fix numbers here, but be assured all this was a very large amount. He," the doctor pointed his finger at me, "he was supposed to tell us where the tipping point was, but he didn't. It would have saved us."

The Nolan interrupted him. "If the young lad had betrayed his employer, Master Till, and signal the - what do you call it? - the tipping point to you, Sir, what would have happened then?"

"We would have made our rightful profit."

"And who would have lost that amount instead?"

"Somebody else. But I do not represent somebody else."

"It appears to me that you, Doctor Borelli, suffered your loss primarily not just on greed alone, but also on account of placing your trust on young Antonio here. Did you have a mutual agreement regarding his duties to you?"

"Not in the legal sense, no."

"Were you aware, Doctor Borelli, that young Mister Parker had an occupational obligation to Master Till at that time?"

"Yes, of course I was."

"As we have not yet established the culpability of Master Till, it may be premature to throw aspersions at anyone. On the contrary, it may appear to some of us that you, Sir, attempted to lead Antonio away from his responsibilities to his employer so you could collect your - what did you call it again? - your rightful profit. As this profit was entirely based upon an illegality to begin with, the word 'rightful' should be handled with utmost circumspection. Can anyone shed light on this situation so that we might find out once and for all the degree of culpability involved? Yes, I see Bernie raised her hand. Go ahead, Bernie."

She turned the Talking Wand between her fingers, gently stroking the beauty of its design. "We are all talking in circles. This cane," she began, "was refurbished in one of the bijouterie working for Master Till. Look at the sheer beauty of style, its arresting craftsmanship; I can only assume that it must have come from very gifted hands. Who discovered these hands? Then look around you. Crosley was a dump. Why? Because its people were depressed, downhearted, dispirited. Suddenly everything changes. There is a wedding on an festive barge; there is a beautiful building, a wonderfully entertaining show. Suddenly there is laughter, joy..." She did not finish her sentence - enough was said.

Il Nolano took off his reading glasses and looked at Bernie for some time. Finally he asked: "You are a banker, are you not, Bernie?"

"Yes, I am a banker."

"As a banker, would it not be your first responsibility to regulate the flow of capital and make certain that it is always returned to its rightful owner? Should a financial institution be in any way responsible for the discovery of artisanship or an entertaining act?"

Bernie replied without hesitation. "You are right, Sir, in a very narrow sense it should not. However, speaking as a custodian of accumulated wealth, it would be my larger obligation to see to it that any moneys in the system have the greatest effectiveness for public benefit. If the accumulation of funds in private hands leads to capitalistic dictatorship and tyranny it will, in the long run, impoverish the human spirit and wealth to the detriment of all."

"Your philosophy may not be shared by all."

"This is true. Those who are in control of huge funds have a vested interest in spreading misleading conjectures which are favourable only to themselves. Furthermore, they will do their utmost to sabotage the education of the working classes which created their wealth to begin with. Without scholastic fundamentals these people would lack the required knowledge to make intelligent choices and so can be manipulated at will. The advantaged classes will then substitute superficialities for the losses of common wealth."

"Please enlighten us."

"It had happened before. *Panem et cirsensis*, the Romans said. Give them bread and games; it diverts their attention. What happened when their society was dumbed down? The real power of the nation came from their productive classes, not from those who owned their wealth. Eventually cynicism took over, the power of the state ebbed and the invincible Roman Empire collapsed. Even those who had amassed great wealth came to grief. No, there is no law against profit; but who, in the end, owns our society?"

"There, she said it herself. We don't have a law against making a profit," Dr. Borelli shouted from the sideline without the protocol of the Wand. "The way I see it, we even have an obligation to do so. There are two sides to every issue."

Il Nolano turned to Oscar Wilde. "I'm not sure I fully understand what goes on here. Are we talking out of both sides of our mouth? Please, give us your impression based on Bernie's statement." Resignedly he added almost inaudibly: "Perhaps that will explain something."

The poet was not yet finished with his writing, but the group waited patiently until he caught up. Finally he was ready and cleared his throat. "She held my bâton with obvious erotic, sensuous pleasure, her fingers…"

"No, no, Mister Wilde, give us just the last exchange between Bernie and Doctor Borelli."

"Right. It appears that, in the name of fairness, every speculation, every philosophical hypothesis requires two opposing opinions to face each other. This malaise is called 'playing the devil's advocate'. The confrontation is assumed to be between two equals, where in reality such equality does not exist. One may say that, on the one hand, the pestilence killed half the population of Europe, but, on the other, it reduced the number of the unemployed for generations. While this statement is factual, it neglects to point out the imbalance between millions of lives lost versus the expense of an effective employment insurance system. To rephrase the above: never have two opinions - it only confuses the issue. Or in other words: in order to see two sides of the coin one must be both cross-eyed and myopic."

"That will do for now, Mister Wilde. Now I know even less than I did before. We haven't heard from all of you yet, but we must get our discussion on track again. If you please, let us get back to the issues. Monsieur Eiffel, you are so evidently silent. How do you see Master Till?"

Gus was ready. "The little fat man there? He was an absolute disaster. He didn't know from one day to the next what he wanted. Actually, I got much of my instructions through Tony here. If at all possible, Tony was a worst disaster yet, but at least he was consistent. He claims to be an engineer, but honestly, what kind of a matchbook university did he go through, if any, hm? He wanted me to weld under water, just so he could save on the cost of a caisson. Sure, you can weld under water, but how about metal carbonisation which would embrittle the steel beams? Did he not realise that just such embrittlement was the true culprit in the Titanic disaster? What kind of a hare-brained quickie course of metallurgy did that young man ever waltz through? None. I had to weasel around his advice and quietly added a bracket here, a gusset there. Even put in two extra beams and hid the costs in the 'Sundries' account. The building was to hold a thousand people - dancing. Swinging. The tuned frequency of the entire structure was nine cycles per second! Far, far too low. According to my numbers the harmonics should have been at least seventeen cycles. On top of it, he never once considered the dynamic load of..."

Again the monk had to interrupt. "At this stage we are mostly concerned with Master Till, if you don't mind. I understand that there is a petition by Dr. Borelli to place young Antonio into the centre of interest in due time. I am not entertaining this new request yet. Please, Monsieur Eiffel, carry on."

"The Professor, as everybody called him? Basically he was just a windbag. 'Do it this way' and next day 'do it that way', you never knew what came tomorrow. Still, he got everybody excited and busy and curious. He would throw a handful of inspirational fluff into the air, and before you knew how it happened everybody caught part of the thrill. A thrill it was, definitely. Mister Norstad said that he was given a lot of rope. That's exactly what the Professor did to all of us. It was as if he threw us into the lake and then watched how fast we could learn to swim. In the end we all turned out to be expert swimmers, and if one of us was in trouble, there always was somebody else around to rescue him. I had for a long time suspected that there was a lot more hidden behind that man than he pretended to be. He was an extraordinary person. If he had asked us all to... to throw our shoes into the river, we probably would have done that as well. He had that effect."

Il Nolano added: "You may be pleased to hear, Monsieur Eiffel, that he once did exactly that, and he did it while dancing on a rope spanning a river no less. However, I notice that Master Till wants to say something." Nodding to Eulenspiegel: "Let us now hear your pre-empt, Master Till; you have the floor."

Till Eulenspiegel slowly rose from his seat and approached the podesta. "Father Bruno, I have full confidence that this durbar will be fair and just, and that you will strive for truth rather than facts. The facts are clear: I have misdirected much money."

He casually walked some paces towards Grietje, then past Lauris, Mr. Busby, Gus, me, all down the line until he stood directly opposite Joe. "Joe, why are you here? Not just here at this durbar, but here in this world of ours?"

Joe briefly closed his eyes, then admitted: "I don't know."

Eulenspiegel made a quick quarter turn, pointed his finger at Wilde and called out: "Oscar Wilde, why are you here?" Walking towards the scribe until he could nearly touch him: "Why?"

The two men locked eyes silently. Seconds ticked by, yet it remained absolutely still in the room.

Finally Eulenspiegel broke the tension. "The sins of omission, Mister Wilde. A mind like yours, and yet, what did we get? A few quotes, a bit of farce written for the Victorian stage, a fairy tale now and then, parlour jokes and much self-pity. Much self-pity. Any semi-competent hack could have produced as much in a year or two, yet you wasted a whole lifetime on what? On what exactly, Mister Wilde? We expected so much and received so little. I had hopes that you would stand up and resume your art here. Why did you fail at your second chance, Mister Wilde?"

The reply was nearly inaudible. "I froze up."

"Louder, Mister Wilde! Don't you realise that you have obligations? You were given a talent and you stole from us by keeping all for yourself." Turning towards Father Bruno. "This man wasted that of which he was only a custodian. He stole from us - no, not money. Money is mere bookkeeping entry, electronic digits, nothing but numbers. Mister Wilde stole much more than numbers. He stole some of our cultural heritage. He stole wisdom though he had so much wisdom to spare."

Eulenspiegel now faced Dr. Borelli. "Yes, Doctor, I picked your pockets. I should now say that I'm sorry, but I don't. I'm glad I cleaned you out. But let's look at the merchandise first. What would you and your group - what was it again? Right, the Security Exchange Company, what would you have bought with all that money? More power, more control which you would have used to buy more power and more control. In other words, Doctor Borelli, you wanted to buy more money with money of which you already had more than you could possibly ever use. Doesn't it make you a little bit sick in your stomach?" He pointed at Bernie. "She has it now. Tell me, Bernie, are you up to your old tricks again? What will you buy with all your money, Bernie? Tell us!"

"I don't know yet," Bernie answered. "I know how to make it, I have yet to learn how to spend it well."

"Then what is your dream? Tell us your dream, Bernie."

Bernie looked around the circle and her eyes linked with Dr. Borelli's. "You and I are cast from different moulds," she addressed him. "We do not have much affection for each other, yet we should work together nevertheless. We would be under constant tension, which would energise us. Can you work under tension, Doctor Borelli?"

"I will never work with you for any reason."

"With your focus, your connections, your drive to win at all cost, we might be able to put my money to good use. Listen carefully, Doctor Borelli: this is a peace offering."

"I don't think so. You are annoyingly presumptuous, young lady."

Bernie insisted. "How about financing Master Till Eulenspiegel? How about setting him up in Vesper? How about a global entertainment syndicate, Mister Borelli?"

Eulenspiegel interrupted them. "Absolutely not. I'm not a business enterprise. I am a jester. I appear when most needed and when least expected." Turning towards Grietje he continued. "Grietje, you are the most disappointed. Why?"

"I put my heart into it."

"When was the last time you put your heart into anything? Tell me, child."

Grietje fidgeted with her pen, drew little figures on her note pad and bit on her lower lip. Don't cry now - not now, not where everyone can see me. "When I was a small child I had crayons. I drew up little dresses and cut them out, stuck them on my doll. The nuns came and took them away."

"You searched for your lost crayons all your life, Grietje. Those crayons were symbols of your passion. And now, suddenly, you rediscover this passion. You are angry because you believe I have taken it away from you again, don't you? There are millions of coloured pencils, Grietje. Find them. Go for it; fill your life with passion."

Eulenspiegel slowly walked to his centre chair again and sat down. Always filled to the brim with boundless energy, suddenly he looked exhausted. His eyes lingered on some pictures on the walls, then stared into nothingness. "I am tired," he allowed. "Can we break?"

Father Bruno answered. "Of course we can. We all know who we are and how we relate to each other. I, too, tire easily now. We shall adjourn until tomorrow morning ten o'clock. Adjourned."

CHAPTER THIRTY-FIVE

B ernie had to talk to me. "Come, you must help me. We have only half a day and if we act quickly, we can still pull it off." She explained to me what to do and how to do it: beat up on the entire Security Exchange Company and make them squirm in agony. "Tony, Darling, my bank holds much of their wealth in cash and papers. They invest in services, oil, gas and hydro-electricity. They have just lost most their convertibles and may be near collapse. My bank also holds a small amount of similar shares. I'll panic-sell them. You, Tony Sweetheart, you will sit somewhere else and buy. You buy all you can catch with my money. I know it's not legal, but to hell with cosmetic niceties. I'm a banker; I don't have to be nice."

Looking at me quizzically, she added: "He turned me down. I came to him with an olive branch but that bastard actually turned me down. He shall regret that."

Bernie sold the Northern Telepipes shares in suspicious chunks, kept selling them as they nose-dived down first to 92, then, as the Asian markets opened, plummeted towards the fifty-loonie mark. During the night it slipped out of sight and I began to buy in at three loonies. At the same time the news was all over the newspapers. Vesper's and Crosley's year-long negotiations have broken down, they reported with great flourish.

Open warfare was now expected, as all trade deals between these financial juggernauts collapsed and the Sovereign Bank sold their energy assets. Insider trading was suspected but never chastised. At zero-four hours the share price had plummeted to penny stock and

I had seventy-two percent of them. Only frightened low-volume investors hung on in terrified stupefaction, not knowing what to do next.

"Don't worry, Tony dear, it'll be up again in a year. He's in free-fall now. All we can do is sit back and wait for the splat." Her fist hit her open hand. Splat.

Bernie was still on the 'phone but I had just sunk into sheer exhaustion when it rang again; this time it was for me. "Anthony? This is Hanna. We must do something quick. Yes, I know it's only five o'clock but this is urgent. I know what must be done."

When she showed up at my old walk-up apartment minutes later, she displayed no surprise to find Bernie at my place as well. And she came with bad news.

Dr. Borelli had plans to have the Professor kidnapped in the morning, she said, lock him up somewhere else and slowly suck every penny out of the man. That done, he would be terminated by hired goons. Borelli is a monster, she said, and would do anything to get his revenge. She had her eyes on him for years already, she claimed, working for him to earn his trust, watching him, secretly exploring his business dealings. Now was the time to get him.

"We must hustle Master Till out. Now, this very minute. And I'm the only one who can actually do it."

Although the guards had given the Professor a free rein within the building, including receiving guests, leaving Eulenspiegel Hall unescorted was another matter. Ted came up the stairs. "That V3 is still up there on the roof. But there are all those vents sticking out everywhere, and exhaust fans, and this and that. And it's still dark now".

"At the Eastern side, there's a flat portion. Five feet wide." I tried hard to recall the blueprints which had gone through my hands so many times.

"How far from there to the drop?"

I paced off the space from the window in my kitchen to the opposite wall in the living room. "About like this. And there's also this skirt all around. It sticks up about this high." I pointed to my knees.

"What's it made of?"

"Three millimetre anodised aluminium sheeting with anchor gussets spaced at sixty centimetres over centres."

The Majestic was still moored there with lots of tools stowed below. Welding material, crowbars, wrenches, couple of sledge hammers and lots of rope. "It's just a matter of getting the stuff from there onto the roof," Ted explained.

Bernie looked at Miss Hanna. "You're not thinking... That's crazy. It's far too short. You're going to kill yourself."

Miss Hanna shrugged her shoulders. "Never lost a passenger yet. Besides, I know a trick or two."

"That's crazy," Bernie insisted.

"But more important: how do we get him far away?" Miss Hanna asked.

"I still say you're going to kill yourself."

"Oh, you are all such imbeciles. Of course there's danger the moment one gets out of bed. Get used to it. If you can't face your own mortality you'll never enter Valhalla."

Bernie sensed that her warnings fell on deaf ears, so she reluctantly relented. "Oh Hanna, you are such a bully. But I must first call Nellie Smith. This time I really need her help."

We all met again in the parking lot of Eulenspiegel Hall just as the sun threw its first golden rays over the rooftops of the city: Ted, Bernie, Miss Hanna and myself and, roused by Ted, also Joe, Marlene and Wolfgang in their rusted station wagon. Gus came in his sporty Horch which threw up a cloud of dust and gravel as it sliced around the corner.

Getting past the lone guard was easier than anticipated. I had the official authorisation to enter at will, Gus claimed that he had to follow up on a report of a leak in the roof, and Ted, as Master of the Majestic which lay moored at the jetty, could claim special privileges any time of the day. Bernie and Miss Hanna requested to be allowed to further secure her gyroplane should they find it necessary, but the best justification came from Joe who insisted to have Marlene and Wolfgang try out a new song-and-dance number on stage for the upcoming Festival of Carnations.

"And Miss Hanna here," Joe explained to one of the guards, "she's Master Till's new nurse. Besides, she'll also be our audience response stand-in to tell us how it sounds from the spectator's seat. You may all come as well. The more people we have in the audience, the better we can fine-tune the PA system."

In the end we convinced the guards of our innocence and we all were admitted to enter. Wolfgang went straight onto the stage, opened the grand piano and fingered out a few chords. "How's that for volume?" he asked in his high-pitched voice. Suddenly he looked very secure in his ways.

"Very good," came the answer from the onlookers which now consisted of Master Till who briefly joined them, and from Miss Hanna, five guards, the driver of the van who had come to deliver breakfast and two policemen which happened to pass in their patrol car and were invited in to enjoy the show. In the auditorium they were also prevented from observing the roof.

Bernie, Gus, Ted, Miss Hanna and I stayed with the group just long enough until Wolfgang hammered out a rolling barrelhouse solo and Marlene delivered the fitting tap dance number which could have been lifted straight out of the Storyville Quarters of New Orleans.

We only stayed for a minute, then quietly stole ourselves away and clambered onto the roof. Gus knew exactly what was needed: a bolt cutter, block and tackle and an adjustable wrench, all to be found in the belly of Ted's Majestic. First we cut the gyroplane's mooring lines and, huffing and puffing, lifted it off the landing pad, over a couple of fans and onto the roof itself, then pushed it towards the north-east corner of the building. Miss Hanna removed three cotter pins and castellated nuts which secured the undercarriage to the fuselage but left the couplings in place. This way the aircraft still had the temporary use of its three bicycle wheels.

Gus took the bolt cutter and made a few short snips in the aluminium gussets. "It's not how much you cut, but where," he instructed his crew. Next he attached one end of the block-and-tackle to the skirting and the other diagonally across the roof to the welded rebar rungs. We pulled and the aluminium facing opened as easily and as noiselessly as a sardine can. Time elapsed from the moment we had left the auditorium: seven minutes.

Just at this moment Master Till came up the ladder. No, there were no objections from the guards, he said, then climbed onto the banana seat with unexpected agility as if he had done this sort of thing a hundred times while Miss Hanna kissed me squarely on the mouth. "Thank you," she said. "I never dreamed you would amount to much, but you did your job well."

With that she seated herself in front of Master Till. It was quiet now in the auditorium below and we waited a few seconds until we heard Marlene's voice coming from the powerful speakers. "My next number…" Her words were suddenly drowned out by a long ear-piercing feedback squeal.

"Now!" said Miss Hanna, pulling the starter cord. The engine revved up briefly while the feedback from below still shrieked, mixed with some popping sounds of tapping the microphone's diaphragm. On Miss Hanna's hand signal I gave the giro prop a powerful spin.

"Sorry for that," we heard Marlene say over the engine noise which soon turned into a gentle snarl. "The volume, you know. It's set for a full auditorium, and this will not happen again. My next number is an old chantey sung by sailors when they trimmed their sails as they prepared to return to their home ports. It is called 'Rolling home'." Wolfgang laid down a thundering arpeggio intro.

Miss Hanna revved the engine once more, the V3 jerked forward, began to roll, noisily rattled over some stray piece of sheet metal, became faster, faster, then fish-tailed over the roof edge and plunged out of sight with the foot-high V3 markings flapping against the thin aluminium frame in a sudden crosswind. We waited to hear the splash. Seconds later it came - splash.

"Shit," said Ted.

Bernie grabbed my arm, squeezed it. "Oh no!" she cried out. "I told her she was crazy."

Gus was the only one at that far side of the roof and he was able to see what happened. As he told us moments later when we got together again on the parking lot: "There it came, and you know the roof is not level at the East side. It has seven degree slope for drainage, and the plane skidded sideways a lot. With bicycle tires, what…"

"Cut that out!" Ted urged him on.

"There it came and it skidded a lot." He accented his story with flailing hand motions. "Like this."

"Gus, we know that."

"Patience, patience. I'll tell you everything. There it came…"

"We know. It skidded."

"…and it bounced up and down, and then…"

"Skidded some more."

"Oui, it did. And it picked up a bit of speed, and then it rolled over the edge and straight down. Fell down like a stone. It's over twenty meters from there to the water."

"Then what?"

"And down it went, straight down, nose first. It twisted a bit as it went, probably by a gust of wind. Nearly pushed it against the building. And then, I don't really know how Hanna did it, but just before I thought they would surely hit the water, the nose pulled up a bit, and the carriage fell off and hit the water with a big splash. And then, finally, the nose came up a little more, a little higher, and higher, and then... I think she must have touched the water also, but when I looked again that thing was still flying, maybe just a foot above the lake. Then it finally levelled out and flew straight into the sunrise like a bloody rocket ship. Mon dieu, it was so bright I couldn't see what happened next. Magnifique."

"Dammit," said Bernie, "she did it again."

CHAPTER THIRTY-SIX

"Shall we come to order? Please, all sit down. Surely he will appear any moment now. Assoyez-vous, Monsieur Wilde. Herr Doktor, bitte setzen sie sich. Please. We'll wait for another fifteen minutes. You up there in the galleries - if you don't stop agitating and shouting I'll have you cleared out. Sit down! All of you!"

At this moment a messenger appeared, approached the monk, had a short discussion and left again.

"Quiet! Quiet there!" Pause. "Master Till is unavoidably detained. Any volunteers to substitute for him?" Il Nolano looked straight at me and I felt the blood rushing to my ears.

Somehow the monk didn't look surprised, and for a moment I thought he even had a hint of a smile. "We have this obscure regulation which permits a stand-in to temporarily replace our person of interest. Anybody?" He scanned his group but only saw cast-down eyes and gentle head shaking, then he turned back at me again.

"I will," I replied resignedly when our eyes met once more.

The monk nodded. "You should be honoured to take his place. But I am glad you come on your own free will, else I would have drafted you. You look quite tired, Mister Parker. Let the records show that young Parker has volunteered."

I glanced at Bernie who stifled a yawn and discretely stuck up her thumb as a sign of victory, then she turned to the monk. "We were up all night," she explained.

"So I understand. Come and think of it," he replied, "that's one of the pleasures I missed." Addressing me again: "We are now one person short. Do we have anyone who might take your own place? We can subscribe one at random from the galleries, but I have never been in favour of asking a complete stranger to search for the nucleus of any problem."

I responded. "When I set up this durbar, I had one other person in mind, but he rejected my appeal. He had played a large part in almost every aspect of this affair, but I'm afraid I cannot motivate him. He's afraid of you, Sir."

"Does he think then that I'm a monster?"

"On the contrary. He can't stand your goodness. Monsters, he thinks, he can slay. He says some people call you a saint. Behind your back, of course. He has no religion. He simply can't deal with that."

"Did he actually say that?"

"He put it differently."

"Exactly, how did he put it then?"

"He said 'I can't take any of that holy-holy shit'."

Il Nolano chuckled. "Neither can I. Go, get him. Let's reconvene tomorrow at two. And get some sleep. You all look exhausted."

✳   ✳   ✳

Ted was adamant when I begged him. He kept repeating over and over again that he did not want to 'face this holy piece of something-or-other,' as he put it, but I appealed to his curiosity. "You steal books," I finally shouted at him. "Don't tell me that you're not curious."

In the end Ted agreed to a very brief meeting with Il Nolano. "Maybe I owe you one, but please, Tony, promise to get me out of there the moment you see me suffer."

Now Ted and I were in the pawnbroker's overstuffed antique living room, facing the monk Giordano Bruno. "Did those Christmas lights work out to your satisfaction," Ahasverus started the conversation as he placed Ted in his own big comfortably stuffed chair. Ted nodded, keeping his eyes on the monk for fear that he might suddenly jump up and devour him. Instead, Il Nolano shook his hand and poured each of us a glass of tea with a tot or two of rum. Finally he took the bull by its horns.

"Ted," he opened, "what exactly scares you about me? Come out with it now. You can tell me, and I assure you that I have heard it all before."

Ted squirmed a bit, but then blurted out: "It's this god-fixation, you know, this obsession with deity. I simply can't hack it, Your Honour."

"First of all, you don't call me 'Your Honour'. Call me Giordano and I'll call you Ted, if that's all right with you." He bowed conspiratorially toward Ted.

"Yes Sir, that's okay."

"No 'sir this' and no 'sir that'. Call me Giordano. Go ahead, try it on for size."

"Yes, Giordano."

"There; sounds much better already. Next we have to straighten out this god fixation thing. I don't believe in such mystical entity myself. Yes, yes, I'm a monk and this sounds odd, but I believe that the real god is in everything we see, touch, smell. It's in the atoms and molecules and the energy which holds all those pieces together. The bare fact that there is anything at all, that's the ultimate power. There could have been an empty universe and nobody would complain. The god in whose image we are supposed to have been created, the divinity of a thousand faces... If there is such a thing, that's an abstraction, an invention to scare the living daylights out of all of us. There is no Almighty in the heavens or anywhere else - never has been, never will be. Or, if you like, there is a god in everything, including in ourselves. I respect only the forces and laws of the universe. People like me are called Pantheists."

"Is that what bugged the pope?"

"That and more. I had a problem with two of them, you know, and it vexed them no end. But it had absolutely nothing to do with religion. It had everything to do with power politics. Either I or the whole Roman Catholic hierarchy had to go. The popes did what was expedient. But tell me about yourself. You were a miner, right?"

"The coal mines. They were the closest thing to hell down there. Hot and stinking and sticky; dark and dangerous. There's not even a decent place to shit. I never told anybody before, but I am claustrophobic. I feared each new day. Look at me, I'm a pretty tough guy, but each day going down there I shook with fear. Now and then I would throw up. They thought it was the drink but it was fear. I never told anyone the truth."

"Doing it in spite of your fears, that's your real strength. You are an exceptionally courageous man, Taddeus Ramelov, and I would be proud if you'd call me your friend."

"But you and I, we are not equals."

"We are all different, all unique, that is true, but at the same time, all of us are such stuff as dreams are made on…"

"Is the Bard here too?"

"Does infomercials now. Steak knifes and electronic fly swatters. - May I call you my friend?"

"Yes, Father, I wish you would."

"And it's Giordano. Remember that."

✳   ✳   ✳

Il Nolano rose and looked around his refurbished 10-person durbar ring. "First I must read to you a short telegram which I have just received. It's from Eulenspiegel, and it reads: 'Having good time being back home in Kneitlingen. Till'."

The monk put the paper down and looked quizzically at his audience before he continued. "He must have counted the words on this telegram, found them to be only nine, one short of the prepaid minimum, and then decided to add the tenth. It reads 'Hahaha'." He put the telegram down again, puzzled and humoured by the absurdity. "I wonder if I'll ever begin to understand this man. Still, I am both delighted and saddened by this turn of events, and happy that he now has finally gone home again. Yet I am saddened that I could not have blessed him personally. Some day, somewhere, somebody might want to explain to all of us who this astounding visitor among us was."

Stunned silence blanketed the room. After a while some rustling noises were heard coming from the balcony section. As we looked up we saw the guests and reporters in the gallery quietly rise to their feet, one by one, then even Grietje rose, and all the others except Dr. Borelli who stared motionless at the ceiling with seething anger.

The monk sat down and continued. "However, we shall carry on and do our part to conclude this durbar. We have a new member here. Please, tell us who you are."

"My name is Aleksandr Sergeyevich Pushkin. I am the Captain of the Majestic. Call me Ted." He bowed awkwardly and sat down.

The monk continued: "Pushkin – hm. I thought so all the time. Sit down, all of you. We also have young Antonio Parker replacing Master Till. I believe he has a lot to tell us. Is anybody objecting?"

"Yes, I am." The voice came from Doctor Borelli who had regained his composure. "I have my own suit against that man there, this Parker. I have a long list..."

The monk was short-tempered after these stressful delays. "It seems that nothing we do here pleases you. Does it, Doctor Borelli. We are not here to grind axes."

"With all due respect, Mister Bruno, I do have a legal claim and I insist on having my day before the bar. If I must bundle my demand with the farce of this spectacle here, I may consider to come to some mutual agreement. That is, if we can find an equitable solution."

"Very well, then. Let's bundle them up. You better agree now, Doctor. We will deal with the two different issues in tandem, starting with the conclusion of the Eulenspiegel affair. And only if young Parker agrees to it will we tackle the second issue, namely the... The - what was that again, Doctor Borelli?"

"The criminal duplicity of that man."

"That man happens to sit in for Master Till now. Only when we have completed with that durbar shall we turn our attention to what you call duplicity. And only if young Parker is in complete agreement with this arrangement as well."

"I am," I said. "I'm ready for that. Any time. You can mix or match it, Sir, it's all the same event anyway."

"So be it then. Now we deal with the original durbar before we change our focus. May I finally say 'amen' to that?" He looked around the group, soliciting signs of assent all around. "You up there, you in the galleries. Do you think this would be a fair procedure? Come, come, somebody please speak up."

After a short mumbled exchange of propositions a voice came from up there. "Why do you ask us? We are mostly reporters and a few visitors; why would it matter what we think."

"It matters in so far as it makes me more comfortable to know we are following a free exchange of ideas instead of facing a kangaroo court. So, what sayest thou?"

After a few minutes of hushed debates in the gallery came the answer. "We up here agree that it would be fair if all parties consent to combine the proceedings, as long as they are clearly separated from each other and conducted in sequence. But we bargain for the condition that both the litigant and the defendant can opt out of this arrangement instantly if any one of them so desires."

Finally the session was underway. Marlene was the first to hold the Talking Wand. "I am very happy that the Professor - and, please, let me continue to call him the Professor - that he is not here in person. I would blush to tell him that I love and adore him. Now I look at myself in the mirror, in shop windows, in polished marble columns even and I love me. I love myself, I love the Professor, I love my husband, my child, my audience. I love to be what I am and who I am."

Marlene sat down and had to blow her nose. She then pointed the bâton to her husband. "What do you think, Joe?"

Joe took his time to answer. "Well, it's all irrelevant now, but I never was a welder before. Now I am one. The day he made me a naval architect he brushed past me - he had been a ventriloquist once, you know - and then he said in a voice only I could hear: 'Now Joe, pull up your socks and go through with it. I'll kick your balls if you don't.' How did he know my fears?" Joe shook his head. "I have no idea, but I came home that night and there on the door steps was an arc-welder and some angle iron and rebars and books and stuff, and when the week was over I could weld. The strangest thing is, I don't even like welding. The iron smoke stinks and I hate this type of work. But I loved doing it just the same."

"What would you have preferred to do instead," the monk asked.

"To be a stage director or an impresario. I found out that I'm good at it. Or I would have liked to make moving pictures. I don't know why exactly, but I believe I am a storyteller at heart, and this would be one way to explain the often unexplainable. I am also thinking about Marlene. I would like to cast her in a play. A dramatic role. Unfortunately it takes a lot of money which I don't have. I never took enough out of the pot when it was still full; and of course, I have not yet discussed this with Marlene either. What do you make of all this?" He looked straight at his wife. She said nothing but smiled modestly and nodded.

"What does it cost to make a movie," Bernie interrupted his monologue.

"A good, tight movie costs about four, five hundred thousand. A really bad one with lots of bodies, dead and alive, a helicopter and an orgy of car crashes would run into millions, though."

Bernie scribbled on something in front of her, then handed Joe the short slip of paper. "Here, Joe. And keep that show running; same arrangement as with the Professor."

Joe was stunned. "Even with the credit cards?"

Bernie nodded. "You are in charge from here on. Get off the pot now, or else."

"Or else she'll kick your balls," I added over my left shoulder, emphasising the word 'she'.

Il Nolano scanned his ring. "We have all had our say, and I believe we should close... Yes? What is it?"

A mail courier had entered the council chamber, approached Il Nolano and whispered something in his ears. The monk nodded and with his head pointed to Bernie, whereupon the courier handed Bernie a large manila envelope. She took it and before opening looked at Il Nolano who nodded permission. She slowly opened the envelope - it was empty. "May I have the floor for ten seconds, please?"

"Yes, you may. No need for the - the.."

"My *bâton de marche*," Oscar Wilde helped out.

Bernie held up the empty envelope. "This is a pre-arranged signal for the following announcement: The Security Exchange Company is filing for insolvency. They have ceased operations."

CHAPTER THIRTY-SEVEN

Reporters were bunching up outside the door. Before Bernie and I faced the mob she had to make a short phone call. "Nellie? I couldn't get to you sooner, just arrived myself. - Yes, exactly as I thought. They are bankrupt. - Thank you, Nellie. Tell Bessie that I thank her also. I had no idea she could fly executive jets. I owe you one, I owe you a big one. And, as you know, I never broke my promise. - Yes, he's just standing next to me." Turning to me: "She says you're pretty smart yourself - for a white guy." Back to her phone, "I'll remember that. - Oh, they are waiting outside this door. - Yes, very soon." The lid of her cell phone snapped shut as we pushed the exit door open.

"Is it true, Miss Robinson, that your bank now holds a vast number of the shares of the Security Exchange Company?" one reporter asked, only to be elbowed aside by another inquiring: "Did you personally benefit from insider trading..." A third one with powerful lungs drowned out all others: "What are you planning to do with your majority ownership in the energy sector?"

Bernie was ready for her impromptu press conference. "On behalf of the Sovereign Bank I have this statement to make: The collapse of the Security Exchange Company has not affected the viability of the Sovereign Bank negatively. On the contrary, in a stock swap the Sovereign Bank now holds the majority of their shares, leaving all other assets of the Bata Global Bank intact. Our representatives are resuming discussions regarding the stalled trade agreements with the City of Vesper. Currently under debate are enhanced commerce options for both, Vesper as well as the City of Crosley. We also came to an understanding with respect to the disputed territories."

"What will you be negotiating next, Miss Robinson?"

There was this dangerous sweet smile again. "On the planning schedules are improved road conditions and pipeline expansions. The Sovereign Bank has been able to secure the export concessions for our surplus water reserves and is investigating possible swaps with the surplus energy resources of the City of Vesper."

"Miss Robinson, is there any truth to the rumour that you personally had prior conferences with representatives of the City of Vesper?"

"Yes, this is true. We held preliminary discussion with the objective of combining the military forces of both cities under the command of General Smith of the Vesper Liberation Commands which would result in lower expenditures for both cities. This is expected to reduce taxes on all sides."

"Who will finance these expansions?"

"The Sovereign Bank will initially underwrite the construction of the pipelines. Energy prices will temporarily have to rise marginally. However, enhanced competition will eventually bring those costs down and are expected to level out below current prices – barring inflationary pressures, of course. The road extension will be financed by charging a reasonable silicon tax which will be rescinded as soon as the outstanding debts are repaid and legitimate profits for the investors have been secured."

"Is it true, Miss Robinson, that you have a personal interest in all these transactions."

"Of course, as CEO of the Sovereign Bank I will have a moderate but indirect interest in the outcome of the proceedings. However, I state categorically that the public interest will be protected. There is absolutely no dispute on this subject."

"How much of the Sovereign Bank assets are your personal property?"

"This is restricted private information."

"According to a certain Doctor Borelli, he alleges that you are planning to reduce the availability of electric power. This, he claims, will bring it below the present demand which will increase consumer prices. Is there any truth in his allegations?"

"Doctor Borelli is a sore loser." She threw one of her infectious smiles into her audience. "He may become the centre of an investigation into his participation in shady investment schemes himself. There is no account of what he may invent next."

"Do you know a certain Mister Parker?"

"Yes, of course I do. He is standing right next to me. I am a facilitator in his integration council and we have kept in contact on a regular basis."

"Mister Parker, are you a squatter?"

Bernie answered instead. "Yes, he is."

"Mister Parker, did you or did you not buy the down-rated energy shares with moneys made available through the Sovereign Bank?"

Bernie was unperturbed. "Mister Parker had been instrumental in putting our negotiations on track again."

"Can Mister Parker speak for himself?"

Bernie did not release her microphone. "Thank you, thank you for coming. All details will be release by my bank in due time. Thank you." And with that she turned away, me in tow. We had barely entered my car when I asked her: "Is it true that you plan to reduce electric power just so you can raise prices?"

She laughed. "They all do it. If you sell energy of any sort you would be a fool to produce enough. Worse yet, if you have a surplus on hand you'll only get into a price cutting war. Nobody wins that way. Of course we'll have to reduce the output."

"By how much?"

"Six percent. Remember this number, Darling. Six percent."

"And what's so special about six percent?"

"That's the threshold of everything. That's the number of unemployed you want to have. Keeps the workers in line. Any lower and they'll ask for better pay or whatever spooky ideas get into their heads. Conversely, any higher and some smart-ass do-gooder will increase welfare benefits or soup kitchens and soon nobody needs to work at all any more. If you handle the money of the masses, you have to be very careful how you dole it out. - Please start your car, Honey. Those reporters - they might catch up if they see us lingering about."

"And for energy?"

"Same six percent, and keep it steady and even. You cut it any tighter and they'll invent some energy-efficient this-or-that. On the other hand, you give them more slack and they start comparing prices again. No good can ever come of that. You must keep them a bit frightened. You don't want them to shop around. That creates competition, and we are all better off without it."

"Isn't competition the bedrock of our consumer society?"

"Only if you're the buyer. It's terribly inconvenient if you are the seller."

"Is competition not the power that spins the wheels of our industry?"

"Yea, and the chocolate Easter Bunny lays coloured marzipan eggs. No, Dear, you must always stay on top of your commerce. You can't let them just do what's best for them. I say, give them their illusions but control their money."

I put the car into gear. "How can you do such a thing?"

"Oops. I think you bumped that thing behind you."

"Bernie, how can you exploit the public so shamelessly?"

"That's easy, Honey. First you create some effective slogans about conservation and such. Use smaller light bulbs, buy energy-efficient appliances, you know. All those little things which neither make sense nor save energy in any meaningful way. But keep your eyes on actual consumption and always make sure you supply just below demand. And it's terribly important to finance the tree huggers and the clean air promoters and those with grassroots support. That risk-free gesture puts you on the side of the angels."

"Damn it, Bernie, you're just like any other politician."

"What have you against conservation?"

"You always answer the wrong questions."

"There are only so many good answers, so I pick the ones that work the best. - What was your question again, Darling?"

"Will you eventually supply enough energy to fill all demands?"

"Yes, of course, Love. But first we have to upgrade our equipment. Naturally, a few generators will be taken out of service so we can service them. We will also look at wind power and other renewable energy resources. Careful, Love. You are driving erratically."

"That's all? Just look?"

"At first, yes. Conduct the proper studies."

"And then, what?"

"What 'what'?"

"What will you do after you looked at wind power? When you have finished all your studies, what then?"

"Careful, Honey. That light! It's red!"

Tire squeals. "After you looked and studied and all, Bernie, what then? Will you go for wind power?"

"Of course, I will. We just need to secure the relevant patents first, that's all. If we don't plan carefully, somebody else takes all the profits. Don't forget, I'm a banker."

"First secure all patents?"

"And existing contracts, naturally. Careful, Honey."

"You are completely heartless."

"Heartless? I'm just an average banker and that, my friend, that's the backbone of our system. You want heartless? Go to the pharmaceuticals. That's heartless!"

"Suppose people will revolt?"

"Excellent. Let them. Applaud them. Even finance some of them. Makes you look even-handed. Someone may blow up a pipeline or a hydro tower here and there. Get some good politicians on your side, you know, the ones who kiss babies and talk a lot about liberty and family values and our way of life."

"Then you'll generate even less energy."

"See what I mean? These things are self-correcting and nobody will blame us to raise prices. It's an easy sale. Everybody must have energy, so it's a low-risk high-profit investment. Just remember the six percent - that is, within a point or two. And then it's time to sell shares. Let the market forces determine the price."

"And the money you make? What will you do with all that?"

"Careful, Baby. I don't like the way you drive. – The money? We'll use it to finance democracy, make sure that our money empowers those who are on our side. It's called free enterprise. Finance even those who blow up something here and there. Dole out five percent of your profits. That's a legitimate business expense, and it shows everybody that you hold no grudges. Besides, it's a tax deduction. Of course, we'll give meaningful tax breaks and investment incentives only to those who actually count." I looked at her with utter surprise. "Did you not talk constantly about public interests coming first and all that gibberish? How about finding art in far off places?"

"Go, it's green now. Please, keep your eyes forward, Darling."

"What about finding..."

"Tony, my Love, that was - oh, watch out! You nearly hit that kid on the bike. Please drive carefully, will you, Honey? You'll yet turn me into a nervous wreck. - Public interest? Sure I said that. I have to say these things. It's expected of me; after all, I'm the CEO. This is still an open and democratic society, I want to point out, and that's free speech. Surely, you don't want to introduce socialism now! Be happy that we managed to tear it out of Borelli's hide. Imagine if we had not succeeded."

"Then what?"

"Tony, Darling, then he would have done the same. Now we'll do it instead, and that makes all the difference. - Please, Love. Aren't you driving on the wrong side of the road?"

CHAPTER THIRTY-EIGHT

'Military Coup in Vesper', the newspapers headlined. According to the reports, General Smith rolled up in her one remaining Tiger Five tank, shot up the two cultured marble lions to the left and right of Vesper's city hall main entrance, drove up the 23 steps and demanded immediate resignation of the ruling august assemblage. Should they refuse she'll drive her war machine straight through those beautiful oak portals, and from there without further ado over the polished marble floors and into the council chambers. She charged the office holders with fermenting continued hostilities with Crosley, budget overruns, decay of the city's infrastructure, accepting bribes, offensive parking regulations and, after a law against stupidity had been enacted, wide-ranging financial mismanagement. In the end, a new political line-up was installed and the just-fired civil servants recited a modified oath or were safely moved to some far-flung trade commissions. The lions were replaced by the ones they had already in storage for just such an occasions, a Victory Holiday was declared for the next day, and by nightfall everything was back to normal. TV reportage showed General Smith sitting boldly on the turret of her tank, signing autographs and telling every reporter with a microphone: "Things will be democratic from now on."

※　　※　　※

The mood at the pawnbroker's place was sombre. I decided to take the bull by its horns and find out exactly what Il Nolano had planned, if anything. Mrs. Kimmelbaum cleared away the few supper dishes, then asked the pawnbroker: "Is there anything else I can do for you?"

"No, my Dear. Thank you for coming over tonight. I really appreciate your kindness."

"I can come anytime, you know."

"That would be wonderful if you did," he said, then accompanied her out and through the hallway into the store where they talked in muted tones. Now and then a few words would drift through the drapes which separated the living room from the hallway. "Mister Ahasverus, that's way too much - yes, of course I can come tomorrow - very much. And good night to you too, Sir."

"She's such a dear," the pawnbroker remarked as he re-entered the room. "She's not much of a cook though, but perhaps I'll teach her."

"I didn't know you could cook," Father Giordano said. "But then, why not. You had enough time to learn it." Looking at me and pointing at my laptop: "Thank you for bringing that machine. I want you to give me two hours of your time. We have to rework something that has been on my mind for years already."

The pawnbroker interceded. "Can it not wait? Our young friend looks worn-out."

I shook my head. There was something in the air, something unsaid, ominous, threatening. "Not just tired, I am terrified. Would anybody know tomorrow's outcome?" What is the monk holding back? Of course, he knew. He did not have to wait for the next day to make up his mind; he was already certain. I was absolutely sure of it and tried to read the answer in his eyes. Perhaps there was a hint, but I could not decipher it. Even the tea didn't make me feel at ease.

Seeing that Il Nolano was not ready to respond to my question, Ahasverus addressed me: "Don't think about Bernie. She will change her mind many more times. She's a wilful child; a cat playing with her plush new toys." Then, trying to tone down the tension, he turned to the monk. "You don't want to bring up Aristotle again, do you? You know what that did to you the last time you worked him over."

"Yes, I do. And I have a confession to make," Il Nolano answered after a pause.

The pawnbroker rose, poured some of his very old cognac and handed us each a snifter. "You? A stubborn old coot like you? A Dominican monk confessing to a Jew? Surely, that must be a historic first. Very well then, confess away." He started pacing the room.

"Do you remember, my dear friend, how we debated timelessness and infinity of the universe? I still don't want to give up on the first, but I concede that I was in error on infinity. I was wrong."

Ahasverus stopped instantly, snifter cradled in his hands. "You were wrong? Listen to him, Anthony. He's confessing that he made a mistake. 'I was wrong' he just said; we all heard it. Three simple little words, but why now? Why could that obstinate mule not have said that to them there four centuries ago? 'I was wrong'. It's so easy to say." Turning to the monk. "You know where all your troubles come from, don't you? You're nothing but an arrogant dogmatist. That's what you are. An obnoxious, arrogant dogmatist."

"And you, Ahasverus, you are a constant whiner. There you are, complaining again. Now sit down, for crying out loud. You make me nervous with your pacing. What got into you tonight?"

"I'm uptight, that's all."

"You're always uptight. You're always looking over your shoulder, even now, even here. Sit down!"

The pawnbroker finally steered towards his armchair and sat down, constraining himself from drumming the side table with his fingers. Finally Il Nolano was ready to continue.

"I wept the day I saw my error, and even now it still pains me that I could have made such a fundamental blunder. The universe is finite. Big but finite. There may even be other universes beside our own, each one of which contains a billion galaxies and nebulas. There may be billions of universes - and there may also be just this one and no more. Whatever the final count may be, it will nevertheless be finite although we cannot express such large numbers mathematically." The tick-tock of the big clock emphasised the quietness of the room.

The monk took a slow sip before he continued. "Which brings me to Aristotle. In his mind everything was essentially made from only four basic elements: water, air, earth and fire. And you know what? He was a fake. He didn't even come up with this one all by himself; he stole it. Empedocles had said the same thing a hundred years earlier. Four elements, he said, but old Ari didn't get it right. He ignored the other thing Empedocles said. He ignored Attraction and Repulsion, the magnetism that pulls them together and the forces that pushes them apart. He completely ignored the dynamics of it. No wonder his theory fell apart. I can see clearly now that he was grasping for symbols which did not exist. Not then, not even today, so we must find them for him now. We need to deal with three major classes. Aristotle took care of only two of them: the abstract and the material but he forgot the dynamics."

"Attraction and Repulsion? I hate myself for asking this, knowing that I won't understand a word you say." Ahasverus put the snifter to his nose to savour the richness of the cognac. "What about them?"

"Of course you will. And Antonio will put it all down on his machine there. Old Ari didn't have the convenience of such apparatus. They were only a few steps beyond clay tablets then. I wouldn't forgive myself if I didn't exploit this opportunity to finally have my say."

"Say it then; spit it out. And make it short. You know how you tire me out with your convoluted..."

The monk interrupted him. "He wanted to define the human spirit, not just the outer world around us. Fire stood for the eternal quest, he must have reasoned, and earth for the rock of knowledge and certainty. One leads to the other. After the fire has burned out, the ashes return to the earth. It's as symbolic as that. And water? Fluidity. That's the desire, the want, the need. Which leaves only the air. Tell me, Ahasverus, what would you think air might mean?"

The pawnbroker took a slow sip, put down his glass, first looked at me, then at the monk. "The opposite of need? Plenitude. Abundance. That which spills over."

The monk laughed. "Absolutely. See how easy it is? That's all the definition old Ari had at the time, he just got the symbols wrong so we need to invent some of our own. And then we must finally put Attraction and Repulsion back into the system. Antonio, show me what you have on your machine."

I let the laptop come to speed, then hesitated. Something was underfoot, and for some reason I had a premonition of an inescapable disaster. Should I contribute anything at my own peril?

The monk grew restless; I could sense it. "Antonio? Are you ready?"

"Why is that important now?" I asked, hoping that my question would delay whatever lay ahead. "Why should we worry about stuff like that?"

"Why? Why do we need to find out what's in the nucleus of an atom? Why do we want to know what's behind those stars? Why are we curious? Because we must. Because that's both our curse and our salvation. It is our destiny. – Now, Antonio, let us begin. What would you suggest for the symbol of fire, the quest?"

I could stall no longer. This was not a cat-and-mouse game, this was my own fate coming forward and I must let it happen.

"Fire? How about double question marks, the quest? And double exclamation marks for earth, the answer."

Now it was Giordano who jumped up. "Brilliant! Exactly! I had a hunch this devilish equipment had some utility. Now air. The wind. The abundance, the power."

I came up with two plus signs, ++, the abundance. And once I was at it, I added ~~ for water, the hungry ocean to tear it all away again.

The old monk was jubilant. "Oh, you are so right." He turned towards his friend. "Look, Ahasverus, look how easy it was. That only leaves magnetism to add. The loadstone, as they called it then. The Chinese already used it to navigate the oceans."

The pawnbroker objected. "There you go again. There was nothing about magnets in Aristotle's dicta if my memories serve me right. Mind you, he was before me and I only knew of him by hearsay."

The monk sat down again, leaning back with his eyes closed, slowly nipping the cognac. "And that's why he couldn't bring it up himself. Magnetism – the energy to attract or reject. The push and pull to make it all work. Without an engine it's only so much stuff, but give it energy and it becomes the keystone of creation. The four elements and the power of the atom. That is all we need to explain the universe. The basic laws which clarify all, even something as complicated as the secrets of life itself. Ahasverus, my dear old friend, now Antonio and I must hunker down for awhile and work this out. Go to bed. Sleep. We have a little work to do and you'll only be in the way."

Turning, he peered at me over the rim of his glasses, slowly set down his snifter and said: "Antonio, our time has come. Let's get to work."

CHAPTER THIRTY-NINE

All hell broke loose. "I want his head," Dr. Borelli shouted, pointing at me in the centre seat. "I want him destroyed, eliminated, punished with utmost severity."

Father Bruno interrupted him. "You, Sir, are not privileged to talk now. You will sit down and shut up!"

"I demand my pound of flesh." He hammered the table with his fist. "I know exactly what went on. If I don't see justice done here I shall take matters in my own hand."

"You will sit down and be quiet, or I will have you removed from this assembly. This is not a court and we are not here to pass judgement."

"If you don't serve me justice instantly, I shall go after you personally. Yes you, Bruno."

The monk looked at him for a minute, then calmly said: "Do you really believe that I will be intimidated by someone like you, Doctor Borelli? Hm?" He gently smiled, then turned towards the scribe. "Please call the guards and have this man escorted out."

The guards must have been alerted earlier as Dr. Borelli was hustled out in seconds. His tumultuous protests could still be heard momentarily after they closed the doors behind him.

Now Il Nolano turned his full attention towards me "You have been at the centre of much of what went on. Am I correct?"

Suddenly I was the focus of the whole assembly, and instant fear gripped me like a vice. I knew the moment I dreaded had come. "Yes Sir, that is correct." I could hear my own heart beat in terror.

"Antonio, you are twenty years old. Look around this room. What do you see?"

I turned my head, even looked up into the galleries crowded with reporters, columnists, and spectators. It seemed to be a mere blur. I see nothing special, I wanted so say, but the words stuck in my throat. Unbearable panic of the pending unknown overwhelmed me; my hands began to shake and I had to hold on to the edge of the table to steady myself. "Nothing," I managed to voice almost inaudibly.

Il Nolano continued. "Except for the child here, you are the youngest person in this room. Do we all understand correctly that you are a squatter, that you are here by mistake?"

I nodded, sweat suddenly breaking out, running down my forehead.

"Much of what you did, Antonio, you did in youthful exuberance and innocence. All of what you did was done with the best of intentions, and most of it benefited us all, even myself. Still a wrong had been done, although now you may not perceive it as such. A wrong had been done which we have an obligation to correct while we still can." Nodding to a guard: "Yes, send him in."

Max, my first friend here, the devoted servant of Miss Lynch entered and briskly walked to the podesta, cupping his hand and whispering into his ear. I tried to catch his eyes, but Max avoided my glance. It was now deadly still in the room. Hot moisture running down my back, I searched the eyes of my other friends, Ted, Bernie, Marlene, all of them. Only Lauris responded, but his eyes were floating in tears.

The monk nodded, then continued. "Please, send in Miss Lynch." That word struck like a lightening bolt.

She entered and sat down stiffly in the chair, which until just two minutes ago had been occupied by Dr. Borelli.

"Miss Lynch, you and I had a short conversation over the 'phone late last night. Would you please tell us the essence of our communication?"

Miss Lynch cleared her throat, quickly glanced at the entire durbar, then focused her eyes on me. "You asked me if I had been the courier for young Anthony Parker, and I said yes. You asked me further if it was true that he was a squatter, and again I answered in the affirmative." Here she paused, uncertain as how to continue.

"And then, Miss Lynch? Please, carry on."

Addressing the monk: "And then you asked me if the window was still open."

"What window are we talking about?"

"The time window to Level One, Sir."

"And what did you reply?"

Miss Lynch inhaled deeply before she continued. "And I replied 'yes'. I told you that it was still open."

"Open for how long?"

"For another two hours from now, Sir. It is closing in one hundred and twenty-nine minutes."

"Please tell us what else we had discussed."

"You had asked me if I would be prepared to undo my programming error to which I also replied affirmatively. Furthermore, you asked me if I fully understood the consequences of this action."

"Do you, Miss Lynch, fully understand the consequences of your planned action?"

"Yes, I do."

"Have you come to peace with your decision?"

"Yes, Father, I have."

Il Nolano looked up to the gallery. "You up there, the reporters and the ones with the microphones and the cameras, pay attention. I want you to report this event truthfully." He turned to Miss Lynch again. "When you freed young Antonio Parker from his seat, was it apparent to you that he would then become a squatter? Take your time, Miss Lynch. I do not want to press you for an answer if this causes you undue anxiety."

Miss Lynch had her response ready. "Yes, Father Giordano, it was clear to me at the time that I was contravening our established code. I also knew that I would eventually be held accountable for my misjudgement."

"And yet, you went ahead with it anyway, did you not?"

"Yes, I did."

"Why?"

"Perhaps he would not have survived until the rescue would come in the morning. I had compassion for him. I did not want him to fade away. I knew at the moment that eventually I would have to pay the price."

"And yet, you agree to go through with it?"

"Yes, I agree on my own free will."

Il Nolano rose; the whole Ring rose. "Please, Antonio Parker, stand up."

I was stricken down by barely controlled fear. I tried to rise, but my legs would not obey. Oscar Wilde rushed to my side. "My dearest, dearest friend," he whispered, "here, take my bâton. Yes, yes, I promised to give it back. Hang on! Never let it go!" He put his arms around me and helped me up.

The monk spoke slowly, each word as heavy as the lead of alchemists which never turned into gold. "Antonio Parker, I shall now pronounce my decree. You have been an unwanted guest in our society, living a fate which was not your own. It is my duty as the podesta of this durbar to undo this error and to send you back to the place from which you had come. You shall be taken from here to your former existence on Level One. Your courier, Miss Lynch, will now return you to the place where she had found you. Arrivederci, my dear friend. May a good star guide your way."

✳   ✳   ✳

I hear something, noises, commotion, a voice. "Over there. I see another seat. Over there... There in the trees."

Thrashing of somebody working his way through thick undergrowth. Static cracking of a radiophone. A flat, rasping reply: "...have that again?"

I try to open my eyes but they are caked shut with dried blood.

The voice from nearby: "Another one. Wedged into these branches here. Double seat. Fairly intact, it seems."

Crrrch. "...bodies?"

"Hold on, I'm getting closer. - Yes, two. A couple. Both hanging upside down. The man seems to have a stick wedged... Let's see now - wedged under the armrests."

"A stick?"

"Like a walking cane."

Crrrch. "... numbers?"

"Four A and B." I feel a rocking motion. "I'll try and turn them around. Woman, dead. - Wait a minute. George! George!"

Shouting: "Stretcher! One is alive. I need a stretcher. We have a live one!"

I am lifted slightly, turned sideways. Hang onto the cane, hang on. Somebody addresses me. "Sir? - Sir? - Can you hear me? Sir?"

I manage to force one eyelid partially open, a slit only, then hear a second person approaching, out of breath. The same voice as before again, now closer to my ear. "Sir, can you hear me?" I see part of his face, broad, unshaven, close enough to notice the pores of his skin, feel his breath. He turns away, shouting. "He has eye movement."

Voice number two from behind: "… older, about sixty. - No, just the man." Nearer: "Sir, can you hear me? Do you have pain?" Pain? No, I have no pain. I try to smile.

"We'll ease you out of your seat now. The chopper will be here in a few minutes. Sir, please let go of that stick."

Voice number one again: "Please, Sir, you must let go of that stick. We cannot take you down from there if you don't. - Sir? - Sir!"

Number two: "What's he holding onto? What's that thing there?"

Number one: "Look at that! How did it get on board? A beautiful old walking cane."

The End